I0592126

John Jamieson

Wallace or the Life and Acts of Sir William Wallace of Ellerslie

John Jamieson

Wallace or the Life and Acts of Sir William Wallace of Ellerslie

ISBN/EAN: 9783337017194

Printed in Europe, USA, Canada, Australia, Japan

Cover: Foto ©Raphael Reischuk / pixelio.de

More available books at **www.hansebooks.com**

THE BRUCE;

AND

WALLACE;

PUBLISHED

FROM TWO ANCIENT MANUSCRIPTS
PRESERVED IN THE LIBRARY OF THE FACULTY
OF ADVOCATES.

WITH

NOTES, BIOGRAPHICAL SKETCHES,
AND A GLOSSARY.

A NEW EDITION.

IN TWO VOLUMES.

VOL. II.

GLASGOW:
MAURICE OGLE & CO.
1869.

WALLACE;

OR,

THE LIFE AND ACTS

OF

SIR WILLIAM WALLACE,

OF ELLERSLIE.

BY HENRY THE MINSTREL.

PUBLISHED FROM A MANUSCRIPT DATED M.CCCC.LXXXVIII.

WITH

NOTES, AND PRELIMINARY REMARKS.

BY JOHN JAMIESON, D.D.,

FELLOW OF THE ROYAL SOCIETY OF EDINBURGH,
OF THE SOCIETY OF THE ANTIQUARIES OF SCOTLAND, AND
THE AMERICAN ANTIQUARIAN SOCIETY.

A NEW EDITION.

GLASGOW:
MAURICE OGLE & CO.
1869.

PRELIMINARY REMARKS,

THE LIFE OF THE AUTHOR,

AND

CHARACTER OF THE WORK.

So little is known, with respect to Henry the Minstrel, that I can scarcely pretend to add any thing to the meagre account which has been given of him by former writers. As we cannot certainly fix the time, we can form no conjecture even as to the place, of his birth. Almost all that can be viewed as an historical record concerning him, is that with which we are supplied by Major. Integrum librum, he says, Guillelmi Vallacei Henricus, a natiuitate luminibus captus, meae infantiae tempore cudit; et quæ vulgo dicebantur, carmine vulgari, in quo peritus erat, conscripsit; (ego autem talibus scriptis solum in parte fidem impertior); qui historiarum recitatione coram principibus victum et vestitum quo dignus erat nactus est. Hist. Lib. IV. c. 15. "Henry, who was blind from his birth, in the time of my infancy composed the whole *Book of William Wallace;* and committed to writing in vulgar poetry, in which he was well skilled, the things that were commonly related of him. For my own part, I give only partial credit to writings of this description. By the recitation of these, however, in the pre-

a

sence of men of the highest rank, he procured, as he indeed deserved, food and raiment."

This account, as it merely respects the recitation of his poem, is not inconsistent with what Henry himself says, when he asserts his independence in the composition of it, and declares that the motive by which he was chiefly actuated, was a patriotic desire to preserve the memory of the illustrious deeds of Wallace from oblivion.

> All worthi men at redys this rurall dyt,
> Blaym nocht the buk, set I be wnperfyt.
> I suld hawe thank, sen I nocht trawaill spard;
> For my laubour na man hecht me reward;
> Na charge I had off king nor othir lord;
> Gret harm I thocht his gud deid suld be smord.
> I haiff said her ner as the process gais;
> And fenyeid nocht for frendschip nor for fais.
> Costis herfor was no man bond to me;
> In this sentence I had na will to be, &c.
> *Wallace*, B. XI. v. 1432.

Mr. Pinkerton has given 1470 as the date when it may be supposed that Henry appeared in the character of an author. It is generally admitted, indeed, that Major was born in the year 1469. Henry, by reason of his blindness, could not himself have written his poetical effusions; and it may reasonably be supposed, from his dependent and ambulatory mode of life, that he could not employ an amanuensis properly qualified for the task. Hence may we account for the obscurity, and even for the apparent absurdity, of some passages in his work. Bating these imperfections, his descriptions are often so vivid, and his images so just, that he undoubtedly ranks higher, as a poetical writer, than either Barbour or Wyntown, who had all the advantages of a liberal education, such, at least, as the times could afford.

Mr. Pinkerton has thus expressed his sentiments concerning

this work: " It has great merit for the age, and is eminently
curious. The language in a few places is not sense. When,
by altering a word or two, the sense may be restored, attention
to this will not only be allowable, but laudable in any proper
editor; especially when we consider the singularity of the case,
and that the poem is very good sense everywhere, save in perhaps a dozen lines at most." List of Scotish Poets, xc.

The late elegant author of *Specimens of Early English Poets*
has remarked; " That a man *born blind* should excel in any
science is extraordinary, though by no means without example;
but that he should become an excellent poet, is almost
miraculous; because the soul of poetry is description. Perhaps, therefore, it may be easily assumed, that Henry was not
inferior in point of genius either to Barbour or Chaucer, nor
indeed to any poet of any age or country." Ellis's Spec. Vol. I.
p. 354.

As the venerable Minstrel could not himself have written his
poem, succeeding ages have never had it in their power to view
him in his proper character. It is unquestionable, however,
that he has not, in any edition hitherto published, appeared to
such advantage as he might have done. Almost every editor,
from the time of Andro Hart downward, used the same unpardonable liberty with his work as with that of Barbour, in
attempting to render it more intelligible, by substituting for
terms, which had become obsolete, or were going into desuetude,
others more generally known. Thus, from gross misapprehension, the very sense of the poet was often lost. Even the edition of Perth, A. 1790, which professes to be an exact transcript
from the MS., is still more inaccurate than that of the year
1714.

Although, from his disastrous circumstances, the principal
fountain of knowledge was shut up to poor Henry, it is evident
that he had made trial of every other within his reach. Knowing the facts of his blindness, itinerary life, and oral publication

of his poetry, the generality of readers, it may be presumed
have previously formed a contemptuous idea of the author, as
if he had been a common ballad-singer, and have either read
his book under the influence of this prepossession, or thrown i
aside as unworthy of their attention. But it should be recol
lected, that the rank of a bard or minstrel was once very high
among our forefathers; and that, although it had considerably
fallen in repute by the time that Henry flourished, he dic
nothing that was deemed unworthy of the character when a
its highest elevation. The language of Major has, it would
appear, been understood according to the prejudices of ou
own time, not according to the sense which it must still have
borne even in that age in which Henry lived, notwithstanding
the Act of James II. A. 1449, against "bardis, or vthirs siclyke
rinnaris about." Acts, Parl. X. c. 21. "He procured food
and raiment by the recitation of his compositions." Is this
any thing different from what was invariably accounted the
privilege of minstrels? Did Henry recite his poetry to the
vulgar; did he stroll through cities, towns, or villages with
this view? Not a hint of this kind is given; the very reverse
is implied in the specification made by the historian. He
recited his compositions "in vulgar poetry" indeed, but it was
coram principibus, "in the presence of princes," or "men of the
highest rank." Major uses the most honourable term that he
could select, to show that even the most exalted in the king
dom did not deem themselves degraded by admitting the
Minstrel into their presence, or by listening to his poetica
narrative. He indeed says; Quæ *vulgo* dicebantur, carmine
vulgari, in quo peritus est, conscripsit; but he does not mear
by this to affix a stigma on Henry's style of writing. The use
of the term *vulgari*, if not merely a *paronomasia* on the pre
ceding one *vulgo*, can signify nothing more than that Henry
did not write, as he himself did, in the language of the learned
which would have been lost even on men of the highest rank

in that age. He does not mean to say that the diction of the Minstrel was low, and thus adapted merely to the *vulgar;* for then men of all ranks spoke in the same manner: but that his work, as being a collection of what was *commonly* related in Scotland concerning Wallace, was composed in the vernacular tongue. When he uses 'the phrase, *in quo peritus est,* he is not to be understood as uttering so gross a solecism, as to say that Henry was well skilled in the language of the lower classes, but that he was an adept in Scottish poetry; for it is evident that *in quo* more immediately refers to *carmine.* He designs to throw as little discredit on him by the phrase, *victum et vestitum nactus est.* For all that he could mean to assert by it is, that as the tables of the great were open to him, where, in former times at least, a minstrel had the prerogative of an honourable seat, he had also, by established custom from time immemorial, as good a right to claim the raiment allotted to his vocation as the baron had to exact military service from his vassals. Hence, when speaking of this procurement, he qualifies his language by the following insertion,—*quo dignus erat;* applicable not merely to the hereditary claim of minstrels, but to the peculiar merit of Henry as sustaining this character.

I will not pretend to exculpate Henry from the charge of credulity. Far more, however, has been said as to his ignorance than can be well supported. We have no other standard of the measure of his knowledge than his own work; and this, there is every reason to think, much disfigured by unavoidable corruptions. But even judging from this, we have sufficient evidence that, from his early years, he must diligently have used all the means of information which were properly within his reach. He seems to have been pretty well acquainted with that kind of history which was commonly read in that period. He alludes to the history of Hector, of Alexander the Great, of Julius Cæsar. Book VIII. 845, 886, 961, &c., and to that of Charlemagne, whose army, at Ronceval in Navarre, being

betrayed by Ganelon, was defeated by the Saracens, Book VIII.
1256. XI. 837. V. Dict. de Trevoux, vo. *Rouncevaux*. With
the romances that were most popular in that age he was perhaps
as well acquainted as Barbour.   He seems to have been
familiar with that of *Alexander;* as, like the latter, he refers to
Gaudifer, Book X. 342.   V. Note on *The Bruce*, B. II. 468.

His acquaintance with the popular romances is perhaps still
more apparent from his style of writing.   As it abounds, much
more than that of Barbour, with poetical allusions to the face
of nature, which the poor Minstrel had never beheld, to the
change of the seasons, to the supposed influence of the planets
or of the constellations; it is more richly strewed with the more
peculiar phraseology of the writers of romance; whence a
stranger to our chronology might be induced to view the Life
of Wallace as of an older date than *The Bruce*, although nearly
a century later.   We meet with a variety of terms or phrases
in *Wallace*, which, from the difference of his habits, do not
seem to have been familiar with the good Archdeacon of Aberdeen, as *frekis, frekis on fold; bane and lyre; brycht*, and *frely
of fassoun*, for a fair maid, &c. &c.

It is necessary to observe, that the Minstrel's mode of expression is often very elliptical.   In order to understand his
meaning, the reader must therefore recollect, that he very commonly omits the pronouns, whether personal or relative.   This,
to those who are not familiar with the ancient style, has given
given him an air of absurdity, and has induced the idea of his
being far more illiterate than we can reasonably suppose him
to have been.   Let us take an example or two among many.

> The defendouris, was off sa fell defens,
> Kepyt thar toun with strenth and excellens.—B. VIII. 803.

The principal assertion is not, that the defenders were
powerful in defence; but that they, being so powerful in

defence, guarded their town well. The reader must supply *quha*, or *who*, after *defendouris*.

> The mar, kepyt the port of that willage,
> Wallace knew weill, and send him his message.—B. IV. 359.

" Wallace was well acquainted with the mayor, *who* kept the port of that village."

The only means that occurred to me for rendering the sense of such elliptical passages more obvious, was to throw in a comma; as, after *The mar*, in the passage quoted.

It cannot be denied that the feelings of the reader are often harrowed up by the coarse description which the Minstrel gives of the warlike deeds of his hero, and by the delight which he seems to take in those merciless scenes in which the English were the immediate sufferers. But great allowance must be made for him, not merely from the barbarism of the time in which he wrote, and from his want of such opportunities of refinement as even Barbour enjoyed, but from the soreness which every thorough Scotchman still felt, in consequence of the unpardonable treachery, violence, and ferocity of Edward the First, and of those employed under him, and the disgraceful stigma they had endeavoured to fix on a nation that had been always independent and always extremely jealous of its liberty. If the manners of the age do not form a sufficient apology for the cruelty ascribed to Wallace himself; it should be recollected that Scotland had no other chance of liberation from the usurpation of Edward than by the diminution of the number of the invaders, and that it was impossible for a few partisans to retain prisoners. Old Wyntown honestly defends Wallace on the grounds of the provocation given to him, and of his owing the English nothing.

> In all Ingland thare wes noucht thane
> As Willame Walays swa lele a mane.

> Quhat he dyd agayne that natyown,
> Thai made hym prowocatyown :
> Na to thame oblyst nevyr wes he
> In fayth, falowschype, na lawté :
> For in hys tyme, I hard well say,
> That fykkil thai ware all tyme of fay.
>
> *Cronykil,* B. VIII. c. 20, v. 9.

There is a prayer at the beginning of the poem, which had been prefixed by the transcriber. It is thus given in Perth edition, Notes, p. 1.

> Jesu, salvator! ex Jussu mihi exponere, ad
> Finem dignum, prædictum Librum, atque benign-um.

The first line has been injured in the binding of the MS.; but it would seem that it should rather be read thus :

> Jhesu saluator, tu sis michi auxiliator,
> Ad finem dignum librum perduc atque benignum.

In all the editions of this work which I have seen, it is divided into twelve books; which are subdivided into chapters or sections, with rubrics prefixed, pointing out the principal matter of each division. I have observed the plan of the MS., which confines the work to eleven books, without any rubrics. Some, indeed, are marked on the margent; but evidently in a different hand-writing, by some early proprietor of the MS.

Mr Pinkerton has said; The first and best edition I have yet seen is, *imprentit at Edinburgh, be Robert Lekprevik, at the expensis of Henrie Charteris: and ar to be sauld in his buith, on the north syde of the gait abone the throne* [*trone?*] *Anno Do.* MD. LXX. 4to. black letter. A fine copy of this edition is in the British Museum among Queen Elizabeth's books: this has no title-page; but the second title is, *The Actis and Deidis of the illuster and vailyeand Campioun Schir William Wallace, Knicht of Ellerslie.*" List of Scotish Poets, xc, xci.

This edition I have never had an opportunity of inspecting.

The oldest that I have seen, after every possible inquiry, is an imperfect one in quarto, formerly the property of Mr George Paton, of the Customs here, now in my possession. It wants the title-page, part of the first leaf, and the last sheet, which must have contained about fifteen pages, besides being imperfect in one or two other places. The title, printed on page first, seems to have been the same with the second title of Edit. 1570, with this difference, that in mine Wallace is denominated " the *maist* illuster," &c. Besides that of 1570, Mr Pinkerton mentions only another edition in 4to, Edin. 1594. I have therefore ventured to quote this as the edition of that year.

Dr Mackenzie seems either to have been unacquainted with any prior edition, or to have preferred this to that of 1570; although, from his known character as a writer, it is most probable that he had never compared the editions to which he refers. " This book, he says, " being highly esteem'd amongst the vulgar, has had many impressions; but the best are these, viz. that printed in the year 1594, and Andrew Hart's, in the year 1620, both printed at Edinburgh, and that at Glasgow in the year, 1699." &c.

Besides the edition of 1594, I have compared the MS. with Hart's, 1620; and with one printed by Gedeon Lithgow, Edinburgh, 1648, which I have not seen mentioned by any writer. It is a neat edition, in small 8vo, black letter, pp. 343, in the square form of our more early publications. It has an introduction, entitled *The Printer to the Reader*, considerably larger than that prefixed to Hart's, as it extends to nineteen pages. This contains an abridgment of the History of Scotland from the portentous death of Alexander III. A. 1285, to the year 1318. I have also consulted the Edinburgh edition of 1673, printed by Andrew Anderson, in twelves, pp. 252. This is considerably inferior in execution to the one last mentioned, although it seems to have been taken from it, with some slight changes of the orthography. The introduction to the former is

reprinted *verbatim;* but there is added, after the Table of
Contents, a poetical address of " Scrimger to Wallace, by reason
of the false Mentcith captive at London," and the reply of
" Wallace to Scrimger, his Baner-man." The following page
contains a curious wood-cut of Wallace in armour, with his bow
and quiver.

Mr Pinkerton mentions also editions at Edinburgh 1601,
Aberdeen 1630, and Glasgow 1665, in 8vo. He adds; " There
are many editions of the present [eighteenth] century, but bad.
The very worst is that of Edinburgh, 1758, 4to., which the
printer very expertly reduced to modern spelling, and printed
in black letter, and in quarto; being exactly, in every point,
the very plan which he ought not to have followed. The same
sagacious personage gave Barbour's Poem in the same way;
and neither selling, (how could they?) the booksellers sometimes tear out the title, and palm them upon the ignorant as
old impressions." List of Scot. Poets, *ut sup.*

This is the edition which is here quoted in the Notes as that
of 1714. For I have been assured, on good authority, that this
edition, as well as that of *The Bruce,* was printed by Robert
Freebairn, printer to his Majesty, in the year 1714 or 1715;
but that, as he engaged in the rebellion in the year last mentioned, before the work was ready for publication, they were
suffered to lie in a bookseller's ware-house till A. 1758, when
they were published, either without titles, or with titles bearing
the false date of this year. As to the merit of these editions, I
am under the necessity of differing from Mr Pinkerton. To
me, the editions printed by Freebairn appear more correct than
any of the preceding ones, and his Wallace even preferable to
the Perth edition, A. 1790; as, bating the liberty used with
regard to the orthography, they, in a great variety of instances,
give the sense of the original writers more accurately, having
evidently been collated with the MSS. of *The Bruce* and *Wallace*
in the Advocates' Library.

I flattered myself, that I might have had it in my power to have enriched this work by some valuable communications from the British Museum. Although, through the good offices of the Earl of Aberdeen, one of the trustees of this national repository, search has been made, nothing of importance has been discovered in regard to this period of our history. Henry Ellis, Esq. of the Museum, who, in the most obliging manner, offered every assistance in his power, has in a letter addressed to his Lordship, furnished two extracts from MSS., which have a claim to attention, at least as matters of curiosity. I shall take the liberty of communicating them in his own language:—

" I find nothing in the King's, the Cottonian, or the Harleian Collections ; but among the Donation Manuscripts, No. 4934, (in the first volume of Francis Peck's Collections for a Supplement to Dugdale's Monasticon), is a transcript of ' Prioris Alnwicensis de Bello Scotico apud Dumbarr, tempore Regis Edwardi I. Dictamen, sive Rithmus Latinus quo de Willielmo Wallace, Scotico illo Robin Whood, plura, sed invidiose, canit.' It is somewhat in the manner of Walter de Mapes, as your Lordship will perceive by the following specimens; and consists of sixty stanzas.

I.

' Ludere volentibus ludens paro Liram,
De Mundi malitia Rem demonstro miram;
Nil quod nocet, refero; Rem gestam requiram:
Scribo novam Satiram, set sic ne seminet Iram.   } MORUS.

46.

Falsus Dux Fallacie convocavit Cetum,
(Sciensque abierit Rex noster trans Fretum)
Cremare Northumbriam statuit Decretum:
Sepe videmus, ait, post Gaudia rumpere Fletum.   } OMER US.

47.

Luge nunc, Northumbria nimis desolata,
Facta es ut vidua Filiis orbata!
Vescy, Morley, Summerville, Bertram sunt in Fata!
O quibus, O quantis, O qualibet es viduata!   } OVID. OMER.

48.

In te, cum sis vidua, cunei Scotorum
Redigunt in cinerea prædia proborum;
Willelmus de Wallia dux est indoctorum,
Gaudia stultorum cumulant augmenta dolorum.   } CART.

49.

Ad Augmenta Sceleris actenus patrati,
Alnewyk dant ignibus viri scelerati;
Circumquaque cursitant velut insensati: } VERITAS EVANGELICA.
Electi pauci sunt, multi vero vocati.'

" The above are the chief allusions in the poem to historical facts.

" There is another manuscript in the same collection, No. 1226, without a title-page, but apparently a composition of the time of King Charles the First, principally relating to the period of Scottish history in question. The work is divided into two books, and as it is possible that Dr Jamieson may know what it is from its contents, I will trouble your Lordship with the heads of the different chapters, the numbers of which are irregular.

‘ Of the strif and debate that chanced betweine Robert de Bruce and John Ballioll, and how Edward Longshanks inwadit Scotland.’   Chap. 1.

‘ Of the walliant deadis of Williame Wallace, in the defence of his Contrie.’   Chap. 2.

‘ How Williame Wallace past to St Johnstone, and of the strange Combattis he had withe Englismen in that Jornay.’ Chap. 3.

‘ How William Wallace past in the sowthe Contrie and wone Lowmabane, and of his ficht with Englis men in the way, and how he tuik the Castell of Craford.’   Chap. 4.

‘ How the Englismen mowrdrit the gentill woman his wife,’ &c.   Chap. 5.

‘ How the Englishemen bound trwis withe Wallace.’ &c. Chap. 6.

'How William Wallace slew Mackfadyean and his hoill armye,' &c. Chap. 7.

'Of the most famous battell at Estirwilling Brige,' &c. Chap. 8.

'Of the famous Jornay and Wictories that William Wallace had into England,' &c. Chap. 9.

'How William Wallace past into France,' &c. Chap. 10.

'Of the great Wictories that Sr William Wallace had after he come forthe of France.' Chap. 11.

'How the Lord Steward encowntred King Edward.' &c. Chap. 12.

" 'The second part of the work begins,

'Of the most famous Wictories that the Lord Fraser had against the Englishmen.' Chap. 1.

'Of the great Wictorie Sr William Wallace obtained in France, and of his returne againe into Scotland.' Chap. 2.

'How Sr William Wallace slew yong Botler,' &c. Chap. 3.

'How Sr William Wallace beseaged St Johnston.' Chap. 4.

'How Sr William Wallace was betrayed by the false Menteithe.' Chap. 5.

'Of the famos raigne of King Robert de Bruise.' Chap. 6.

'How King Edward 3 of England inwadit Scotland, and was expellet again.' Chap. 7.

" Several chapters follow, ' Of Love,' 'The politick Law,' &c."

He also mentions a volume in the Cotton Library, marked Claud. D. VII. in which the 13th article is a chronicle written, or rather compiled, with additions, by a Canon of Lanercost priory, illustrative of the ravages in Cumberland towards the latter end of the reign of Edward the First. Several extracts having been made from this for the use of Mr Lysons, he found them extremely valuable, and containing more for his purpose than could be found in print.

Being anxious to bring forward every authentic information that

I could possibly collect concerning Wallace, I lately transmitted
to Mr Ellis a few queries, especially regarding the Lanercost
MS., which had occurred to me in consequence of his former
obliging communication; and, while I feel myself deeply in-
debted to him for the trouble he has taken, and for the prompt-
ness of his reply, I cannot pretend to give the substance of it
in any language so appropriate as that which he has himself
used.

" I must tell you that the Chronicle of Lanercost is a manuscript of peculiar intricacy in its contractions. The first
mention which I find in it of William Wallace is in 1297,
fol. 208 b. 'Vix sex mensium tempus elapsum extitit a gravi
sacramento supradicto quo se Albanacti fidelitati ac subjectioni
Regis Anglorum astrinxerant, cum rediviva perfidorum malitia
ad alias versutias ingenium acuit. Nam presul Ecclesiæ Glas-
cuensis proprio agnomine dictus Robertus Wyscardus, semper
in proditione primus, cum senescallo primæ' (the word *primæ*
is dotted under as if to be erased,) 'terræ nomine Jacobo, novam
sibi finxerunt audaciam, quinimo novam proditionis famam,
fidem Regi præstitam manifeste infringere non audentes, *quen-
dam virum sanguineum Wills. Waleis*, qui prius fuerat in Scotia
princeps latronum, contra Regem insurgere fecerunt et Papam
in sui adjutorium congregare.'

" Then follows the battle of Stirling, in which the notice of
the slain contains the following anecdote: ' Inter quos cedidit
thesaurarius Angliæ Hugo de Kersyngham, de cujus corio ab
occipite usque ad talum Wills. Waleis latam corrigiam sum
fecit, ut inde sibi faceret cingulum ensis sui.' The subsequent
entrance of the Scots into Northumberland is of course noticed,
but generally, and without any mention of Wallace's name.
The mention of the retreat of the English to Berwick opens the
account of transactions under the year 1298. It is there said,
' Wills. Waleis non tenuit eis fidem.'

" The Chronicle next mentions, that Edward having settled

a truce with the King of France returned, and collecting his army, marched towards Scotland. ' In festo autem beatæ Mariæ Magdalenæ occurrerunt ei Scoti apud Faukirk cum toto robore suo, *duce eorum Willelmo Waleis superius nominato.*' The defeat is then detailed in few words. Some wretched Latin verses follow, of which I give you the only specimen concerning Wallace, viz.—

> ' Sub duce de genere gens Scotia degeneravit,
> Quæ famam temere foedusque fidem violavit.
> Postquam Willelmus Wallens nobilitavit,
> Nobilitas prorsus Scottorum degeneravit.'

"Such are the scanty materials relating to Wallace's history in the Chronicle of Lanercost.

" In 1306, fol. 211 b, we read, ' Dominus autem Symon Freser Scottus adductus London, prius fuit tractus, postea suspensus, tertio decapitatus, et caput ejus positum super pontem London juxta caput Willelmi Waleis.' In the same year the Earl of Athol's head (Comes de Athetel) was placed above that of William Wallace; and in 1307 it is said, ' In die autem sancto Paschæ Dungallus factus est miles, et infra eandem septimanam captus est dominus *Johannes Waleis* et ad Regem apud Karl. adductus, qui misit eum London ut ubi caperet idem judicium quod prius acceperat frater suus Willelmus.' " Fol. 212.

We have a similar account in the St Albans Chronicle.

" How Johne, that was Wyllyam Waleys brother, was put to dethe.

" As the gretteste masteyrs of Scotlonde were thus doon to euyll dethe, and destroyed for theyr falsnesse, Johan. that was Wyllyam Waleys brother, was take and doon vnto deth, as Syr Johan erle of Alethes [Athol] was." Sign. q. vi. b. Edit. 1502.

This account, as regarding *Johannes Waleis*, must certainly be viewed as a mistake of the writers of these Chronicles. It has originated, perhaps, from the circumstance of two *brothers* of Robert Bruce, Thomas and Alexander, being made prisoners by Macdowal at Lochrian in Galloway, 9th February, 1306-7, and carried to Edward at Carlisle, who ordered them to instant execution. Or it may respect Sir Reginald Crawfurd, the *cousin* of Wallace, who was made prisoner with them, and subjected to the same fate. Matthew of Westminster says that their heads were placed on the gates of Carlisle. V. Dalrymple's Annals, II. 19.

The other queries were;—If, from any of the MSS. in the British Museum, there is ground to suppose that Wallace had ever fought with King Edward in England? If any thing occurs that might have given rise to the story, told by Henry, of an interview with the English queen? If there is any hint as to Wallace having opposed the English in Guienne? If there is any proof that Sir John Menteith was concerned in delivering up Wallace to the English? And if it appears that Menteith acted in concert with Aymer de Valence? To these Mr Ellis gives the following answer:—

" Except at the battle of Falkirk, I see no reason to think that Wallace was ever personally opposed to Edward the First; certainly not during his incursion in 1297, as Edward was then in France. The story of his meeting the queen at St Albans must be a fiction. It is too singular a circumstance, if it had happened, to remain totally unnoticed in any of the English annals. I can find no mention of Wallace's being in Guienne. I think it was not likely that he should be found there. Scotland and the Border gave him full employ for his short career. No concert is at all noticed in the Lanercost MS. between Aymer de Valence and Sir John Menteith."

His important communication, in regard to the concern that Menteith himself had in the base transactions referred to, will be found among the proofs which I have collected on this subject, in the Note on Book XI. ver. 948. p. 402.

Having made some inquiries as to the manuscript No. 1226, formerly mentioned, and suggested that, from its orthography, it seems to claim a date prior to the age of Charles the First; Mr Ellis has favoured me with the following reply:—

"The manuscript in the same collection, Num. 1226, is entirely in prose. It occupies about a hundred leaves in small quarto; but is not paged. From the orthography, the manuscript may be somewhat older than I had supposed. It certainly is not before the time of James the First. I think you are correct in supposing it a copy from Henry the Minstrel. In an address 'To the moist cortews Reader,' the author says, ' al thoche this famous historie hathe beine republished heir to foir by hime which deserws great thankis for so worthie a work, yit the gathering of the said historie in a smaller compass may gif moir content vnto some readers.' &c. From another passage it should seem that additions are interspersed: but evidently without either distinction or authorities."

Mr Ellis also informs me, that the only old edition of Wallace, in the Museum, besides that of 1570, is the one printed at Aberdeen, in 1630. small octavo.

ARGUMENTS

OF

THE DIFFERENT BOOKS.

ARGUMENT OF THE FIRST BOOK.

PROEM, v. 1.—Parentage of Wallace, v. 17.—Bruce and Baliol, v. 47.—Battles of Berwick and Dunbar, v. 85.—Baliol deposed, v. 115.—Wallace slays young Selbie at Dundee, v. 203.—Escapes disguised as an old woman, v. 239.—Arrives, with his mother, at Ellerslie, v. 315.—Adventure, when fishing at the water of Irvine, v. 367.

ARGUMENT OF THE SECOND BOOK.

Wallace slays the churl at Ayr, v. 29.—Also Percy's Steward, v. 84.—Cast into prison in Ayr, v. 153.—Henry's lamentation for him, v. 160.—Thrown over the wall as dead, v. 252.—Recovered by his nurse, v. 258.—Thomas the Rhymer, v. 288.—Wallace, on his way to Riccarton, slays the Squire Longcastle, v. 360.

ARGUMENT OF THE THIRD BOOK.

Wallace revenges the slaughter of his father and brother at Loudoun-hill, v. 40.—Slays the knight Fenwick, v. 175.—Sojourns in Clyde's wood, v. 249.—Makes peace with the English, at the instigation of Sir Ronald Crawfurd his uncle, v. 278.—Slays the buckler-player in Ayr, v. 353.

ARGUMENT OF THE FOURTH BOOK.

Percy's servant slain, v. 31.—Wallace rides towards the Lennox, v. 104.—Visits Earl Malcolm, v. 156.—Character of Fawdoun, v. 185.—The Peel of Gargunnock taken, v. 213.—Wallace crosses Forth, v. 270.—Goes to St. Johnston; and takes the castle of Kinclevin, v. 358.—Battle of Shortwood-shaw, v. 512.—Betrayed by his lemman, escapes from Perth, v. 703.

ARGUMENT OF THE FIFTH BOOK.

Wallace traced by a slouth-hound, v. 23.—Goes to Elcho Park, v. 35.—Slays Fawdoun on suspicion, v. 115.—Kerlé kills Heron, v. 145.—Wallace reaches Gask Hall, v. 175.—Ghost of Fawdoun, v. 192.—Wallace slays Butler, v. 238.—Swims across Forth at Cambuskenneth, v. 304.—Finds shelter at Torwood, v. 319.—Here he meets with his uncle, v. 350.—Visits Sir John the Graham at Dundaff, v. 436.—Master John Blair and Parson Gray, v. 538.—Falls in love with a young lady in Lanark, v. 584.—His reasoning against love, v. 622.—He visits her, v. 672.—The English cut the tails of his horses in Lochmaben, v. 731.—He slays Hugh of Moreland, v. 820.—Graystock follows Wallace with three hundred men, and is slain by Sir John the Graham, v. 860.—Lochmaben Castle taken, v. 992.—Also that of Crawford, v. 1075.

ARGUMENT OF THE SIXTH BOOK.

Dissertation on love, v. 25.—Wallace marries Miss Bradfute, v. 48.—Being assaulted by the English, retreats to Cartlane Craigs, v. 155.—Hesilrig, to revenge the escape of Wallace, murders his wife, v. 191.—Wallace slays Hesilrig, and drives the English out of Lanark, v. 230.—The battle of Biggar, v. 341.—Wallace disguises himself, v. 435.—Chosen guardian of Scotland, v. 767.—Takes a strength on the water of Cree, v. 803.—Also Turnbery Castle in Carrick, v. 834.—Agrees to a truce at Rutherglen, v. 865.—Resides at Cumnock, v. 936.

ARGUMENT OF THE SEVENTH BOOK.

Wallace's vision in Monkton Kirk, v. 57.—Treachery of the English at Ayr, v. 171.—Burning of the Barns, v. 333.—The Friar of Ayr's Benison, v. 471.—Wallace drives Bishop Beck and Percy out of Glasgow, v. 515.—He seeks Macfadyan, and slays old Rukby at Stirling, v. 623.—Earl Malcolm takes Stirling Castle, v. 727.—Macfadyan killed, v. 862.—Council at Ardchattan, v. 875.—Wallace takes St Johnston, v. 958.—Destroys the English at Dunottar, v. 1042.—Burns an hundred ships belonging to them at Aberdeen, v. 1065.—Besieges the Castle of Dundee, v. 1090.—Battle of Stirling-bridge, v. 1134.—Hugh de Cresyngham slain, v. 1196.—Sir John Menteith takes an oath to Wallace, v. 1259.—Cristal of Seatoun, v. 1275.

ARGUMENT OF THE EIGHTH BOOK.

A parliament at Perth, to which Corspatrick refuses to come, v. 1.—Wallace fights with him at Dunbar, v. 86.—Bruce and Beik enter Scotland with an army, v. 139.—They, with Corspatrick, are driven out of the country, v. 380.—Wallace invades England, v. 433.—Advances to York, v. 517. —Demands battle of King Edward, v. 550.—The siege of York, v. 741.— Ramswaith burnt, v. 1008.—Poetical description of morning, v. 1181.— The Queen of England sues to Wallace for peace, v. 1215.—This is granted on certain conditions, v. 1510.—Wallace returns to Scotland, v. 1570.— Invited by the King of France to visit him, v. 1619.

ARGUMENT OF THE NINTH BOOK.

Description of Spring, v. 1.—Wallace sets sail for France, v. 47.—Is attacked by Longueville, the Red Reaver, v. 86.—Takes him prisoner, v. 149. —Goes to Paris, v. 300.—Obtains Longueville's pardon, v. 381.—Passes into Guienne, v. 427.—During his absence the English invade Scotland, v. 550.—He is invited to return, v. 646.—On his return he takes St Johnston, v. 697.—The battle of Black Irnside, v. 779.—Sir John Stewart killed, v. 1103.—Castle of Lochlevin taken, v. 1161.—Also, that of Airth, v. 1281.—Wallace delivers his uncle from prison, v. 1345.—Englishmen burnt in Dunbarton, v. 1376.—The castle kept by Menteith, v. 1395.— Death of the mother of Wallace, v. 1530.—Douglas takes the castle of Sanquhar, v. 1551.—The English lay siege to it, and Douglas is rescued by Wallace, v. 1729.—He lays siege to Dundee, v. 1839.

ARGUMENT OF THE TENTH BOOK.

The battle of Sheriff-muir, v. 19.—Battle of Falkirk, v. 37.—Contention between Wallace and Stewart of Bute, v. 109.—Death of Sir John the Graham, v. 378.—Conference between Wallace and Bruce at Carron, v. 439. —Lamentation of Wallace for the loss of Graham, v. 557.—Edward surprised at Linlithgow, v. 627.—Bruce held in subjection to England, v. 720. —Dundee taken, v. 751.—Wallace resigns his office, v. 762.—Sets sail for France, and meets John of Lynn, v. 797.—The Reaver killed, v. 885.— Menteith engaged to King Edward, v. 972.—Edward invades Scotland, divides the lands, and sends some noblemen to prison, v. 985.—Cumyn enters into a compact with the Bruce, v. 1007.—Different opinions as to the part he acted, v. 1153.

ARGUMENT OF THE ELEVENTH BOOK.

The success of Wallace in Guienne, v. 1.—A French knight seeks to slay him, v. 71.—Wallace slays two champions, v. 149.—His pretended encounter with a lion, v. 195.—He leaves France, and lands at the mouth of Earn, v. 295.—Slays young Butler in Elcho Park, v. 358.—Straits of Wallace and his companions from want of food, v. 553.—Kills five men who come on him while asleep, and provides food for his men, v. 571.—Lays siege to St Johnstoun, and drives the English out of Scotland, v. 707.—Wallange and Menteith plot against Wallace, v. 791.—St Johnstoun taken, v. 854.—Edward Bruce meets Wallace, v. 918.—Wallace invites Robert the Bruce to Scotland, v. 965.—Is betrayed and taken at Rob Royston, v. 995.—Lamentation for the loss of him, v. 1109.—Grief of Longueville, v. 1139.—Robert the Bruce arrives at Lochmaben, v. 1155.—Kills Cumyn, v. 1185.—Vision of a monk of Bury Abbey, v. 1238.—Martyrdom of Wallace at London, v. 1305.—Conclusion, v. 1451.

WALLACE.

BUKE FYRST.

OUR antecessowris, that we suld of reide,
And hald in mynde thar nobille worthi deid,
We lat ourslide, throw werray sleuthfulnes;
And castis ws euir till vthir besynes.
5 Till honour ennymys is our haile entent,
It has beyne scyne in thir tymys bywent;
Our ald ennemys cummyn of Saxonys blud,
That neuyr yeit to Scotland wald do gud,
Bot euir on fors, and contrar haile thair will,
10 Quhow gret kyndnes thar has beyne kyth thaim till.
It is weyle knawyne on mony diuerss syde,
How thai haff wrocht in to thair mychty pryde,
To hald Scotlande at wndyr cuirmar.
Bot God abuff has maid thar mycht to par:
15 Yhit we suld thynk one our bearis befor.
Of thair parablyss as now I say no mor.

We reide of ane rycht famouss of renowne,
Of worthi blude that ryngis in this regioune:
And hensfurth I will my process hald
20 Of Wilyham Wallas yhe haf hard beyne tald.
His forbearis quha likis till wndrestand,

A

Of hale lynage, and trew lyne of Scotland,
Schir Ranald Crawfurd, rycht schirreff of Ayr:
So in hys tyme he had a dochter fayr,
25 And yonge Schir Ranald schirreff of that toune,
His systir fair, off gud famç and ranoune:
Malcom Wallas hir gat in mariage,
That Elrislé than had in heretage,
Auchinbothe, and othir syndry place;
30 The secund O he was of gud Wallace:
The quhilk Wallas fully worthely at wrocht,
Quhen Waltyr hyr of Waillis fra Warayn socht.
Quha likis till haif mar knawlage in that part,
Go reid the rycht lyne of the fyrst Stewart.
35 Bot Malcom gat wpon this lady brycht
Schir Malcom Wallas, a full gentill knycht,
And Wilyame als, as Conus cornykle beris on hand;
Quhilk eftir was the reskew of Scotland.
Quhen it was lost with tresoune and falsness,
40 Our set be fais, he fred it weyle throu grace.

   Quhen Alexander our worthi king had lorn,
Be awentur, his liff besid Kyngorn,
Thre yer in pess the realm stude desolate;
Quharfor thair raiss a full grewous debate.
45 Our prynce Dawy, the erle of Huntyntoun,
Thre dochtrys had that war of gret ranoun;
Off quhilk thre com Bruce, Balyoune, and Hastyng:
Twa of the thre desyryt to be kyng.
Balyoune clamyt of fyrst gre lynialy;
50 And Bruce fyrst male of the secund gre by.
Fol. 1 b To Paryss than, and in Ingland thai send,
Off this gret striff how thai suld haif ane end.
Foly it was, forsuth it happynnyt sa,
Succour to sek of thar alde mortale fa.

55 Eduuarde Langschankis had new begune hys wer
Apon Gaskone, fell awfull in effer:
Thai landis thane he clamde as heretage.
Fra tyme that he had semblit his barnage,
And herd tell weyle Scotland stude in sic cace,
60 He thocht till hym to mak it playn conquace.
Till Noram kirk he come with outyn mar,
The consell than of Scotland meit hym thar.
Full sutailly he chargit thaim in bandoune,
As thar our lord, till hald of hym the croun.
65 Byschope Robert, in his tyme full worthi,
Off Glaskow lord, he said that "we deny
" Ony our lord, bot the gret God abuff."
The king was wrath, and maid hym to ramuff.
Couatus Balyoune folowid on hym fast:
70 Till hald of hym he grantyt at the last.
In contrar rycht, a king he maid hym thar;
Quhar throuch Scotland rapentyt syne full sar.
To Balyoune yhit our lordis wald nocht consent.
Eduuard past south, and gert set his parliment:
75 He callyt Balyoune till ansuer for Scotland.
The wyss lordis gert hym sone brek that band.
Ane abbot past, and gaif our this legiance.
King Eduuard than it tuk in gret greuance.
His ost he rasd, and come to Werk on Twede;
80 Bot for to fecht, as than he had gret drede.
To Corspatryk of Dunbar sone he send,
His consell ast, for he [the] contré kend:
And he was brocht in presence to the king.
Be suttale band thai cordyt of this thing.

85 Erle Patrik than till Berweik couth persew;
Ressawide he was and trastyt werray trew.
The king folowid with his host of ranoun;

Eftir mydnycht at rest wes all the toun.
Corspatryk raiss, the keyis weile he knew,
90 Leit breggis doun, and portculess thai drew;
Set wp yettis syne, couth his baner schaw;
The ost was war, and towart hym thai draw.
Eduuard entrit, and gert sla hastely,
Of man and wiff, sewyn thousand and fyfty,
95 And barnys als: be this fals awentur,
Of trew Scottis chapyt na creatur.
A captayne thair this fals Eduuard maid:
Towart Dunbar, without restyng thai raid;
Quhar gaderyt was gret power of Scotland,
100 Agayne Eduuard in bataill thocht to stand.
Thir four erllis was entrit in that place,
Of Mar, Menteith, Adell, Ross, wpon cace.
Fol. 2 a In that castell the erle gert hald thaim in,
At to thar men with out thai mycht nocht wyn;
105 Na thai to thaim supplëyng for to ma.
The battaillis than to giddyr fast thai ga.
Full gret slauchtyr, at pitté was to se,
Off trew Scottis oursett with sutelté.
Erle Patrik than, quhen fechtyng was fellast,
110 Till our fa turnd, and harmyng did ws mast.
Is nayne in warld, at scaithis ma do mar,
Than weile trastyt in borne familiar.
Our men was slayne with outyn redemptioune;
Throuch thar dedis all tynt was this regioune.
115 King Eduuard past and Corspatrik to Scwne;
And thar he gat homage of Scotland swne:
For nane was left the realme for to defend.
For Jhon the Balyoune to Munross than he send,
And putt hym doune for euir of this kynrik:
120 Than Eduuarde self was callit a roy full ryk.
The croune he tuk apon that sammyne stane

At Gadalos send with his sone fra Spane,
Quhen Iber Scot fyrst in till Irland come.
At Canemor syne king Fergus has it nome;
125 Brocht it till Scwne, and stapill maid it thar,
Quhar kingis was cround aucht hundyr yer and mar,
Befor the tyme at king Eduuard it fand.
This jowell he gert turss in till Ingland;
In Lwnd it sett till witness of this thing;
130 Be conquest than of Scotland cald hym king.
Quhar that stayne is, Scottis suld mastir be:
God chess the tyme Margretis ayr till see!
Sewyn scor thai led off the gretast that thai fand
Off ayris with thaim, and Bruce, out of Scotland.
135 Eduuard gayf hym his faderis heretage;
Bot he thocht ay till hald hym in thrillage.
Baith Blatok Mur was his and Huntyntoun;
Till erle Patrik thai gaif full gret gardoun.
For the frendschipe king Eduuard with hym fand,
140 Protector haile he maid hym of Scotland.
That office than he brukyt bot schort tyme.
I may nocht now putt all thair deid in ryme;
Off cornikle quhat suld I tary lang?
To Wallace agayne now breiffly will I gange.
145 Scotland was lost quhen he was bot a child,
And our set throuch with our ennemyss wilde.
His fadyr Malcom in the Lennox fled;
His eldest sone thedir he with hym led.
Hys modyr fled with him fra Elrislé,
150 Till Gowry past, and duelt in Kilspyndé.
The knycht hir fadyr thedyr he thaim sent
Till his wncle, that with full gud entent
In Gowry duelt, and had gud lewyng thar;
Ane agyt man, the quhilk resawyt thaim far.
155 In till Dundé Wallace to scule thai send,

Fol. 2 b Quhill he of witt full worthely was kend.
      Thus he conteynde in till hys tendyr age;
      In armys syne did mony hie waslage,
      Quhen Saxons blude into this realm cummyng,
160 Wyrkand the will of Eduuard that fals king,
      Mony gret wrang thai wrocht in this regioune,
      Distroyed our lordys, and brak thar byggynnys doun.
      Both wiffis, wedowis, thai tuk all at thair will,
      Nonnys, madyns, quham thai likit to spill.
165 King Herodis part thai playit in to Scotland,
      Off yong childer that thai befor thaim sand.
      The byschoprykis, that war of gretast waile,
      Thai tuk in hand of thar archbyschops haile:
      No for the Pape thai wald no kyrkis forber,
170 Bot gryppyt all be wiolence of wer.
      Glaskow thai gaif, as it our weile was kend,
      To dyocye in Duram to commend.
      Small benifice that wald thai nocht persew,
      And for the richt full worthy clerkis thai slew;
175 Hangitt barrownnys and wroucht full mekill cayr:
      It was weylle knawyn, in the Bernys of Ayr,
      Auchtene score putt to that dispitfull dede:
      Bot God abowyn has send ws sum ramede.
      The remembrance is forthir in the taile.
180 I will folow apon my process haile.

      Willyham Wallace, or he was man of armys,
      Gret pitté thocht that Scotland tuk sic harmys.
      Mekill dolour it did hym in hys mynde;
      For he was wyss, rycht worthy, wicht and kynd:
185 In Gowry duelt still with this worthy man.
      As he encressyt, and witt haboundyt than,
      In till hys hart he had full mekill cayr,
      He saw the Sothroun multipliand mayr;

And to hym self offt wald he mak his mayne.
190 Off his gud kyne thai had slane mony ane.
Yhit he was than semly, stark and bald;
And he of age was bot auchtene yer auld.
Wapynnys he bur, outhir gud suerd or knyff;
For he with thaim hapnyt richt offt in stryff.
195 Quhar he fand ane without the othir presance,
Eftir to Scottis that did no mor grewance;
To cut his throit, or steik hym sodanlye,
He wayndyt nocht, fand he thaim fawely.
Syndry wayntyt, bot nane wyst be quhat way;
200 For all to him thar couth na man thaim say.
Sad of contenance he was bathe auld and ying,
Litill of spech, wyss, curtass and benyng.
Wpon a day to Dundé he was send;
Off cruelness full litill thai him kend.
205 The constable a felloun man of wer,
Fol. 3 a That to the Scottis did full mekill der,
Selbye he hecht, dispitfull and owtrage.
A sone he had ner twenty yer of age:
Into the toun he wsyt euerlik day;
210 Thre men or four thar went with him to play;
A hely schrew, wanton in his entent.
Wallace he saw, and towart him he went;
Liklé he was, richt byge and weyle beseyne,
In till a gyde of gudly ganand greyne.
215 He callyt on hym, and said; "Thou Scot, abyde;
" Quha dewill the grathis in so gay a gyde?
" Ane Ersche mantill it war thi kynd to wer;
" A Scottis thewtill wndyr thi belt to ber;
" Rouch rewlyngis apon thi harlot fete.
220 " Gyff me thi knyff; quhat dois thi ger so mete?"
Till him he yeid, his knyff to tak him fra.
Fast by the collar Wallace couth him ta;

Wndyr his hand the knyff he bradit owt,
For all his men that semblyt him about:
225　Bot help him selff he wsyt of no remede;
With out reskew he stekyt him to dede.
The squier fell: of him thar was na mar.
His men folowid on Wallace wondyr sar:
The press was thik, and cummerit thaim full fast.
230　Wallace was spedy, and gretlye als agast;
The bludy knyff bar drawin in his hand,
He sparyt nane that he befor him fand.
He knew the hous his eyme had lugit in;
Thedir he fled, for owt he mycht nocht wyn.
235　The gude wyff than within the closs saw he;
And, " Help," he cryit, " for him that deit on tre;
" The yong captane has fallyn with me at stryff."
In at the dur he went with this gud wiff.
A roussat goun of hir awn scho him gaif
240　Apon his weyd, at coueryt all the layff;
A soudly courche our hed and nek leit fall;
A wowyn quhyt hatt scho brassit on with all;
For thai suld nocht lang tary at that in;
Gaiff him a rok, syn set him doun to spyn.
245　The Sothroun socht quhar Wallace was in drede;
Thai wyst nocht weylle at quhat yett he in yeide.
In that same houss thai socht him beselye;
Bot he sat still, and span full conandly,
As of his tym, for he nocht leryt lang.
250　Thai left him swa, and furth thar gait can gang,
With hewy cheyr and sorowfull in thocht:
Mar witt of him as than get couth thai nocht.
The Inglis men, all thus in barrat boune,
Bade byrne all Scottis that war in to that toun.
255　Yhit this gud wiff held Wallace till the nycht,
Maid him gud cher, syne put hym out with slycht.

Fol. 3 b Throw a dyrk garth scho gydyt him furth fast;
In cowart went and vp the wattyr past;
Forbure the gate for wachis that war thar.
260 His modyr bade in till a gret dispar.
Quhen scho him saw scho thankit hewynnis queyn,
And said; "Der sone, this lang quhar has thow beyne?"
He tald his modyr of his sodane cass.
Than wepyt scho, and said full oft, 'Allas!
265 'Or that thow cessis thow will be slayne with all.'
"Modyr," he said, "God reuller is of all.
"Unsouerable are thir pepille of Ingland;
"Part of thar ire me think we suld gaynstand."
His eme wist weyle that he the squier slew;
270 For dreid thar of in gret langour he grew.
This passit our, quhill diueris dayis war gane:
That gud man dred or Wallace suld be tane:
For Suthroun ar full sutaille euirilk man.
A gret dyttay for Scottis thai ordand than;
275 Be the lawdayis in Dundé set ane ayr:
Than Wallace wald na langar soiorne thar.

His modyr graithit hir in pilgrame weid;
Hym[selff] disgysyt syne glaidlye with hir yeid;
A schort swerd wndyr his weid priualé.
280 In all that land full mony fays had he.
Baith on thar fute, with thaim may tuk thai nocht.
Quha sperd, scho said to Sanct Margret thai socht,
Quha serwit hir.   Full gret frendschipe thai fand
With Sothroun folk: for scho was of Ingland.
285 Besyd Landoris the ferrye our thai past
Syn throw the Ochell sped thaim wondyr fast.
In Dunfermlyn thai lugyt all that nycht.
Apon the morn, quhen that the day was brycht,
With gentill wemen hapnyt thaim to pass,

290 Off Ingland born, in Lithquhow wounnand was.
　　The captans wiff, in pilgramage had beyne,
　　Fra scho thaim mett, and had yong Wallace sene,
　　Gud cher thaim maid; for he was wondyr fayr,
　　Nocht large of tong, weille taucht and debonayr.

295 Furth tawkand thus of materis that was wrocht,
　　Quhill south our Forth with hyr son scho thaim bro
　　In to Lithkow thai wald nocht tary lang;
　　Thar leyff thai tuk, to Dunypace couth gang.
　　Thar duelt his eyme, a man of gret richess.

300 This mychty persone, hecht to name Wallas,
　　Maid thaim gud cher, and was a full kynd man,
　　Welcummyt thaim fair, and to thaim tald he than,
　　Dide him to witt, the land was all on ster;
　　Trettyt thaim weyle, and said; " My sone so der,

305 " Thi modyr and thow rycht heir with me sall bide,
　　" Quhill better be, for chance at may betyde."
Fol. 4 a Wallace ansuerd, said; ' Westermar we will:
　　' Our kyne ar slayne, and that me likis ill;
　　' And othir worthi mony in that art:

310 ' Will God I leiffe, we sall ws wreke on part.'
　　The persone sicht, and said; " My sone so fre,
　　" I cannot witt how that radress may be."
　　Quhat suld I spek of frustir? as this tyd,
　　For gyft of gud with him he wald nocht bide.

315 His modyr and he till Elrislé thai went.
　　Vpon the morn scho for hir brothyr sent,
　　In Corsby duelt and schirreff was of Ayr.
　　Hyr fadyr was dede, a lang tyme leyffyt had thar;
　　Hyr husband als at Lowdoun-hill was slayn.

320 Hyr eldest sone, that mekill was of mayn,
　　Schir Malcom Wallas was his nayme but less,
　　His houch senons thai cuttyt in that press;
　　On kneis he faucht, felle Inglismen he slew;

Till hym thar socht may fechtaris than anew;
325 On athyr side with speris bar him doun;
Thar stekit thai that gud knycht of renoun.
On to my taile I left. At Elrislé
Schir Ranald come son till his sistyr fre,
Welcummyt thaim hayme, and sperd of hir entent.
330 Scho prayde he wald to the lord Persye went,
So yrk of wer scho couth no forthir fle,
To purchess pes, in rest at scho mycht be.
Schyr Ranald had the Perseys protectioune,
As for all part to tak the remissioune.
335 He gert wrytt ane till his systir that tyde.
In that respyt Wallas wald nocht abyde:
Hys modyr kyst, scho wepyt with hart sar,
His leyff he tuk, syne with his eyme couth far.
Yonge he was, and to Sothroun rycht sauage;
340 Gret rowme thai had, dispitfull and wtrage.
Schir Ranald weylle durst nocht hald Wallas thar;
For gret perell he wyst apperand war:
For thai had haile the strenthis of Scotland;
Quhat thai wald do durst few agayne thaim stand.
345 Schyrreff he was, and wsyt thaim amang;
Full sar he dred or Wallas suld tak wrang:
For he and thai couth neuir weyle accord.
He gat a blaw, thocht he war lad or lord,
That proferryt him ony lychtlynes;
350 Bot thai raparyt our mekill to that place.
Als Ingliss clerkis in prophecyss thai fand,
How a Wallace suld putt thaim of Scotland.
Schir Ranald knew weill a mar quiet sted,
Quhar Wilyham mycht be bettir fra thair fede,
355 With his wncle Wallas of Ricardtoun,
Schir Richard hecht, that gud knycht off renoun.
Fol. 4 b Thai landis hayle than was his heretage,

Bot blynd he was, (so hapnyt throw curage,
Be Ingliss men that dois ws mekill der;
360 In his rysyng he worthi was in wer.)
Throuch hurt of waynys, and mystyrit of blud.
Yeit he was wiss, and of his conseil gud.
In Feuiryer Wallas was to him send;
In Aperill fra him he bownd to wend.
365 Bot gud serwice he dide him with plesance,
As in that place was worthi to awance.

So on a tym he desyrit to play.
In Aperill the thre and twenty day,
Till Erewyn wattir fysche to tak he went;
370 Sic fantasye fell in his entent.
To leide his net, a child furth with him yeid;
But he, or nowne, was in a fellowne dreid.
His suerd he left, so did he neuir agayne;
It dide him gud, supposs he sufferyt payne.
375 Off that labour as than he was nocht sle:
Happy he was, tuk fysche haboundanlé.
Or of the day ten houris our couth pass,
Ridand thar come, ner by quhar Wallace wass,
The lorde Persye, was captane than off Ayr;
380 Fra thine he turnde and couth to Glaskow fair.
Part of the court had Wallace labour seyne,
Till him raid fyve cled in to ganand greyne,
And said sone; " Scot, Martyns fysche we wald hawe."
Wallace meklye agayne ansuer him gawe;
385 ' It war resone, me think, yhe suld haif part:
' Waith suld be delt, in all place, with fre hart.'
He bad his child, " Gyff thaim of our waithyng."
The Sothroun said; ' As now of thi delyng
' We will nocht tak, thow wald giff ws our small.'
390 He lychtyt doun, and fra the child tuk all.

Wallas said than; " Gentill men gif ye be,
" Leiff ws sum part, we pray for cheryté.
" Ane agyt knycht serwis our lady to day;
" Gud frend, leiff part and tak nocht all away."

395 ' Thow sall haiff leiff to fysche, and tak the ma,
' All this forsuth sall in our flyttyng ga.
' We serff a lord; thir fysche sall till him gang.'
Wallace ansuerd, said; " Thow art in the wrang."
' Quham thowis thow, Scot? in faith thow serwis a blaw.'

400 Till him he ran, and out a suerd can draw.
Willyham was wa he had na wappynis thar,
Bot the poustaff, the quhilk in hand he bar.
Wallas with it fast on the cheik him tuk
Wyth so gud will, quhill of his feit he schuk.

405 The suerd flaw fra him a fur breid on the land.
Wallas was glad, and hynt it sone in hand;
And with the swerd awkwart he him gawe
Wndyr the hat, his crage in sondre drawe.

Fol. 5 a Be that the layff lychtyt about Wallas;

410 He had no helpe, only bot Goddis grace.
On athir side full fast on him thai dange;
Gret perell was giff thai had lestyt lang.
Apone the hede in gret ire he strak ane;
The scherand suerd glaid to the colar bane.

415 Ane othir on the arme he hitt so hardely,
Quhill hand and suerd bathe on the feld can ly.
The tothir twa fled to thar hors agayne;
He stekit him was last apon the playne.
Thre slew he thar, twa fled with all thair mycht

420 Eftir thar lord; bot he was out of sycht,
Takand the mure, or he and thai couth twyne.
Till him thai raid onon, or thai wald blyne,
And cryit; " Lord, abide; your men ar martyrit doun
" Rycht cruelly, her in this fals regioun.

425 " Fyve of our court her at the wattir baid,
   " Fysche for to bryng, thocht it na profyt maid.
   " We ar chapyt, bot in feyld slayne are thre."
   The lord speryt; ' How mony mycht thai be?'
   " We saw bot ane that has discumfyst ws all."
430 Than leuch he lowde, and said; ' Foule mot yow fall;
   ' Sen ane yow all has putt to confusioun.
   ' Quha menys it maist, the dewyll of hell him droun;
   ' This day for me, in faith, he beis nocht socht.'
   Quhen Wallas thus this worthi werk had wrocht,
435 Thar horss he tuk, and ger that lewyt was thar;
   Gaif our that crafft, he yeid to fysche no mar;
   Went till his eyme, and tauld him of this dede.
   And he for wo weyle ner worthit to weide;
   And said; " Sone, thir tythingis syttis me sor;
440 " And be it knawin, thow may tak scaith tharfor."
   ' Wncle,' he said, ' I will no langar byde;
   ' Thir Southland horss latt se gif I can ride.'
   Than bot a child, him serwice for to mak,
   Hys emys sonnys he wald nocht with him tak.
445 This gude knycht said; " Deyr cusyng, pray I the,
   " Quhen thow wanttis gud, cum fech ynewch fra me."
   Syluir and gold he gert on to him geyff.
   Wallace inclynys, and gudely tuk his leyff.

EXPLICIT LIBER PRIMUS,
ET INCIPIT SECUNDUS.

BUKE SECUND.

Yong Wallace fulfillit of hie curage;
In pryss of armys desirous and sauage;
Thi waslage may neuir be forlorn,
Thi deidis are knawin, thocht that the warld had suorn:
5 For thi haile mynde, labour and besynes,
Was set in wer, and werray rychtwisnes;
· And felloune loss of thi deyr worthi kyn.
Fol. 5 b The rancour more remaynde thi mynd with in.
It was his lyff, and maist part of his fude,
10 To se thaim sched the byrnand Sothroun blude.
Till Auchincruff with outyn mar he raid,
And bot schort tyme in pess at he thar baid.
Thar duelt a Wallas, welcummyt him full weill;
Thocht Ingliss men thar of had litill feille.
15 Bathe meite and drynk at his wille he had thar.
In Laglyne wode, quhen that he maid repayr,
This gentill man was full oft his resett;
With stuff of houshald strestely he thaim bett.
So he desirit the toune of Air to se,
20 His child with him; as than na man had he.
Ay next the wode Wallace gert leiff his horss;
Syne on his feit yeid to the merkat corss.
The Persye was in the castell of Ayr
With Ingliss men, gret nowmber and repayr:
25 Our all ye toune rewlyng on thair awne wiss,
Till mony Scot thai did full gret suppriss.

Aboundandely Wallace amang thaim yeid;
The rage of youth maid him to haf no dreid.
A churll thai had, that felloune byrdyngis bar;
30 Excedandlye he wald lyft mekill mar
Than ony twa that thai amang thaim fand;
And als be wss a sport he tuk in hand:
He bar a sasteing in a boustous poille:
On his braid bak of ony wald he thoile,
35 Bot for a grot, als fast as he mycht draw.
Quhen Wallas herd spek of that mery saw,
He likyt weill at that mercat to be,
And for a strak he bad him grottis thre.
The churll grantyt, of that proferr was fayn.
40 To pay the siluer Wallas was full bayne.
Wallas that steing tuk wp in till his hand;
Full sturdely he coud befor him stand,
Wallace, with that, apon the bak him gaif,
Till his ryg bayne he all in sondyr draif.
45 The carll was dede: of him I spek no mar.
The Ingliss men semblit on Wallace thair,
Feill on the feld of frekis fechtand fast;
He vnabasyt, and nocht gretlie agast,
Vpon the hed ane with the steing hitt he,
50 Till bayn and brayn he gert in pecis fle.
Ane othir he straik on a basnat of steille,
The tre to raiff and fruschit euiredeille.
His steyng was tynt, the Ingliss man was dede;
For his crag bayne was brokyn in that stede.
55 He drew a suerd at helpit him at neide,
Throuch oute the thikest of the press he yeid;
And at his horss full fayne he wald haif beyne.
Twa sarde him maist that cruell war and keyne.
Wallace raturnd as man of mekyll mayne;
Fol. 6 a 60 And at a straik the formast has he slayne.

The tothir fled, and durst him nocht abide;
Bot a rycht straik Wallace him gat that tid:
In at the guschet brymly he him bar;
The grounden suerd throuch out his cost it schar.
65 Fyve slew he thar, or that he left the toune:
He gat his horss, to Laglyne maid him boune,
Kepyt his child, and leyt him nocht abide;
In saufté thus on to the wod can ride.
Feille folowit him on hors, and eik on futte,
70 To tak Wallace: bot than it was no butte;
Couert of treis sawit him full weille.
Bot thar to bid than coude he nocht adeille
Gud ordinance, that serd for his estate,
His cusyng maid at all tyme, ayr and late,
75 The Squier Wallace in Auchincruff that was;
Baith bed and meite he maid for thaim to pass,
As for that tyme that he remanyt thar;
Bot sar he langit to [se] the toune of Ayr.
Thedyr he past apon the mercate day;
80 Gret God gif he as than had beyne away!

His emys serwand to buy him fysche was send,
Schir Ranald Craufurd, schirreff than was kend.
Quhen he had tane of sic gud as he bocht,
The Perseys stwart sadly till him socht,
85 And said; "Thow Scot, to quhom takis thow this thing?"
'To the schirreff.' he said. "Be hewynnys king,
"My lord sall haiff it; and syne go seke the mar."
Wallace on gaite ner by was walkand thar:
Till him he yeid, and said; 'Gud freynd, pray I the,
90 'The schirreffis serwand thow wald lat him be.'
A hetfull man the stwart was of blude:
And thoucht Wallace chargyt him in termys rude.
"Go hens, the Scot, the mekill dewill the speid;

B

"At thi shrewed wss thow wenys me to leid."
95 A huntyn staff in till his hand he bar;
Thar with he smat on Willyham Wallace thair.
Bot for his tre litill sonyhé he maid,
Bot be the coler claucht him with outyn baid.
A felloun knyff fast till his hart straik he;
100 Syn fra him dede schot him doun sodanlé:
Catour sen syne he was, but weyr, no mar.
Men of armess on Wallace semblit thar,
Four scor was sett in armyss buskyt boune,
On the merket day, for Scottis to kepe the toune.
105 Bot Wallace bauldlye drew a suerd of wer,
In to the byrneis the formast can he ber,
Throuch out the body stekit him to dede;
And syndry ma, or he past of that stede.
Ane othir awkwart a large straik tuk [he] thar,
110 Abown the kne, the bayne in sondir schar.
The thrid he straik throuch his pissand of maile,
The crag in twa; no weidis mycht him waill.
Fol. 6 b Thus Wallace ferd als fers as a lyoun.
Than Inglissmen, that war in bargane, boune
115 To kepe the gait with speris rud and lang;
For dynt of suerd thai durst nocht till hym gang.
Wallace was harnest on his body weyle;
Till him thai socht with hedis scharp of steyle,
And fra his strenth enwerounde him about;
120 Bot throu the press on a side he went out,
On till a wall that stude by the se syde;
For weyle or wo thar most he nedis abide.
And off thar speris in pecis part he schar.
Than fra the castell othir help come mar.
125 Atour the dike thai yeid on athir side,
Schott doun the wall; no socour was that tyde.
Than wist he nocht of no help, bot to de;

To wenge his dede amang thaim louss yeid he,
On athyr part in gret irc hewand fast.
130 Hys byrnyst brand to byrstyt at the last,
Brak in the heltis, away the blaid it flaw;
He wyst na wayne, bot out his knyff can draw.
The fyrst he slew, that him in hand has hynt;
And othir twa he stekit with his dynt.
135 The remanand with speris to him socht,
Bar him to ground, than forthir mycht he nocht.
The lordis bad that thai suld nocht him sla;
To pyne him mar thai chargyt him to ta.
Thus in thar armyss, supposs that he had suorne,
140 Out off the garth befors thai haff him borne.
Thus gud Wallace with Inglissmen was tane,
In falt of helpe, for he was him allayne:
He coud nocht cheyss, sic curage so hym bar,
Frewill fortoun thus broucht him in the snar;
145 And falss Inwye, ay contrar rychtwisnes,
That wiolent god full of doubilnes.
Thai fenyeit goddis Wallace neuir knew:
Gret rychtwisness him ay to mercy drew.
His kyn mycht nocht him get for na kyn thing,
150 Mycht thai hawe payit the ransoune of a king.
The more thai bad, the mor it was in wayne.
Off thar best men that day sewyn has he slayne.
Thai gert set him in till a presoune fell;
Off his turment gret payne it war to tell.
155 Ill meyt and drynk thai gert on till hym gyff,
Gret merwaille was lang tyme gif he mycht leyff:
And ek thar to he was in presoune law,
Quhill thai thocht tyme on him to hald the law.
Leyff I him thar in to that paynfull sted.
160   Gret God abowe till him send sum ramede!
The playne compleynt, the pittows wementyng!

The wofull wepyng that was for his takyng!
The tormentyng of euery creatur!
"Alas," thai said, "how suld our lyff endur?
165 "Be fortoun armess has left him in thrillage:
Fol. 7 a "The flour of youth in till his tendir age.
"Lefand as now a chiftane had we nane,
"Durst tak on hand, bot yong Wallace alayne.
"This land is lost; he caucht is in the swar,
170 "The Apersé of Scotland left in cayr!"

Barrell heryng and wattir thai him gawe,
Quhar he was set in to that vgly cawe.
Sic fude for him was febill to commend.
Than said he thus; 'All weildand God, resawe
175 'My petows spreit and sawle amang the law!
'My carneill lyff I may nocht thus defend.
'Our few Sothroune on to the dede I drawe.
'Quhen so thow will, out of this warld I wend;
'Giff I suld now in presoune mak ane end.
180   'Eternaile God, quhy suld I thus wayis de;
'Syne my beleiff all haile remanys in the,
'At thin awn will full worthely was wrocht?
'Bot thow rademe, na liff thai ordand me,
'Gastlye Fadyr, that deit apon the tre,
185 'Fra hellis presoune with thi blud ws bocht;
'Quhi will thow giff thi handéwark for nocht;
'And mony worthy in to gret payne we se?
'For off my lyff ellys no thing I roucht.
'O wareide suerd, of tempyr neuir trew,
190 'Thi fruschand blaid in presoune sone me threw:
'And Inglissmen our litill harm has tayne.
'Off ws thai haiff wndoyne may than ynew;
'My faithfull fadyr dispitfully thai slew,
'My brothir als, and gud men mony ane.

195 ' Is this thi dait, sall thai our cum ilkane?
   ' On our kynrent, deyr God, quhen will thow rew;
   ' Sen my pouer thus sodandlye is gane.
     ' All worthi Scottis, almychty God yow leid,
   ' Sen I no mor in wyage may you speid!
200 ' In presoune heir me worthis to myscheyff.
   ' Sely Scotland, that of helpe has gret neide,
   · Thi· natioune all standis in a felloun dreid.
   ' Off wardlynes all thus I tak my leiff.
   ' Off thir paynys God lat you neuir preiff,
205 ' Thocht I for wo all out off witt suld weid!
   ' Now othir gyft I may none to you gyff.'
    O der Wallace, wmquhill was stark and stur,
   Thow most o neide in presoune till endur.
   Thi worthi kyn may nocht the saiff for sold.
210 Ladyis wepyt, that was bathe mylde and mur,
   In fureous payne, the modyr that the bur:
   For thou till hir was fer derer than gold.
   Hyr most desyr was to be wndyr mold.
   In wardlynes quhi suld ony ensur?
b 215 For thow was formyt forsye on the feld.
    Compleyn, Sanctis thus, as your sedull tellis;
   Compleyn to hewyn with wordis that nocht faillis:
   Compleyne your woice wnto the God abuffe;
   Compleyne for him in to that sitfull sell is;
220 Compleyne his payne in dolour thus that duellis;
   In langour lyis, for losyng of thar luff,
   Hys fureous payne was felloune for to pruff.
   Compleyne also, yhe birdis, blyth as bellis,
   Sum happy chance may fall for your behuff.
225   Compleyne, lordys, compleyne, yhe ladyis brycht,
   Compleyne for him that worthi was and wycht,
   Off Saxons sonnys sufferyt full mekill der.
   Compleyne for him was thus in presone dicht

And for na causs, bot, Scotland, for thi rycht.
230 Compleyne also, yhe worthi men of wer,
Compleyne for hym that was your aspresper;
And to the dede fell Sothroun yeit he dicht:
Compleyne for him your triumphe had to ber.
Celimus was maist his geyeler now.
235 In Inglissmen, allace, quhi suld we trow,
Our worthy kyn has payned on this wyss?
Sic reulle be rycht is litill [till] allow:
Me think we suld in barrat mak thaim bow
At our power, and so we do feill syss.
240 Off thar danger God mak ws for to ryss,
That weill has wrocht befor thir termyss, and now!
For thai wyrk ay to wayt ws with suppryss.
Quhat suld I mor of Wallace turment tell;
The flux he tuk in to thar presoune fell?
245 Ner to the dede he was likly to drawe.
Thai chergyt the geyler nocht on him to duell,
Bot bryng him wp out of that vgly sell
To jugisment, quhar he suld thoill the law.
This man went doun, and sodanlye he saw,
250 As to hys sycht, dede had him swappyt snell;
Syn said to thaim, " He has payit at he aw."
Quhen thai presumyt he suld be werray ded,
Thai gart serwandys, with outyn langer pleid,
With schort awiss on to the wall him bar:
255 Thai kest him our out of that bailfull steid,
Off him thai trowit suld be no mor ramede,
In a draff myddyn, quhar he remannyt thar.
His fyrst noryss, of the Newtoun of Ayr,
Till him scho come, quhilk was full will of reid,
260 And thyggyt leiff away with him to fayr.
In to gret ire thai grantyt hir to go.
Scho tuk him wp with outyn wordis mo,

And on a caar wnlikly him thai cast:
Atour the wattir led him with gret woo,
265 Till hyr awin houss with outyn ony hoo.
Scho warmyt wattir, and hir serwandis fast
His body wousche, quhill filth was of hym past.
Fol. 8 a His hart was wicht, and flykeryt to and fro,
Als his twa eyne he kest wp at the last.
270 His fostyr modyr, lowed him our the laiff,
Did mylk to warme, his liff giff scho mycht saiff;
And with a spoyn gret kyndnes to him kyth.
Hyr dochtir had of twelf wokkis ald a knayff;
Hir childis pape in Wallace mouth scho gaiff.
275 The womannys mylk recomford him full swyth:
Syn in a bed thai brocht him fair and lyth.
Rycht couertly thai kepe him in that caiff,
Him for to sawe so secretlye thai mycht.
    In thar chawmyr thai kepyt him that tide;
280 Scho gart graith wp a burd be the houss side,
Wyth carpettis cled, and honowryt with gret lycht:
And for the woice in euiry place suld bide,
At he was ded, out throuch the land so wide,
In presence ay scho wepyt wndyr slycht;
285 Bot gudely meytis scho graithit him at hir mycht.
And so befel in to that sammyn tid,
Quhill forthirmar at Wallas worthit wycht.
    Thomas Rimour in to the Faile was than,
With the mynystir, quhilk was a worthi man:
290 He wsyt oft to that religiouss place.
The peple demyt of witt mekill he can;
And so he told, thocht at thai bliss or ban,
Quhilk hapnyt suth in many diuerss cace,
I can nocht say, be wrang or rychtwisnas,
295 In rewlle of wer, quhethir thai tynt or wan;
It may be demyt be diuisioun of grace.

Thar man that day had in the merket bene,
On Wallace knew this cairfull cass so kene.
His mastyr speryt, quhat tithingis at he saw.
300 This man ansuerd; " Of litill hard I meyn."
The mynister said; ' It has bene seildyn seyn,
' Quhar Scottis and Ingliss semblit bene on raw,
' Was neuir yit, als fer as we coud knaw,
' Bot othir a Scott wald do a Sothroun teyne,
305 ' Or he till him, for awentur mycht faw.'
"Wallas," he said, " ye wist tayne in that steid;
" Out our the wall I saw thaim cast him deide,
" In presoune famyst for fawt of fude."
The mynister said, ' with hart hewy as leid;
310 ' Sic deid to thaim, me think, suld foster feid;
' For he was wicht, and cummyn of gentill blud.'
Thomas ansuerd; " Thir tythingis ar noucht gud;
" And that be suth, my self sall neuir eit breid,
" For all my witt her schortlye I conclud."
315 ' A woman syne of the Newtoun of Ayr,
' Till him scho went fra he was fallyn thar;
' And on hir kneis rycht lawly thaim besocht,
' To purchess leiff scho mycht thine with him fayr.
Fol. 8 b ' In lychtlyness tyll hyr thai grant it thair.
320 ' Our the wattyr on till hir houss him brocht,
' To beryss him als gudlye as scho mocht.'
Yhit Thomas said; " Than sall I leiff na mar,
" Giff that be trow, be God, that all has wrocht."
The mynister herd quhat Thomas said in playne.
325 He chargyt him than; ' Go, speid the fast agayne
' To that sammyn houss, and werraly aspye.'
The man went furth, at byddyng was full bayne;
To the Newtoun to pass he did his payn,
To that ilk houss; and went in sodanlye.
330 About he blent on to the burd him bye.

This woman raiss, in hart scho was [nocht] fayn.
Quha aw this lik he bad hir nocht deny.
 " Wallace," scho said, " that full worthy has beyne."
Than wepyt scho, that peté was to scyne.
335 The man thar to gret credens gaif he nocht:
Towart the burd he bowned as he war teyne.
On kneis scho felle, and cryit; ' For Marye scheyne,
· Let sklandyr be, and flemyt out of your thocht.'
This man hir suour; " Be him that all has wrocht,
340 " Mycht I on lyff him anys se with myn eyn,
" He suld be saiff, thocht Ingland had hym socht."
 Scho had him wp to Wallace by the dess;
He spak with him, syne fast agayne can press
With glaid bodword, thar myrthis till amend.
345 He told to thaim the first tithingis was less.
Than Thomas said; ' Forsuth, or he decess,
' Mony thousand in feild sall mak thar end.
' Off this regioun he sall the Sothroun send;
' And Scotland thriss he sall bryng to the pess:
350 'So gud off hand agayne sall neuir be kend.'
 All worthi men, that has gud witt to waille,
Be war that yhe with myss deyme nocht my taille.
Perchance ye say, that Bruce he was none sik.
He was als gud, quhat deid was to assaill,
355 As off his handis, and bauldar in battaill.
Bot Bruce was knawin weyll ayr off this kynrik;
For he had rycht, we call no man him lik.
Bot Wallace thriss this kynrik conquest haile,
In Ingland fer socht battaill on that rik.

360 I will ratorn to my mater agayne.
Quhen Wallace was ralesched off his payne,
The contré demyd haile that he was dede;
His derrest kyn nocht wist of his ramede.

Bot haile he was, likly to gang and ryd.

365 In to that place he wald na langar byde.

His trew kepar he send to Elrislé;

Eftir him thar he durst nocht lat hyr be:

Hir dochtir, als thar serwand, and hir child,

He gart thaim pass on to his modyr myld.

Fol. 9 a 370 Quhen thai war gayne, na wapynnys thar he saw

To helpe him with, quhat auentur mycht befaw.

A rousty suerd in a noik he saw stand,

With outyn belt, but boss, bukler, or band.

Lang tyme befor it had beyne in that steid;

375 Ane agyt man it left quhen he was dede.

He drew the blaid, he fand it wald bitt weill;

Thocht it was foule, nobill it was of steyll.

"God helpis his man; for thou sall go with me,

"Quhill bettir cum; will God full sone may be!"

380 To Schyr Ranald as than he wald nocht fair;

In that passage offt Sothroun maid repar.

At Rycardtoun full fayn he wald hawe beyne,

To get him horss and part of armour scheyne.

On thedyrwart as he bownyt to fair,

385 Thre Inglissmen he met ridand till Ayr,

In thair wiage at Glaskow furth had beyne;

Ane Longcastell, that cruell was and keyne,

A bauld squier, with him gud yemen twa.

Wallace drew by, and wald haiff lattyn thaim ga.

390 Till him he raid, and said dispitfully;

"Thow Scot, abide, I trow thow be sum spy;

"Or ellis a theyff, fra presens wald the hid."

Than Wallace said, with sobyr wordis, that tid:

'Schir, I am seik, for Goddis luff latt me ga!'

395 Langcastell said; "Forsuth it beis nocht sa.

"A felloune freik thow semys in thi fair;

"Quhill men the knaw, thow sall with me till Ayr."

Hynt out his suerd, that was of nobill hew,
Wallace with that, at hys lychtyn, him drew;
400 Apon the crag with his suerd has him tayne;
Throw brayne and seyne in sondyr straik the bayne.
Be he was fallyn, the twa than lichtyt doun;
To wenge his dede to Wallace maid thaim boun.
The tayne of thaim apon the hed he gaiff,
405 The rousty blaid to the schulderis him claiff.
The tothir fled, and durst no langer bide;
With a rud step Wallace coud eftyr glide.
Our thourch his rybbis a seker straik drewe he,
Quhill leuir and lounggis men mycht all redy se.
410 Thar horss he tuk, bathe wapynnys and armour;
Syne thankit God with gud hart in that stour.
Syluer thai had, all with him has he tayne,
Him to support; for spendyng had he nayne.
In to gret haist he raid to Ricardtoun,
415 A blyth semblay was at his lychtyn doun.
Quhen Wallace mett with Schyr Richart the knycht,
For him had murnit quhill feblit was his mycht.
His thre sonnys of Wallace was full fayne;
Thai held him lost, yit God him sawth agayne.
420 His eyme, Schyr Ranald, to Rycardtoun come fast;
The wemen, told, by Corsby as thai past,
Off Wallace eschaipe, syne thar wiage yeid.
ol. 9 b Schyr Ranald yit was in a felloune dreid:
Quhill he him saw, in hart he thocht full lang;
425 Than sodanlye in armys he couth him fang.
He mycht nocht spek, but kyst him tendyrlye;
The knychtis spreit was in ane extasye,
The blyth teris tho bryst for his eyne two;
Or that he spak, a lang tyme held him so:
430 And at the last rycht freindfully said he;
" Welcum, neuo, welcum deir sone to me.

" Thankit be he that all this warld has wrocht,
" Thus fairlye the has out of presoune brocht."
His modyr come, and othir freyndis enew,
435 With full glaid will, to feill thai tithingis true.
Gud Robert Boyd, that worthi was and wicht,
Wald nocht thaim trew, quhill he him saw with sycht.
Fra syndry part thai socht to Ricardtoun.
Feille worthi folk, that war of gret renoun.
440 Thus leiff I thaim in myrth, blyss and plesance,
Thankand gret God off his fre happy chance.

EXPLICIT LIBER SECUNDUS,
ET INCIPIT TERCIUS.

BUKE THRYD.

In joyowss Julii, quhen the flouris suete,
Degesteable, engenered throu the heet,
Baith erbe and froyte, busk and bewis, braid
Haboundandlye in euery slonk and slaid;
5 Als bestiall, thar rycht courss till endur,
Weyle helpyt ar be wyrkyn off natur,
On fute and weynge ascendand to the hycht,
Conserwed weill be the Makar of mycht;
Fyscheis in flude refeckit rialye
10 Till mannys fude, the warld suld occupye.
Bot Scotland sa was waistit mony day,
Throw wer sic skaith, at labour was away.
Wictaill worth scant or August coud apper,
Throu all the land, that fude was hapnyt der:
15 Bot Inglissmen, that richess wantyt nayne,
Be caryage brocht thair wictaill full gud wayne;
Stuffit houssis with wyn and gud wernage;
Demaynde this land as thair awne heretage;
The kynryk haile thai rewllyt at thar will.
20 Messyngeris than sic tithingis brocht thaim till;
And tald Persye, that Wallace leffand war,
Off his eschaip fra thar presoune in Ayr.
Thai trowit rycht weill he passit was that steid;
For Longcastell and his twa men was deid.
25 He trowit the chance that Wallace so was past.

In ilka part thai war gretly agast,
Throw prophesye that thai had herd befor.
Lord Persye said; "Quhat nedis wordis mor?
"Bot he be cest he sall do gret merwaill.
30 "It was the best for king Eduuardis awaill,
"Mycht he him get to be his steidfast man,
"For gold or land; his conquest mycht lest than.
Fol. 10 a "Me think beforce he may nocht gottyn be;
"Wyssmen the suth be his eschaip may se."
35 Thus deyme [thai] him in mony diuerss cass.
We leiff thaim her, and spek furth of Wallass.
In Rycardtoun he wald no langer byde,
For freindis consaill, nor thing that mycht betide.
And quhen thai saw that it awaillit nocht,
40 His purposs was to wenge him, at he mocht,
On Sothron blud, quhilk has his eldris slayne.
Thai latt him wyrk his awn will in to playne.
Schir Richart had thre sonnys, as I yow tald.
Adam, Rychart, and Symont that was bald.
45 Adam, eldest, was growand in curage;
Forthward, rycht fayr, auchtene yer of age;
Large off persone; bath wiss, worthi and wicht:
Gude king Robert in his tyme maid him knycht.
Lang tyme eftir in Brucis weris he baid,
50 On Inglissmen moné gud iorné maid.
This gud squier with Wallace bound to ryd;
And Robert Boid, quhilk wald no langar bide
Vndir thrillage of segis of Ingland.
To that falss king he had neuir maid band.
55 Kneland was thar, ner cusyng to Wallace,
Syne baid with him in mony peralouss place;
And Eduuard Litill, his sistir sone so der;
Full weill graithit in till thar armour cler.

With thar serwandis fra Ricardtoun thai raid
60 To Mawchtlyne mur, and schort tyme thar abaid;
    For freindis thaim tauld, was bound wndir trewage,
    That Fenweik was for Perseys caryage:
    With in schort tyme he will bryng it till Ayr
    Out off Carleile; he had resawyt it thair.
65 That plesyt Wallace in his hart gretumlye;
    Wytt yhe thai war a full glaid cumpanye.
    Towart Lowdoun thai bownyt thaim to ride:
    And in a schaw, a litill thar besyde,
    Thai lugyt thaim, for it was nere the nycht,
70 To wache the way als besyly as thai mycht.
    A trew Scot, quhilk hosteler houss thair held,
    Wnder Lowdon, as myn autor me teld,
    He saw thar come, syne went to thaim in hye;
    Baithe meite and drynk he brocht full priwalye:
75 And to thaim tald the cariage in to playn;
    Thair forrydar was past till Ayr agayne,
    Left thaim to cum with pouer of gret waille,
    Thai trowit be than thai war in Awendaille.
    Wallace than said, we will nocht soiorne her,
80 Nor change no weid, bot our ilk dayis ger.
    At Corssentoun the gait was spilt that tide;
    For thi that way behowid thaim for to ride.
    And fra the tyme that he of presoune four,
    Gude souir weide dayly on him he wour:
85 Gude lycht harness, fra that tyme, wsyt he euir;
    For sodeyn stryff, fra it he wald nocht seuir.
ol. 10 b A habergione vndyr his goune he war,
    A steylle capleyne in his bonet but mar;
    His glowis of plait in claith war couerit weill,
90 In his doublet a closs coler of steyle;
    His face he kepit, for it was euir bar,
    With his twa handis, the quhilk full worthi war,

In to his weid, and he come in a thrang :
Was na man than on fute mycht with him gang.
95 So growane in pith, off pouer stark and stur,
His terryble dyntis war awfull till endur.
Thai trast mar in Wallace him allane,
Than in a hundreth mycht be off Ingland tayne.
The worthi Scottis maid thar no soiornyng,
100 To Lowdoun hill past in [the] gray dawyng;
Dewysyt the place, and putt thair horss thaim fra;
And thocht to wyn, or neuir thin to ga:
Send twa skowrrouris to wesy weyll the playne;
Bot thai rycht sone raturnde in agayne,
105 To Wallace tald that thai war cummand fast.
Than thai to grounde all kneland at the last,
With humyll hartis prayit with all thair mycht,
To God abowne to help thaim in thar rycht.
Than graithit thai thaim till harnes hastely
110 Thar sonyeit nane of that gud chewalrye.
Than Wallace said; " Her was my fadyr slayne;
" My brothyr als, quhilk dois me mekill payne;
" So sall my selff, or wengit be but dreid.
" The traytour is her, [the] causs was off that deid."
115 Than hecht thai all to bide with hartlye will.
Be that the power was takand Lowdounhill.
The knycht Fenweik conwoide the caryage;
He had on Scottis maid mony schrewide wiage.
The sone was rysyne our landis schenand brycht.
120 The Inglissmen so thai come to the hycht;
Ner thaim he raid, and sone the Scottis saw.
He tald his men, and said to thaim on raw;
" Yhonne is Wallace, that chapit our presoune;
" He sall agayne be drawyn throu the toune.
125 " His hede mycht mar I wait, weill pless the king,
" Than gold, or land, or ony warldly thing."

He gart serwandes bide with the cariage still;
Thai thocht to dawnt the Scottis at thar will.
Nyne scor he led in harnes burnyst brycht;
130 And fyfty was with Wallace in the rycht.
Vnraboytyt the Sothroun was in wer;
And fast thai cum, fell awfull in affer.
A maner dyk, off stanys thai had maid,
Narrowyt the way quhar throuch thai thikar raid.
135 The Scottis on fute tuk the feld thaim befor;
The Sothroun saw thar curage was the mor.
In prydefull ire thai thoucht our thaim to ryde;
Bot othyr wyss it hapnyt in that tide.
On athir side to giddyr fast thai glaid;
11 a 140 The Scottis on fute gret rowme about thaim maid,
With ponyeand speris throuch platis prest of steylle;
The Inglissmen, that thoucht to weng thaim weylle,
On harnest horss about thaim rudely raide;
That with wness wpone thar feit thai baid.
145 Wallace the formast in the byrneis bar;
The grounden sper throuch his body schar.
The shafft to schonkit off the fruschand tre;
Dewoydyde sone, sen na bettir mycht be.
Drew suerdis syne, bathe hewy, scharp and lang;
150 On athyr syd full cruelly thai dang.
Fechtand at anys in to that felloune dout,
Than Inglissmen enverond thaim about;
Beforce etlyt throuch out thaim for to ryde.
The Scottis, on fute that baldly couth abyde,
155 With suerdis schar throuch habergeons full gude,
Vpon the flouris schot the schonkan blude,
Fra horss and men throw harness burnyst beyne.
A sair sailyie forsuth thair mycht be seyne:
Thai traistyt na lyff bot the lettir end.
160 Off sa few folk gret nobilness was kend,

c

To gydder baid defendand thaim full fast;
Durst nane seuer quhill the maist press was past.
The Inglissmen, that besye was in wer,
Beforss ordand in sondyr thaim to ber.

165 Thair cheyff chyftan feryt als ferss as fyr,
Throw matelent, and werray propyr ire;
On a gret horss, in till his glitterand ger,
In fewtir kest a fellone aspre sper
The knycht Fenweik, that cruell was and keyne;

170 He had at dede off Wallace fadyr beyne,
And his brodyr that douchty was and der.
Quhen Wallace saw that falss knycht was so ner,
His corage grew in ire as a lyoune.
Till him he ran, and fell frekis bar he doune;

175 As he glaid by, aukwart he couth hym ta,
The and arson in sondyr gart he ga.
Fra the coursour he fell on the fer syd;
With a staff suerd Boyd stekit him that tyde.
Or he was dede, the gret press come so fast,

180 Our him to grounde thai bur Boyd at the last.
Wallace was ner, and ratornde agayne
Hym to reskew, till that he raiss off payne;
Wichtly him wor, quhill he a suerd had tayne.
Throu out the stour thir twa in feyr ar gayne.

185 The ramanand apon thaim folowit fast;
In thar passage fell Sothron maid agast.
Adam Wallace, the ayr off Ricardtoun,
Straik ane Bewmound, a squier of renoun,
On the pyssan, with his hand burnyst bar,

190 The thrusande blaid his halss in sonder schayr.
The Inglissmen, thocht thar chyftayn was slayne,

Fol. 11 b Bauldly thai baid, as men mekill off mayn.
Reth horss repende rouschede frekis wndir feit;
The Scottis on fute gert mony loiss the suete.

195 Wicht men lichtyt thaim selff for to defend;
    Quhar Wallace come thar deide was litill kend.
    The Sothroune part so frusched was that tide,
    That in the stour thai mycht no langar bide.
    Wallace in deide he wrocht so worthely,
200 The squier Boid, and all thair chewalry,
    Litill, Kneland, gert off thair enemyss de.
    The Inglissmen tuk playnly part to fle;
    On horsis some, to strenthis part, can found
    To socour thaim, with mony werkand wound.
205 A hundreth dede in feild was lewyt thar,
    And thre yemen that Wallace menyde fer mar;
    Twa was off Kyle, and ane of Conyngayme,
    With Robert Boide to Wallace com fra hayme.
    Four scor fled, that chapyt on the south syde.
210 The Scottis, in place that bauldly couth abyde,
    Spoilyed the feld, gat gold and othir ger,
    Harnes and horss, quhilk thai mysteryt in wer.
    The Ingliss knawis thai gart thar caryage leid
    To Clidis forest: quhen thai war out off dreid,
215 Thai band thaim fast with wedeis sad and sar,
    On bowand treis hangyt thaim rycht thar.
    He sparyt nane that abill was to wer;
    Bot wemen and preystis he gart thaim ay forber.
    Quhen this was doyne, to thar dyner thai went,
220 Off stuff and wyne that God had to thaim sent.
    Ten scor thai wan of horss that cariage bure;
    With flour and wyne als mekill as thai mycht fur,
    And othir stuff that thai off Carleile led.

    The Sothron part out off the feild that fled,
225 With sorow socht to the castell off Ayr,
    Befor the lord, and tauld him off thair cair;
    Quhat gud thai lost, and quha in feild was slayne,

Throw wicht Wallace that was mekill off mayne;
And how he had gart all thar serwandis hang.
230 The Persye said; " And that squier lest lang,
" He sall ws exille out off this contré cleyne;
" Sa dispitfull in wer was neuir seyne.
" In our presounc her last quhen that he was,
" Our slouthfully our keparis leit him pass.
235 " Thus stuff our land, I fynde may nocht weill be;
" We mon ger bryng our wittaill be the se.
" Bot loss our men, it helpis ws rycht nocht;
" Thar kyne may ban that euir we hydder socht."
Lat I thaim thus, blamand thar sory chance,
240 And mar to sper of Scottis mennys gouernance.
Quhen Wallace had weyle wenquist to the playne
The falss terand that had his fadyr slayne;
Fol. 12 a His brothyr als, quhilk was a gentill knycht,
Othir gud men befor to dede thai dycht;
245 He gert dewyss, and prowide thar wictaille;
Baith stuff and horss that was of gret awaille,
To freyndis about preualye thai send,
The ramanand full glaidlye thar thai spend.
In Clydis wode thai soiornyt twenty dayis,
250 Na Sothren that tyme was persawyt in thai wais,
Bot he tholyt dede that come in thar danger:
The worde of him walkit baith fer and ner.
Wallace was knawin on lyff leyffand in playne,
Thocht Inglissmen tharoff had gret payne.
255 The erle Persye to Glaskow couth he fair,
With wyss lordis, and held a consell thair.
Quhen thai war mett, weylle ma na ten thousand,
Na chyftane was that tyme durst tak on hand,
To leide the range on Wallace to assaill.
260 He speryt about, quhat was the best consaill.
Schir Amar Wallange, a falss traytour strange,

In Bothwell duelt, and thar was thaim amange.
He said; " My lorde, my consaill will I giff;
" Bot ye do it, fra scaith ye may nocht scheyff,
265 " Yhe mon tak pess, with out mar tarying,
" As for a tyme we may send to the king."
The Persye said; ' Of owr trewis he will nane.
' Ane awfull chyftane trewly he is ane;
' He will do mair, in faith, or that he blyne:
270 ' Sothroun to sla he thinkis it na syne.'
Schir Amar said; " Trewis it wordis tak;
" Quhill eft for him prowisioune we may mak.
" I knaw he will do mekill for his kyne;
" Gentryss and trewtht ay restis him within.
275 " His wncle Schyr Ranald may mak this band.
" Gyff he will nocht, racunnyss all his land
" On to the tym that he this werk haiff wrocht."
Schir Ranald was sone to that consell brocht;
Thai chargyt him to mak Wallace at pess,
280 Or he suld pass to Londone with outyn less.
Schir Ranald said; " Lordis, yhe knaw this weill,
" At my commande he will nocht do a deill.
" His worthi kyn dispitously ye slew,
" In presone syne ner to the dede him threw.
285 " He is at large, and will nocht do for me,
" Thocht ye tharfor rycht now suld ger me de."
Schir Amar said; ' Thir lordis sone sall send
' On to the king, and mak a finall end
' Off his conquest, forsuth he will it haiff.
290 ' Wallace na thou ma nocht this kynrik saiff.
' Mycht Eduuard king get him, for gold or land,
' To be his man, than suld he bruk Scotland.'
12 b The lordis bad cess; " Thow excedis to that knycht
" Fer mair be treuth than it is ony rycht.
295 " The wrang conquest our king desiris ay;

"On hym or vs it sall be seyne some day.
"Wallace has rycht, bathe force and fair fortoun:
"Ye hard how he eschapyt our presoune."
Thus said that lord, syne prayit Schyr Ranald fair
300 To mak this pess; "Thou schirreff art of Ayr.
"As for a tyme we may awisit be:
"Vndyr my seylle I sall be bound to the
"For Inglissmen, that thai sall do him nocht,
"Nor to no Scottis, less it be on thaim socht."
305 Schir Ranald wist he mycht thaim nocht ganestand;
Off lord Persye he has resauit this band.
Perseys war trew, and ay off full gret waill,
Sobyr in pess, and cruell in battaill.
Schir Ranald bownyde vpon the morne but baid,
310 Wallace to seke in Clydis forest braid.
So he him fand bownand to his dyner.
Quhen thai had seyne this gud knycht was so ner,
Weyle he him knew, and tauld thaim quhat he was;
Meruaille he had quhat gart him hiddyr pass,
315 Maide him gud cheyr of meyttis fresche and fyne.
King Eduuardis self could nocht get bettir wyn
Than thai had thar, warnage and wenysoune
Off bestiall in to full gret fusioun.
Syn eftir mett, he schew thaim of hys deide,
320 How he had beyne in to so mekill dreid.
"Now," he said, "wyrk part of my consaill;
"Tak pess a quhill, as for the mair awaill.
"Bot thou do so, forsuth thou dois gret syne,
"For thai ar set till wndo all thi kyn."
325 Than Wallace said till gud men him about;
'I will no pess for all this felloune dout,
'Bot gif it pless bettir to yow than me.'
The squier Boide him ansuerd sobyrle;
"I gif conseill, or this gud knycht be slayne,

330 "'Tak pess a quhill, supposs it do ws payne."
So said Adam the ayr of Rycardtoune;
And Kneland als grantyt to thair opynyoun.
With thair consent Wallace this pess has tayne,
As his eyme wrocht, till ten moneth war gayne.

335 Thar leyff thai tuk, with conforde into playn;
Sanct Jhone to borch thai suld meyt haill agayn,
Boyde and Kneland past to thar placis hayme;
Adam Wallace to Ricardtoun by nayme;
And Wilyham furth till Schir Ranald can ride,

340 And his houshald, in Corsby for to bide.
This peess was cryede in August moneth myld:
Yhet god of battaill furius and wild,

Fol. 13 a Mars, and Juno ay dois thair besynes,
Causer of wer, wyrkar of wykitnes;

345 And Venus als the goddess of luff,
Wytht ald Saturn, his coursis till appruff.
Thir four scansyte of diuerss complexioun,
Bataill debaite, inwy and destructioun,
I can nocht deyme for thar malancoly.

350 Bot Wallace weille coude nocht in Corsby ly,
Hym had leuir in trauaill for to be;
Rycht sar he langyt the toune of Ayr to se.

Schir Ranald past fra hame apon a day.
Fyfteyne he tuk, and to the toune went thai;

355 Couerit his face, that no man mycht him knaw:
Nothing him roucht how few ennymyis him saw.
In souir weide disgysyt weill war thai.
Ane Inglissman, on the gait, saw he play
At the scrymmagis a bukler on his hand.

360 Wallace ner by in falouschipe couth stand.
Lychtly he sperde; "Quhi, Scot, dar thow nocht preiff?"
Wallace said; 'Ya, sa thow wald gif me leiff.'

"Smyt on," he said, " I defy thine actioune."
Wallace tharwith has tane him on the croune,
365 Throuch bukler, hand, and the harnpan also,
To the schulderis, the scharp suerd gert he go.
Lychtly raturnd till his awne men agayne.
The wemen cryede; "Our bukler player is slaine."
The man was dede; quhat nedis wordis mair?

370 Feille men of armys about him semblit thair,
Sewyn scor at anys agayne sextene war sett:
Bot Wallace sone weill with the formest mett,
With ire and will on the hede has him tayne,
Throuch the brycht helm in sondyr bryst the bayne.

375 Ane othir braithly on the breyst he bar;
His burnyst blaid throuch out the body schar.
Gret rowme he maid, his men war fechtand fast;
And mony a growme thai maid full sair agast:
For thai war wicht, and weill wsyt in wer;

380 Off Inglissmen rycht bauldly doun thai ber.
On thair enemyss gret martirdome thai maik,
Thar hardy chiftane so weill couth wndyrtak,
Quhat Inglissman, that baid in till his gait,
Contrar Scotland maid neuir mar debait.

385 Felle frekis on fold war fellyt wndyr feit;
Off Sothroune blude lay stekit in the streit.
New pouir come fra the castell that tyde:
Than Wallace drede, and drew towart a side.
With gude will he wald escheu a suppriss;

390 For he in wer was besy, wicht and wiss.
Harness and hedis he hew in sonderys fast;
Beforce out off the thikest preyss thai past.
Wallace raturnyde behynde his men agayne,
At the reskew feile enemyss hass he slayne.

395 His men all samyn he out off perill brocht,
Fol. 13 b Fra his enymyss, for all the pouer thai mocht.

To thar horss thai wan but mair abaide;
For danger syne to Laglyne wode thai raid.
Twenty and nyne thai left in to that steide,
400 Off Sothroun men that bertynit war to dede.
The ramaynand agayne turnyt that tide;
For in the woode thai durst nocht him abyde.
Towart the toune thai drew with all thair mayn,
Cursand the pess thai tuk befor in playne.
405 The lord Persye in hart was gretlye grewyt.
His men supprisyt agayne to him relewyt;
And feille war dede in to thair armour cler,
Thre of his kyne that war till him full der.
Quhen he hard tell of thair gret grewance,
410 Thar selff was causs of this myschefull chance,
Murnyng he maid, thoucht few Scottis it kend.
A herald than to Schyr Ranald he send,
And tald till him of all thair sodeyne cass;
And chargyt him tak souerté of Wallas,
415 He suld him kepe fra merket toune or fair,
Quhar he mycht best be out of thair repair.
The Sothroun wist that it was wicht Wallace,
Had thaim our set in to that sodand cass:
Thair trewis for this thai wald nocht brek adeill.
420 Quhen Wallace had this chance eschewit weill,
Vpon the nycht fra Lagleyne hayme he raid;
In chaumeris sone thair residence thai maid.
Vpon the morn, quhen that the day was lycht,
Wicht Wallace went with Schyr Ranald.   The knycht
425 Schew him the wryt lord Persie had him sent.
" Deir sone," he said, " this war my haile entent,
" That thow wald grant, quhill thir trewis war worne,
" Na scaith to do till Inglissman that is born;
" Bot quhar I pass dayly thou bid with me."
430 Wallace ansuerd; 'Gud Schyr, that may nocht be.

' Rycht laith I war, deyr wncle, you to greiff;
' I sall do nocht till tyme I tak my leyff,
' And warn you als or that I fra you pass.'
His eyme and he thus weill accordyt was.
435 Wallace with him maid his continuance;
Ilk wicht was blyth to do till him plesance.
In Corsby thus he resyd thaim amang
Thai sextene dayis, suppos him thoucht it lang.
Thocht thai mycht pless him as a prince or king,
440 In his mynde yit remanyt ane othir thing.
He saw his enemys maistris in this regioune,
Mycht nocht him pless thocht he war king with croune.
Thus leyff [I] him with his der freyndis still;
Off Inglissmen of sumpart spek I will.

EXPLICIT LIBER TERCIUS,
ET INCIPIT QUARTUS.

BUKE FEYRD.

In September, the humyll moneth suette,
Quhen passyt by the hycht was off the hette,
ol. 14 a Wictaill and froyte ar rypyt in aboundance,
As God ordans to mannys gouernance.
5 Sagittarius with his aspre bow,
Be the ilk syng weryté ye may know
The changing courss quhilk makis gret deference;
And lewyss had lost thair colouris of plesence.
All warldly thing has nocht bot a sesoune;
10 Both erbe and froyte mon fra hewyn cum doun.
In this ilk tyme a gret consell was sett
In to Glaskow quhar mony maistris mett,
Off Ingliss lordis, to statute this cuntré.
Than chargyt thai all schirreffis thar to be.
15 Schir Ranald Crawfurd behowide that tyme be thar,
For he throw rycht was born schirreff of Ayr.
His der neuo that tyme with hym he tuk,
Willyham Wallace, as witness beris the buk;
For he na time suld be fra hys sycht,
20 He luffyt him with hart and all hys mycht.
Thai graith thaim weill with out langar abaid.
Wallace sum part befor the court furth raid,
With him twa men that douchtye war in deid;
Our tuk the child Schyr Ranaldis sowme couth leid.
25 Softlye thai raid quhill thai the court suld knaw.
So sodeynly at Hesilden he saw

The Perseys sowme, in quhilk gret ryches was;
The horss was tyryt, and mycht no forthyr pass.
Fyve men was chargit to keipe it weill all tid;
30 Twa wass on fute, and thre on horss couth ride.
The maistir man at thair serwand can sper;
" Quha aw this sowme? the suth thou to me ler."
The man ansuerd, with outyn wordis mair;
' My lordis,' he said, ' quhilk schirreff is of Ayr.'
35 " Sen it is his, this horss sall with ws gang
    " To serwe our lord, or ellis me think gret wrang;
    " Thocht a subiet in deid wald pass his lord,
    " It is nocht lewyt be na rychtwiss racord."
Thai cutt the brayss and leyt the harness faw.
40 Wallace was ner; quhen he sic reueré saw,
He spak to thaim with manly contenance.
In fayr afforme, he said, but wariance;
' Ye do vs wrang, and it in tyme of pess;
' Off sic rubry war suffisance to cess.'
45 The Sothron schrew in ire ansuerd him to;
    " It sall be wrocht as thow may se ws do.
    " Thow gettis no mendis; quhat wald thow wordis mar?"
Sadly awisit Wallace remembrith him thar
On the promyss he maid his eyme befor:
50 Resoun him rewllyt, as than he did no mor.
The horss thai tuk for awentur mycht befall,
Laid on thar sowme, syne furth the way couth call.
Thar tyryt sowmir so left thai in to playne.
Wallace raturnd towart the court agayne;
55 In the mursyde sone with his eyme he mett,
Fol. 14 b And tauld how thai the way for his man sett:
    " And war noucht I was bonde in my legiance,
    " We partyt noucht thus for all the gold in France.
    " The horss thai reft quhilk suld your harness ber."
60 Schir Ranald said; ' That is bot litill der.

'We may get horss and [vthir] gud in playne;
'And men be lost, we get neuir agayne.'
Wallace than said; "Als wisly God me sawe,
"Off this gret myss I sall amendis hawe;
65 "And nothir latt for pess na your plesance.
"With witness her I gif vp my legiance:
"For cowardly ye lik to tyne your rycht;
"Your selff sone syne to dede thai think to dycht."
In wraith thar with away fra him he went.
70 Schyr Ranald was wiss, and kest in his entent;
And said I will byde at the Mernys all nycht:
So Inglissmen may deyme ws no wnrycht,
Gyff ony be deide befor ws vpon cass,
That we in law may bide the rychtwisnass.
75 His luging tuk; still at the Mernyss baid;
Full gret murnyng he for his neuo maid.
Bot all for nocht; quhat mycht it him awaill?
As in till wer he wrocht nocht his consaill.
Wallace raid furth, with him twa yemen past;
80 The sowmer man he folowid wondyr fast;
Be est Cathcart he our hyede thaim agayne.
Than knew thai weille that it was he in playne,
Be horss and weide, that argownd thaim befor.
The fyve to thaim retornde with outyn mor.
85 Wallace to ground fra his courser can glide;
A burnyst brand he bradyt out that tyde.
The maistir man with sa gud will straik he,
Bathe hatt and hede he gert in sondyr fle.
Ane othir fast apon the face he gaiff,
90 Till dede to ground, but mercy, he him draiff.
The thrid he hyt with gret ire in that steid;
Fey on the feld he has him left for deid.
Wallace slew thre; by that his yemen wicht,
The tothir twa derfly to dede thai dycht.

95 Syne spoilyeid thai the harnaiss or thai wend,
   Off siluer and gold aboundandlye to spend.
   Jowellis thai tuk, the best was chosyn thar,
   Gud horss and geyr; syne on thair wayis can fayr.
   Than Wallace said; " At sum strenth wald I be."
100 Our Clid that tyme thar was a bryg of tre;
   Thiddir thai past in all thair gudlye mycht:
   The day was gayne, and cummyn was the nycht.
   Thai durst nocht weylle ner Glaskow still abide;
   In the Lennox he tuk purposs to ryde.
105 And so he dyde, syne lugyt thaim that nycht,
   As thai best mowcht, quhill that the day was brycht.
Fol. 15 a Till ane ostrye he went, and soiorned thar
   With trew Scottis, quhilk at his freindis war.
   The consaill mett rycht glaidly on the morn;
110 Bot fell tithingis was brocht Persie beforne.
   His men war slayne, his tresour als bereft
   With fell Scottis, and thaim na jowellis left.
   Thai demede about off that derff doutouss cass;
   The Sothren said; " Forsuth, it is Wallas."
115 The schirreffis court was cumand to the toune,
   And he as ane for Scot of most renoune.
   Thai gert go seik Schyr Ranald in that rage;
   Bot he was than yeit still at herbryage.
   Sum wiss men said; " Heroff na thing he kend:
120 " The men war slayne rycht at the townis end."
   Schyr Ranald come by ten houris of the day.
   Befor Persye than seir men brocht war thai:
   Thai folowit him of felouny that was wrocht;
   The siyss of this couth say to him rycht nocht.
125 Thai demede about of that feill sodeyne cass,
   Befor the juge thar he denyit Wallas;
   And so he mycht, he wist nocht quhar he was.
   Fra this consaill my purposs is to pass,

Off Wallace spek, in wyldirnes so wyde;
130 The eterne God his gouernour be and gyde!

   Styll at the place four dayis he soiorned haill,
   Quhill tithingis come till hym fra thair consaill.
   Than statute thai, in ilk steide of the west,
   In thar boundis Wallace suld haiff no rest.
135 His der wncle gret ayth thai gert him suer,
   That he, but leiff, suld no freindschipe him ber:
   And mony othir was full woo that day.
   Robert the Boide stall of the toune his way;
   And Kneland als, befor with him had beyne.
140 Thai had leuir haif seyne him with thair eyne,
   Leyffand in lyff, as thai knew him befor,
   Than of cler gold a fyne mylyone and mor.
   Boid wepyt sor, said; " Our leidar is gayne,
   " Amang our fays he is set him allayne."
145 Than Kneland said; ' Fals fortoun changis fast;
   ' Gret God sen we had euir with him past!'
   Edward Litill in Annadyrdaill is went,
   And wait rycht nocht of this newe jugément.
   Adam Wallace baid still in Ricardtoune.
150 So fell [it] thus with Wallace of renoune;
   He with power partyt merwalusly,
   Be fortoune chance ourturnys doubilly.
   Thar petuouss mene as than couth nocht be bett;
   Thai wyst no wyt quhar that thai suld him get.
155 He left the place, quhair he in lugyng lay;
   Till erle Malcome he went vpon a day.
   The Lennox haile he had still in his hand;
Fol. 15 b Till king Eduuard he had nocht than maid band.
   That land is strait, and maisterfull to wyn;
160 Gud men of armyss that tyme was it within.
   The lord was traist, the men sekyr and trew;

With waik power thai durst him nocht persew.
Rycht glaid he was of Wallace cumpany,
Welcummyt him fayr with worschipe reuerandlye;
165 At his awne will desyryt, gyff he walde
To byde thair still maistyr of his houshald;
Off all his men he suld haile chyftayne be.
Wallace ansuerd; "That war yneuch for me.
" I can nocht byde, my mynde is sett in playne
170 "Wrokyn to be, or ellis de in the payne.
"Our wast contré thar statute is so strang,
"Into the north my purposs is to gang."
Stewyn of Irland than in the Lennox was
With wicht Wallace; he ordynyt him to pass,
175 And othir als that borne war off Argill.
Wallace still thair residence maid a quhill,
Quhill men it wist, and semblit sone him till.
He chargyt nayne bot at thair awne gud will;
For thai war strang: yeitt he couth nocht thaim dreid,
180 Bot resawit all in weris thaim to leid.
Sum part off tham was in to Irland borne,
That Makfadyan had exilde furth beforne :
King Eduuardis man he was suorn, of Ingland,
Off rycht law byrth, supposs he tuk on hand.
185 To Wallace thar come ane that hecht Fawdoun;
Malancoly he was of complexioun,
Hewy of statur, dour in his contenance,
Soroufull, sadde, ay dreidfull but plesance.
Wallace resawit quhat man wald cum him till;
190 The bodelye ayth thai maid him with gud will
Before the erle, all with a gud accord;
And him resawyt as captane and thair lord.
His speciall men, that cum with him fra hayme,
The tayne hecht Gray, the tothir Kerlé be nayme,
195 In his seruice come fyrst with all thair mayne,

To Lowdoun hill quhar that Fenweik was slayne.
He thaim comandyt ay next him to persew;
For he thaim kend rycht hardye, wiss and trew.
His leyff he tuk rycht on a fair maner.
200 The gud erlle than he bad him gyftis ser:
Wallace wald nayne, bot gaiff of his fell syss,
To pour and rych, vpon a gudlye wiss.
Humyll he was, hardy, wiss and fre,
As off rychess he held na propyrté.
205 Off honour, worschipe, he was a merour kend;
Als he off gold had boundandlye to spend.
Wpon his fayis he wan it worthely.
Thus Wallace past, and his gud chewalry.
Sexty he had off lykly men at wage;
16 a 210 Throuch the Lennox he led thaim with curage.
Abown Lekkie he lugyt thaim in a waille.
A strenth thar was quhilk thai thocht till assaill.

On Gargownno was byggyt a small peill,
That warnyst was with men and wittaill weill,
215 Within a dyk, bathe closs, chawmer, and hall;
Capteyne tharoff to nayme he hecht Thrilwall.
Thai led Wallace quhar that this byggynge wass;
He thocht to assaill it, ferby or he wald pass.
Twa spyiss he send to wesy all that land:
220 Rycht laith he was the thing to tak on hand,
The quhilk, beforce, that suld gang hym agayne;
Leuir had he throw awentur be slayne.
Thir men went furth as it was large mydnycht;
About that houss thai spyit all at rycht.
225 The wachman was hewy fallen on sleipe;
The bryg was doun at that entré suld keipe;
The lauboreris latt rakleslye went in.
Thir men retornede, with outyn noyess or dyn,

D

To thair maistir; told him as thai had seyne.
230 Than grathit sone thir men of armyss keyne;
Sadlye on fute on to the houss thai socht,
And entryt in, for lattyn sand thai nocht.
Wicht men assayede, with all thair besy cur,
A loklate bar, was drawyn ourthourth the dur;
235 Bot thai mycht nocht it brek out of the waw.
Wallace was grewyt quhen he sic tary saw.
Sumpart amowet, wraithly till it he went;
Be forss off handis it raist out of the stent;
Thre yerde off breide alss off the wall puld out.
240 Than merweld all his men that war about,
How he dide mair than twenty off thaim mycht.
Syne with his fute the yett he straik wp rycht,
Quhill braiss and band to byrst all at anyss.
Ferdely thai raiss, that war in to thai wanyss.
245 The wachman had a felloune staff of steill,
At Wallace strake, bot he kepyt hym weill.
Rudely fra him he reft it in that thrang,
Dang out his harnyss, syne in the dik him flang.
The remaynand be that was on thair feit;
250 Thus Wallace sone can with the capteyn meite.
That staff he had, hewy and forgyt new,
With it Wallace wpon the hede him threw,
Quhill bayn and brayn all in to sondyr yeid.
His men entryt, that worthy war in deid,
255 In handis hynt, and stekit of the layff.
Wallace commaundede thai suld na wermen saiff.
Twenty and twa thai stekit in that steid.
Wemen and barnyss, quhen that the men war deide,
He gert be tayn, in closs houss kepyt weill,
260 So thai wytht out thar off mycht haiff no feill.
Fol. 16 b The dede bodyes thai put sone out of sycht;
Tuk wp the bryg or that the day was lycht.

In that place baid four dayis or he wald pass;
Wist nane with out how at this mater wass:
265 Spoilyeide that steid, and tuk thaim ganand ger;
Jowellis and gold away with thaim thai ber.
Quhen him thocht tyme, thai ischede on the nycht;
To the next woode thai went with all thair mycht.
The captenys wiff, wemen, and childer thre,
270 Pass quhar thai wald, for Wallas leit thaim be.
In that forest he likit nocht to bide:
Thai bownyt thaim atour Forth for to ride.
The moss was strang, to ryde it was no but:
Wallas was wicht and lychtyt on his fute.
275 Few horss thai had, litill thar off thai roucht:
To sawe thar lywes feill strenthis oft thai socht.
Stewyn of Irland he was thair gyd that nycht
Towart Kyncardyn, syne restit thar at rycht
In a forest, that was bathe lang and wide,
280 Rycht fra the moss grew to the wattir syde.
Eftre the sone Wallas walkit about
Vpon Tetht side, quhar he saw mony rout
Off wyld bestis wauerand in wode and playne.
Sone at a schot a gret hart hass he slayne;
285 Slew fyr on flynt, and graithit thaim at rycht;
Sodeynly thar fresche venesoun thai dycht.
Wictaill thai had, bathe breid, and wyne so cler,
With othir stuff yneuch at thair dyner.
His staff of steill he gaiff Kerly to kepe;
290 Syn passit [thai] our Tetht wattir so depe.
In to Straithern thai entrit sodeynly;
In couert past, or Sothren suld thaim spy.
Quhen at thai fand of Scotlandis aduersouris,
With out respyt cummyn was thair fatell houris.
295 Quham euir thai mett, was at the Ingliss fay,
Thai sparyt nane that was off Ingliss blude;

To dede he yeid thocht he war neuir so gude.'
Thai sawyt nothir knycht, squier, nor knaiff;
300 This was the grace that Wallace to thaim gaiff;
Bot wastyt all be worthynes off wer,
Off that party that mycht weild bow or sper.
Sumpart be slycht, sum throw force thai slew;
Bot Wallace thocht thai stroyit nocht half enew.
305 Siluer thai tuk, and als gold at thai fand,
Othir gud ger full lychtly yeid be hand;
Cuttyt throttis, and in to cuwyss thaim kest,
Put out of sycht, for that him thocht was best.
At the Blakfurd, as at thai suld pass our,
Fol. 17 a 310 A squier come, and with him bernyss four,
Till Doun suld ryde; and wend at thai had beyne
All Inglissmen, at he befor had seyne.
Tithingis to sper he howid thaim amang.
Wallace thar with swyth out a [gude] suerd swang;
315 Vpon the hede he straik with so gret ire,
Throu bayne and brayn in sondyr schar the swyr.
The tothir four in handis sone war hynt,
Derfly to dede stekit or thai wald stynt.
Thar horss thai tuk, and quhat thaim likit best;
320 Spoilyeid thaim bar, syne in the brook thaim kest.
Off this mater no mor tary thai maid,
Bot furth thar way passit with outyn baid.
Thir werlik Scottis, all with one assent,
Northt so our Ern throuch out the land thai went:
325 In Meffan woode thair lugyng tuk that nycht.
Vpon the morn, quhen it was dayis lycht,
Wallace raiss wp, went to the forest side,
Quhar that he sawe full feill bestis abide,
Off wylde and tayme walkand haboundandlye.
330 Than Wallace said; "This contré likis me.
"Wermen may do with fud at thai suld haiff;

" Bot want thai meit, thai rak nocht of the laiff."
Off dyet fayr Wallace tuk neuir kepe;
Bot as it come, welcum was meit and sleip.
335 Sum quhill he had gret sufficience within;
Now want, now has; now losis, now can win;
Now lycht, now sadd; now blisful, now in baill;
In haist, now hurt; now sorroufull, now haill;
Nowe weildand weyle; now calde weddyr, now hett;
340 Nowe moist, now drowth; now wauerand wynd, now weit.
So ferd with hym for Scotlandis rycht full ewyn,
In feyle debait six yeris and monethis sewyn.
Quhen he wan peess, and left Scotland in playne,
The Inglissmen maid new conquest agayne.

345   In frustyr termys I will nocht tary lang.
Wallace agayne wnto his men can gang,
And said; " Her is a land of gret boundance,
" Thankit be God of his hye perwyans.
" Sewyn of yow feris graith sone, and ga with me;
350 " Rycht sor I long Sanct Jhonstoun for to se.
" Stewyn of Irland als, God of hewyn the saiff,
" Maister leiddar I mak the of the laiff.
" Kepe weill my men, latt nane out [of] thi sycht,
" Quhill I agayn sall cum with all my mycht.
355 " Byde me sewyn dayis in this forest strang:
" Yhe may get fude, supposs I duell so lang.
" Sumpart yhe haif, and God will send ws mair."
Thus turnyt he, and to the toune couth fair.
Fol. 17 b The mar, kepyt the port of that willage,
360 Wallace knew weill, and send him his message.
The mar was brocht, saw him a gudlye man;
Rycht reuerandlye he has resawyt thaim than.
At him he speryt, all Scottis gyff thai be.
Wallace said; " Ya, and it is peess trow we."

365 'I grant,' he said, 'that likis ws wondyr weill:
'Trew men of peess may ay sum frendschipe feill.
'Quhat is your nayme? I pray yow tell me it.'
"Will Malcomsone," he said, "sen ye wald witt.
"In Atryk forest has my wonnyng beyne:
370 "Thar I was born amang the schawis scheyne.
"Now I desyr this north land for to se,
"Quhar I mycht find bettyr duellyng for me."
The mar said; 'Schyr, I sper nocht for nane ille;
'Bot feill tithingis oft syiss is brocht ws till
375 'Off ane Wallace, was born in to the west.
'Our kingis men he haldis at gret wnrest,
'Martyris thaim doun, gret peté is to se:
'Out of the trewis, forsuth, we trow he be.'
Wallace than said; "I her spek of that man;
380 "Tithingis off him to you nane tell I can."
For him he gert ane innys graithit be,
Quhar nane suld cum bot his awne men and he.
Hys stwart Kerlye brocht thaim in fusioun
Gude thing eneuch quhat was in to the toun.
385 Alss Inglissmen to drynkyn wald him call,
And commownly he delt nocht thar withall.
In thar presence he spendyt resonably,
Yheit for him self he payit ay boundandlye.
On Scottis men he spendyt mekill gud,
390 Bot nocht his thankis wpon the Sothren blud.
Son he consawyt in his witt prewalye,
In to that land quha wass of maist party.
Schir Jamys Butler, ane agit cruell knycht,
Kepyt Kynclewyn, a castell wondyr wycht.
395 His sone Schyr Jhon than duelt in to the toune,
Vndyr capteyn to Schyr Garrard Heroune.
The wemen alss he wysyt at the last;
And so on ane hys eyne he can to cast,

In the south gait, of fassoun fresche and fayr.
400 Wallace to hir maid preualye repair.
So fell it thus, of the toun or he past,
At ane accorde thai hapnyt at the last.
Wallace with hyr in secré maid him glaid.
Sotheren wist nocht that he sic plesance haid.
405 Offt on the nycht he wald say to him sell;
" This is fer war than ony payn of hell,
" At thus, with wrang, thir dewillis suld bruk our land,
" And we with force may nocht agayne thaim stand.
ol. 18 a " To tak this toune my pouer is to small,
410 " Gret perell als on my self may fall.
" Set we it in fyr, it will wndo my seil,
" Or loss my men; thar is no mor to tell.
" Yhettis ar closs, the dykis depe with all.
" Thocht I wald swyme, forsuth so can nocht all.
415 " This matir now herfor I will ourslyde;
" Bot in this toun I may no langar byde."
Alss men tald him quhen the captayne wald pass
Hayme to Kynclewyn, quharoff glaid he wass.

His leiff he tuk at heris of the toune ;
420 To Meffane wode rycht glaidly maid him boune.
Hiss horn he hynt, and bauldly loud can blaw,
Hiss men him hard, and tharto sone couth draw.
Rycht blyth he wass, for thai war all in feyr;
Mony tithingis at him thai wald nocht speyr.
425 He thaim commaunde to mak thaim redy fast.
In gud array out of the woode thai past;
Towart Kynclewyn thai bownyt thaim that tid.
Syn in a waill that ner was thar besid,
Fast on to Tay his buschement can he draw.
430 In a dern woode thai stellit thaim full law;
Set skouriouris furth the contré to aspye.

Be ane our nowne thre for rydaris went bye.
The wach turned in to witt quhat was his will;
He thaim commaund in couert to bide still:
435 "And we call, Feyr! the houss knawlege will haiff;
"And that may sone be warnyng to the laiff.
"All forss in wer do nocht but gouernance."
Wallace was few; bot happy ordinance
Maid him fell syiss his aduersouris to wyn.
440 Be that the court of Inglissmen com in,
Four scoyr and ten weill graithit in thar ger,
Harnest on horss, all likly men of wer.
Wallace saw weill his nowmir was na ma;
He thankit God, and syne the feild couth ta.
445 The Inglissmen merweild quhat thai suld be;
But fra thai saw thai maid [thaim] for mellé,
In fewtir thai kest scharpe speris at that tide;
In ire thai thoucht atour the Scottis to ryd.
Wallace and his went cruelly thaim agayne.
450 At the fyrst rusche feill Inglissmen war slayne.
Wallace straik ane, with hiss gud sper of steill,
Throw out the cost; the shafft to brak ilk deyll.
A burnyst brand in haist he hyntis out;
Thryss apon fute he thrang throuch all the rout.
455 Stern horss thai steik, suld men of armyss ber;
Sone wndir feit fulyeid was men of wer.
Butler lychtyt him self for to defend,
Witht men of armyss quhilk war full worthi kend.
Fol. 18 b On athyr syde feill frekis war fectand fast.
460 The captayne baid, thocht he war sor agast.
Part of the Scottis be worthines thai slew:
Wallace was wa, and towart him he drew.
His men dred for the Butler bauld and keyn.
On him he socht in ire and propyr teyn;
465 Vpon the hed him straik in matelent:

The burnyst blaid throu his basnett went.
Bathe bayne and brayn he byrst throw all the weid;
Thus Wallace hand deliuerit thaim off dreid.
Yeitt feill on fold was fechtand cruelly:
470 Stewyn of Irland, and all the cheualry,
In to the stour did cruelly and weill;
And Kerlé alss with his gud staff of steill.
The Inglissmen, fra thar cheftayne was slayne,
Thai left the feild and fled in all thair mayn.
475 Thre scoyr war slayne or thai wald leif that steid.
The fleande folk, that wist of no rameid,
Bot to the houss thai fled in all thair mycht;
The Scottis folowit, that worthi war and wycht.
Few men of fenss was left that place to kepe,
480 Wemen and preistis wpon the wall can wepe:
For weill thai wend the flearis was thar lord;
To tak him in thai maid thaim redy ford,
Leit doun the bryg, kest wp the yettis wide.
The frayit folk entrit, and durst nocht byde:
485 Gud Wallace euir he folowit thaim so fast,
Quhill in the houss he entryt at the last;
The yett he wor, quhill cumin was all the rout
Of Ingliss and Scottis; he held na man tharout.
The Inglissmen, that won war in that steid,
490 With outyn grace thai bertnyt thaim to deid.
The capteynis wiff, wemen, and preistis twa,
And yong childer, forsuth thai sawyt no ma;
Held thaim in closs eftir this sodeyn cass,
Or Sothron men suld sege him in that place;
495 Tuk wp the bryg, and closyt yettis fast.
The dede bodyes out of sicht he gart cast,
Baith in the houss, and with out at war dede;
Fyve of hys awne to beryniss he gart leid.

In that castell thar sewyn dayis baide he;
500 On ilka nycht thai spoilycid besylé.
    To Schortwode schaw leide wittaill and wyn wicht,
    And houshald ger, baithe gold and siluer brycht.
    Women, and thai that he had grantyt grace,
    Quhen him thoucht tyme, thai put out of that place.
505 Quhen thai had tayne quhat he likit to haiff,
    Straik doun the yettis and set in fyr the laiff;
    Out off wyndowis stanssouris all thai drew;
    Full gret irne wark in to the wattir threw;
    Burdyn duris and lokis, in thair ire,
510 All werk of tre, thai brynt wp in a fyr:
Fol. 19 a Spylt at thai mycht, brak brig and bulwark dounc.
    To Schortwode schawe in haist thai maid thaim boune;
    Chesyt a strenth, quhar thai thar lugyng maid,
    In gud affer a quhill thar still be baid;
515 Yit in the tounc no wit of this had thai.
    The contré folk, quhen it was lycht of day,
    Gret reik saw ryss, and to Kynclewyn thai socht:
    Bot wallis and stane, mar gud thar fand thai nocht.
    The captennis wiff to Sanct Jhonstoun scho yeid,
520 And to Schyr Garrate scho tauld this felloune deid;
    Alss till hyr son quhat hapnyt was be cass.
    Than demyt thai all that it wass wicht Wallas;
    Off for tyme thar he spyit had the toune.
    Than chargyt thai all, thai suld be redy boune.
525 Harnest on horss in to thair armour cler,
    To seik Wallace thai went all furth in feyr,
    A thousand men weill garnest for the wer,
    Towart the woode rycht awfull in affer,
    To Schortwode schaw, and set it all about,
530 Wytht fyve staillis that stalwart was and stout;
    The sext thai maid a fellon range to leid,
    Quhar Wallace was full worthi ay in deid.

The strenth he tuk, and bade thaim hald it still,
On ilka syde, assailye quha sa will.

535 Schyr Jhon Butler in to the forrest went
With twa hundreth, sor mowit in his entent;
His fadris dede to wenge him giff he mocht,
To Wallace sone with men of armyss socht.
A cleuch thar was, quharoff a strenth thai maid

540 With thuortour treis, [and] bauldly thar abaid.
Fra the ta side thai mycht ische till a playne,
Syn throuch the wode to the strenth pass agayn.
Twenty he had that nobill archaris war,
Agayne sewyn scoyr of Ingliss bowmen sar.

545 Four scoyr of speris ner hand thaim baid at rycht,
Giff Scottis ischit to help thaim at thair mycht.
On Wallace sett a bykkyr bauld and keyn;
A bow he bair was byg and weyll beseyn,
And arrouss als, bath lang and scharpe with aw;

550 No man was thar that Wallace bow mycht draw.
Rycht stark he was, and in to souir ger,
Bauldly [he] schott amang thai men of wer.
Ane angell hede to the hukis he drew,
And at a schoyt the formast sone he sleu.

555 Yngliss archaris, that hardy war and wicht,
Amang the Scottis bykkerit with all thair mycht;
Thar awfull schoyt was felloun for to byd,
Off Wallace men thai woundyt sor that tid.
Few off thaim was sekyr of archary;

560 Bettyr thai war, and thai gat ewyn party,
ol. 19 b In feild to byde, othir with suerd or speyr.
Wallace persauit his men tuk mekill deyr:
He gart thaim change, and stand nocht in to steid;
He kest all wayis to saiff thaim fra the dede.

565 Full gret trauaill vpon him self tuk he;
Off Sothron men feill archaris he gert de,

Off Longcaschyr bowmen was in that place.
A sar archar ay waytit on Wallace,
At ane opyn, quhar he vsyt to repair:
570 At him he drew a sekir schot and sar,
Undyr the chyn, throuch a coler of steill,
On the left side, and hurt his halss sumdeill.
Astonaide he was, bot nocht gretlye agast;
Out fra his men on him he folowit fast;
575 In the turnyng, with gud will hass him tayne
Vpon the crag, in sondyr straik the bayne.
Feill of thaim ma na freyndschip with him fand;
Fyfteyn that day he schot to dede of hys hand.
Be that his arrous waistyt war and gayne;
580 The Ingliss archaris forsuth thai wantyt nayne:
With out thai war thar power to ranew,
On ilka side to thaim thai couth persew.
Wylyham Loran com with a boustouss staill,
Out of Gowry, on Wallace to assaill;
585 Neuo he was, as it was knawin in playn,
To the Butler befor that thai had slayn;
To wenge his eyme he come with all his mycht.
Thre hundreth he led of men in armyss brycht;
To leide the range on fute he maid him ford.
590 Wallace to God his conscience fyrst remord,
Syne comfort thaim with manly contenance;
" Yhe se," he said, " gud schiris, thar ordinance;
" Her is no choss, bot owdir do or de.
" We haiff the rycht, the happyar may it be,
595 " That we sall chaipe with grace out of this land."
The Loran, by that, was redy at his hand.
Be that it was eftir nown of the day,
Feill men of witt to consaill sone yeid thai.
The Sothron kest scharply at ilka side,
600 And saw the wood was nothir lang no wide.

Lychtly thai thought he suld hald it so lang:
Fywe hundreth maid throu it on fute to gang,
Sad men off armess that war off eggyr will;
Schyr Garratis self with out the woode baid still.
605 Schyr Jhon Butler the ta sid chesyt he,
The tothyr Loran with a fell menyhe.
Than gud Wallace, that of help had gret neid,
Was fyfty men in all that felloun dreid.
Ane awfull salt the Sothren son began,
610 About the Scottis socht mony likly man,
With bow, and sper, and swerdis stiff of steill:
On athir side no frendschip was to feill.
Wallace in ire a burly brand can draw,
20 a Quhar feill Sothron war semblit vpon raw,
615 To fende his men with his deyr worthi hand:
The folk was fey that he befor him fand.
Throw the thikkest of the gret preiss he past,
Vpon his enemyss hewand wondyr fast.
Agayne his dynt na weidis mycht awaill;
620 Quham so he hyt was dede with outyn faill.
Off the fersest full braithly bair he doun,
Befor the Scottis that war of gret renoun.
To hald the strenth thai preist, with all thair mycht,
The Inglissmen, that worthi war and wicht.
625 Schir Jhon Butler relewit in agayne,
Swndryt the Scottis and did thaim mekill payn;
The Loran alss that cruell was and keyn.
A sar assay forsuth thar mycht be seyn.
Than at the strenth thai mycht no langer bide,
630 The range so strang come wpon athir syde.
In the thikkest woode thar maid thai felle defens,
Agayn thair fayis so full of wiolens:
Yit felle Sothron left the lyff to wed.

Till a new strenth Wallace and his men fled;
635 On aduersouris thai maid full gret debait,
Bot help thaim self, no socour ellis thai wait.
The Sothron als war sundryt than in twyn;
Bot thai agayne to gidder sone can wyn:
Full sutellye thar ordinance thai maid,
640 The rang agayne bownyt but mar abaid.
The Scottis war hurt, and part of thaim war slayn;
So fair assay thai couth nocht mak agayn.
Be this the host approchand was full ner;
Thus wrandly thai held thaim wpon ster.
645 Quhen Wallace saw the Sothroune was at hand,
Him thocht no tym langar for to stand.
Rycht manfully he graithit has his ger;
Sadly he went agayne the men of wer.
Throw out the stour full fast fechtand he socht,
650 With Goddis grace to wenge him gif he mocht.
Vpon the Butler awfully straik he;
Saiffgarde he gat wndir a bowand tre;
The bowcht in twa he straik, abounc his hede,
Alss to the ground, and feld him in that stede.
655 The haill pouer wpon him com so fast,
At thai beforce reskewit him at the last.
Loran was wa, and thidder fast can draw.
Wallas retornd, sa sodeynly him saw:
Out at a syde full fast till him he yeid;
660 He gat no gyrth for all his burnyst weid:
With ire him straik on his gorgeat off steill,
The trensand blaid to persyt euirydeill
Throu plaitt and stuff, mycht nocht agayn it stand;
Derffly to dede he left him on the land.
Fol. 20 b 665 Hym haif thai lost, thocht Sotheren had it suorn;
For his crag bayne was all in sondyr schorn.
The worthi Scottis did nobilly that day

About Wallace, till he was woun away.
He tuk the strenth magre thar fayis will;
670 Abandonly in bargan baid thar still.
The scry sone raiss, the bald Loran was dede :
Schyr Garrat Heroun tranontit that stede,
And all the host assemblit him about.
At the north side than Wallace ischet owt,
675 With him his men, and bownyt him to ga,
Thankand gret God at thai war partyt sa.
To Cargyll wood thai went that samyn nycht.
Sewyn of his men that day to dede was dycht :
In feld was left of the Sothren sex scoyr ;
680 And Loran als, thair mumyng was the mor.
The rang in haist thai rayit sone agayne :
Bot quhen thai saw thair trauaill was in wayne,
And he was past, full mekill mayne thai maid
To rype the wood, bath wala, slonk, and slaid,
685 For Butleris gold Wallace tuk off befor;
Bot thai fand nocht, wald thai seke euirmor.
Hys horss thai gat, and nocht ellis of thair ger.
With dulfull mayn retorned thir men of wer
To Sanct Jhounston, in sorou and gret cayr.
690 Off Wallace furth me likis to spek mair.

The secunde nycht the Scottis couth thaim draw
Rycht priwaly agayne to Schortwod schaw ;
Tuk wp thair gud, quhilk was put owt of sycht,
Cleithing and stuff, bathe gold and siluer brycht.
695 Vpon thar fute, for horsis was thaim fra ;
Or the son raiss, to Meffen wood can ga.
Thar twa dayis our thar lugyng still thai maid ;
On the thrid nycht thai mowit but mar abaid.
Till Elkok park full sodeynly thai went :
700 Thar in that strentht to bide was his entent.

Than Wallace said, he wald go to the toun ;
Arayit him weill in till a preistlik goun.
In Sanct Jhonstoun disgysyt can he fair,
Till this woman the quhilk I spak of ayr.
705 Off his presence scho rycht reiosit was;
And sor adred how he away suld pass.
He soiornyt thar fra nowne was of the day
Quhill ner the nycht, or that he went away.
He trystyt hyr quhen he wald cum agayne,
710 On the thrid day; than was scho wondyr fayne.
Yeitt he was seyn with enemyss as he yeid;
To Schyr Garraid thai tald off all his deid,
And to Butler, that wald haiff wrokyn beyne.
Than thai gart tak that woman brycht and scheyne,
715 Accusyt hir sar of resset in that cass:
Feyll syiss scho suour, that scho knew nocht Wallass.
Fol. 21 a Than Butler said; "We wait weyle it was he;
" And bot thou tell, in bayle fyre sall thou de.
" Giff thou will help to bryng yon rebell doune,
720 " We sall the mak a lady off renoun."
Thai gaiff till hyr baith gold and siluer brycht;
And said, scho suld be weddyt with ane knycht,
Quham scho desirit, that was but mariage.
Thus tempt thai hir, throu consaill and gret wage,
725 That scho thaim tald quhat tyme he wald be thar.
Than war thai glad; for thai desirit no mar
Off all Scotland, bot Wallace at thair will.
Thus ordaynyt thai this poyntment to fullfill.
Feyle men off armes thai graithit hastelye
730 To kepe the yettis, wicht Wallas till aspye.
At the set trist he entrit in the toune,
Wittand no thing of all this falss tresoune.
Till hir chawmer he went but mair abaid.
Scho welcummyt him, and full gret plesance maid.

735 Quhat at thai wrocht, I can nocht graithly say;
Rycht wnperfyt I am of Venus play:
Bot hastelye he graithit him to gang.
Than scho him tuk, and speryt giff he thocht lang;
Scho askit him that nycht with hir to bid.

740 Sone he said; " Nay, for chance that may betide;
" My men ar left all at mysrewill for me.
" I may nocht sleipe this nycht quhill I thaim se."
Than wepyt scho, and said full oft; 'Allace
' That I was maide, wa worthe the courssit cass!

745 ' Now haiff I lost the best man leiffand is;
' O feble mynd, to do so foull a myss!
' O waryit witt, wykkyt and wariance,
' That me hass brocht in to this myschefull chance!
' Allace,' scho said, ' in warld that I was wrocht!

750 ' Giff all this payne on my self mycht be brocht!
' I haiff seruit to be brynt in a gleid.'
Quhen Wallace saw scho ner of witt couth weid,
In his armess he caucht hir sobrely,
And said ; " Der hart, quha hass mysdoyne ocht, I?"

755 ' Nay, I,' quoth scho, ' hass falslye wrocht this trayn,
' I haiff you sald; rycht now yhe will be slayn.'
Scho tauld [to] him hir tresoun till ane end,
As I haiff said; quhat nedis mair legend?
At hir he speryt, giff scho forthocht it sar.

760 " Wa, ya," scho said, " and sall do euirmar.
" My waryed werd in warld I mon fullfill;
" To mend this myss I wald byrne on a hill."
He comfort hir, and baide hir haiff no dreide.
' I will,' he said, ' haiff sumpart off thi weid.'

765 Hir gowne he tuk on hym, and courchess alss.
21 b ' Will God, I sall eschape this tresoune falss.
' I the forgyff.'   With outyn wordis mair
He kissyt hyr, syne tuk his leiff to fayr.

E

Hys burly brand, that helpyt him offt in neid,
770 Rycht priwalye he hid it wndyr that weid.
To the south yett, the gaynest way, he drew;
Quhar that he fand off armyt men enew.
To thaim he tald, dissemblyt [in] contenance;
"To the chawmer, quhar he was vpon chance,
775 "Speid fast," he said, "Wallace is lokit in."
Fra him thai socht with outyn noyiss or dyn,
To that sammyn houss; about thai can thaim cast.
Out at the yett [than] Wallas gat full fast,
Rycht glaid in hart; quhen that he was with out,
780 Rycht fast he yeide, a stour paiss and a stout.
Twa him beheld, and said; "We will go se;
"A stalwart queyne, forsuth, yon semyss to be."
Him thai folowit throwe the South Ynche thai twa.
Quhen Wallace saw with thaim thar come na ma,
785 Agayne he turnede, and has the formast slayn.
The tothir fled; than Wallas, with gret mayn,
Vpon the hede, with his suerd, has him tayne;
Left thaim bathe dede, syne to the strenth is gayne.
His men he gat, rycht glaid quhen thai him saw;
790 Till thair defens in haist he gart thaim draw;
Deuoydyde him sone of the womannys weid:
Thus chapyt he out of that felloun dreid.

EXPLICIT LIBER QUARTUS,
ET INCIPIT QUINTUS.

BUKE FYFTE.

THE dyrk regioun apperand wondyr fast,
In Nouember, quhen October was past,
The day faillit, throu the rycht courss worthit schort;
Till banyst men that is no gret comfort,
5 With thair power in pethis worthis gang;
Hewy thai think quhen at the nycht is lang.
Thus Wallas saw the nychtis messynger;
Phebus had lost his fyry bemyss cler.
Out of the wood thai durst nocht turn that tyd,
10 For aduersouris that in thair way wald byde.
Wallace thaim tauld that new wer wes on hand;
The Inglissmen was off the toune cummande.
The dure thai brak, quhar thai trowyt Wallace wass;
Quhen thai him myst, thai bownyt thaim to pass.
15 In this gret noyis the woman gat away,
But to quhat steide I can nocht graithlye say.
The Sothroun socht rycht sadlye fra that stede
Throu the South Ynch, and fand thair twa men dede.
Thai knew be that Wallace was in the strenth.
Fol. 22 a 20 About the park thai set on breid and lenth,
With sex hundreth weill graithit in thar armess,
All likly men, to wrek thaim of thair harmess.
A hundreth men chargit, in armes strang,
To kepe a hunde that thai had thaim amang;
25 In Gyllisland thar was that brachell brede,

Sekyr off sent to folow thaim at flede.
So was scho vsyt on Esk and on Ledaill;
Quhill scho gat blude no flëyng mycht awaill.
Than said thai all, Wallace mycht nocht away,
30 He suld be tharis for ocht at he do may.
The ost thai delt in diuerss part that tyde.
Schyr Garrat Herroun in the staill can abide;
Schyr Jhon Butler the range he tuk him till,
With thre hundre quhilk war of hardy will;
35 In to the woode apon Wallace thai yeid.
The worthi Scottis that wer in mekill dreid,
Socht till a place for till haiff yschet out,
And saw the staill enwerounyt thaim about.
Agayne thai went with hydwyss strakis strang,
40 Gret noyiss and dyne was rayssit thaim amang.
Thar cruell deide rycht merwaluss to ken,
Quhen fourtie macht agayne thre hundyr men.
Wallace so weill apon him tuk that tide,
Throw the gret preyss he maid a way full wide;
45 Helpand the Scottis with his der worthi hand:
Fell faymen he left fey vpon the land.
Yheit Wallas lost fyfteyn in to that steid;
And fourtie men of Sothroun part war dede.
The Butleris folk so fruschit was in deid,
50 The hardy Scottis to the strenthis throw thaim yeide.
On to Tay side thai hastyt thaim full fast,
In will thai war the wattir till haiff past.
Halff couth nocht swym that than with Wallas wass;
And he wald nocht leiff ane, and fra thaim pass.
55 Bettir him thocht in perell for to be
Wpon the land, than willfully to se
His men to droun, quhar reskew mycht be nayne.
Agayne in ire to the feild ar thai gayne.
Butler be than had putt his men in ray,

60 On thaim he sett with ane awfull hard assay,
   On athir side with wapynnys stiff off steill.
   Wallace agayne no frendschipe lett thaim feill.
   Bot do or de, thai wist no mor socour;
   Thus fend thai lang in to that stalwart stour.
65 The Scottis chyftayne was yong, and in a rage,
   Vsyt in wer, and fechtis with curage.
   He saw his men off Sothroun tak gret wrang,
22 b Thaim to raweng all dreidles can he gang:
   For mony off thaim war bledand wondyr sar.
70 He couth nocht se no help apperand thar,
   Bot thair chyftayne war putt out off thair gait;
   The bryme Butler so bauldlye maid debait.
   Throu the gret preyss Wallace to him socht:
   His awful deid he eschewit as he mocht.
75 Vndyr ane ayk, wyth men about him set:
   Wallace mycht nocht a graith straik on him gett:
   Yeit schede he thaim, a full royd slope was maid.
   The Scottis went out, no langar thar abaid.
   Stewyn off Irland, quhilk hardy was and wicht,
80 To helpe Wallace he did gret preyss and mycht;
   With trew Kerlé, douchty in mony deid;
   Wpon the grounde feill Sothroun gert thai bleid.
   Sexty war slayne of Inglissmen in that place,
   And nyne off Scottis thair tynt was throuch that cace.
85 Butleris men so stroyit war that tide,
   In to the stour he wald no langar bide.
   To get supple he socht on to the staill:
   Thus lost he thar a hundreth of gret waill.
   As thai war best arayand Butleris rout,
90 Betuex parteys than Wallace ischit out;
   Sexteyn with him, thai graithit thaim to ga;
   Off all his men he had lewyt no ma.
   The Inglissmen has myssyt hym; in hy

The hund thai tuk, and folowit haistely.
95 At the Gask woode full fayne he wald haiff beyne;
Bot this sloth brache, quhilk sekyr was and keyne,
On Wallace fute folowit so felloune fast,
Quhill in thar sicht thai prochit at the last.
Thar horss war wicht, had soiorned weill and lang
100 To the next woode twa myil thai had to gang,
Off vpwith erde; thai yeid with all thair mycht;
Gud hope thai had for it was ner the nycht.
Fawdoun tyryt, and said, he mycht nocht gang.
Wallace was wa to leyff him in that thrang.
105 He bade him ga, and said the strenth was ner;
Bot he tharfor wald nocht fastir him ster.
Wallace in ire on the crag can him ta
With his gud suerd, and strak the hed him fra.
Dreidless to ground derfly he duschit dede.
110 Fra him he lap, and left him in that stede.
Sum demys it to ill, and othyr sum to gud;
And I say her, into thir termyss rude,
Bettir it was he did, as thinkis me.
Fyrst, to the hunde it mycht gret stoppyn be.
115 Als Fawdoun was haldyn at [gret] suspicioun;
For he was haldyn of brokill complexioun.
Rycht stark he was, and had bot litill gayne.
Fol. 23 a Thus Wallace wist: had he beyne left allayne,
And he war fals, to enemyss he wald ga;
120 Gyff he war trew, the Sothroun wald him sla.
Mycht he do ocht bot tyne him as it was?
Fra this questioun now schortlye will I pass.
Deyme as yhe lest, ye that best can and may;
I bott raherss as my autour will say.

125   Sternys, be than, began for till apper,
The Inglissmen was cummand wondyr ner;

Fyve hundreth haill was in thair chewalry:
To the next strenth than Wallace couth him hy.
Stewyn off Irland, wnwitting of Wallas,
130 And gud Kerlé, baid still ner hand that place,
At the mur syde, in till a scrogghy slaid,
Be est Dipplyne quhar thai this tary maid.
Fawdoun was left besid thaim on the land;
The power come, and sodeynly him fand:
135 For thair sloith hund the graith gait till him yeid,
Off othir trade scho tuk as than no heid.
The sloith stoppyt, at Fawdoune still scho stude;
Nor forthir scho wald, fra tyme scho fand the blud.
Inglissmen dempt, for ellis thai couth nocht tell,
140 Bot at the Scottis had fochtyn amang thaim sell.
Rycht wa thai war that losyt was thair sent.
Wallace twa men amang the ost in went;
Dissemblit weylle, that no man suld thaim ken,
Rycht in affer, as thai war Inglissmen.
145 Kerlé beheld on to the bauld Heroun,
Vpon Fawdoun as he was lukand doune,
A suttell straik wpwart him tuk that tide,
Wndir the chokkeis the grounden suerd gart glid,
By the gude mayle bathe halss and his crag bayne
150 In sondyr straik; thus endyt that cheftayne.
To grounde he fell, feile folk about him thrang,
Tresoune! thai criyt, traytouris was thaim amang.
Kerlye with that fled out sone at a side;
His falow Stewyn than thocht no tyme to bide.
155 The fray was gret, and fast away thai yeid,
Lawch towart Ern; thus chapyt thai of dreid.
Butler for woo off wepyng mycht nocht stynt.
Thus raklesly this gud knycht [haiff] thai tynt.
Thai demyt all that it was Wallace men,
160 Or ellis him self, thocht thai couth nocht him ken.

" He is rycht ner, we sall him haif but faill;
" This febill woode may him litill awaill."
Fourtie thar past agayne to Sanct Jhonstoun,
With this dede corss, to berysing maid it boune.
165 Partyt thar men, syne diuerss wayis raid;
A gret power at Dipplyn still thar baid.

Fol. 23 b Till Dawryoch the Butler past but let;
At syndry furdis the gait thai wmbeset;
To kepe the wode quhill it was day [thai] thocht.
170 As Wallace thus in the thik forrest socht,
For his twa men in mynd he had gret payne;
He wist nocht weill giff thai wàr tayne or slayne,
Or chapyt haile be ony jeperté.
Threttene war left with him, no ma had he.
175 In the Gask hall thair lugyng haif thai tayne;
Fyr gat thai sone, bot meyt than had thai nane.
Twa scheipe thai tuk besid thaim of a fauld,
Ordanyt to soupe in to that sembly hauld;
Graithit in haist sum fude for thaim to dycht:
180 So hard thai blaw rude hornyss wpon hycht.
Twa sende he furth to luk quhat it mycht be;
Thai baid rycht lang, and no tithingis herd he,
Bot boustouss noyis so brymly blew and fast:
So othir twa in to the woode furth past.
185 Nane come agayne, bot boustously can blaw.
In to gret ire he send thaim furth on raw.
Quhen he allayne Wallace was lewyt thar,
The awfull blast aboundyt mekill mayr.
Than trowit he weill thai had his lugyng seyne;
190 His suerd he drew of nobill mettall keyne,
Syn furth he went quhar at he hard the horne.
With out the dur Fawdoun was him beforn,
As till his sycht, his awne hed in his hand;
A croyss he maid, quhen he saw him so stand

195 At Wallace in the hed he swaket thar;
And he in haist sone hynt [it] by the hair,
Syne out agayne at him he couth it cast;
In till his hart he was gretlye agast.
Rycht weill he trowit that was no spreit of man;
200 It was sum dewill, at sic malice began.
He wyst no waill thar langar for to bide,
Vp throuch the hall thus wicht Wallace can glid,
Till a closs stair; the burdis raiff in twyne,
Fyftene fute large he lap out of that in.
205 Wp the wattir sodeynlye he couth fair;
Agayne he blent quhat perance he sawe thair.
Him thocht he saw Faudoun that hugly syr;
That haill hall he had set in a fyr;
A gret raftre he had in till his hand.
210 Wallace as than no langar walde he stand,
Off his gud men full gret meruaill had he,
How thai war tynt throuch his feyle fantasé.
Traistis rycht weill all this was suth in deide,
Supposs that it no poynt be of the creide.
215 Power thai had witht Lucifer that fell,
The tyme quhen he partyt fra hewyn to hell.
ol. 24 a Be sic myscheiff giff his men mycht be lost,
Drownyt or slayne amang the Ingliss ost;
Or quhat it was in liknes of Faudoun,
220 Quhilk brocht his men to suddand confusioun;
Or gif the man endyt in ewill entent,
Sum wikkit spreit agayne for him present;
I can nocht spek of sic diuinité,
To clerkis I will lat all sic materis be:
225 Bot of Wallace, furth I will yow tell.
Quhen he wes went of that perell fell,
Yeit glaid wes he that he had chapyt swa:
Bot for his men gret murnyng can he ma;

Flayt by him self to the Maker off buffe,
230 Quhy he sufferyt he suld sic paynys pruff.
He wyst nocht weill giff it wes Goddis will,
Rycht or wrang his fortoun to fullfill:
Hade he plesd God, he trowit it mycht nocht be
He suld him thoill in sic perplexité.
235 Bot gret curage in his mynd euir draiff,
Off Inglissmen thinkand amendis to haiff.

As he was thus walkand be him allayne
Apon Ern side, makand a pytuouss mayne,
Schyr Jhone Butler, to wache the furdis rycht,
240 Out fra his men of Wallace had a sicht.
The myst wes went to the montanys agayne;
Till him he raid; quhar at he maid his mayne
On loude he sperde; "Quhat art thow walkis that gait?"
'A trew man, Schyr, thocht my wiagis be layt;
245 'Erandis I pass fra Doun to my lord,
'Schir Jhon Sewart; the rycht for [till] record,
'In Doune is now, new cummyn fra the king.'
Than Butler said; "This is a selcouth thing.
"Thou leid all out, thow has beyne with Wallace;
250 "I sall the knaw, or thou cum of this place."
Till him he stert the courser wondyr wicht,
Drew out a suerd, so maid [hym] for to lycht.
Abowne the kne gud Wallas has him tayne,
Throw the and brawn in sondyr straik the bayne;
255 Derflly to dede the knycht fell on the land.
Wallace the horss sone sesyt in his hand,
Ane awkwart straik syne tuk him in the sted,
His crag in twa; thus was the Butler dede.
Ane Inglissman saw thair chiftayne wes slayn;
260 A sper in reyst he kest with all his mayne,
On Wallace draiff, fra the horss him to ber.

Warly he wrocht, as worthi man in wer:

· The sper he wan with outyn mor abaid;

24 b On horss he lap, and throw a gret rout raid.

265 To Dawryoch he knew the forss full weill.

Befor him come feyll stuffyt in fyne steill:

He straik the fyrst but baid in the blasoune.

Quhill horss and man bathe flet the wattir doune.

Ane othir sone doune fra his horss he bar,

270 Stampyt to grounde, and drownyt with outyn mar.

The thrid he hyt in his harness of steyll,

Throw out the cost; the sper to brak sumdeyll.

The gret power than efftir him can ryd:

He saw na waill no langar thar to byd.

275 His burnyst brand braithly in hand he bar.

Quham he hytt rycht, thai folowit him no mar.

To stuff the chass feyll frekis folowit fast;

Bot Wallace maid the gayast ay agast.

The mur he tuk, and throw thair power yeid;

280 The horss was gud, bot yeit he had gret dreid

For failyeing or he wan to a strenth.

The chass was gret, scalyt our breid and lenth;

Throw strang danger thai had him ay in sycht.

At the Blakfurd thar Wallace doune can lycht;

285 His horss stuffyt, for the way was depe and lang;

A large gret myile wichtly on fute couth gang.

Or he was horst, rydaris about him kest;

He saw full weyll lang swa he mycht nocht lest.

Sad men in deid wpon him can renew;

290 With retornyng that nycht twenty he slew.

The forseast ay rudely rabutyt he,

Kepyt hys horss, and rycht wysely can fle;

Quhill that he cum the myrkest mur amang.

His horss gaiff our, and wald no forthyr gang.

295 Wallace on fute tuk him with gud entent:

The horss he straik, or that he fra him went;
His houch sennownnis he cuttyt all atanyss,
And left him thus besyde the standand stanys;
For Sotheron men no gud suld off him wyn.
300 In heich haddyr Wallace and thai can twyn.
Throuch that doun with to Forth sadly he soucht.
Bot sodandly thar come in till his thocht,
Gret power wok at Stirlyng bryg off tre.
Seychand he said; "No passage is for me.
305 " For want off fude, and I haiff fochtyn lang,
" On wer men now me thynk no tyme to gang.
" At Kamyskynnett I sall the wattir till;
" Lat God abowne do with me quhat he will!
" In to this land lang[er] I may nocht byd."
310 Tary he maid sum part on Forthis syd;
Tuk off his weid, and graithit him but mar;
Hys swerd he band, that wondyr scharply schar,
Amang his ger, be his schuldrys on loft.
Fol. 25 a Thus in he went, to gret God prayand oft,
315 Off his hye grace the causs to tak on hand.
Our the wattyr he swame to the south land;
Arayede him sone; the sessone was rycht cauld,
For Piscis was in tyll his dayis of auld.

Our thwort the Kerss to the Torwode he yeide;
320 A wedow thar duelt that helpyt him in neid.
Thiddyr he come or day begouth to daw,
Till a wyndow, and prewaly couth caw.
Thai sperd his nayme; bot tell thaim wald he nocht,
Quhill scho hir selff ner till his langage socht.
325 Fra tyme scho wist at it was wicht Wallace,
Reiossyt scho wes, and thankit God off his grace.
Scho sperd sone, quhy he was him allayne.
Murnand, he said; "As now may haiff I nane."

Scho askyt him, quhar at his men suld be.

330 " Feyr deyme," he said, " go get sum meit for me;

" I haiff fastyt syne yhisterday at morn :

" I dreid full sar that my men be forlorn.

" Gret part off thaim to the dede I saw dycht."

Scho gat him meyt in all the haist scho mycht.

335 A woman he cald, and als with hyr a child ;

Syne bade thaim pass agayne thai wayis wild,

To the Gask-hall, tithingis for to sper,

Giff part war left of his men in to fer ;

And scho suld fynd a horss sone in hir gait.

340 He bad thaim se giff that place stud in stait :

Tharoff to her he had full gret desyr,

Be causs he thocht that it was all in fyr.

Thai passyt furth with outyn tary mar.

Him for to rest, Wallace ramaynit thar.

345 Refreschit he wes with meyte, drynk, and with heit;

Quhilk causyt him throuch naturall courss to weit

Quhar he suld sleipe, in sekyrnes to be.

The wedow had off hyr awne sonnys thre.

Fyrst twa off thaim scho send to kepe Wallace ;

350 And gert the thrid go sone to Dwnypace ;

And tald his eyme, that he was hapnyt thar.

The persone yeid to se of his weyllfar.

Wallace to sleipe [was] laid in the wood syde ;

The twa yong men with out hym ner couth byd.

355 The persone come ner, and thar maner saw ;

Thai beknyt him to quhat stede he suld draw.

The rone wes thik that Wallace slepyt in ;

About he yeid, and maid bot litill dyn.

So at the last of him he had a sycht,

360 Full prewalye how that his bed was dycht.

He him beheld, and said syne to him sell ;

" Her is merwaill, quha likis it to tell ;

Fol. 25 b " That a persone, be worthines of hand,
    " Trowys to stop the powér of Ingland.
365 " Now falss fortoune, the myswyrkar of all,
    " Be awentur has gyffyn him a fall,
    " At he is left with out supple of ma;
    " A cruell wyff with wapynnys mycht him sla."
    Wallace him herd, quhen his slepe ouerpast;
370 Fersly he rayss, and said till him als fast;
    ' Thou leid, falss preyst, war thow a fa to me,
    ' I wald nocht dreid sic othir ten as the.
    ' I haiff had mar syne yhistirday at morn,
    ' Than syk sexty war semblyt me beforn.'
375 His eyme him tuk, and went furth with Wallace :
    He tald till him off all his paynfull cace.
    ' This nycht,' he said, ' I was left me allayne,
    ' In feyle debait with enemyss mony ane.
    ' God at his will my liff did ay to kepe :
380 ' Our Forth I swame, that awfull is and depe.
    ' Quhat I haiff had in wer befor this day,
    ' Presoune and payne, to this nycht was bot play;
    ' So bett I am with strakis sad and sar;
    ' The cheyle wattir vrned me mekill mar;
385 ' Eftir gret blud throu heit in cauld was brocht,
    ' That off my lyff almost no thing I roucht.
    ' I meyn fer mar the tynsell off my men,
    ' Na for my selff, mycht I suffir sic ten.'
    The persone said ; " Der sone, thow may se weyll,
390 " Langar to stryff it helpis nocht adeyll,
    " Thi men ar lost, and nayne will with the ryss;
    " For Goddis [saik,] wyrk as I sall dewyss.
    " Tak a lordschipe, quhar on at thow may liff;
    " King Eduuard wald gret landis to the giff."
395 ' Wncle,' he said, ' off sic wordis no mar ;
    ' This is no thing bot eking off my car.

‘ I lik bettir to se the Sothren de,
‘ Than gold or land that thai can giff to me.
‘ Trastis, rycht weyll of wer I will nocht cess,
400 ‘ Quhill tyme that I bryng Scotland in to pess,
‘ Or de tharfor, in playne to wndrestand.’
So come Kerlé, and gud Stewyn of Irland ;
The wedowis sone to Wallace he thaim broucht.
Fra thai him saw, of na sadnes thai roucht ;
405 For perfyt joy thai wepe with all thair eyne ;
To ground thai fell, and thankit hewynnys queyn.
Als he was glaid for reskew off thaim twa ;
Off thair feris leyffand was left no ma.
Thai tald him that Schyr Garrat wes dede ;
410 How thai had weyll eschapyt of that stede.
Throuch the Oychall thai had gayne all that nycht,
Fol. 26 a Till Quenysferry, or that the day was brycht ;
How a trew Scot, for kyndnes off Wallace,
Brocht thaim sone oure, syne kend thaim to that place :
415 Als Kerlé wyst, gyff Wallace leyffand war,
Nere Dwnypace that he suld fynd him thar.
The persone gart gud purwiance for thaim dycht.
In the Torwode thai lugyt all that nycht ;
Quhill the woman, that Wallace north had send,
420 Retornd agayne, and tald him till ane end,
Quhat Inglissmen in the way scho fand dede :
Feyll was fallyn fey in mony syndry stede.
The horss scho saw that Wallace had berefft,
And the Gask hall standand as it was left,
425 With out harme, nocht sterd off it a stane ;
Bot off his men gud tithingis scho gat nane.
Tharoff he grewyt gretlyc in that tyd :
In the forrest he wald no langar bid.
The wedow him gaiff part off siluer brycht ;
430 Twa of hyr sonnys, that worthi war and wycht.

The thrid scho held becauss he lakit age,
In wer as than mycht nocht wyn wesselage.
The persone than gat thaim gud horss and ger:
Bot wa he was, his mynd was all in wer.

435 Thus tuk he leyff with owtyn langar abaid:
In Dundaff mur that sammyn nycht he raid.
Schir Jhone the Grayme, quhilk lord wes of that land,
Ane agyt knycht had made nane othir band;
Bot purchest pess in rest he mycht bide still,
440 Tribute payit full sore agayne his will.
A sone he had, bathe wyss, worthi and wicht;
Alexander the ferss at Berweik maid him knycht,
Quhar schawyn wes off battaill till haif beyne,
Betuex Scottis and the bauld Persie keyne.
445 This yong Schyr Jhone rycht nobill wes in wer
On a braid scheyld his fadyr gert him swer,
He suld be trew till Wallace in all thing,
And he till him, quhill lyff mycht in thaim ryng.
Thre nychtis thar Wallace baid out off dreid;
450 Restyt him weill, swa had he mekill neid.
On the ferd day he wald no langar bide:
Schir Jhone the Grayme bownyt with him to ryd;
And he said; nay, as than it suld nocht be:
"A playne part yeit I will nocht tak on me.
455 "I haiff tynt men throw my [ouer] rakless deid:
"A brynt child mayr sayr the fyr will dreid.
"Freyndis haiff I sum part in Clyddysdaill;
"I will go se quhat may thai me awaill."
Schir Jhon ansuerd; 'I will your consaill do;
Fol. 26 b 460 'Quhen yhe se tyme, send priwale me to:
'Than I sall cum with my power in haist.'
He him betuk on to the haly Gaist,
Saynct Jhone to borch, thai suld meite haill and sound.

Out off Dundaff he and thir four couth found;
465 In Bothwell mur that nycht remaynyt he,
With ane Craufurd that lugyt him preualé.
Wpon the morn to the Gilbank he went;
Rasauit was with mony glaid entent:
For his deyr eyme, yong Auchinlek, duelt thar,
470 Brothyr he was to the schirreff off Ayr.
Quhen auld Schyr Ranald till his dede wes dycht,
Than Auchinlek weddyt that lady brycht,
And childyr gat, as storyess will record,
Off Lesmahago, for he held off that lord.
475 Bot he wes slayne, gret peté wes the mar,
With Perseys men, in [to] the toun of Ayr.
His sone duelt still, than nynetene yeris off age,
And brokit haille his fadris heretage.
Tribute he payit for all his landis braid,
480 To lord Persie, as hys brodyr had maid.

I leyff Wallace, with his der wncle still;
Off Inglissmen yeit sum thing spek I will.
A messynger sone throw the contré yeid,
To lord Persie thai tald this fellone deid;
485 Kynclewyn was brynt, brokyn, and castyn doun,
The captayn dede off it and Saynt Jhonstoun;
The Loran als, at Schortwod schawis scheyn;
In to that land, gret sorow has beyne seyn
Throuch wicht Wallace, that all this deid has done;
490 "The toune he spyit, and that forthocht we sone.
"Butler is slayne, with douchty men and deyr."
In aspre spech the Persye than can speyr;
"Quhat worth of him? I pray you graithlye tell."
'My lord,' he said, 'rycht thus the case befell.
500 'We knaw for treuth he was left him allayne;
'And, as he fled, he slew full mony ayne.

F

'The horss we fand, that him that gait couth ber;
'Bot of hym self no othyr word we her.
'At Styrlyng bryg we wait he passit nocht;
505 'To dede in Forth he may for vs be brocht.'
Lorde Persye said; " Now suthlye that war syne;
" So gud of hand is nayne this warld within.
" Had he tayne pess, and beyne our kingis man,
" The haill empyr he mycht haiff conquest than.
510 " Gret harme it is, our knychtis that ar ded;
" We mon ger se for othir in thair sted.
" I trow nocht yeit at Wallace losyt be:
Fol. 27 a " Our clerkys sayis, he sall ger mony de."
The messynger said; ' All that suth has beyne;
515 'Mony hundreth, that cruell war and keyne,
'Sene he begane, ar lost with out ramede.'
The Persye said; " Forsuth he is nocht ded;
" The crukis off Forth he knawis wondyr weylle;
" He is on lyff, that sall our natioune feill.
520 " Quhen he is strest, than can he swym at will;
" Gret strenth he has, bathe wyt and grace thartill."
A messynger the lord chargyt to wend;
And this commaunde in wryt with him he send.
Schir Jhone Sewart gret schirreff than he maid
525 Off Sanct Jhonstoun, and all thai landis braid.
In till Kynclewyn thar duelt nane agayne;
Thar wes left nocht bot brokyn wallis in playne.
Leiff I thaim thus reulland the landis thar;
And spek I will off Wallace glaid weillfar.
530 He send Kerle to Schyr Ranald the knycht,
Till Boyd and Blayr that worthi war and wicht,
And Adam als, his cusyng, gud Wallace;
To thaim declarde of all this paynfull cass.
Off his eschaipe out off that cumpany,
535 Rycht wondyr glaid was this gud chewalry:

Fra tyme thai wyst that Wallace leiffand was,
Gude expensis till him thai maid to pass.
Maister Jhone Blayr was offt in that message,
A worthy clerk, bath wyss and rycht sawage.
540 Lewyt he was befor in Paryss toune.
Amang maistris in science and renoune.
Wallace and he at hayme in scule had beyne;
Sone eftirwart, as verité is seyne,
He was the man that pryncipall wndirtuk,
545 That fyrst compild in dyt the Latyne buk
Off Wallace lyff, rycht famouss of renoune;
And Thomas Gray persone off Libertoune.
With him thai war, and put in story all,
Offt ane or bath, mekill of his trauaill;
550 And tharfor her I mak off thaim mencioune.
Master Jhone Blayr to Wallace maid him boune;
To se his heyle his comfort was the mor,
As thai full oft togyddyr war befor.
Syluer and gold thai gaiff him for to spend;
555 Sa dyde he thaim frely, quhen God it send.
Of gud weylfayr as than he wantyt nane.
Inglissmen wyst he was left him allane.
Quhar he suld be was nayne off thaim couth say,
Drownyt or slayne, or eschapyt away:
560 Tharfor off him thai tuk bot litill heid;
Thai knew him nocht, the less he was in dreid.
ol. 27 b All trew Scottis gret fauour till him gaiff,
Quhat gude thai had he mysterit nocht to craiff.

The pess lestyt, that Schyr Ranald had tayne;
565 Thai four monethis it suld nocht be out gane.
This Chrystismess Wallace ramaynyt thar,
In Laynrik oft till sport he maid repair.
Quhan that he went fra Gilbank to the toune,

And he fand men that was off that falss nacioune,
570 To Scotland thai dyde neuir grewance mar;
Sum stekyt thai, sum throttis in sondyr schar.
Feill war sone dede, bot nanc wyst quha it was;
Quham he handlyt he leyt no forthir pass.
Thar Hesylryg duelt, that curssyt knycht to waill:
575 Schyrreff he was off all the landis haill,
Fellounc, owtragc, dispitfull in his deid;
Mony off him tharfor had mekill dreid.
Merwaill he thocht quha durst his peple sla,
With out the toune he gert gret nowmir ga.
580 Quhen Wallace saw that thai war ma than he,
Than did he nocht but salust curtaslé.
All his four men bar thaim quietlik,
Na Sotheron couth deme thaim myss, pur no rik.
In Lanryk duelt a gentill woman thar,
585 A madyn myld, as my buk will declar,
Off auchteyn yeris ald or litill mor off age;
Alss born scho was till part off heretage.
Hyr fadyr was off worschipe and renoune,
And Hew Braidfute he hecht of Lammyngtoune,
590 As feylle othyr was in the contré calld;
Befor tyme thai gentill men war off ald.
Bot this gud man, and als his wiff wes ded.
The madyn than wyst off no othyr rede,
Bot still scho duelt on trewbute in the toune,
595 And purchest had king Eduuardis protectioune;
Serwandys with hyr, off freyndis at hyr will.
Thus leyffyt scho without desyr off ill;
A quiet houss, as scho mycht hald in wer,
For Hesylryg had done hyr mekill der;
600 Slayne hyr brodyr, quhilk eldast wes and ayr.
All sufferyt scho, and rycht lawly hyr bar;
Amyabill, so benyng, war, and wyss,

Curtass and swete, fulfillyt of gentryss,
Weyll rewllyt off tong, rycht haill of contenance,
605 Off wertuouss scho was worthi till awance;
Hummylly hyr led, and purchest a gud name,
Off ilkyn wicht scho kepyt her fra blame.
28 a Trew rychtwyss folk a gret fauour hir lent.
Apon a day, to the kyrk as scho went,
610 Wallace hyr saw, as he his eyne can cast.
The prent off luff him punyeit at the last,
So asprely, throuch bewté off that brycht,
With gret wness in presence bid he mycht.
He knew full weyll hyr kynrent and hyr blud,
615 And how scho was in honest oyss and gud.
Quhill wald he think to luff hyr our the laiff,
And othir quhill he thocht on his dissaiff,
How that hys men was brocht to confusioun,
Throw his last luff he had in Saynct Jhonstoun.
620 Than wald he think to leiff and lat our slyd:
Bot that thocht lang in hys mynd mycht nocht byd.
He tauld Kerlé off his new lusty baille,
Syne askit hym off his trew best consaill.
"Maister," he said, "as fer as I haiff feyll,
625 "Off lyklynes it may be wondyr weill.
"Sen ye sa luff, tak hir in mariage;
"Gudlye scho is, and als has heretage.
"Supposs at yhe in luffyng feill amyss,
"Gret God forbede it suld be so with this."
630 'To mary thus I can nocht yeit attend:
'I wald of wer fyrst se a finaill end.
'I will no mor allayne to my luff gang;
'Tak tent to me, or dreid we suffer wrang.
'To proffer [luff] thus sone I wald nocht preffe;
635 'Mycht I leyff off, in wer I lik to leyff.
'Quhat is this luff? no thing bot folychnes;

' It may reiff men bathe witt and stedfastnes.'
Than said he thus; ' This will nocht graithly be,
' Amors and wer at anys to ryng in me.
640 ' Rycht suth it is, stude I in blis off luffe,
' Quhar dedis war I suld the bettir pruff.
' Bot weyle I wait, quhar gret ernyst is in thocht,
' It lattis wer in the wysest wys be wrocht;
' Less gyf it be, bot only till a deid:
645 ' Than he that thinkis on his luff to speid,
' He may do weill, haiff he fortoun and grace.
' Bot this standis all in ane othir cass;
' A gret kynryk with feill fayis our set,
' Rycht hard it is amendis for to get
650 ' At anys of thaim, and wyrk the observance
' Quhilk langis luff, and all his frewill chance.
' Sampill I haif; this me forthinkis sar:
' I trow to God it sall be so no mar.
' The trewth I knaw off this, and hyr lynage;
Fol. 28 b 655 ' I knew nocht hyr, tharfor I lost a gage.'

To Kerlé he thus argownd in this kynd:
Bot gret desyr remaynyt in till his mynd,
For to behald that frely off fassoun.
A quhill he left, and come nocht in the toun;
660 On othir thing he maid his witt to walk,
Prefand giff he mycht off that languor slalk.
Quhen Kerlé saw he sufferit payne for thi,
" Der schyr," he said, " ye leiff in slogardy;
" Go se youre luff, than sall yhe get comfort."
665 At his consaill he walkit for to sport,
On to the kyrke quhar scho maid residence.
Scho knew him weille; bot, as of eloquence,
Scho durst nocht weill in presens till him kyth,
Full sor scho dred or Sotheron wald him myth:

670 For Hesilryg had a mater new begone,
    And hyr desirde in mariage till his sone.
    With hir madyn thus Wallace scho besocht
    To dyne with hyr, and prewaly hym brocht
    Throuch a garden scho had gart wyrk off new:
675 So Ingliss men nocht off thair metyng knew.
    Than kissit he this gudlé with plesance;
    Syne hyr besocht rycht hartly of quentance.
    Scho ansuerd hym, with humyll wordis wise;
    " War my quentance rycht worthi for till pryse,
680 " Yhe sall it haiff, als God me saiff in saille.
    " Bot Inglissmen gerris our power faill,
    " Throuch violence of thaim and thair barnage,
    " At has weill ner destroyit our lynage."
    Quhen Wallace hard hyr plenye petously,
685 Agrewit he was in hart rycht gretumly.
    Bathe ire and luff him set in till a rage;
    Bot nocht forthi he soberyt his curage.
    Off his mater he tald, as I said ayr,
    To that gudlye, how luff him strenyeit sar.
690 Scho ansuerd him rycht resonably agayne,
    And said; " I sall to your seruice be bayne,
    " With all plesance, in honest causis haill;
    " And I trast yhe wald nocht set till assaill,
    " For yhoure worschipe, to do me dyshonour,
695 " And I a maid; and standis in mony stour,
    " Fra Inglissmen to saiff my womanheid;
    " And cost has maid to kepe me fra thar dreid.
    " With my gud will I wyll no lemman be
    " To no man born, tharfor me think suld yhe
700 " Desyr me nocht bot intill gudlynes.
    " Perchance ye think I war to law perchass
    " For tyll attend to be your rychtwyss wyff.
29 a " In your seruice I wald oyss all my lyff.

" Her I beseik, for your worschipe in armys,
705 " Yhe charge me nocht with no wngudly harmys;
" Bot me defend, for worschipe off your blude."
Quhen Wallace weyll hyr trew tayll wnderstud,
As in a part hym thocht it was resoun,
Off hyr desir tharfor till conclusioun,
710 He thankit hyr, and said; ' Gif it mycht be,
' Throuch Goddis will, that our kynryk war fre,
' I wald yow wed with all hartlie plesance;
' But as this tym I may nocht tak sic chance.
' And for this causs none othir now I crayff:
715 ' A man in wer may nocht all plesance haiff.'
Off thar talk than I can tell yow no mar
To my purposs, quhat band that thai maid thar.
Conclud thai thus, and syne to dyner went.
The sayr grewans ramaynyt in his entent;
720 Loss off his men, and lusty payne off luff.
His leiff he tuk at that tyme to ramuff.

Syne to Gilbank he past or it was nycht.
Apon the morn, with hys four men, him dycht;
To the Corhed with out restyng he raid,
725 Quhar his nevo Thom Haliday him baid;
And Litill alss Eduuard, his cusyng der,
Quhilk was full blyth quhen he wyst him so ner,
Thankand gret God that send him saiff agayne;
For mony demyt he was in Strathern slayne.
730 Gud cher thai maid all out thai dayis thre.
Than Wallace said, that he desirde to se
Lowmaban toun and Ynglissmen that was thar;
On the ferd day thai bownyt thaim to far.
Sexteyne he was of gudlé chewalré;
735 In the Knok wood he lewyt all bot thre.
Thom Halyday went with him to the toun;

Eduuard Litill and Kerlé maid thaim boun,
Till ane ostrye Thom Halyday led thaim rycht,
And gaiff commaund thair dyner suld be dycht.
740 Till her a mess in gud entent thai yeid;
Off Inglissmen thai trowit thar was no dreid.
Ane Clyffurd come, was emys sone to the lord,
And four with him, the trewth for to record.
" Quha awcht thai horss?" in gret heithing he ast;
745 He was full sle, and ek had mony cast.
The gud wyff said, till [haiff] applessyt him best;
' Four gentill men is cummyn owt off the west.'
" Quha dewill thaim maid so galy for to ryd?
" In faith, with me a wed thar most abide.
750 " Thir lewit Scottis has leryt litill gud :
29 b " Lo ! all thair horss ar schent for faut off blud."
In to gret scorn with outyn wordis mayr,
The taillis all off thai four horss thai schayr.
The gud wyff cryede, and petuously couth gret.
755 So Wallace come, and couth the captayne mete.
A woman tald how thai his horss had schent,
For propyr ire he grew in matelent.
He folowid fast, and said; " Gud freynd, abid,
" Seruice to tak for thi craft in this tyde.
760 " Marschell thou art with out commaund off me;
" Reward agayne, me think, I suld pay the;
" Sen I off laitt now come owt off the west
" In this cuntré, a barbour off the best
" To cutt and schaiff, and that a wondyr gude;
765 " Now thow sall feyll how I oyss to lat blude."
With his gud suerd the captayn has he tayn,
Quhill horss agayne he marscheld neuir nayn.
A nothir sone apon the hed strak he,
Quhill chaftis and cheyff vpon the gait can fle.
770 Be that his men the tothir twa had slayne;
Thar horss thai tuk, and graithit thaim full bayne,

Out off the toun; for dyner baid thai nayne.
The wyff he payit, that maid so petuouss mayne.
Than Inglissmen, fra that chyftayne wes dede,
775 To Wallace socht fra mony syndry stede.
Off the castell come cruell men and keyne.
Quhen Wallace has thair sodand semlé seyne,
Towart sum strenth he bownyt him to ryd;
For than him thocht it was no tyme to byd.
780 Thar horss bled fast, that gert him dredyng haiff:
Off his gud men he wald haif had the laiff.
To the Knok-woode with owtyn mor thai raid,
Bot in till it no soiornyng he maid:
That wood as than was nothir thik no lang.
785 His men he gat; syn lychtyt for to gang
Towart a hicht, and led thar horss a quhill.
The Inglissmen was than within a myill,
On fresche horsis rydand full hastely;
Sewyn scor and ma was in thair chewalry.
790 The Scottis lap on, quhen thai thar power saw,
Frawart the south thaim thocht it best to draw.
Than Wallace said; " It is no witt in wer,
" With our power to byd thaim bargane her.
" Yon are gud men, tharfor I rede that we
795 " Estuirmar seik, quhill God send sum supplé."
Halyday said; ' We sall do your consaille;
' Bot sayr I dreid or thir hurt horss will fayll.'
The Inglissmen, in burnyst armour cler,
Fol. 30 a Be than to thaim approchyt wondyr ner.
800 Horssyt archaris schot fast, and wald nocht spar;
Off Wallace men thai woundyt twa full sar.
In ire he grew, quhen that he saw thaim bleid;
Him self retornde, and on thaim sone he yeid.
Sexteyn with him that worthi was in wer,
805 Off the formast rycht freschly doun thai ber.
At that retorn fyfteyn in feild war slayne;

The laiff fled fast to thair power agayne.
Wallace folowid, with his gud chewalrye;
Thom Halyday, in wer was full besye,
810 A buschement saw that cruell was to ken,
Twa hundreth haill off weill gerit Inglissmen.
" Wncle," he said, " our power is to smaw;
" Off this playne feild I consaill you to draw:
" To few we ar agayne yon fellone staill."
815 Wallace relewit full sone at his consaill.

At the Corheid full fayne thai wald haif beyne;
Bot Inglissmen weyll has thair purposs seyne.
In playne battaill thai folowid hardely;
In dangir thus thai held thaim awfully.
820 Hew of Morland on Wallace folowid fast;
He had befor maid mony Scottis agast,
Haldyn he was off wer the worthiast man,
In north Ingland with thaim was leiffand than.
In his armour weill forgyt off fyne steill,
825 A nobill cursour bur him bath fast and weill.
Wallace retorned besyd a burly ayk,
And on him set a fellone sekyr straik;
Baith cannell bayne and schuldir blaid in twa,
Throuch the myd cost, the gud suerd gert he ga.
830 His speyr he wan, and als the coursour wicht,
Syne left his awn, for he had lost his mycht.
For lak off blud he mycht no forthir gang.
Wallace on horss, the Sotheron men amang,
His men relewit, that douchty was in deid,
835 Him to reskew out off that felloune dreid.
Cruell strakis forsuth thar mycht be seyne
On athir syde, quhill blud ran on the greyne.
Rycht peralous the semlay was to se:
Hardy and hat contenyt the fell mellé.

840 Skew and reskew off Scottis and Ingliss alss;
    Sum kerwyt bran in sondyr, sum the hals;
    Sum hurt, sum hynt, sum derffly dong to dede:
    The hardy Scottis so steryt in that sted,
    With Halyday on fute bauldly that baid,
Fol. 30 b 845 Amang Sotheron a full gret rowme thai maid.
    Wallas on horss, in hand a nobill sper,
    Out throuch thaim raid, as gud chyftayne in wer.
    Thre slew he thar, or that his sper was gayne:
    Than his gud suerd in hand sone has he tayne,
850 Hewyt on hard with dyntis sad and sar;
    Quhat ane he hyt grewyt the Scottis no mar.
    Fra Sotheron men be naturall resone knew,
    How with a straik a man euir he slew,
    Than merweld thai he was so mekill off mayne;
855 For thar best man in that kynd he had slayne,
    That his gret strenth agayne him helpyt nocht,
    Nor nane othir in contrar Wallace socht.
    Than said thai all; " Lest he in strenth wntayne,
    " This haill kynryk he wyll wyn him allayne."
860 Thai left the feild, syne to thair power fled,
    And tald thair lord how ewill the formest sped,
    Quhilk Graystok hecht, was new cummyn in the land;
    Tharfor he trowit nane durst agayne him stand.
    Wondyr him thocht, quhen that he saw that sicht,
865 Quhy his gud men for sa few tuk the flycht.
    At that retorn twenty in feild was tynt,
    And Morland als; tharfor he wald nocht stynt,
    Bot folowed fast with thre hundreth but dreid;
    And swour he suld be wengit on that deid.
870 The Scottis wan horss, becaus thair awne couth faill;
    In flëyng syne chesd thaim the maist awaill.
    Owt off that feild thus wicht Wallas is gayn;
    Off his gud men he had nocht losyt ayne:

Fyve woundyt wes, yeit blythly furth thai raid.
875 Wallace a space behynd thaim ay he baid:
And Halyday prewyt weill in mony place;
Sib sister sone he wes to gud Wallace.
Warly thai raid, and held thar horss in aynd;
For thai trowide weyll Sotheron wald afaynd
880 With haill power at anys on thaim to sett:
Bot Wallace kest thair power for to let;
To brek thar ray he besyit hym full fast.
Than Inglissmen so gretly wes agast,
That nane off thaim durst rusch out off the staill;
885 All in aray held thaim to gidder haill.
The Sotheron saw, how that so bandounly
Wallace abaid ner hand thar chewalry.
Be Morlandis horss thai knew him wondyr weill;
Past to thar lord, and tauld him euirilkdeill.
890 " Lo Schyr," thai said, " forsuth yon sammyn is he,
" That with his hand gerris so mony de!
" Haiff his horss grace apon his feyt to bid,
Fol. 31 a " He dredis nocht throw fyve thousand to ryd.
" We rede ye cess, and folow him no mar,
895 " For drede that we repent it syn full sar."
He blamyt thaim, and said; ' Men weyll may se,
' Cowartis ye ar, that sor so few wald fle.'
For thar consaill yeit leiff thaim wald he nocht;
In gret ire he apon thaim sadly socht,
900 Wailland a place quhar he mycht bargane mak.
Wallace was wa apon him for to tak,
And he so few, to bid thaim on a playne;
At Quenysbery he wald haiff beyne full fayne.
Apon him self he tuk full gret trawaill
905 To fend his men, gyff that mycht ocht awaill.
A suerd he drew, rycht manlik him to wer,
Ay wayttand fast gyff he mycht get a sper;

Now her, now thar, befor thaim to and fra.
His horss gaiff our, and mycht no forthir ga.

910   Rycht at the skyrt off Quenysbery befell,
Bot wpon grace, as my autor will tell;
Schir Jhone the Grayme, that worthi wes and wicht,
To the Corhed come on the tothir nycht;
Thretty with him off nobill men at wage.

915 The fyrst dochtyr he had in mariage
Off Halyday was nevo to Wallace.
Tithandis to sper Schyr Jhone past off that place,
With men to spek, quhar thai a tryst had set,
Rycht ner the steid quhar Scottis and Yngliss mete.

920 Ane Kyrk Patryk, that cruell was and keyne,
In Esdaill wood that half yer he had beyne.
With Ingliss men he couth nocht weyll accord;
Off Torthorowald he barron wes and lord.
Off kyn he was, and Wallace modyr ner,

925 Off Craufurd syd that mydward had to ster.
Twenty he had off worthi men and wicht.
Be than Wallace approchit to thair sycht.
Schir Jhon the Grayme, quhen he the cownter saw,
On thaim he raid, and stud bot litill aw;

930 His gudfadyr he knew rycht wondyr weyll,
Kest doun his sper, and sonyeit nocht a deyll.
Kyrk patryk alss, with worthi men in wer,
Fyfty in fronte at anyss doun thai ber.
Throuch the thikkest off thre hundreth thai raid,

935 On Sotheron men full gret slauchter thai maid,
Thaim to reskew that was in fellone thrang.
Wallace on fute the gret power amang,
Gud rowme he gat, throuch help off Goddis grace.
The Sotheron fled, and left thaim in that place.

Fol. 31 b 940 Horsis thai ran to stuff the chass gud spede,

Wallace and his that douchty wes in dede.
Graystok tuk flycht on stern horss and stout;
A hundreth held to gydder in a rout.
Wallace on thaim full sadly couth persew;
945 The fleyng weyll off Ingliss men he knew,
At ay the best wald pass with thair chyftayne.
Befor him he fand gud Schyr Jhone the Grayme,
Ay strykand doun quham euir he mycht ourhy.
Than Wallace said; " This is bot waist foly,
950 " Comons to slay, quhar chyftayns gayis away;
" Your horss is fresche, tharfor do as I say.
" Gud men yhe haiff ar yeit in nobill stait:
" To yon gret rout, for Goddis luff, had your gait;
" Sowndyr thaim sone, we sall cum at your hand."
955 Quhen Schyr Jhon had his tayll weyll wndirstand,
Off nane othir fra thine furth tuk he heid;
To the formast he folowid weill gud speid.
Kyrk Patryk als consideryt thar consaill,
Than chargyt thair men, " All folow on the stayll."
960 At his command full sone with hym thay met;
Sad straikys and sayr apon thaym sadly set.
Schyr Jhone the Grayme to Graystok fast he socht;
Hys pryss pissan than helpyt him rycht nocht.
Vpon the crage a graith straik gat him rycht;
965 The burly blaide was braid and burnyst brycht,
In sonder kerwyt the mailyeis off fyne steyll,
Throwch bayne and brawne it prochyt euirilkdeill;
Dede with that dent to the erd doun him draiff.
Be that Wallace was semland with the laiff.
970 Derfly to dede feyle frekys thar he dycht;
Rayss neuir agayne quhat ane at he hyt rycht.
Kyrkpatryk than, Thom Halyday, and thair men,
Thar douchty deid was nobill for to ken.
At the Knokheid the bauld Graystok was slayne,

975 And mony man quhilk wes off mekill mayne.
    To saiff thair lyff part in the wood is past;
    The Scottis men than relewit to gidder fast.
    Quhen that Wallace with Schyr Jhone Grayme wes met,
    Rycht gudlye he with humylness him gret;
980 Pardown he ast off the repreiff befor,
    In to the chass; and said, he suld no mor
    Formacioune mak off him that was so gud.
    Quhen that Schyr Jhon Wallace weyll wndirstud,
    " Do away," he said, " tharoff as now no mar;
985 " Yhe dyd full rycht; it was for our weylfar.
    " Wysar in weyr ye ar all out than I;
Fol. 32 a " Fadyr in armess ye ar to me forthi."
    Kyrk patryk syne, that wes his cusyng der,
    He thankit hym rycht on a gud maner.
990 Nocht ane was lost off all thair chewalry;
    Schir Jhone the Grayme to thaim come happely.

      The day was downe, and prochand wes the nycht;
    At Wallace thai askit his consaill rycht.
    He ansuerd thus; " I spek bot with your leiff;
995 " Rycht laith I war ony gud man to greyff.
    " Bot thus I say, in termes schort for me,
    " I wald sailye, giff ye think it may be,
    " Lowmaban houss, quhilk now is left allayne;
    " For weyll I wait power in it is lewyt nayne.
1000 " Carlaucrok als yeit Maxwell has in hand;
    " And we had this, thai mycht be bath a wand
    " Agayne Sotheroun, that now has our cuntré.
    " Say quhat ye will, this is the best, think me."
    Schir Jhone the Grayme gaiff fyrst his gud consent;
1005 Syne all the layff, rycht with a haill entent.
    To Lowmaban rycht haistely thai ryd.
    Quhen thai cum ner, nocht half a myill besid,

The nycht was myrk; to consaill ar thai gayne:
Off mwne nor stern gret perans was thar nayne.
1010 Than Wallace said; " Methink, the land at rest;
" Thom Haliday, thow knawis this cuntré best:
" I her no noyis of feyll folk her about;
" Tharfor I trow we ar the less in dout."
Haliday said; ' I will tak ane with me,
1015 ' And ryde befor, the maner for to se.'
Watsone he callit; ' With me thow mak the boun;
' With thaim thow was a nychtbour off this toun.'
" I grant I was with thaim agayne my will,
" Myn entent is euir to do thaim ill."
1020 Unto the yeitt thir twa pertly furth raid;
The portar come with owt langar abaid.
At Jhone Watsone sone tythandis he couth ass;
Opyn, he bad, the captayne cummand was.
The yett, but mayr, wnwysly he wp drew.
1025 Thom Haliday sone be the craig him threw;
And with a knyff he stekit him to dede;
In a dyrk holl kest him doun in that sted.
Jhone Watsone syne has hynt the keyis in hand.
The power than with Wallace wes cummand;
1030 Thai entryt in, befor thaim fand no ma,
Excep wemen, and sympill serwandis twa.
. 32 b In the kyching scudleris lang tyme had beyne;
Sone thai war slayne.   Quhen the ladie had thaim seyne,
" Grace," scho cryit, " for hym that deit on tre."
1035 Than Wallace said; ' Mademe, your noyis lat be.
' To wemen yeit we do bot litill ill;
' Na yong childir we lik for to spill.
' I wald haiff meit; Haliday, quhat sayis thow?
' For fastand folk to dyne gud tym war now.'
1040 Gret purwiance was ordand thaim befor,
Bath breid and aylle, gud wyne and othir stor.

G

To meyt thai bownyt, for thai had fastyt lang;
Gud men off armes in to the closs gert gang.
Part fleand folk on fute, that fra thaim glaid
1045 On the Knok heid, quhar gret mellé was maid,
Ay as thai come Jhon Watsone leit thaim in,
And doun to dede with outyn noyis or din:
Na man left thar that was off Ingland born.
The castell weyll thai wesyt on the morn;
1050 For Jhonstoune send, a man off gud degre:
Secund dochtir forsuth weddyt had he
Off Halidays, nere neuo to Wallace;
Gret captayne [than] thai maid him off that place.
Thai leyffit him thar in till a gud aray,
1055 Syne wsched furth wpon the secund day.
Wemen had leyff in Ingland for to fayr.
Schyr Jhon the Grayme and gud Wallace couth cair
To the Corhed, and lugyt all that nycht.
Wpon the morn the sone wes at the hycht,
1060 Eftir dyner thai wald na langer byde,
Thar purposs tuk in Craufurd mur to ryd;
Schir Jhon the Grayme, with Wallace that was wycht.
Thom Haliday agayne retorned rycht
To the Corhall, and thar remanyt but dred.
1065 Na Sotheroun wyst prynsuall quha did this dede.
Kyrk patrik past in Aisdaill woddis wyd;
In saufté thar he thoucht he suld abid.

Schyr Jhone the Grayme, and gud Wallace in feir,
With thaim fourtye off men in armes cleir,
1070 Throuch Craufurd mur as that thai tuk the way,
On Ingliss [men] thar mynd ramaynit ay.
Fra Crawfurd Jhon the wattir doune thai ryd;
Ner hand the nycht thai lychtyt apon Clyd:
Thar purposs tuk in till a quiet waill.

1075 Than Wallace said; " I wald we mycht assaill
"Craufurd castell, with sum gud jepertè.
"Schir Jhon the Grayme, how say yhe best may be?"
This gud knycht said; 'And the men war with out,

ol. 33 a 'To tak the hous thar is bot litill doubt.'

1080 A squier than rewllyt that lordschip haill,
Off Cummyrland borne, his name was Martyndaill.
Than Wallace said; " My selff will pass in feyr,
"And ane with me, off herbrè for to speyr.
"Folow on dreich, giff that we mystir ocht."

1085 Edward Litill with his mastir furth socht
Till ane oystry, and with a woman met.
Scho tald to thaim that Sothroune thar was set:
'And ye be Scottis, I consaill yow pass by;
'For, and thai may, yhe will get ewill herbry.

1090 'At drynk thai ar, so haiff thai bene rycht lang;
'Gret worde thar is of Wallace thaim amang.
'Thai trew that he has found hys men agayne:
'At Lowchmaban feyll Inglis men ar slayne.
'That houss is tynt; that gerris thaim be full wa:

1095 'I trow to God that thai sall swne tyne ma.'
Wallace sperd, of Scotland giff scho be.
Scho said him; 'Ya, and thinkis yet to se
'Sorow on thaim, throw help off Goddis grace.'
He askit hyr, quha was in to the place.

1100 'Na man of fens is left that houss within,
'Twenty is her, makand gret noyis and dyn.
'Allace,' scho said, 'giff I mycht anys se,
'The worthy Scottis maist maister in it to be.'
With this woman he wald no langar stand;

1105 A bekyn he maid, Schyr Jhon come at his hand.
Wallace went in, and bad *Benedicite*.
The capteyne speryt; " Quhat bellamy may thow be,

"That cummys so grym? sum tithandis till vs tell.
"Thow art a Scot; the dewyll thi natiounc quell."
1110 Wallace braid out his suerd with outyn mar;
In to the breyst the bryme captayne he bar,
Throuch out the cost, and stekit him to ded.
Ane othir he hyt awkwart vpon the hed.
Quham euir he strak he byrstyt bayne and lyr;
1115 Feill off thaim dede fell thwortour in the fyr.
Haisty payment he maid thaim on the flur;
And Eduuard Litill kepyt weill the dur.
Schir Jhon the Graym full fayne wald haiff beyne in;
Eduuard him bad at the castell begyne;
1120 "For off thir folk we haiff bot litill dreid."
Schir Jhon the Grayme fast to the castell yeid.
Wallace rudly sic routis to thaim gaiff,
That twenty men derffly to dede thai draiff.
Fyfteyne he straik, and fyfteyne has he slayne;
1125 Edward slew fyve quhilk was off mekill mayne.
Fol. 33 b To the castell Wallace had gret desyr.
Be that Schir Jhone had set the yett in fyr;
Nane wes tharin at gret defens couth ma,
Bot wemen fast sar wepand in to wa.
1130 With out the place ane ald bulwark was maid;
Wallace yeid our with out langar abaid.
The wemen sone he sauffyt fra the dede;
Waik folk he put, and barnys, off that stede.
Off purwiaunce thai fand litill or nane;
1135 Befor that tyme thar wictaill was all gayne.
Yeit in that place thai lugyt still that nycht;
Fra oystré broucht sic gudis as thai mycht.
Wpon the morn the houss thai spoilye fast,
All thing that doucht out off that place thai cast.
1140 Tre wark thai brynt, that was in to tha wanys;

Wallis brak doun that stalwart war off stanys;
Spylt at thai mycht, syne wald no langar bid:
On till Dundaff that sammyn nycht thai ryde;
And lugit thar with myrthis and plesance,
1145 Thankand gret God that lent thaim sic a chance.

EXPLICIT LIBER QUINTUS,
ET INCIPIT SEXTUS.

BUKE SEXT.

Than passit was wtass off Feuiryher,
And part off Marche off rycht degestioune;
Apperyd than the last moneth off wer,
The syng off somir with his suet sessoun.
5 Be that Wallace off Dundaff maid him boune;
His leyff he tuk, and to Gilbank can fair.
The rewmour raiss throuch Scotland vp and doune,
With Ingliss men, that Wallace leiffand war.
    In Aperill quhen cleithit is, but weyne,
10 The abill grounde be wyrking off natur,
And woddis has won thar worthy weid off greyne.
Quhen Nympheus, in beldyn off his bour,
With oyle and balm fullfillit off suet odour,
Faunis materis, as thai war wount to gang,
15 Walkyn thair courss in euery casuall hour,
To glaid the huntar with thair merye sang.
    In this samyn tyme to him approchit new
His lusty payne, the quhilk I spak off ayr,
Be luffis cass, he thoucht [for] to persew
20 In Laynryk toune, and thidder he can fayr:
At residence a quhill ramaynit thair
In hyr presence as I said off befor;
Thocht Inglissmen was grewyt at his repayr,
Yeit he desyrd the thing that sat him sar.
Fol. 34 a 25   The feyr off wer rewllyt him on sic wiss;
He likit weyll with that gudlye to be;

Quhill wald he think off danger for to ryss,
And othir quhill out of hir presens fle.
" To cess off wer it war the best for me;
30 " Thus wyn I nocht bot sadnes on all syde.
" Sall neuir man this cowartyss in me se,
" To wer I will, for chance that may betyd.
    " Quhat is this luff? it is bot gret myschance,
" That me wald bryng fra armess wtterly.
35 " I will nocht loss my worschip for plesance;
" In wer I think my tyme till occupy:
" Yeit hyr to luff I will nocht lat for thy;
" Mor sall I desyr hyr frendschip to reserue,
" Fra this day furth than euir befor did I,
40 " In fer off wer quhethir I leiff or sterue."
    Quhat suld I say, Wallace was playnly set
To luff hyr best in all this warld so wid;
Thinkand he suld off his desyr to get;
And so befell be concord in a tid,
45 That scho [was] maid at his commaund to bid;
And thus began the styntyn off this stryff:
Begynnyng band, with graith witnes besyd,
Myn auctor sais, scho was his rychtwyss wyff.
    Now leiff in pees, now leiff in gud concord!
50 Now leyff in blyss, now leiff in haill plesance!
For scho be choss has bath hyr luff and lord.
He thinkis als, luff did him hye awance,
So ewynly held be fauour the ballance,
Sen he at will may lap hyr in his armyss.
55 Scho thankit God off hir fre happy chance,
For in his tyme he was the flour off armys.
    Fortoune him schawit hyr fygowrt doubill face,
Feyll syss or than he had beyne set abuff:
In presounc now, delyuerit now throw grace,
60 Now at vmess, now in to rest and ruff;

Now weyll at wyll, weyldand his plesand luff,
As thocht him selff out off aduersité;
Desyring ay his manheid for to pruff,
In curage set apon the stagis hye.

65   The werray treuth I can nocht graithly tell,
In to this lyff how lang at thai had beyne:
Throuch naturall courss off generacioune befell,
A child was chewyt thir twa luffaris betuene,
Quhilk gudly was, a maydyn brycht and schene;

Fol. 34 b 70 So forthyr furth, be ewyn tyme off hyr age,
A squier Schaw, as that full weyll was seyne,
This lyflat man hyr gat in mariage.

Rycht gudly men come off this lady ying.
Forthyr as now off hyr I spek no mar.

75 Bot Wallace furth in till his wer can ryng,
He mycht nocht cess, gret curage so him bar;
Sotheroun to sla for dreid he wald nocht spar,
And thai oft syss feill causis till him wrocht,
Fra that tyme furth, quhilk mowit [hym sa sar,

80 That neuir in warld out of his mind was brocht.]
Now leiff thi myrth, now leiff thi haill plesance;
Now leiff thi bliss, now leiff thi childis age;
Now leiff thi youth, [now] folow thi hard chance;
Now leyff thi lust, now leiff thi mariage;

85 Now leiff thi luff, for thow sall loss a gage
Quhilk neuir in erd sall be redemyt agayne;
Folow fortoun, and all hir fers owtrage;
Go leiff in wer, go leiff in cruell payne.

Fy on fortoun, fy on thi frewall quheyll;
90 Fy on thi traist, for her it has no lest;
Thow transfigowryt Wallace out off his weill,
Quhen he traistyt for till haiff lestyt best.
His plesance her till him was bot a gest;
Throw thi fers courss, that has na hap to ho,

95 Him thow our threw out off his likand rest,
Fra gret plesance, in wer, trawaill, and wo.
What is fortoune, quha dryffis the dett so fast?
We wait thar is bathe weill and wykit chance.
Bot this fals warld, with mony doubill cast,
100 In it is nocht bot werray wariance;
It is nothing till hewynly gowernance.
Than pray we all to the Makar abow,
Quhilk has in hand off justry the ballance,
That he vs grant off his der lestand lowe.
105 Her off as now forthyr I spek no mar,
Bot to my purposs schortly will I fayr.

Tuelff hundreth yer, tharto nynté and sewyn,
Fra Cryst wes born the rychtwiss king off hewyn,
Wilyham Wallace in to gud liking gais,
110 In Laynrik toun amang his mortaill fais.
The Ingliss men, that euir fals has beyne,
With Hesilryg, quhilk cruell was and keyn,
And Robert Thorn, a felloune sutell knycht,
Has founde the way, be quhat meyn best thai mycht,
35 a 115 How that thai suld mak contrar to Wallace
Be argument, as he come vpon cace
On fra the kyrk, that was without the toune,
Quhill thar power mycht be in harness boune.
Schyr Jhon the Grayme, bathe hardy, wyss, and trew,
120 To Laynrik come, gud Wallace to persew;
Off his weyllfayr as he full oft had seyne.
Gud men he had in cumpany fyfteyne,
And Wallace nyne; thai war na feris ma.
Wpon the morn wnto the mess thai ga,
125 Thai and thar men graithit in gudly greyn;
For the sesson sic oyss full lang has beyne.
Quhen sadly thai had said thar deuotiounc,

Ane argwnde thaim, as thai [went] throuch the toun,
The starkast man that Hesylryg than knew,
130 And als he had off lychly wordis ynew.
He salust thaim, as it war bot in scorn;
" Dewgar, gud day, bone Senyhour, and gud morn!"
' Quhom scornys thow?' quod Wallace, ' quha lerd the?'
" Quhy, schir," he said, " come yhe nocht new our se?
135 " Pardown me than, for I wend ye had beyne
" Ane inbasset to bryng ane wncouth queyne."
Wallace ansuerd; ' Sic pardoune as we haiff
' In oyss to gyff, thi part thow sall nocht craiff.'
" Sen ye ar Scottis, yeit salust sall ye be;
140 " Gud deyn, dawch Lard, bach lowch banyoch a de."
Ma Sotheroune men to thaim assemblit ner.
Wallace as than was laith to mak a ster.
Ane maid a scrip, and tyt at his lang suorde:
' Hald still thi hand,' quod he, ' and spek thi word.'
145 " With thi lang suerd thow makis mekill bost."
' Tharoff,' quod he, ' thi deme maid litill cost.'
" Quhat causs has thow to wer that gudlye greyne?"
' My maist causs is bot for to mak the teyne.'
" Quhat suld a Scot do with sa fair a knyff?"
150 ' Sa said the prest that last janglyt thi wyff;
' That woman lang has tillit him so fair,
' Quhill that his child worthit to be thine ayr.'
" Me think," quod he, " thow drywys me to scorn."
' Thi deme has beyne japyt or thow was born.'
155 The power than assemblyt thaim about;
Twa hundreth men that stalwart war and stout.
The Scottis saw thair power was cummand;
Schir Robert Thorn and Hesilryg at hand,
The multitude wyth wappynys burnist beyne.
Fol. 35 b 160 The worthi Scottis, quhilk cruell was and keyne,

Amang Sotherone sic dyntis gaiff that tyd,
Quhill blud on breid byrstyt fra woundis wyd,
Wallace in stour wes cruelly fechtand;
Fra a Sotheroune he smat off the rycht hand:
165 And quhen that carle off fechtyng mycht no mar,
With the left hand in ire held a buklar.
Than fra the stowmpe the blud out spurgyt fast,
In Wallace face aboundandlye can out cast;
In to gret part it marryt hym off his sicht.
170 Schyr Jhone the Grayme a straik has tayne him rycht,
With hys gud suerd, vpon the Sotherone syr,
Derffly to ded draiff him in to that ire.
The perell was rycht awfull, hard, and strang;
The stour enduryt merwalusly and lang.
175 The Inglissmen gaderit fellone fast;
The worthi Scottis the gait left at the last.
Quhen thai had slayne and woundyt mony man,
Till Wallace in, the gaynest way thai can,
Thai passit swne, defendand tham richt weill;
180 He and Schyr Jhone, with suerdis stiff off steill,
Behind thair men, quhill thai the yett had tayne.
The woman than, quhilk was full will off wayne,
The perell saw, with fellone noyis and dyne,
Gat wp the yett, and leit thaim entir in.
185 Throuch till a strenth thai passit off that stede.
Fyftye Sotheroun wpon the gait was dede.
This fayr woman did besines, and hir mycht,
The Ingliss men to tary with a slycht,
Quhill that Wallace on to the wood wes past;
190 Than Cartlane craggis thai persewit full fast.
Quhen Sotheroun saw that chapyt was Wallace,
Agayne thai turnyt, the woman tuk on cace,
Put hir to dede, I can nocht tell yow how;
Off sic mater I may nocht tary now.

195 Quhar gret dulle is, bot rademyng agayne,
    Newyn off it is bot ckyng of payne.
    A trew woman, had scruit hir full lang,
    Out off the toune the gaynest way can gang;
    Till Wallace tald how all this dede was done.
200 The paynfull wo socht till hys hart full sone;
    War nocht for schayme he had socht to the ground,
    For bytter baill that in his breyst was bound.
    Schir Jhone the Grayme, bath wyss, gentill, and fre,
    Gret murnynge maid, that peté was to se;
Fol. 36 a 205 And als the laiff that was assemblit thar,
    For pur sorou wepyt with hart full sar.
    Quhen Wallace feld thar curage was so small,
    He fenyeit him for to comfort thaim all.
    "Cess, men," he said, "this is a butlass payne;
210 "We can nocht now chewyss hyr lyff agayne."
    Wness a word he mycht bryng out for teyne;
    The bailfull teris bryst braithly fra his eyne.
    Sichand he said; "Sall neuir man me se
    "Rest in till eyss, quhill this deid wrokyn be,
215 "The saklace slauchter off hir, blith and brycht.
    "That I awow to the Makar off mycht,
    "That off that nacioune I sall neuir forber,
    "Yhong nor ald, that abill is to wer;
    "Preystis no wemen I think [nocht] for to sla,
220 "In my defaut bot thai me causing ma.
    "Schir Jhon," he said, "lat all this murnyng be,
    "And for hir saik thair sall ten thousand de.
    "Quhar men may weipe, thar curage is the less;
    "It slakis ire off wrang thai suld radres."

225   Off thar complaynt as now I say no mar;
       Off Awchinlek off Gilbank duelland thar.
       Quhen he hard tell off Wallace wexatioune,

To Cartlane wood with ten men maid him boune.
Wallace he fand sum part with in the nycht;
230 To Laynryk toune in all haist thai thaim dycht.
The wache off thaim as than had litill heid;
Partyt thair men, and diuerss gatis yeid.
Schir Jhone the Grayme, and his gud cumpany,
To Schyr Robert off Thorn full fast thai hy.
235 Wallace and his to Hesilrige sone past,
In a heich houss quhar he was slepand fast;
Straik at the dure with his fute hardely,
Quhill bar and braiss in the flour he gart ly.
The schirreff cryt; " Quha makis that gret deray?"
240 'Wallace,' he said, 'that thow has socht allday.
'The womannis dede, will God, thow sall der by.'
Hesilrige thocht it was na tyme to ly;
Out off that houss full fayne he wald haiff beyne.
The nycht was myrk, yeit Wallace has him seyne,
245 Freschly him straik, as he come in gret ire,
Apon the heid, birstit throuch bayne and lyr.
The scherand suerd glaid till his coler bayne,
Out our the stayr amang thaim is he gayne.
36 b Gude Awchinlek trowit nocht that he was dede;
250 Thryss with a knyff stekit him in that stede.
The scry about raiss rudly on the streyt;
Feyll off the layff war fulyeit wndir feyt.
Yong Hesilryg and wicht Wallace is met;
A sekyr strak Wilyham has on him set,
255 Derffly to dede off the stair dang him doune.
Mony thai slew that nycht in Laynrik toune.
Sum grecis lap, and sum stekit with in,
Aferd thai war with hidwiss noyis and dyne.
Schir Jhone the Grayme had set the houss in fyr,
260 Quhar Robert Thorn was brynt wp bayne and lyr.
Twelf scor thai slew that was off Ingland born;

Wemen thai lewit and preistis, on the morn,
To pass thar way, off blyss and gudis bar;
And swor that thai agayne suld cum no mar.

265 Quhen Scottis hard thir fyne tythingis off new,
Out off all part to Wallace fast thai drew;
Plenyst the toun quhilk was thair heretage.
Thus Wallace straiff agayne that gret barnage.
Sa he begane with strenth and stalwart hand,

270 To chewyss agayne sum rowmys off Scotland.
The worthy Scottis, that semblyt till him thar,
Chesit him for cheyff, thar chyftayne and ledar.
Amer Wallang, a suttell terand knycht,
In Bothwell duelt, king Eduuardis man full rycht.

275 Murray was out, thocht he was rychtwyss lord
Off all that land, as trew men will racord.
In till Aran he was duelland that tyd;
And othir men, in this land durst nocht bide.
Bot this fals knycht in Bothwell wonnand was;

280 A man he gert sone to king Eduuard pas,
And tald him haill off Wallace ordinance,
How he had put his pepill to myschance.
And playnly was ryssyn agayne to ryng.
Grewit tharat rycht gretly wes the king;

285 Throuch all Ingland he gart his doaris cry
Power to get; and said, he wald planly
In Scotland pass, that rewme to statut new.
Feill men off wer till him full fast thai drew.
The queyne feld weill how that his purpos was;

290 Till him scho went, on kneis syne can him ass,
He wald desist, and nocht in Scotland gang;
He suld haiff dreid to wyrk so felloune wrang:

Fol. 37 a   "Crystyne thai ar, yone is thar heretage;
"To reyff that croune that is a gret owtrage."

295 For hyr consaill at hayme he wald nocht byde;

His lordis hym set in Scotland for to ryde.
A Scottis man, than duellyt with Eduuard,
Quhen he hard tell that Wallace tuk sic part,
He staw fra thaim as priualé as he may;
300 In to Scotland he come apon a day,
Sekand Wallace he maid him reddy boune.
This Scot was born at Kyle in Rycardtoune;
All Ingland cost he knew it wondyr weill,
Fra Hull about to Brysto euirilk deill;
305 Fra Carleill throuch Sandwich that ryoll stede,
Fra Douer our on to Sanct Beis hede.
In Pykarté and Flandrys he hade beyne,
All Normondé and Frans haill he had seyne;
A pursiwant till king Eduuard in wer,
310 Bot he couth neuir gar him his armes ber.
Off gret statur, and sum part gray wes he;
The Inglissmen cald him bot Grymmysbé.
To Wallace come, and in to Kile him fand;
He tald him haill the tithandis off Ingland.
315 Thai turnyt his nayme, fra [that] tyme thai him knew,
And cald him Jop; off ingen he was trew;
In all his tyme gud seruice in him fand;
Gaiff him to ber the armés off Scotland.
Wallace agayne in Cliddisdaill sone raid,
320 And his power semblit with outyn baid,
He gart commaund, quha that his pes wald tak,
A fre remyt he suld ger to thaim mak,
For alkyn deid that thai had doyne beforn.
The Perseis peess and Schyr Ranaldis wes worn.
325 Feill till him drew that bauldly durst abid,
Off Wallace kyn, fra mony diuerss sid.
Schir Ranald than send him his power haill;
Him selff durst nocht be knawine in battaill
Agayne Sotheroun, for he had maid a band,

330 Lang tyme befor, to hald off thaim his land.
    Adam Wallace past out off Ricardtoun,
    And Robert Boid, with gud men off renoun.
    Off Cunyngayme and Kille come men off waill,
    To Laynrik socht, on horss a thousand haill.
335 Schyr Jhone the Grayme, and his gud chewalré,
    Schir Jhone off Tynto, with men that he mycht be,
    Gud Awchinlek, that Wallace wncle was,
    Mony trew Scot with that chyftayne couth pass;
    Thre thousand haill off likly men in wer,
340 And feill on fute quhilk wantyt horss and ger.

Fol. 37 b   The tyme be this was cummand apon hand;
    The awfull ost, with Eduuard off Ingland,
    To Beggar come, with sexté thousand men,
    In wer wedis that cruell war to ken.
345 Thai playntyt thar feild with tentis and pailyonis,
    Quhar claryowns blew full mony mychty sonis;
    Plenyst that place with gud wittaill and wyne,
    In cartis brocht thar purwiance dewyne.
    The awfull king gert twa harroldis be brocht,
350 Gaiff thaim commaund, in all the haist thai mocht,
    To charge Wallace, that he sulde cum him till,
    Witht out promyss, and put him in his will;
    " Be causs we wait he is a gentill man,
    " Cum in my grace, and I sall saiff him than,
355 " As for his lyff, I will apon me tak;
    " And efftir this, gyff he couth scruice mak,
    " He sall haiff wage that may him weill suffice.
    " That rebald wenys, for he has done supprice
    " To my pepill oft apon awentur,
360 " Agaynys me [that] he may lang endur.
    " To this proffyr gaynstandand giff he be,
    " Her I awow he sall be hyngyt hye."

A yong squier, was brothir to Fehew,
He thocht he wald dysgysit [ga] to persew,
365 Wallace to se that tuk so hie a part;
Born sister sone he was to king Eduuart.
A cot off armes he tuk on him but baid;
With the harroldis full prewaly he raid
To Tynto hill with outyn residens,
370 Quhar Wallace lay with his folk at defence.
A likly ost, as of sa few, thai fand;
Till hym thai socht, and wald no langar stand:
"Gyff ye be he that rewllis all this thing,
"Credence we haiff brocht fra our worthi king."
375 Than Wallace gert thre knychtis till him call,
Syne red the wryt in presens off thaim all.
To thaim he said; "Ansuer ye sall nocht craiff;
"Be wryt or word quhilk likis yow best till haiff?"
'In wryt,' thai said, 'it war the liklyast.'
380 Than Wallace thus began to dyt in hast:
"Thow reyffar king chargis me throw cass,
"That I suld cum, and put me in thi grace.
"Gyff I gaynstand, thow hechtis till hyng me:
"I wow to God, and euir I may tak the,
385 "Thow sall be hangyt, ane exempill to geiff
"To kingis off reyff, als lang as I may leiff.
"Thow profferis me thi wage for till haiff:
"I the defy, power and all the laiff,
"At helpis the her, off thi fals natioun.
390 "Will God, thow sall be put off this regioune,
Fol. 38 a "Or de tharfor, contrar thocht thow had suorne.
"Thow sall ws se or nyne houris to morn,
"Battaill to gyff, magre off all thi kyn;
"For falsly thow sekis our rewme to wyn."
395 This wryt he gaiff to the harraldis but mar,
And gud reward he gart delyuer thaim thar.

Bot Jop knew weyll the squier yong Fehew,
And tald Wallace, for he wes euir trew.
Than he command, that thai suld sone thaim tak:
400 Him selff began a sair cusyng to mak.
 "Squier," he said, "sen thow has fenyeit armys;
 "On the sall fall the fyrst part off thir harmys,
 "Sampill to geyff till all thi fals natioune."
Apon the hill he gert thaim set him downe,
405 Straik off his hed, or thai wald forthyr go.
To the herrold said syne with outyn ho;
 "For thow art falss till armys and maynsuorn,
 "Throuch thi chokkis thi tong sall be out schorn."
Quhen that was doyne, than to the thrid said he;
410 "Armyss to juge thow sall neuir graithly se."
He gert a smyth, with his turkas rycht thar,
Pow out his eyne, syne gaiff thaim leiff to far.
 "To your falss king thi falow sall thou leid;
 "With my ansuer turss him his newois heid:
415 "Thus sar I drede the king, and all his bost."
His dum falow [led] hym on to thair ost.
Quhen king Eduuard his herroldis thus has seyne,
In propyr ire he wox ner wode for teyne,
That he nocht wyst on quhat wiss him to wreke;
420 For sorow almaist a word he mycht nocht spek.
A lang quhill he stud wrythand in a rage;
On loud he said; "This is a fell owtrage,
 "This deid to Scottis full der it sall be boucht;
 "Sa dispitfull in warld was neuir wroucht.
425 "Off this regioun I think nocht for to gang,
 "Quhill tyme that I sall se that rybald hang,"
Lat I him thus in till his sorow duell;
Off thai gud Scottis schortly I will yow tell.
Furth fra his men than Wallace rakit rycht;
430 Till him he cald Schyr Jhon Tynto the knycht,

And leit him witt, to wesy him selff wald ga
The Ingliss ost, and bad him tell na ma,
Quhat euir thai speryt, quhill that he come agayne.
Wallace dysgysit thus bownyt our the playne.
435 Betwix Cultir and Bygar as he past,
He was [sone] war quhar a werk man come fast,
Dryfande a mere, and pychars had he to sell.
38 b " Gud freynd," he said, " in treuth will thow me tell,
" With this chaffar quhar passis thow treuly."
440 ' Till ony, Schyr, quha likis for to by ;
' It is my crafft, and I wald [sell] thaim fayne.'
" I will thaim by, sa God me saiff fra payne ;
" Quhat price lat her, I will tak thaim ilkayne."
' Bot half a mark, for sic pryss haiff I tayne.'
445 " Twenty shillingis," Wallace said, " thow sall haiff ;
" I will haiff mer, pycharis and als the laiff.
" Thi gowne and hoiss in haist thow put off syne,
" And mak a chang, for I sall geyff the myne ;
" And thi ald hud, becauss it is thred bar."
450 The man wend weyll that he had scornyt him thar.
" Do, tary nocht, it is suth I the say."
The man kest off his febill weid off gray,
And Wallace his, and payit siluer in hand.
" Pass on," he said, " thou art a proud merchand."
455 The gown and hoiss in clay that claggit was,
The hude heklyt, and maid him for to pass.
The qwhipe he tuk, syne furth the mar can call ;
Atour a bray the omast pot gert fall,
Brak on the ground. The man lewch at his fair ;
460 ' Bot thow be war, thow tynys off thi chaiffair.'
The sone be than was passit out off sicht,
The day our went, and cummyn was the nycht.
Amang Sotheroun full besyly he past ;
On athir side his eyne he gan to cast,

465 Quhar lordis lay, and had thair lugeyng maid.
    The kingis palyone, quhar on the libardis baid,
    Spyand full fast, quhar his awaill suld be,
    And couth weyll luk and wynk, with the ta E.
    Sum scornyt him, sum gleid carll cald him thar;
470 Agrewit thai war for thair herroldis mysfayr.
    Sum sperd at him, how [he] sald off the best.
    " For fourty pens," he said, " quhill thai may lest."
    Sum brak a pott, sum pyrlit at his E.
    Wallace fled out, and prewalé leit thaim be:
475 On till his ost agayne he past full rycht.
    His men be than had tane Tynto the knycht;
    Schyr Jhon the Grayme gert bynd him wondyr fast,
    For he wyst weill he was with Wallace last.
    Sum bad byrn him, sum hang him in a cord;
480 Thai swor that he had dissawit thair lord.
    Wallace be this was entryt thaim amang;
    Till him he yeid, and wald nocht tary lang.
    Syne he gart louss him off thai bandis new,
    And said, he was baith suffer, wyss and trew.
Fol. 39 a 485 To souper sone thai bownd but mar abaid.
    He tald to thaim quhat market he had maid;
    And how at he the Sotheroun saw full weill.
    Schyr Jhon the Grayme displessit was sumdeill,
    And said till him: " Nocht chyftaynlik it was,
490 " Throw wilfulnes, in sic perell to pas."
    Wallace ansuerd; ' Or we wyn Scotland fre,
    ' Baith ye and I in mor perell mon be,
    ' And mony othir, the quhilk full worthi is.
    ' Now off a thing we do sumpart amys.
495 ' A litill slepe I wald fayne that we had;
    ' With yone men syne luk how we may ws glaid.'
    The worthi Scottis tuk gud rest quhill ner day;
    Than raiss thai wp, till ray sone ordand thai.

The hill thai left, and till a playne is gayne;
500 Wallace him selff the wantguard he has tayne:
With him was Boid and Awchinlek but dreid,
With a thousand off worthi men in weid.
Alss mony syne in the mydwart put he;
Schir Jhon the Grayme he gert thar ledar be:
505 With him Adam young lord off Ricardtoun,
And Somerwaill a squier off renoun.
The thrid thousand in [the] rerward he dycht,
Till Waltir gaiff off Newbyggyn the knycht;
With him Tynto that douchty wes in deid,
510 And Daui son off Schyr Waltir, to leid.
Behynd thaim ner, the fute men gert he be;
And bade thaim bid, quhill thai thar tyme mycht se:
" Ye want wapynnys and harnes in this tid;
" The fyrst cowntir ye may nocht weill abid."
515 Wallace gert sone the chyftaynis till him call;
This charg he gaiff, for chance that mycht befall,
Till tak no heid to ger, nor off pylage,
" For thai will fle as wod [men] in a rage.
" Wyne fyrst the men, the gud syne ye may haiff;
520 " Than tak na tent off cowatyss to craiff.
" Throuch cowatyss sum lossis gud and lyff;
" I commaund yow forber sic in our stryff.
" Luk that ye saiff na lord, capteyne, nor knycht;
" For worschipe wyrk, and for our eldris rycht.
525 " God blyss ws, [that] may we in sic wiage
" Put thir falss folk out off our heretage."
Than thai inclynd all with a gudly will;
His playne commaund thai hecht for to fullfill.

l. 39 b   On the gret ost thir partice fast can draw,
530 Cumand to thaim, out off the south, thai saw:
Thre hundreth men, in till thar armour cler,

The gaynest way to thaim approchit ner.
Wallace said sone, thai war na Inglissmen;
For by this ost the gatis weyll thai ken.
535 Thom Haliday thai men he gydyt rycht;
Off Anadderdaill he had thaim led that nycht.
His twa gud sonnis, Wallas and Rudyrfurd,
Wallace was blyth fra he had hard thair wourd;
So was the laiff off his gud chewalry.
540 Jarden thar come in till thar cumpany;
And Kyrkpatrik, befor in Esdaill was;
A weyng thai war in Wallace ost to pass.
The Ingliss wach, that nycht had beyne on steir,
Drew to thair ost rycht as the day can per.
545 Wallace knew weill, for he befor had seyne,
The kings palyon, quhar it was buskit beyne.
Than with rych horss the Scottis vpon thaim raid:
The fyrst cownter so gret abaysing maid,
That all the ost was stunyst of that sicht;
550 Full mony ane derffly to ded was dicht.
Feill off thaim was as than out off aray;
The mair haisté and awfull was the fray.
The noyis rouschit throuch straikis that thai dang.
The rewmour raiss so rudly thaim amang,
555 That all the ost was than in poynt to fle.
The wyss lordis, fra thai the perell se,
The fellone fray, all rasyt wes about;
And how thar king stud in so mekill dout;
Till his palyone, how mony thousand socht,
560 Him to reskew be ony way thai mocht!
The erle of Kent that nycht [had] walkand beyne,
With fyve thousand off men in armour cleyne;
About the king full sodandly thai gang,
And traistis weyll, the sailye wes rycht strang.
565 All Wallace folk in wyss off wer was gud,

In to the stour sone lychtyt quhar thai stud.
Quham euir thai hyt, na harnes mycht thaim stynt,
Fra thai on fute semblit with suerdis dynt;
Off manheid thai in hartis cruell was,
570 Thai thocht to wyn, or neuir thine to pass.
Feill Inglissmen before the king thai slew.
Schir Jhon the Grayme come with his power new
Amang the ost; with the mydwart he raid;
Gret martyrdome on Sotheroun men thai maid.
575 The rerward than set on sa hardely,
Fol. 40 a With Newbyggyn, and all the chewalry;
Palyone rapys thai cuttyt in to sowndyr,
Borne to the ground, and mony smoryt owndir.
The fute men come, the quhilk I spak off ayr,
580 On frayt folk set strakis sad and sayr:
Thocht thai befor wantyt bath horss and ger,
Anewch thai gat, quhat thai wald waill to wer.
The Scottis power than all to gyddir war;
The kingis palyon brymly doun thai bar.
585 The erle off Kent, with a gud ax in hand,
Into the stour full stoutly couth he stand
Befor the king, makand full gret debait:
Quha best did than, he had the heast stait.
The felloune stour so stalwart was and strang,
590 Thar to contened marwalusly and lang.
Wallace him saw, full sadly couth persew,
And at a straik the cheiff chyftayne he slew.
The Sotheron folk fled fast, and durst nocht byd;
Horssit thair king and off the feild couth ride
595 Agaynis his will, for he was laith to fle;
In to that tyme he thocht nocht for to de.
Off his best men four thousand thar was dede,
Or he couth fynd to fle and leiff that stede.
Twenty thousand with him fled in a staill.

600 The Scottis gat horss, and folowit that battaill
    Throuch Cultir hope; or tyme thai wan the hycht,
    Feill Sotheroun folk was marryt in thair mycht,
    Slayne be the gait as thair king fled away.
    Bathe fair, and brycht, and rycht cler was the day,
605 The sonc ryssyn, schynand our hill and daill.
    Than Wallace kest quhat was his grettest waill,
    The fleand folk, that off the feild fyrst past,
    In to thair king agayne releiffit fast.
    Fra athir sid so mony semblit thar,
610 That Wallace wald lat folow thaim no mar;
    Befor he raid, gart his folk turn agayne.
    Off Inglissmen sewyn thousand thar was slayne.
    Than Wallace ost agayne to Beggar raid,
    Quhar Inglissmen gret purwians had maid.
615 The jowalré, as it was thiddir led,
    Palyonis and all thai leiffit quhen thai fled.
    The Scottis gat gold, gud, ger, and othir wage;
    Relewyt thai war, at partit that pilage.
    To meit thai went, with myrthis and plesance;
Fol. 40 b 620 Thai sparyt nocht king Eduuardis purweance.
    With solace syne a litill sleyp thai ta;
    A prewa wach he gart amang thaim ga.
    Twa kukis fell, thair lyffis for to saiff,
    With dede corssys that lay wnputt in graiff:
625 Quhen thai saw weyll the Scottis war at rest,
    Out off the feild to steill thaim thocht it best.
    Full law thai crap, quhill thai war out off sicht;
    Eftir the ost syne ran in all thair mycht.
    Quhen that the Scottis had slepyt bot a quhill,
630 Than raiss thai wp, for Wallace dredyt gyll.
    He said to thaim; " The Sotherone may persewe
    " Agayne to ws, for thai ar folk enew,
    " Quhar Ingliss men prowisioune makis in wer.

"It is full hard to do thaim mekill der.
635 "On this playne feild we will thaim nocht abid;
"To sum gud strenth my purpos is to ryd."
The purweance, that left was in that stede,
To Ropis Bog he gert serwandis it lede,
With ordinance at Sothroun broucht in thar.
640 He with the ost to Dawis schaw can far;
And thar ramaynede a gret space off the day.
Off Ingliss men yeit sum thing will I say.

As king Eduuart throuch Cultir hoppis socht,
Quhen he persawit the Scottis folowed nocht,
645 In Jhonnys greyne he gert the ost ly still;
Feill fleand folk assemblit sone him till.
Quhen thai war met, the king ner worthis mad,
For his der kyn that he thar lossyt had;
His twa emys in to the feild was slayne,
650 His secund sone that mekill was off mayne.
His brothir Hew was kelyt thar full cald;
The erle off Kent. that cruell berne and bald,
With gret worschip tuk ded befor the king;
For him he murnyt, als lang as he mycht ryng.
655 At this semlay as thai in sorow stand,
The twa kukis come sone in at his hand,
And tald till him how thai enchapyt war:
"The Scottis all as swyne lyis droukyn thar,
"Off our wycht wyne ye gert ws thidder led;
660 "Full weill we may be wengit off thar ded.
"A payne our lywis, it is suth that we tell:
"Raturne agayne, ye sall fynd thaim your sell."
He blamyt thaim; and said, na witt it was,
That he agayne for sic a taill sud pass.
665 'Thar chyftayne is rycht marwalus in wer;

Fol. 41 a ' Fra sic perell he can full weill thaim ber.
     ' To sek him mar as now 1 will nocht ryd;
     ' Our meit is lost, tharfor we may nocht byd.'
     The hardy duk off Longcastell and lord,
670 "Soucrane," he said, " till our consaill concord.
     " Gyff this be trew, ye haiff the mar awaill;
     " We may thaim wyne, and mak bot lycht trawaill.
     " War yon folk ded, quha may agayne ws stand?
     " Than neid we nocht for meit to leiff the land."
675 The king ansuerd; ' I will nocht rid agayne,
     ' As at this tyme, my purpos is in playne.'
     The duk said; " Schir, gyff ye contermyt be,
     " To mowff yow mor it afferis nocht for me.
     " Commaund power agayne with me to wend;
680 " And I off this sall se a finaill end."
     Ten thousand haill he chargyt for to ryd;
     ' Her in this strenth all nycht I sall yow bid.
     ' We may get meit off bestiall in this land;
     ' Gud drynk as now we can nocht bryng to hand.'
685 Off Westmorland the lord had mett him thar,
     On with the duk he graithit him to fair.
     At the fyrst straik with thaim he had nocht beyne;
     With him he led a thousand weill beseyne.
     A Pykart lord was with a thousand bowne;
690 Off king Edward he kepyt Calyss toun.
     This twelf thousand on to the feild can fair.
     The twa captans sone mett thaim at Beggair,
     With the haill stuff off Roxburch and Berweike.
     Schir Rawff Gray saw at thai war Sotheron leik,
695 Out off the south approchit to thair sicht;
     He knew full weill with thaim it was nocht rycht.
     Amer Wallange with his power come als,
     King Eduuardis man, a tyrand knycht and fals.

Quhen thai war mett thai fand nocht ellis thar,
700 Bot dede corssis, and thai war spulyeit bar.
Than marueld thai quhar at the Scottis suld be;
Off thaim about perance thai couth nocht se:
Bot spyis thaim tald, that come with Schyr Amar,
In Dawis schaw thai saw thaim mak repair.
705 The fers Sotheroun sone passit to that place;
The wach wes war, and tald [it] to Wallace.
He warnd the ost out off that wood to ryd,
In Roppis bog he purpost for to byd.
A litill schaw wpon the ta syd was,
710 That men on fute mycht off the bog out pass.
Fol. 41 b Thar horss thai left in to that litill hauld.
On fute thai thocht the moss that thai suld hauld.
The Ingliss ost had weill thar passage seyne,
And folowed fast with cruell men and keyne.
715 Thai trowit that bog mycht mak thaim litill waill,
Growyn our with reyss, and all the sward was haill.
On thaim to ryd thai ordand in gret ire;
Off the formest a thousand, in the myre,
Off horss with men, was plungyt in the deipe.
720 The Scottis men tuk off thair cummyng kepe;
Upon thaim set with strakis sad and sar,
Yeid nane away off all that entrit thar.
Lycht men on fute apon thaim derffly dang;
Feill wndyr horss was smoryt in that thrang,
725 Stampyt in moss, and with rud horss ourgayne.
The worthy Scottis the dry land than has tayne.
Apon the laiff fechtand full wondyr fast,
And mony groyme thai maid full sar agast.
Than Inglissmen, that besy was in wer,
730 Assailyeit sar thaim fra the moss to ber,
On athir syd; bot than it was no but.
The strenth thai held rycht awfully on fut,

Till men and horss gaiff mony grewous wound;
Feyll to the dede thai stekit in that stound.

735 The Pykart lord assailyeit scharply thar,
Vpon the Grayme, with strakis sad and sar.
Schir Jhone the Grayme, with a staff suerd off steill,
His brycht byrneis he persyt euirilkdeill,
Throuch all the stuff, and stekit him in that sted:

740 Thus off his dynt the bauld Pykart is ded.
The Ingliss ost tuk playne purposs to fle;
In thar turnyng the Scottis gert mony de.
Wallace wald fayne at the Wallang haiff beyne;
Off Westmorland the lord was thaim betweyne:

745 Wallace on him he set ane awfull dynt,
Throuch basnet stuff, that na steill mycht it stynt;
Derffly to dede he left him in that place.
The fals knycht thus eschapit throuch this cace.
And Robert Boid has with a captayne mett

750 Off Berweik, than a sad straik on him set
Awkwart the crag, and kerwyt the pissane,
Throuch all his weid in sondyr straik the bane.
Feill horssyt men fled fast, and durst nocht byd:
Raboytit ewill, on to thar king thai rid.

755 The duk him tald off all thair jornay haill:
His hart for ire bolnyt for byttir baill;
Haill he hecht he suld neuyr London se,
On Wallace deid quhill he rawengit be,
Or loss his men agayne as he did ayr.

760 Thus socht he south with gret sorou and cair;
At the Byrkhill a litill tary maid;
Syne throuch the land but rest our Sulway raid.
The Scottis ost a nycht ramanyt still;
Apon the morn thai spulyete, with gud will,

765 The dede corssis; syne couth to Braid wood fayr,
At a consaill thre dayis soiornyt thar.

Fol. 42 a

At Forest kyrk a metyng ordand he;
Thai chesd Wallace Scottis wardand to be,
Traistand he suld thair paynfull sorow cess.
770 He rasawyt all that wald cum till his pess.
Schir Wilyham come that lord off Douglas was,
Forsuk Eduuard, at Wallace pess can ass;
In thair thrillage he wald no langar be:
Trewbut befor till Ingland payit he.
775 In contrar Scottis with thaim he neuir raid;
Fer bettir cher Wallace tharfor him maid.
Thus tretyt he, and cheryst wondyr fair
Trew Scottis men that fewté maid him thar;
And gaiff gretly feill gudis at he wan;
780 He warndit nocht till na gud Scottis man.
Quha wald rebell, and gang contrar the rycht,
He punyst sar, war he squier or knycht.
Thus marwalusly gud Wallas tuk on hand;
Lykly he was, rycht fair and weill farrand,
785 Mandly and stout, and tharto rycht liberall,
Plesand and wiss in all gud gouernall.
To sla, forsuth, Sotheroun he sparyt nocht;
To Scottis men full gret profyt he wrocht.
In to the south sone efftir passit he;
790 As him best thocht he rewllyt that contré.
Schirrais he maid that cruell was to ken,
And captans als, off wiss trew Scottis men.
Fra Gamlis peth the land obeyt him haill,
Till Ur wattir, bath strenth, forest, and daill.
795 Agaynis him in Galloway hous was nayne,
Except Wigtoun, byggyt off lyme and stayne.
That captayne hard the reullis off Wallace;
Away be sey, he staw out off that place,
Lewyt all waist, and couth in Ingland wend.
800 Bot Wallace sone a kepar till it send,

A gud squier; and to nayme he was cald
Adam Gordone, as the storie me tald.

A strenth thar was on the wattir off Cre,
With in a roch, rycht stalwart wrocht off tre;
Fol. 42 b 805 A gait befor mycht no man to it wyn,
But the consent off thaim that duelt within.
On the bak sid a roch and wattir was;
A strait entré forsuth it was to pass.
To wesy it Wallace him selff sone went;
810 Fra he it saw, he kest in his entent
To wyn that hauld; he has chosyne a gait,
That thai with in suld mak litill debait.
His power haill he gerd bid out off sycht,
Bot thre with him qwhill tyme that it was nycht.
815 Than tuk he twa, quhen that the nycht was dym,
Stewyn off Irland, and Kerlé, that couth clyme
The wattir wnder; and clame the roch so strang:
Thus entrit thai the Sothrone men amang.
The wach befor tuk na tent to that syd:
820 Thir thre in feyr sone to the port thai glid.
Gud Wallace than straik the portar him sell;
Dede our the roch in to the dik he fell;
Leit doun the brig, and blew his horne on hycht.
The buschement brak, and come in all thar mycht;
825 At thair awne will sone entrit in that place;
Till Inglissmen thai did full litill grace.
Sexty thai slew; in that hald was no ma,
Bot ane auld preist, and sympill wemen twa.
Gret purweance was in that roch to spend;
830 Wallace baid still quhill it was at ane end:
Brak doune the strenth, bath bryg, and bulwark all;
Out our the roch thai gert the temyr fall;
Wndid the gait, and wald no langar bid.

In Carrik syne thai bownyt thaim to rid;
835 Haistit thaim nocht, bot sobyrly couth fair
Till Towrnbery; thar captane was at Ayr
With lord Persie, to tak his consaill haill:
Syne fyrd the yett, na succour mycht awaill.
A prest thar was, and gentill wemen with in,
840 Quhilk for the fyr maid hiddewis noyis and dyn.
"Mercy," thai cryit, "for him that deit on tre!"
Wallace gert slaik the fyr, and leit thaim be.
, To mak defens na ma was lewyt thar :
· He thaim commaund out off the land to far;
845 Spulyeit the place, and spilt all at thai mocht.
Apon the morn in Cumno sone thai socht;
To Laynrik syne, and set a tyme off ayr,
Mysdoaris feill he gert be punyst thar.
To gud trew men he gaiff full mekill wage;
850 His brothir sone put to his heretage;
Fol. 43 a To the blak crag in Cumno past agayne;
His houshauld set with men off mekill mayne.
Thre monethis thar he duellyt in gud rest;
Suttell Sotheroune fand weill it was the best
855 Trewis to tak; for till enchew a chans
To furthir this, thai send for knycht Wallans
Bothwell yeit that tratour kepyt still;
And Ayr all haill was at the Perseis will ;
The byschope Beik in Glaskow duellyt thar,
860 Throucht gret supple off the captayne off Ayr.
Erll off Stamffurd, was chanslar off Ingland,
With Schyr Amar this trawaill tuk on hand,
To procur pess be ony maner off cace.
A saiff condyt thai purchest off Wallace.
865 In Ruglen kyrk the tryst than haiff thai set,
A promes maid to meit Wallace but let.
The day off this approchit wondyr fast;

The gret chanslar and Amar thidder past:
Syne Wallace come, and his men weill beseyn,
870 With him fyfty arayit all in greyne.
Ilkane off thaim a bow and arrowis bar,
And lang suerdis, the quhilk full scharply schar.
In to the kyrk he gert a preyst rewess;
With humyll mynd rycht mekly hard a mess:
875 Syne wp he raiss and till ane alter went,
And his gud men full cruell off entent.
In ir he grew, that traitour quhen he sawe;
The Inglissmen off his face stud gret aw.
Witt reullyt him, that he did no owtrage.
880 The erlle beheld fast till his hye curage;
Forthocht sum part that he come to that place,
Gretlye abaysit for the vult off his face.
Schir Amer said; " This spech ye mon begyne;
" He will nocht bow to na part off your kyn.
885 " Sufferyt ye ar, I trow yhe may spek weill.
" For all Ingland he will nocht brek adeyll
" His saiff cwndyt, or quhar he makis a band."
The chanslar than approfferit him his hand.
Wallace stud still, and couth na handis ta;
890 Frendschipe to thaim na liknes wald he ma.
Schir Amar said: ' Wallace, yhe wndyrstand,
' This is a lord, and chanslar off Ingland;
' To salus him ye may be propyr skill.'
With schort awyss he maid ansuer him till:
895 " Sic salusyng I oyss till Ingliss men
" Sa sall he haiff, quhar euir I may him ken
" At my power; that God I mak awow,
" Out off souerance gyff that I had him now.
" Bot for thi lyff, and all his land so braid,
900 " I will nocht brek this promess that is maid.
Fol. 43 b " I had leuir at myn awn will haiff the,

" With out condyt, that I mycht wrokyne be
" Off thi fals deid, thou dois in this regiounc,
" Than off pur gold a kingis gret ransoune.
905 " Bot, for my band, as now I will lat be.
" Chanslar, schaw furth quhat ye desyr of me."
The chanslar said ; ' The most causs of this thing,
' To procur peess I am send fra our king,
' With the gret scill, and woice off hys parliament ;
910 ' Quhat I bynd her oure barnage sall consent.'
Wallace ansuerd ; " Our litill mendis we haiff,
" Syne off oure rycht ye occupy the laiff.
" Quytcleyme our land, and we sall nocht deny."
The chanslar said ; ' Off na sic chargis haiff I ;
915 ' We will gyff gold, or oure purpose suld faill.'
Than Wallace said ; " In waist is that trawaill.
" Be fauour gold we ask nayne off your kyn ;
" In wer off you we tak that we may wyn."
Abaissid he was to mak ansuer agayne.
920 Wallace said ; " Schyr, we jangill bot in wayne.
" My consell gyffis, I will na fabill mak,
" As for a yer a finaill pess to tak.
" Nocht for my self, that I bynd to your seill,
" I can nocht trow that euir ye will be leill ;
925 " Bot for pur folk gretlye has beyne supprisyt,
" I will tak peess, quhill forthir we be awisit."
Than band thai thus ; thar suld be no debait,
Castell and towne suld stand in that ilk stait,
Fra that day furth, quhill a yer war at end :
930 Sellyt this pess, and tuk thar leyff to wend.
Wallace fra thine passit in to the west,
Maid playne repair quhar so him likit best ;
Yeit sar he dred or thai suld him dissaiff.
This endentour to Schyr Ranald he gaiff,

I

935   His der wncle, quhar it mycht kepit be;
      In Cumno syne till his duellyng went he.

EXPLICIT LIBER SEXTUS,
INCIPIT SEPTIMUS.

BUKE SEWYND.

, In Feueryher befell the sammyn cace,
That Inglissmen tuk trewis with Wallace.
This passyt our till Marche till end was socht.
The Inglismen kest all the wayis thai mocht,
5 With sutteltẻ and wykkit illusione,
The worthi Scottis to put to confusioune.
In Aperill the king off Ingland come
In Cvmmyrland of Pumfrat fro his home;
In to Carleill till a consell he yeid,
10 Quhar off the Scottis mycht haiff full mekill dreid.
Fol. 44 a Mony captane that was off Ingland born,
Thidder thai past, and semblit thar king beforn;
Na Scottis man to that consell thai cald,
Bot Schyr Amer, that traytour was off ald.
15 At him thai sperd, how thai suld tak on hand
The rychtwyss blud to scour out off Scotland.
Schir Amer said; " Thair chyftayne can weill do,
" Rycht wyss in wer, and has gret power to;
" And now this trew gyffis thaim sic hardyment,
20 " That to your faith thai will nocht all consent.
" Bot wald ye do rycht as I wald yow ler,
" This pess to thaim it suld be sald full der."
Than demyt he, the fals Sotheroun amang,
How thai best mycht the Scottis barownis hang.
25 For gret bernys that tyme stud in till Ayr,
Wrocht for the king, quhen his lugyng wes thar;

Byggyt about, that no man entir mycht,
Bot ane at anys, nor haiff off othir sicht.
Thar ordand thai thir lordis suld be slayne;
30 A justice maid, quhilk wes of mekill mayne.
To lord Persye off this mattir thai laid.
With sad awyss agayne to thaim he said;
" Thai men to me has kepit treuth so lang,
" Desaitfully I may nocht se thaim hang.
35 " I am thar fa, and warn thaim will I nocht;
" Sa I be quytt, I rek nocht quhat yhe wrocht.
" Fra thine I will, and towart Glaskow draw,
" With our byschope to her off his new law."
Than chesyt thai a justice fers and fell,
40 Quhilk Arnwlff hecht, as my auctour will tell,
Off South hantoun, that huge hie her and lord;
He wndretuk to pyne thaim with the cord.
Ane othir ayr in Glaskow ordand thai,
For Cliddisdaill men, to stand that sammyn day:
45 Syne chargyt thaim, in all wayis ernystfully,
Be no kyn meyne Wallace suld nocht chaip by.
For weill thai wyst, and thai men war ourthrawin,
Thai mycht at will bruk Scotland as thair awin.
This band thai cloiss wndre thair seillis fast;
50 Syne south our mur agayn king Edward past.
The new justice rasawit was in Ayr:
The lord Persye can on to Glaskow fayr.
This ayr was set in Jun the auchtand day,
And playnly cryt, na fre man war away.
55 The Scottis marweld, and pess tane in the land,
Quhy Inglissmen sic maistir tuk on hand.
Schir Ranald set a day befor this ayr,
At Monktoun kyrk; his freyndis mett him thar.
Fol. 44 b Wilyham Wallace on to the tryst couth pass,
60 For he as than wardane off Scotland was.

This maistir Jhone a worthi clerk was thar;
He chargyt his kyne for to byd fra that ayr.
Rycht weill he wyst, fra Persey fled that land,
Gret perell was till Scottis apperand.

65 Wallace fra thaim [in] to the kyrk he yeid;
Pater Noster, Aue, he said, and Creid.
Sync to the grece he lenyt him sobyrly;
Apon a sleip he slaid full sodandly.
Kneland folowed, and saw him fallyn on sleip;

70 He maid na noyis, bot wysly couth him kepe.
In that slummir, cummand him thocht he saw
Ane agit man, fast towart him couth draw;
Sone be the hand he hynt him haistelé,
" I am," he said, " in wiage chargit with the."

75 A suerd him gaiff off burly burnist steill;
" Gud sone," he said, " this brand thou sall bruk weill."
Off topastone him thocht the plumat was;
Baith hilt and hand all glitterand lik the glas.
" Der sone," he said, " we tary her to lang;

80 " Thow sall go se quhar wrocht is mekill wrang."
Than he him led till a montane on hycht;
The warld him thocht he mycht se with a sicht.
He left him thar, syne sone fra him he went.
Tharoff Wallace studiit in his entent;

85 Till se him mar he had still gret desyr.
Tharwith he saw begyne a felloune fyr,
Quhilk braithly brynt on breid throu all the land,
Scotland atour, fra Ross to Sulway sand.
Than sone till him thar descendyt a qweyne,

90 Inlumyt lycht, schynand full brycht and scheyne.
In hyr presens apperyt so mekill lycht,
At all the fyr scho put out off his sycht;
Gaiff him a wand off colour reid and greyne,
With a saffyr sanyt his face and eyne.

95   " Welcum," scho said, " I cheiss the as my luff.
    " Thow art grantyt, be the gret God abuff,
    " Till help pepill that sufferis mekill wrang:
    " With the as now I may nocht tary lang.
    " Thou sall return to thi awne oyss agayne;
100   " Thi derrast kyne ar her in mekill payne.
    " This rycht regioun thow mon redeme it all:
    " Thi last reward in erd sall be bot small.
    " Let nocht tharfor, tak redress off this myss:
    " To thi reward thou sall haiff lestand blyss."
105 Off hir rycht hand scho betaucht him a buk;
    Humylly thus hyr leyff full sone scho tuk;
    On to the cloud ascendyt off his sycht.
Fol. 45 a Wallace brak vp the buk in all his mycht.
    In thre partis the buk weill writyn was;   .
110 The fyrst writtyng was gross letteris off bras,
    The secound gold, the thrid was siluer scheyne.
    Wallace merueld quhat this writyng suld meyne.
    To rede the buk he besyet him so fast,
    His spreit agayne to walkand mynd is past;
115 And wp he raiss, syne sodandly furth went.
    This clerk he fand, and tald him [his] entent
    Off this wisioun, as I haiff said befor,
    Completly throuch.   Quhat nedis wordis mor?
    " Der sone," he said, " my witt vnabill is
120   " To runsik sic, for dreid I say off myss.
    " Yeit I sall deyme, thocht my cunnyng be small:
    " God grant na chargis efftir my wordis fall!
    " Saynct Androw was, gaiff the that suerd in hand;
    " Off sanctis he is wowar off Scotland.
125   " That montayne is, quhar he the had on hycht,
    " Knawlage to haiff off wrang that [thow] mon rych
    " The fyr sall be fell tithingis, or ye part,
    " Quhilk will be tald in mony syndry art.

" I can nocht witt quhat qweyn at it suld be,

130 " Quhethir fortoun, or our lady so fre.

" Lykly it is, be the brychtnes scho brocht,

" Modyr off him that all this warld has wrocht.

" The prety wand, I trow be myn entent,

" Assignes rewlle and cruell jugément.

135 " The red colour, quha graithly wndrestud,

" Betaknes all to gret battaill and blud:

" The greyn, curage that thow art now amang,

" In strowbill wer thou sall conteyne full lang.

" The saphyr stayne, scho blissit the with all,

140 " Is lestand grace, will God, sall to the fall.

" The thrynfald buk is bot this brokyn land,

" Thou mon rademe be worthines off hand.

" The bras lettris betakynnys bot to this,

" The gret oppress off wer and mekill myss,

145 " The quhilk thow sall bryng to the rycht agayne;

" Bot thou tharfor mon suffer mekill payne.

" The gold takynnis honour and worthinas,

" Wictour in armys, that thou sall haiff be grace.

" The siluer schawis cleyne lyff, and hewynys blyss;

150 " To thi reward that myrth thou sall nocht myss.

" Dreid nocht tharfor, be out off all dispayr.

" Forthir as now her off I can no mair."

He thankit hym, and thus his leyff has tayne;

45 b Till Corsbé syne with his wncle raid hayme.

155 With myrthis thus all nycht thai soiornyt thar.

Apon the morn thai graith thaim to the ar;

And furth thai ryd, quhill thai come to Kingace.

With dreidfull hart thus sperit wicht Wallace

At Schyr Ranald, for the charter off pees.

160 " Neuo," he said, " thir wordis ar nocht les.

" It is lewyt at Corsbé, in the kyst

" Quhar thou it laid; tharoff na othyr wist."
Wallace ansuerd; 'Had we it her to schaw,
' And thai be falss, we suld nocht entir awe.'
165 " Der sone," he said, "I pray the pass agayne;
" Thocht thou wald send, that trawaill war in wayne:
" Bot thou, or I, can nane it bryng this tid."
Gret grace it was maid him agayne to ryd.
Wallace raturnd, and tuk with him bot thre;
170 Nane off thaim knew this endentour bot he.
Wnhap him led, for bid him couth he nocht;
Off fals dissayt this gud knycht had na thocht.
Schir Ranald raid but restyng to the town,
Wittand na thing off all this falss tresown.
175 That wykked syng so rewled the planait;
Saturn was than in till his heast stait.
Aboune Juno in his malancoly,
Jupiter, Mars, ay cruell off inwy,
Saturn as than awansyt his natur.
180 Off terandry he power had and cur;
Rebell renkis in mony seir regioun;
Trubbill weddyr makis schippis to droune,
His drychyn is with Pluto in the se;
As off the land, full off iniquité,
185 He waknys wer, waxyng off pestilence,
Fallyng off wallis with cruell wiolence,
Pusoun is ryff, amang thir othir thingis;
Sodeyn slauchter off empriouris and kingis.
Quhen Sampsone powed to grond the gret piller,
190 Saturn was than in till the heast sper.
At Thebes als off his power thai tell,
Quhen Phiorax sank throuch the erd till hell.
Off the Troianis he had full mekill cur,
Quhen Achilles at Troy slew gud Ectur,
195 Burdeous schent, and mony citeis mo;

His power yeit it has na hap to' ho.
In braid Brytane feill wengeance has beyne seyne;
Off this and mar, ye wait weill quhat I meyn.
Bot to this hous, that stalwart wes and strang,
200 Schir Ranald come, and mycht nocht tary lang.
ol. 46 a A bawk was knyt all full of rapys keyne;
Sic a towboth sen syn was neuir seyne.
Stern men was set the entré for to hald;
Nayne mycht pass in, bot ay as thai war cald.
205 Schir Ranald fyrst, to mak fewté for his land,
The knycht, went in, and wald na langar stand:
A rynnand cord thai slewyt our his hed,
Hard to the bawk, and hangyt him to ded.
Schyr Bryss the Blayr next with hys eyme in past;
210 On to the ded thai haistyt him full fast,
Be he entrit, hys hed was in the swar;
Tytt to the bawk, hangyt to ded rycht thar.
The third entrit, that peté was for thy,
A gentill knycht, Schyr Neill off Mungumry;
215 And othir feill off landit men about.
Mony yeid in, bot na Scottis com out.
Off Wallace part, thai putt to that derff deid,
Mony Craufurd sa endyt in that steid.
Off Carrik men Kennadyss slew thai alss;
220 And kynd Cambellis, that neuir had beyne falss.
Thir rabellit nocht contrar thair rychtwiss croun;
Sotheroun for thi thaim putt to confusioun;
Berklais, Boidis, and Stuartis off gud kyn:
Na Scott chapyt that tyme that entrit in.
225 Vpon the bawk thai hangit mony par,
Be sid thaim ded in the nuk kest thaim thar.
Sen the fyrst tyme that ony wer wes wrocht,
To sic a dede so mony sic yeid nocht
Vpon a day, throuch curssit Saxons seid:

230 Vengeance off this throuch out that kynrik yeid.
    Grantyt wes fra God in the gret hewyn,
    Sa ordand he that law suld be thair stewyn.
    To falss Saxons, for thair fell jugément,
    Thar wykkydnes our all the land is went.
235 Yhe nobill men, that ar off Scottis kind,
    Thar petous dede yhe kepe in to your mynd;
    And ws rawenge, quhen we ar set in thrang.
    Dolour it is her on to tary lang.
    Thus auchtene scor to that derff dede thai dycht,
240 Off barronis bald, and mony worthi knycht.
    Quhen thai had slayne the worthiast that was thar,
    For waik peple thai wald na langar spar:
    In till a garth kest thaim out off that sted,
    As thai war born, dispulyeit, bar, and ded.
245 Gud Robert Boid on till a tawern yeid,
    With twenty men that douchty war in deid,
    Off Wallace houss, full cruell off entent;
    He gouernyt thaim quhen Wallace was absent.
    Kerlé turnyt with his mastir agayne,
Fol. 46 b 250 Kneland and Byrd, that mekill war off mayne.
    Stewyn off Irland went furth; apon the streit
    A trew woman full sone with him couth meit.
    He speryt at hir, quhat hapnyt in the ayr.
    " Sorou," scho said, " is nothing ellis thar."
255 Ferdly scho ast, " Allace! quhar is Wallace?"
    ' Fra ws agayne he passit at Kingace.'
    " Go warn his folk, and haist thaim off the toun;
    " To kepe him selff I sall be reddy boun."
    With hir as than no mar tary he maid;
260 Till his falowis he went with outyn baid.
    And to thaim tald off all this gret mysfair.
    To Laglane wood thai bownyt with outyn mar.
    Be this Wallace wes cummand wondir fast;

For his freyndis he was full sar agast.
265 On to the bern sadly he couth persew
Till entir in, for he na perell knew.
This woman than apon him loud can call;
" O fers Wallace, feill tempest is befall.
" Our men ar slayne, that peté is to se,
270 " As bestiall houndis hangit our a tre;
" Our trew barrounis be twa and twa past in."
Wallace wepyt for gret loss off his kyne.
Than with wness apon his horss he baid;
Mair for to sper to this woman he raid.
275 ' Der nece,' he said, ' the trewth giff thow can tell,
' Is my eyme dede, or hou the cace befell?'
" Out off yon bern," scho said, " I saw him borne,
" Nakit, laid law on cald erd, me beforn.
" His frosty mouth I kissit in that sted;
280 " Rycht now manlik, now bar, and brocht to ded.
" And with a claith I couerit his licaym;
" For in his lyff he did neuir woman schayme.
" His systir sone thou art, worthi and wicht;
" Rawenge thar dede, for Goddis saik, at thi mycht:
285 " Als I sall help, as I am woman trew."
' Der wicht,' he said, ' der God, sen at thou knew
' Gud Robert Boid, quhar at thou can him se;
' Wilyham Crawfurd als giff he lyffand be.
' Adam Wallace wald help me in this striff,
290 ' I pray to God send me [thaim] all in liff;
' For Marys saik bid thaim sone cum to me.
' The justice innys thow spy for cheryté;
' And in quhat feir that thai thair lugyne mak.
' Son efftir that we will our purposs tak
·295 ' In to Laglane, quhilk has my succour beyne.
' Adew market, and welcum woddis greyne!'

Her off as than till hir he spak no mair;
His brydill turnyt, and fra hir can he fair:
Sic murnyng maid for his der worthi kyn,

Fol. 47 a 300 Him thocht for baill his breyst ner bryst in twyn.
As he thus raid in gret angyr and teyne,
Off Inglissmen thar folowed him syfteyn,
Wicht, wallyt men, at towart him couth draw,
With a maser, to tach him to the law.

305 Wallace raturnd in greiff and matelent;
With his suerd drawyn amang thaim sone he went.
The myddyll off ane he mankit ner in twa;
Ane othir thar apon the hed can ta;
The thrid he straik, and throuch the cost him claiff;

310 The ferd to ground rycht derffly ded doun he draiff;
The fyft he hit with gret ire in that sted;
With out reskew dreidles he left thaim ded.
Than his thre men had slayn the tothir fyve.
Fra thaim the laiff eschapit in to lyff;

315 Fled to thair lord, and tald him off this cass.
To Laglane wode than ridis wicht Wallas.
The Sotheroun said, quhat ane that he hit rycht,
With out mercye, dredles, to ded wes dycht.
Merwell thai had sic strenth in ane suld be;

320 Ane off thair men at ilk straik he gert de.
Than demyt thai, it suld be Wallace wicht.
To thar langage maid ansuer ane ald knycht;
" Forsuth," he said, " be he chapyt this ayr,
" All your new deid is eking off our cair."

325 The justice said, quhen thar sic murmur raiss;
' Yhe wald be ferd, and thar come mony faiss,
' That for a man me think yow lik to fle,
' And wait nocht yeit in deid gyff it be he.
' And thocht it be, I cownt him bot full lycht;

330 ' Quha bidis her, ilk gentill man sall be knycht:
    ' I think to deill thair landis haill to morn
    ' To yow about, that ar off Ingland born.'

    The Sotheron drew to thar lugyng but mar;
    Four thousand haill that nycht was in till Ayr.
335 In gret bernyss, biggyt with out the toun,
    The justice lay, with mony bald barroun.
    Than he gert cry about thai waynys wide,
    Na Scottis born amang thaim thar suld bid.
    To the castell he wald nocht pass for eyss,
340 Bot soiornd thar with thing that mycht him pleyss.
    Gret purwians be se to thaim was bocht,
    With Irland ayle, the mychteast couth be wrocht.
    Na wach wes set, be caus thai had na dout
    Off Scottis men that leiffand was with out.
345 Lawberand in mynd thai had beyne all that day,
    Off ayle and wyne yneuch chosyne haiff thai:
    As bestly folk tuk off thaim selff no keip;
    In thair brawnys sone slaid the sleuthfull sleip;
    Throuch full gluttré in swarff swappyt lik swyn.
l. 47 b 350 Thar chyftayne than was gret Bachus off wyn.
    This wyss woman besy amang thaim was;
    Feill men scho warnd and gart to Laglayne pass,
    Hyr selff formest, quhill thai with Wallace met.
    Sum comfort than in till his mynd was set;
355 Quhen he thaim saw, he thankit God off micht.
    Tithandis he ast; the woman tald him rycht;
    " Slepand as swyn ar all yone fals menyhe;
    " Na Scottis man is in that cumpané."
    Than Wallace said; ' Giff thai all droukyn be,
360 ' I call it best with fyr sor thaim to se.'
    Off gud men than thre hundreth till him socht;
    The woman had tald thre trew burges, at brocht

Out off the toun, with nobill aile and breid,
And othir stuff, als mekill as thai mycht leid.
365 Thai eit and drank, the Scottis men at mocht.
The noblis than Jop has to Wallace brocht.
Sadly he said; " Der freyndis, now you se,
" Our kyn ar slayne, tharoff is gret peté;
" Throuch feill murthyr, the gret dispite is mor;
370 " Now sum rameid I wald we set tharfor.
" Supposs that I was maid wardane to be,
" Part ar away sic chargis put to me;
" And ye ar her, cummyn off als gud blud,
" Als rychtwis born be awentur, and als gud,
375 " Alss forthwart, fair, and als likly off persoun,
" As euir was I; tharfor till conclusioun,
" Latt ws cheyss fyve off this gud cumpany;
" Syne caflis cast quha sall our master be."
Wallace and Boyd, and Craufurd off renoun,
380 And Adam als than lord off Ricardtoun;
His fadyr than wes wesyed with seknes,
God had him tayne in till his lestand grace;
The fyft Awchinlek, in wer a nobill man;
Caflis to cast about thir fyve began.
385 It wald on him, for ocht thai cuth dewyss.
Continualy, quhill thai had castyn thryss.
Than Wallace raiss, and out a suerd can draw;
He said, " I wow to the Makar off aw,
" And till Mary, his modyr wirgyne cler,
390 " My wnclis dede now sall be sauld full der,
" With mony ma off our der worthi kyn.
" Fyrst, or I eit or drynk, we sall begyn;
" For sleuth nor sleip sall nayne remayne in me,
" Off this tempest till I a wengeance se."
395 Than all inclynd rycht humyll off accord,
And him resawit as chyftayne and thair lord.

Wallace a lord he may be clepyt weyll,
Thocht ruryk folk tharoff haff litill feill;
Na deyme na lord, bot landis be thair part.
48 a 400 Had he the warld, and be wrachit off hart,
He is no lord as to the worthines;
It can nocht be, but fredome, lordlyknes.
At the Roddis thai mak full mony ane,
Quhilk worthy ar, thocht landis haiff thai nane.
405 This discussyng I leiff herroldis till end;
On my mater now brieffly will I wend.
Wallace commaunde a burgess for to get
Fyne cawk eneuch, that his der nece mycht set
On ilk yeit, quhar Sotheroun wer on raw.
410 Than twenty men he gert fast wetheis thraw,
Ilk man a pair, and on thair arme thaim threw;
Than to the toune full fast thai cuth persew.
The woman past befor thaim suttelly;
Cawkit ilk yett, that thai neid nocht gang by.
415 Than festnyt thai with wetheis duris fast,
To stapill and hesp, with mony sekyr cast.
Wallace gert Boid ner hand the castell ga,
With fyfté men, a jeperté to ma.
Gyff ony ischet, the fyr quhen that thai saw,
420 Fast to [the] yett he ordand thaim to draw.
The laiff with him about the bernys yheid.
This trew woman thaim seruit weill in deid,
With lynt and fyr, that haistely kendill wald;
In euir ilk nuk thai festnyt blesis bald.
425 Wallace commaund till all his men about,
Na Sotheron man at thai suld lat brek out:
Quhat euir he be, reskewis off that kyn
Fra the rede fyr, him selff sall pass tharin.
The lemand low sone lanssyt apon hycht.
430 " Forsuth," he said, " this is a plessand sycht;

" Till our hartis it suld be sum radress:
" War thir away, thar power war the less."
On to the justice him selff loud can caw;
" Lat ws to borch our men fra your fals law,
435 " At leyffand ar, that chapyt fra your ayr.
" Deyll nocht thar land, the wnlaw is our sayr.
" Thou had no rycht, that sall be on the seyne."
The rewmour raiss with cairfull cry and keyne.
The bryme fyr brynt rycht braithly apon loft;
440 Till slepand men that walkand was nocht soft.
The sycht with out was awfull for to se:
In all the warld na grettar payne mycht be,
Than thai with in, insufferit sor to duell,
That euir was wrocht, bot purgatory or hell.
445 A payne off hell weill ner it mycht be cauld,
Mad folk with fyr hampryt in mony hauld.
Feill byggyns brynt. that worthi war and wicht;
Gat nane away, knaiff, capitane, nor knycht.
Quhen brundis fell off raftreis thaim amang,
Fol. 48 b 450 Sum rudly raiss in byttir paynys strang;
Sum nakyt brynt, bot beltless all away;
Sum neuir raiss, bot smoryt quhar thai lay;
Sum ruschyt fast, till Ayr gyff thai mycht wyn,
Blyndyt in fyr, thar deidis war full dym.
455 The reik mellyt with fylth off carioune,
Amang the fyr, rycht foull off offensioune.
The peple beryt lyk wyld bestis in that tyd,
Within the wallis, rampand on athir sid;
Rewmyd in reuth, with mony grysly grayne;
460 Sum grymly gret, quhill thar lyff dayis war gayne.
Sum durris socht the entré for to get;
Bot Scottis men so wysly thaim beset,
Gyff ony brak, be awntur, off that steid,
With suerdis sone bertnyt thai war to dede;

465 Or ellys agayne beforce drewyn in the fyr:
     Thar chapyt nayne bot brynt wp bayne and lyr.
     The stynk scalyt off ded bodyis sa wyde,
     The Scottis abhord ner hand for to byd;
     Yeid to the wynd, and leit thaim ewyn allayne,
470 Quhill the rede fyr had that fals blude ourgayne.
     A frer Drumlay was priour than off Ayr;
     Sewyn scor with him that nycht tuk herbry thar,
     In his innys; for he mycht nocht thaim let.
     ·Till ner mydnycht a wach on thaim he set;
475 Him selff wouk weyll quhill he the fyr saw ryss:
     Sum mendis he thocht to tak off that suppryss.
     Hys brethir sewyn till harnes sone thai yeid,
     Hym selff chyftayne the ramanand to leid.
     The best thai waill off armour and gud ger;
480 Syne wapynnys tak, rycht awfull in affer.
     Thir aucht freris in four partis thai ga,
     With suerdis drawyn, till ilk houss yeid twa.
     Sone entrit thai quhar Sotheroune slepand war,
     Apon thaim sett with strakis sad and sar.
485 Feill frekis thar thai freris dang to dede,
     Sum nakit fled, and gat out off that sted,
     The wattir socht, abaissit out off slepe.
     In the furd weill, that was bath wan and depe,
     Feyll off thaim fell, that brak out off that place,
490 Dowkit to grounde, and deit with outyn grace.
     Drownyt and slayne war all that herbryt thar,
     Men callis it yeit, "The Freris blyssyng off Ayr."
     Few folk off waill was lewyt apon cace
     In the castell; lord Persye fra that place,
495 Befor the ayr, fra thine to Glaskow drew;
     Off men and stuff it was to purwa new.
     Yeit thai within, saw the fyr byrnand stout,

K

With schort awiss ischet, and had na dout.
The buschement than, as weryouris wyss and wicht,
500 Leit thaim allayne, and to the houss past rycht.
Fol. 49 a Boyd wan the port, entryt and all his men;
Keparis in it was left bot nyne or ten.
The formast sone hym selff scsyt in hand,
Maid quyt off hym, syne slew all at thai fand.
505 Off purwyaunce in that castell was nayne;
Schort tyme befor Persye was fra it gayne.
The erll Arnulff had rasawit that hauld,
Quhilk in the toune was brynt to powder cauld.
Boyd gert ramayn off his men twenty still,
510 Him selff past furth to witt off Wallace will,
Kepand the toune, quhill nocht was lewyt mar
Bot the woode fyr, and beyldis brynt full bar.
Off lykly men, that born was in Ingland,
Be suerd and fyr, that nycht deit fyve thousand.

515   Quhen Wallace men was weill to gydder met,
" Gud freyndis," he sayd, " ye knaw that thar wes s
" Sic law as this now in to Glaskow toune,
" Be byschope Beik, and Persye off renoun.
" Tharfor I will in haist we thidder fair;
520 " Off our gud kyn [sum] part ar lossyt thair."
He gert full sone the burges till him caw,
And gaiff commaund in generall to thaim aw.
In kepyng thai suld tak the houss off Ayr,
And " hald it haill quhill tyme that we her mayr;
525 " To byd our king castellys I wald we had;
" Cast we doun all, we mycht be demyt our rad."
Thai gart meit cum, for thai had fastyt lang;
Litill he tuk, syne bownyt thaim to gang.
Horsis thai cheyss, that Sotheroun had brocht thar,

530 Anew at will; and off the toune can fair.
    Thre hundreth haill was in his cumpany.
    Rycht wondir fast raid this gud chewalry
    To Glaskow bryg, that byggyt was off tre;
    Weyll passit our or Sotheroun mycht thaim se.
535 Lorde Persye wycht, that besy wes in wer,
    Semblyt his men fell awfull in affer.
    Than demyt thai that it was wicht Wallace,
    He had befor chapyt throw mony cace.
    The byschope Beik, and Persye that was wicht,
540 A thousand led off men in armyss brycht.
    Wallace saw weill quhat nowmyr semblit thar,
    He maid his men in twa partis to fair;
    Graithit thaim weill without the townys end.
    He callit Awchinlek, for he the passage kend.
545 " Wncle," he said, " be besy in to wer.
    " Quhethir will yhe the byschoppys taill wpber,
    " Or pass befor, and tak his benysone?"
    He ansuerd hym, with rycht schort provision,
    ' Wnbyschoppyt yeit, for suth I trow ye be;
550 ' Your selff sall fyrst his blyssyng tak for me:
49 b ' For sekyrly ye scruit it best the nycht.
    ' To ber his taill we sall in all our mycht.'
    Wallace ansuerd; " Sen we mon sindry gang,
    " Perell thar is and ye bid fra ws lang;
555 " For yone ar men will nocht sone be agast.
    " Fra tyme we meit, for Goddis [saik] haist yow fast.
    " Our disseueryng I wald na Sotheroune saw;
    " Behynd thaim cum, in [throw] the Northeast raw.
    " Gud men off wer ar all Northummyrland."
560 Thai partand thus tuk othir be the hand.
    Awchinlek said; ' We sall do at we may;
    ' We wald ilk ill to byd oucht lang away.

' A boustous staill betwix ws sone mon be;
' Bot to the rycht all mychty God haiff E!'

565 Adam Wallace and Awchinlek was boune,
Sewyn scor with thaim, on the baksid the toune.
Rycht fast thai yeid, quhill thai war out off sycht:
The tothir part arrayit thaim full rycht.
Wallace and Boid the playne streyt wp can ga.

570 Sotheroun marweld be causs thai saw na ma;
Thar senyhe cryit vpon the Persys syde,
With byschop Beik that bauldly durst abide.
A sayr semlay was at that metyng seyne,
As fyr on flynt it ferryt thaim betwcyne.

575 The hardy Scottis rycht awfully thaim abaid;
Brocht feill to grounde throuch weid that weill was
Perssyt plattis with poyntis stiff off steill;
Befors off hand gert mony cruell kneill.
The strang stour raiss, as reik, vpon thaim fast,

580 Or myst, throuch sone, vp to the clowdis past.
To help thaim selff ilkayne had mckill neid.
The worthy Scottis stud in fellone dreid;
Yeit forthwart ay thai pressit for to be,
And thai on thaim, gret wondyr was to se.

585 The Perseis men, in wer was oysit weill,
Rycht fersly faucht, and sonycit nocht adeill.
Adam Wallace and Awchinlek com in,
And partyt Sotheron rycht sodeynly in twyn;
Raturnd to thaim as noble men in wer.

590 The Scottis gat rowme, and mony doun thai ber;
The new cowntir assailyeit thaim sa fast,
Throuch Inglissmen maid sloppys at the last.
Than Wallace selff, in to that felloune thrang,
With his gud swerd, that hewy was and lang,

595 At Perseis face with a gud will he bar;
Bath bayne and brayne the forgyt steill throw sch

Four hundreth men, quhen lord Persie was dede,
Out off the gait the byschope Beik thai lede,
For than thaim thocht it was no tyme to bid,
600 By the Frer kyrk, till a wode fast besyd.
In that forest forsuth thai taryit nocht;
50 a On fresche horss to Bothwell sone thai socht.
Wallace folowed with worthi men and wicht;
Forfouchtyn thai war and trawald all the nycht.
605 Yeit feill thai slew in to the chace that day;
The byschope selff and gud men gat away.
Amar Wallang reskewit him in that place;
That knycht full oft did gret harme to Wallace.
Wallace began off nycht ten houris in Ayr;
610 On day be nyne in Glaskow semlyt thair;
Be ane our nowne at Bothwell yeit he was,
Repreiffit Wallang or he wald forthir pass;
Syne turnd agayne, as weyll witnes the buk;
Till Dundaff raid, and thar restyng he tuk;
615 Tald gud Schyr Jhon off thir tithandis in Ayr:
Gret mayne he maid he was nocht with him thar.
Wallace soiornd in Dundaff at his will,
Fyve dayis out, quhill tithandis come him till,
Out off the hycht, quhar gud men was forlorn;
620 For Bouchane raiss, Adell, Menteth, and Lorn,
Apon Argyll a fellone wer thai mak;
For Eduuardis saik thus can thai wndirtak.

The knycht Cambell in Argyll than wes still,
With his gud men, agayne king Eduuardis will;
625 And kepyt fre Lowchow his heretage:
Bot Makfadyan than did him gret owtrage.
This Makfadyan till Inglissmen was suorn;
Eduuard gaiff him bath Argill and Lorn.
Falss Jhon off Lorn to that gyft can concord:

630 In Ingland than he was new maid [anc] lord.
     Thus falssly he gaiff our his heretage,
     And tuk at London off Eduuard grettar wage.
     Dunkan off Lorn yeit for the landis straiff,
     Quhill Makfadyan ourset him with the laiff;
635 Put him off force to gud Cambell the knycht,
     Quhilk in to wer was wyss, worthi, and wicht.
     Thus Makfadyan was entrit in to Scotland,
     And marwalusly that tyrand tuk on hand,
     With his power, the quhilk I spak off ayr.
640 Thai four lordschippis all semlyt till him thair.
     Fyftene thousand off curssyt folk in deid,
     Off all gaddryn, in ost he had to leid:
     And mony off thaim was out off Irland brocht,
     Barnyss nor wyff thai peple sparyt nocht;
645 Waistyt the land als fer as thai mycht ga;
     Thai bestly folk couth nocht bot byrn and sla.
     In to Louchow he entryt sodeynly.
     The knycht Cambell maid gud defens for thi;
     Till Crage Vuyn with thre hundir he yeid;
650 That strenth he held, for all his cruell deid;
Fol. 50 b Syne brak the bryg, quhar thai mycht nocht out p
     Bot throuch a furd, quhar narow passage was.
     Abandounly Cambell agayne thaim baid,
     Fast vpon Aviss that was bathe depe and braid.
655 Makfadyane was apon the tothir syd,
     And thar on force behuffit him for to byd;
     For at the furde he durst nocht entir out,
     For gud Cambell mycht set him than in dout.
     Makfadyane socht, and a small passage fand;
660 Had he lasar, thai mycht pass off that land,
     Betuix a roch and the gret wattir sid,
     Bot four in front; na ma mycht gang nor rid.
     In till Louchow wes bestis gret plenté;

A quhill he thocht thar with his ost to be,
665 And othir stuff that thai had with thaim brocht.
Bot all his crafft awailyeit him rycht nocht.
Dunkane off Lorn has seyne the sodeyne cace;
Fra gud Cambell he went to seik Wallace,
Sum help to get off thar turment and teyne.
670 To gydder before in Dundé thai had beyne,
Lerand at scule in to thair tendyr age.
He thocht to slaik Makfadyanys hic curage.
Gylmychell than with Dunkan furth him dycht;
Agyd he was, and fute man wondyr wicht.
675 Sone can thai witt quhar Wallace lugyt was;
With thair complaynt till his presence thai pass.
Erll Malcom als the Lennox held at ess;
With his gud men to Wallace can he press.
Till him thar come gud Rychard off Lundy;
680 In till Dundaff he wald no langar ly.
Schir Jhon the Graym als bownyt him to ryd.
Makfadyanis wer so grewit thaim that tid,
At Wallace thocht his gret power to se,
In quhat aray he reullyt that cuntré.
685 The Rukbé than he kepit with gret wrang
Stirlyng castell, that stalwart wes and strang.
Quhen Wallace come be sowth it in a waill,
Till erll Malcome he said he wald assaill.
In diuerss partis he gert seuer thar men,
690 Off thair power that Sotheroun suld nocht ken.
Erll Malcome baid in buschement out off sicht.
Wallace with him tuk gud Schyr Jhone the knycht,
And a hundreth off wyss wer men but dout;
Throuch Stirlyng raid, gyff ony wald ysche out.
695 Towart ye bryg the gaynest way thai pass.
Quhen Rukbé saw quhat at thair power was,
He tuk sewyn scor off gud archaris was thar,

Wpon Wallace thai folowed wondyr sayr;
At fell bykkyr thai did thaim mekill der.

700 Wallace in hand gryppyt a nobill sper;
Agayne raturnd and has the formast slayne.
Schir Jhon the Grayme, that mekill was off mayne,
Amang thaim raid with a gud sper in hand.
The fyrst he slew that he befor him fand;

705 Apon a nothir his sper in sowndyr yeid;
A suerd he drew quhilk helpyt him in neid.
Yngliss archaris apon thaim can ranew,
That his gud horss with arrowis sone thai slew;
On fute he was.   Quhen Wallace has it seyne,

710 He lychtyt sone, with men off armys keyne,
Amang the rout fechtand full wondyr fast.
The Inglissmen raturnyt at the last.
At the castell thai wald haiff [beyne] full fayne;
Bot erll Malcome, with men off mekill mayne,

715 Betuix the Sotheroun and the yettis yeid;
Mony thai slew that douchty wes in deid.
In the gret press Wallace and Rukbé met;
With his gud suerd a straik apon him set;
Derffly to dede the ald Rukbé he draiff.

720 His twa sonnys chapyt amang the laiff.
In the castell be awentur thai yeid,
With twenty men; na ma chapyt that dreid.
The Lennox men, with thair gud lord at was,
Fra the castell thai said thai wald nocht pass:

725 For weill thai wyst it mycht nocht haldyn be,
On na lang tyme; forthi thus ordand he.
Erll Malcom tuk the houss, and kepyt that tyd.
Wallace wald nocht fra his fyrst purpos bid;
Instance he maid to this gud lord and wyss,

730 Fra thine to pass he suld on nakyn wyss,
Quhill he had tane Stirlyng the castell strang;

Trew men him tald he mycht nocht hald it lang.
Than Wallace thocht was maist on Makfadyane;
Off Scottis men he had slayne mony ane.
735 Wallace awowide, that he suld wrokyn be
On that rebald, or ellis tharfor to de.
Off tyrandry king Eduuard thocht him gud;
Law born he was, and off law simpill blud.
Thus Wallace was sar grewyt in his entent;
740 To this jornay rycht ernystfully he went.
At Stirlyng bryg assemlyt till hym rycht
Twa thowsand men, that worthi war and wycht.
Towart Argyll he bownyt him to ryd;
Dunkan off Lorn was thair trew sekyr gid.
745 Off ald Rukbé, the quhilk we spak off ayr,
Twa sonnys on lyff in Stirlyng lewit thair:
Quhen thai brethir consawit weill the rycht,
51 b This houss to hald that thai na langar mycht,
For causs quhi thai wantyt men and meit,
750 With erll Malcome thai kest thaim for to treit.
Grace off thair lyff, and thai that with thaim [was];
Gaiff our the houss, syne couth in Ingland pass,
On the thrid day that Wallace fra thaim raid.
With king Eduuard full mony yer thai baid;
755 In Brucis wer agayne come in Scotland;
Stirlyng to kepe the toune off thaim tuk on hand.
Mencione off Bruce is oft in Wallace buk;
To fend his rycht full mekill payne he tuk.
Quhar to suld I her off tary ma?
760 To Wallace furth now schortlye will I ga.

Dunkan off Lorne Gilmychall fra thaim send,
A spy to be, for he the contré kend.
Be our party was passit Straithfulan.
The small fute folk began to irk ilkane;

765 And horss, off fors, behuffyt for to faill.
     Than Wallace thocht that cumpany to waill.
     " Gud men," he said, '· this is nocht meit for ws;
     " In brokyn ray and we cum on thaim thus,
     " We may tak scaith, and harme our fayis bot small;
770 " To thaim in lik we may nocht semble all.
     " Tary we lang, a playne feild thai will get;
     " Apon thaim sone sa weill we may nocht set.
     " Part we mon leiff ws folowand for to be;
     " With me sall pass our power in to thre."
775 A hundyr fyrst till him selff he has tayne,
     Off westland men, was worthi knawin ilkane.
     To Schyr Jhon Graymc als mony ordand he,
     And fyve hundreth to Rychard off Lundye.
     In that part was Wallace off Ricardtoun;
780 In all gud deid he was ay redy boun.
     Fyve hundreth left, that mycht nocht with thaim ga,
     Supposs at thai to byd was wondyr wa.
     Thus Wallace ost began to tak the hicht;
     Our a montayne sone passit off thar sicht.
785 In Glendowchar thair spy met thaim agayn,
     With lord Cambell; than was our folk rycht fayn.
     At that metyng gret blithnes mycht be seyne;
     Thre hundreth he led that cruell was and keyne.
     He comford thaim, and bad thaim haiff no dreid:
790 " Yon bestly folk wantis wapynnys and weid;
     " Swne thai will fle, scharply and we persew."
     Be Louchdouchyr full sodeynly thaim drew.
     Than Wallace said; " A lyff all sall we ta;
     " For her nayne will fra his falow ga."
795 The spy he send, the entré for to se;
     Apon the moss a scurrour sone fand he.
Fol. 52 a To scour the land Makfadyane had him send;
     Out off Cragmor that day he thocht to wend.

Gylmychall fast apon him folowed thar,

800 With a gud suerd, that weill and scharply schar;
Maid quyt off him, at tithandis tald he nane:
The out spy thus was lost fra Makfadyhane.
Than Wallace ost apon thair fute thai lycht;
Thar horss thai left, thocht thai war neuir so wicht;

805 For moss and crag thai mycht no langar dre.
Than Wallace said; "Quha gangis best lat se."
Throuch out the moss delyuerly thai yeid;
Syne tuk the hals, quharoff thai had most dreid.
Endlang the schoir ay four in frownt thai past,

810 Quhill thai with in assemblit at the last.
Lord Cambell said; "We haiff chewyss this hauld;
"I trow to God thair wakynning sall be cauld.
"Her is na gait' to fle yone peple can,
"Bot rochis heich, and wattir depe and wan."

815 Auchtene hundreth off douchty men in deid
On the gret ost, but mar process, thai yeid,
Fechtand in frount, and mekill maistry maid;
On the frayt folk buskyt with outyn baid.
Rudly till ray thai ruschit thaim agayne;

820 Gret part off thaim wes men off mekill mayne.
Gud Wallace men sa stowtly can thaim ster,
The battaill on bak fyve akyr breid thai ber;
In to the stour feill tyrandis gert thai kneill.
Wallace in hand had a gud staff off steyll;

825 Quhom euir he hyt to ground brymly thaim bar;
Romde him about a large rude and mar.
Schir Jhon the Grayme in deid was rycht worthy;
Gud Cambell als, and Rychard off Lundy,
Adam Wallace, and Robert Boid in feyr,

830 Amang thair fayis, quhar deidis was sald full der.
The felloun stour was awfull for to se;
Macfadyane than so gret debait maid he,

With Yrage men, hardy and curageous,
The stalwart stryff rycht hard and peralous;

835 Boundance of blud fra woundis wid and wan;
Stekit to deid on ground lay mony man.
The ferfast thar ynewch off fechtyn fand;
Twa houris large into the stour thai stand,
At Jop him selff weill wyst nocht quha suld wyn.

840 Bot Wallace men wald nocht in sowndyr twyn;
Till help thaim selff thai war off hardy will;
Off Yrage blud full hardely thai spill;
With feyll fechtyn maid sloppys throuch the thrang.

Fol. 52 b On the fals part our wicht wer men sa dang,

845 That thai to byd mycht haiff no langar mycht.
The Irland folk than maid thaim for the flycht;
On craggis clam, and sum in wattir flett:
Twa thousand thar drownyt with outyn lett.
Born Scottis men baid still in to the feild;

850 Kest wappynys [fra] thaim, and on thar kneis kneild:
With petouss woice thai cryt apon Wallace,
For Goddis saik to tak thaim in his grace.
Grewyt he was; bot rewth off thaim he had,
Resauit thaim fair with contenance full sad.

855 " Off our awne blud we suld haiff gret pete;
" Luk yhe sla nane off Scottis will yoldyn be.
" Off outland men lat nane chaip with the liff."
Makfadyane fled, for all his felloun stryff,
On till a cave, within a clyfft off stayne,

860 Wndyr Cragmor, with fyftene is he gayne.
Dunkan off Lorn his leyff at Wallace ast;
On Makfadyane with worthi men he past.
He grantyt him to put thaim all to ded:
Thai left nane quyk, syne brocht Wallace his hed;

865 Apon a sper throuch out the feild it bar.
The lord Cambell syne hynt it by the har;

Heich in Cragmor he maid it for to stand,
Steild on a stayne for honour off Irland.
The blessit men, that was off Scotland borne,
870 Fwnde at his faith Wallace gert thaim be sworn;
Restorit thaim to thar landis, but less :
He leit sla nayne that wald cum till his pes.
Eftir this deid in Lorn syne couth he fayr;
Reullyt the land had beyne in mekill cayr.

875   In Archatan a consell he gert cry,
Quhar mony man socht till his senyory.
All Lorn he gaiff till Duncan, at was wicht,
And bad him hald [in] Scotland with the rycht :
" And thow sall weill bruk this in heretage.
880 " Thi brothir sone at London has grettar wage ;
" Yeit will he cum. he sall his landis haiff.
" I wald tyne nayne that rychtwisnes mycht saiff."
Mony trew Scot to Wallace couth persew :
At Archatan fra feill strenthis thai drew.
885 A gud knycht come, and with him men sexté ;
He had beyn oft in mony strang jeperté
With Inglissmen, and sonyeid nocht adeill.
Ay fra thar faith he fendyt him full weill ;
Kepyt him fre, thocht king Eduuard had suorne ;
53 a 890 Schir Jhon Ramsay, that rychtwyss ayr was borne
Off Ouchterhous, and othir landis was lord,
And schirreff als, as my buk will record ;
Off nobill blud, and alss haill ancestré ;
Contenyt weill with worthi chewalré.
895 In till Straithern that lang tyme he had beyne,
At gret debait agaynys his enemyss keyne ;
Rycht wichtly wan his lewing in to wer :
Till him and his Sotheroun did mekill der :
Weill eschewit. and sufferyt gret distress.

900 His sone was calld the flour of courtlyness;
As witnes weill in to the schort tretty
Eftir the Bruce, quha redis in that story.
He rewllit weill bathe in to wer and pess;
Alexander Ramsay to nayme he hecht, but less.
905 Quhen it wes wer, till armes he him kest;
Wndir the croun he wes ane off the best:
In tyme off pees till courtlynes he yeid;
Bot to gentrice he tuk nayne othir heid.
Quhat gentill man had nocht with Ramsay beyne;
910 Off courtlynes thai cownt him nocht a preyne.
Fredome and treuth he had as men would ass;
Sen he begane na bettyr squier was.
Roxburch hauld he wan full manfully;
Syne held it lang, quhill tratouris tresonably
915 Causit his dede, I can nocht tell yow how;
Off sic thingis I will ga by as now.
I haiff had blayme to say the suthfastnes;
Tharfor I will bot lychtly ryn that cace,
Bot it be thing that playnly sclanderit is;
920 For sic I trew thai suld deyme me no myss.
Off gud Alexander as now I spek no mar.
His fadyr come, as I tald off befor:
Wallace off hym rycht full gud comford hais;
For weill he coud do gret harmyng till his fais.
925 In wer he was rycht mekill for to pryss;
Besy and trew, bath sobyr, wicht, and wyss.
A gud prelat als to Archatan socht;
Off his lordschip as than he brukyt nocht.
This worthi clerk, cummyn off hie lynage,
930 Off Synclar blude, nocht fourty yer off age,
Chosyne he was be the Papis consent;
Off Dunkell lord was maid with gud entent.
Bot Inglissmen, that Scotland gryppit all,

Off benyfice thai leit him bruk bot small.
935 Quhen he saw weill tharfor he mycht nocht mwte,
53 b To saiff his lyff thre yer he duelt in But;
　　Leifyde as he mycht, and kepyt ay gud part,
　　Wndir saifté off Jamys than lord Stewart,
　　Till gud Wallace, quhilk Scotland wan with payne,
940 Restord this lord till his leyffing agayne;
　　And mony ma, that lang had beyne ourthrawin,
　　Wallace thaim put rychtwisly to thair awin.
　　The small ost alss, the quhilk I spak off ayr,
　　In to the hycht that Wallace lewyt thar,
945 Come to the feild quhar Makfadyane had beyne,
　　Tuk at was left, baithe weid and wapynnys scheyne;
　　Throw Lorn syne past als gudly as thai can:
　　Off thair nowmyr thai had nocht lost a man.
　　On the fyft day thai wan till Archatan,
950 Quhar Wallace baid with gud men mony ane.
　　He welcummyt thaim apon a gudly wyss,
　　And said thai war rycht mekill for to pryss.
　　All trew Scottis he honourit in to wer;
　　Gaiff that he wan, hym selff kepyt no ger.

955　　Quhen Wallace wald no langar soiorn thar,
　　Fra Archattan throu out the land thai far
　　Towart Dunkell, with gud men off renoun;
　　His maist thocht than was haill on Sanct Jhonstoune.
　　He calld Ramsai, that gud knycht off gret waill;
960 Sadly awysyt, besocht him off consaill:
　　" Off Saynct Jhonstoun now haiff I in remembrance;
　　" Thar I haiff beyne, and lost men apon chance:
　　" Bot ay for ane we gert ten off thaim de.
　　" And yeit me think that is no mendis to me;
965 " I wald assay, off this land or we gang,
　　" And lat thaim witt thai occupy her with wrang."

Than Ramsay said; 'That toune thai may nocht kep
'The wallis ar laych, supposs the dyk be depe.
'Ye haiff enewch, that sall thaim cummyr sa;
970 'Fyll wp the dyk, that we may playnly ga
'In haill battaill, a thowsand our at anys:
'Fra this power thai sall nocht hald yon wanys.'
Wallace was glaid that he sic comfort maid;
Furth talkand thus on to Dunkell thai raid.
975 Four dayis thar thai lugyt with plesance,
Quhill tyme thai had forseyne thair ordinance.
Ramsay gert byg strang bestials off tre,
Be gud wrychtis the best in that cuntré:
Quhan thai war wrocht, betaucht thaim men to leid
980 The wattir doun, quhill thai come to that steid.
Schir Jhon Ramsay rycht gudly was thair gid,
Fol. 54 a Rewillyt thaim weill at his will for to bid.
The gret ost than about the willage past;
With erd and stayne thai fillit dykis fast.
985 Flaikis thai laid on temyr lang and wicht;
A rowme passage to the wallis thaim dycht.
Feill bestials rycht starkly wp thai raiss;
Gud men of armys sone till assailye gais.
Schir Jhon the Grayme, and Ramsay that was wicht.
990 The turat bryg segyt with all thair mycht;
And Wallace selff, at mydsid off the toyne,
With men of armys thai was to bargane bown.
The Sotheron men maid gret defens that tid,
With artailye, that felloune was to bid.
995 With awblaster, gaynye, and stanys fast,
And hand gunnys rycht brymly out thai cast;
Pwnyeid with speris men off armys scheyn.
The worthi Scotts, that cruell war and keyne,
At hand strakis fra thai to gidder met,
1000 With Sotheroun blud thair wapynnys sone thai wet.

Yeit Inglissmen, that worthi war in wer,
In to the stour rycht bauldly can thaim ber.
Bot all for nocht awailyeid thaim thar deid;
The Scottis throw force apon thaim in thai yeid.
1005 A thousand men our wallis yeid hastely;
In to the toun raiss hidwiss noyis and cry.
Ramsay and Graym the turat yet has wown,
And entrit in, quhar gret striff has begown.
A trew squier, quhilk Rwan hecht be nayme,
1010 Come to the salt, with gud Schyr Jhon the Grayme;
Thretty with him off men that prewit weill,
Amang thair fais with wapynnys stiff off steill.
Quhen at the Scottis semblyit on athir sid,
Na Sotheroun was that mycht thair dynt abid.
1015 Twa thousand sone, was fulyied vnder feit,
Off Sotheroun blud, lay stekit in the streit.
Schir Jhon Sewart saw weill the toune was tynt;
Tuk him to flycht, and wald no langar stynt;
In a lycht barge, and with him men sexté,
1020 The water doun, socht succour at Dundé.
Wallace baid still, quhill the ferd day at morn;
And left nane thar that war off Ingland born.
Riches thai gat off gold and othir gud;
Plenyst the toun agayne with Scottis blud.
1025 Rwan he left thair capteyn for to be;
In heretage gaiff him office to fee
Off all Straithern, and schirreiff off the toun;
Syne in the north gud Wallace maid him boune.
In Abyrdeyn he gert a consaill cry,
1030 Trew Scottis men suld semble hastely.
Till Cowper he raid to wesy that abbay;
The Ingliss abbot fra thine was fled away.
Bischop Synclar, with out langar abaid,
Met thaim at Glammyss, syne furth with thaim he raid.

L

1035 In till Breichyn thai lugyt all that nycht;
      Syne on the morn Wallace gert graith thaim rycht,
      Displayed on breid the baner off Scotland
      In gud aray, with noble men at hand;
      Gert playnly cry, that sawfté suld be nayne
1040 Off Sotheroun blud, quhar thai mycht be ourtayn.
      In playne battaill throuch out the Mernyss thai rid.
      The Inglissmen, at durst thaim nocht abid,
      Befor the ost full ferdly furth thai fle
      Till Dwnottar, a snuk within the se.
1045 Na ferrar thai mycht wyn out off the land.
      Thai semblit thar quhill thai war four thousand;
      To the kyrk rane, wend gyrth for till haiff tayne,
      The laiff ramaynd apon the roch off stayne.
      The byschope than began tretty to ma
1050 Thair lyffis to get, out off the land to ga.
      Bot thai war rad, and durst nocht weill affy;
      Wallace in fyr gert set all haistely,
      Brynt wp the kyrk, and all that was tharin,
      Atour the roch the laiff ran with gret dyn.
1055 Sum hang on craggis rycht dulfully to de,
      Sum lap, sum fell, sum floteryt in the se.
      Na Sotheroun on lyff was lewyt in that hauld,
      And thaim with in thai brynt in powdir cauld.
      Quhen this was done, feill fell on kneis doun,
1060 At the byschop askit absolutioun.
      Than Wallace lewch, said; " I forgiff yow all;
      " Ar ye wer men, rapentis for sa small?
      " Thai rewid nocht ws in to the toun off Ayr;
      " Our trew barrownis quhen that thai hangyt thar."

1065   Till Abyrdeyn than haistely thai pass,
      Quhar Inglissmen besyly flittand was.
      A hundreth schippis, that ruther bur and ayr,
      To turss thair gud, in hawyn was lyand thar.

Bot Wallace ost come on thaim sodeynlye;
1070 Thar chapyt nane off all that gret menyhe;
Bot feill serwandis, in thaim lewyt nane.
. 55 a At ane eb se the Scottis is on thaim gayne;
Tuk out the ger, syne set the schippys in fyr:
The men on land thai bertynyt bayne and lyr.
1075 Yeid nane away bot preistis, wyffis and barnys;
Maid thai debait, thai chapyt nocht but harmys.
In to Bowchane Wallace maid him to ryd,
Quhar lord Bewmound was ordand for to bid.
Erll he was maid off bot schort tyme befor;
1080 He brukit [it] nocht for all his bustous schor.
Quhen he wyst weill that Wallace cummand was,
He left the land, and couth to Slanys pass;
And syne be schip in Ingland fled agayne.
Wallace raid throw the northland in to playne.
1085 At Crummadé feill Inglissmen thai slew.
The worthi Scottis till hym thus couth persew.
Raturnd agayne, and come till Abirdeyn,
With his blith ost, apon the Lammess ewyn;
Stablyt the land, as him thocht best suld be.
1090 Syne with ane ost he passit to Dundé,
Gert set a sege about the castell strang.
I leyff thaim thar, and forthir we will gang.

Schir Amhar Wallang haistit him full fast,
In till Ingland with his haill houshald past;
1095 Bothwell he left, was Murrays heretage,
And tuk him than bot till King Eduuardis wage:
Thus his awne land forsuk for euirmar;
Off Wallace deid gret tithandis tald he thar.
Alss Englissmen sair murnyt in thar mude,
1100 Had lossyt her bathe lyff, landis, and gud.
Eduuard as than couth nocht in Scotland fair;

Bot Kertyingame, that was his tresorair,
With him a lord, than erll was off Waran,
He chargyt thaim, with nowmeris mony ane
1105 Rycht weill beseyn, in Scotland for to ryd.
At Stirlyng still he ordand thaim to bid,
Quhill he mycht cum with ordinance off Ingland:
Scotland agayne he thocht to tak in hand.
This ost past furth, and had bot litill dreid;
1110 The erle Patrik rasauit thaim at Tweid.
Malice he had at gud Wallace befor
Lang tyme by past, and than incressyt mor:
Bot throuch a cass that hapnyt off his wyff,
Dunbar scho held fra him in to thair striff,
1115 Throuch the supplé off Wallace in to playne:
Bot he be meyne gat his castell agayne
Lang tyme or than, and yeit he couth nocht cess;
Agayne Wallace he prewit in mony press;
With Inglissmen suppleit thaim at his mycht.
Fol. 55 b 1120 Contrar Scotland thai wrocht full gret wnrycht.
Thar mustir than was awfull for to se;
Off sechtand men thousandis thai war sexté.
To Stirlyng past, or thai likit to bid,
To erll Malcome a sege thai laid that tid;
1125 And thocht to kep the commaund off thar king:
Bot gud Wallace wrocht for ane othir thing.
Dundé he left, and maid a gud chyftane,
With twa thousand, to kepe that houss off stayne,
Off Angwiss men, and duellaris off Dundé;
1130 The samyn nycht till Sanct Jhonstoun went he.
Apon the morn till Schirreff mur he raid;
And thar a quhill, in gud aray, thai baid.
Schir Jhon the Grayme, and Ramsay that was wich
He said to thaim; "This is my purpos rycht;
1135 "Our mekill it is to proffer thaim battaill

" Apon a playne feild, bot we haiff sum awaill."
Schir Jhon the Grayme said; ' We haiff wndirtayn,
' With less power, sic thing that weill is gayn.'
Than Wallace said; " Quhar sic thing cummys off neid,
1140 " We suld thank God that makis ws for to speid.
" Bot ner the bryg my purposs is to be,
" And wyrk for thaim sum suttell jeperté."
Ramsay ansuerd : ' The brig we may kepe weill;
' Off way about Sotheroun has litill feill.'
1145 Wallace sent Jop the battaill for to set,
The Twysday next to fetch with outyn let.
On Setterday on to the bryg thai raid,
Off gud playne burd was weill and junctly maid;
Gert wachis wait that nane suld fra thaim pass.
1150 A wricht he tuk, the suttellast at thar was,
And ordand him to saw the burd in twa,
Be the myd streit, that nane mycht our it ga;
On charnaill bandis nald it full fast and sone,
Syne fyld with clay as na thing had beyne done.
1155 The tothir end he ordand for to be,
How it suld stand on thre rowaris off tre,
Quhen ane war out, that the laiff doun suld fall;
Him selff wndyr he ordand thar with all,
Bownd on the trest in a creddill to sit,
1160 To louss the pyne quhen Wallace leit him witt.
Bot with a horn, quhen it was tyme to be,
In all the ost suld no man blaw bot he.
The day approchit off the gret battaill;
The Inglissmen for power wald nocht faill.
1165 Ay sex thai war agayne ane off Wallace;
Fyfty thousand maid thaim to battaill place.
. 56 a The ramaynand baid at the castell still;
Baithe feild and houss thai thocht to tak at will.
The worthi Scottis, apon the tothir side,

1170 The playne feild tuk, on fute maid thaim to bid.
Hew Kertyngayme the wantgard ledis he,
With twenty thousand off likly men to se.
Thretty thousand the erll off Waran had;
Bot he did than as the wyssman him bad;

1175 All the fyrst ost befor him our was send.
Sum Scottis men, that weill the maner kend,
Bade Wallace blaw, and said thai war enew.
He haistyt nocht, bot sadly couth persew,
Quhill Warans ost thik on the bryg he saw.

1180 Fra Jop the horn he hyntyt and couth blaw
Sa asprely, and warned gud Jhon Wricht:
The rowar out he straik with gret slycht;
The laiff yeid doun, quhen the pynnys out gais.
A hidwyss cry amang the peple raiss;

1185 Bathe horss and men in to the wattir fell.
The hardy Scottis, that wald na langar duell,
Set on the laiff with strakis sad and sar,
Off thaim thar our as than souerit thai war.
At the forbreist thai prewit hardely,

1190 Wallace and Grayme, Boid, Ramsay, and Lundy;
All in the stour fast fechtand face to face.
The Sotheron ost bak rerit off that place
At thai fyrst tuk, fyve akyr breid and mar.
Wallace on fute a gret scharp sper he bar;

1195 Amang the thikest off the press he gais.
On Kertyngaym a straik chosyn he hais
In the byrnes, that polyst was full brycht.
The punyeand hed the plattis persyt rycht,
Throuch the body stekit him but reskew;

1200 Derffly to dede that chyftane was adew.
Baithe man and horss at that strak he bar doun.
The Ingliss ost, quhilk war in battaill boun,
Comfort thai lost quhen thair chyftayne was slayn;

And mony ane to fle began in playne.
205 Yeit worthi men baid still in to the sted,
    Quhill ten thousand was brocht on to thair dede.
    Than fled the laiff, and mycht no langar bid;
    Succour thai socht on mony diuerss sid,
    Sum est, sum west, and sum fled to the north.
210 Sewyn thousand large at anys flottryt in Forth,
56 b Plungyt the depe, and drownd with out mercy;
    Nayne left on lyff off all that feill menyhe.
    Off Wallace ost na man was slayne off waill,
    Bot Androw Murray, in to that strang battaill.
215 The south part than, saw at thar men was tynt,
    Als fersly fled as fyr dois off the flynt.
    The place thai left, castell, and Stirlyng toune;
    Towart Dunbar in gret haist maid thaim boune.
    Quhen Wallace ost had won that feild throuch mycht,
220 Tuk wp the bryg, and loussit gud Jhone Wricht;
    On the flearis syne folowed wondyr fast.
    Erll Malcom als out off the castell past,
    With Lennox men, to stuff the chace gud speid.
    Ay be the way thai gert feill Sotheroun bleid;
225 In the Torwod thai gert full mony de.
    The erll off Waran, that can full fersly fle,
    With Corspatrik, that graithly was his gyd,
    On changit horss throuch out the land thai rid,
    Strawcht to Dunbar, bot few with thaim thai led;
230 Mony was slayne our sleuthfully at fled.
    The Scottis horss that had rown wondyr lang,
    Mony gaiff our, that mycht no forthyr gang.
    Wallace and Grayme euir to giddyr baid;
    At Hathyntoun full gret slauchtir thai maid
235 Off Inglissmen, quhen thair horss tyryt had.
    Quhen Ramsay come, gud Wallace was full glad;
    With him was Boid, and Richard off Lundy,
    Thre thousand haill was off gud chewalry;

And Adam als Wallace off Ricardtoune,
1240 With erll Malcome, thai fand at Hathyntoune.
The Scottis men on slauchtir taryt was;
Quhill to Dunbar the twa chyftanys couth pass,
Full sitfully, for thar gret contrar cass.
Wallace folowed till thai gat in that place.
1245 Off thair best men, and Kertyngaym off renoune,
Twenty thousand was dede but redemptioune.
Besyd Beltoun Wallace raturnd agayn,
To folow mar as than was bot in wayn.

In Hathyntoun lugyng thai maid that nycht;
1250 Apon the morn to Stirling passit rycht.
Assumptioun day off Marye fell this cass;
Ay lowyt be our lady off hir grace!
Connoyar offt scho was to gud Wallace,
And helpyt him in mony syndry place.
1255 Wallace in haist, sone efftir this battaill,
A gret aith tuk off all the barrons haill,
That with gud will wald cum till his presens;
He hecht thaim als to bid at thar defens.
Fol. 57 a Schir Jhon Menteth, was than off Aran lord,
1260 Till Wallace come, and maid a playne record;
With witnes thar be his ayth he him band,
Lauta to kep to Wallace and Scotland.
Quha with fre will till rycht wald nocht apply,
Wallace with force pwnyst [thaim] rygorusly;
1265 Part put to dede, part set in prysone strang;
Gret word off him throuch bathe thir regiouns rang.
Dundé thai gat sone be a schort treté,
Bot for thar lywes, and fled away be se.
Ingliss capdans, that houss had in to hand,
1270 Left castellis fre, and fled out off the land.
Within ten dayis efftir this tyme was gayne,
Ingliss captanys in Scotland left was nayne,

Except Berweik, and Roxburch castell wicht;
Yeit Wallace thocht to bryng thai to the rycht.
1275 That tyme thar was a worthi trew barroun,
To nayme he hecht gud Cristall off Cetoun.
In Jedwort wod for saifigard he had beyne,
Agayne Sotheroun full weill he couth opteyn.
In wtlaw oyss he lewit thar but let;
1280 Edruard couth nocht fra Scottis faith him get.
Herbottell fled fra Jedwort castell wicht,
Towart Ingland; thar Cetoun met him rycht.
With fourty men Cristall in bargane baid
Agayne aucht scor, and mekill mastir maid;
1285 Slew that captane, and mony cruell man;
Full gret ryches in that jornay he wan,
Houshald and gold, as thai suld pass away,
The quhilk befor thai kepit mony day.
Jedwort thai tuk; and Ruwan lewit he,
1290 At Wallace will captane off it to be.
Bauld Cetoun syne to Lothiane made repair:
In this storye ye ma her off him mair,
And in to Bruce quha likis for to rede;
He was with him in mony cruell deid.
1295 Gud Wallace than full sadly can dewyss
To rewill the land with worthi men and wyss;
Captans he maid, and schirreffis that was gud,
Part off his kyn, and off trew othir blud.   .
His der cusyng in Edynburgh ordand he,
1300 The trew Crawfurd, that ay was full worthé,
Kepar off it, with noble men at wage;
In Mannuell than he had gud heretage.
Scotland was fre, that lang in baill had beyne,
Throw Wallace won fra our fals enemys keyn.
1305 Gret gouernour in Scotland he couth ryng,
Wayttand a tyme to get his rychtwiss king

Fra Ingliss men, that held him in bandoune,
Lang wrangwysly fra his awn rychtwis croun.

EXPLICIT LIBER SEPTIMUS,
ET INCIPIT OCTAVUS.

BUKE AUCHT.

Fywe monethis thus Scotland stud in gud rest;
A consell cryit, thaim thocht it wes the best
In Sanct Jhonstoun at it suld haldyn be;
Assemblit thar clerk, barown, and bowrugie.
5 Bot Corspatrik wald nocht cum at thair call,
Baid in Dunbar, and maid scorn at thaim all.
Thai spak off him feill wordis in that parlyment.
Than Wallace said; "Will ye her to consent,
" Forgyff him fre all thing that is bypast;
10 " Sa he will cum and grant he has trespast,
" Fra this tyme furth kepe lawta till our croune?"
Thai grant tharto, clerk, burgess, and barroune:
With haill consent thar writyng till him send;
Rycht lawly thus till him thai thaim commend;
15 Besocht him fair, as a peyr off the land,
To cum and tak sum gouernaill on hand.
Lychtly he lowch, in scorn as it had beyn,
And said; "He had sic message seyldyn seyne,
" That Wallace now as gouernowr sall ryng:
20 " Her is gret faute off a gud prince or kyng.
" That king off Kyll I can nocht wndirstand;
" Off him I held neuir a fur off land.
" That bachiller trowis, for fortoun schawis hyr quhell,
" Thar with to lest; it sall nocht lang be weill.
25 " Bot to yow, lordis, and ye will wndirstand,
" I mak yow wyss, I aw to mak na band.

" Als fre I am in this regioun to ryng,

" Lord off myn awne, as euyr was prince or king.

" In Ingland als gret part off land I haiff;

30 " Manrent tharoff thar will no man me craiff.

" Quhat will ye mar?   I warne yow, I am fre;

" For your somoundis ye get no mar off me."

Till Sanct Jhonstone this wryt he send agayne,

Befor the lordis was manifest in playne.

35 Quhen Wallace herd the erll sic ansuer mais,

A gret hate ire throu curage than he tais;

For weyll he wyst thar suld be bot a king

Off this regioun, at anys for to ryng;

" A king off Kyll!" for that he callyt Wallace.

40 " Lordis," he said, " this is ane wncouth cace.

" Be he sufferyt, we haiff war than it was."

Thus raiss he wp, and maid him for to pass.

" God has ws thólyt to do so for the laiff:

Fol. 58 a " In lyff or dede, in faith, him sall we haiff,

45 " Or ger him grant quhom he haldis for his lord;

" Or ellis war schaym in story to racord.

" I wow to God, with eyss he sall nocht be

" In to this realme, bot ane off ws sall de;

" Less than he cum, and knaw his rychtwiss king.

50 " In this regioun weill bathe we sall nocht ryng.

" His lychtly scorn he sall rapent full sor,

" Bot power faill, or I sall end tharfor.

" Sen in this erd is ordand me no rest,

" Now God be juge, the rycht he kennys best."

55 At that consaill langar he tary nocht,

With twa hundreth fra Sanct Jhonston he socht;

To the consaill maid instans or he yeid,

Thai suld conteyn, and off him haiff na dreid.

" I am bot ane, and for gud causs I ga."

60 Towart Kyngorn the gaynest way thai ta;

Apon the morn atour Forth south thai past;
On this wyage thai haistit wondyr fast.
Robert Lauder at Mussilburgh met Wallace,
Fra Inglissmen he kepyt weill his place;
65 Couth nayne him trete, knycht, squier, nor lord,
With king Eduuard to be at ane accord.
On erll Patrik to pass he was full glaid;
Sum said befor the Bass he wald haiff haid.
Gud men come als with Crystell off Cetoun;
70 Than Wallace was four hundreth off renoun.
A squier Lyll, that weill that cuntré knew,
With twenty men to Wallace couth persew,
Besyd Lyntoun; and to thaim tald he than,
The erll Patrik, with mony likly man,
75 At Coburns peth he had his gaderyng maid,
And to Dunbar wald cum with outyn baid.
Than Lawder said, " It war the best, think me,
" Faster to pass, in Dunbar or he be."
Wallace ansuerd; ' We may at laysar ryd;
80 ' With yon power he thinkis bargane to bid.
' And off a thing ye sall weill wndrestand,
' A hardyar lord is nocht in to Scotland:
' Mycht he be maid trew stedfast till a king,
' Be wit and force he can do mekill thing:
85 ' Bot willfully he likis to tyne him sell.'
Thus raid thai furth, and wald na langar duell,
Be est Dunbar, quhar men him tald on cass,
How erll Patrik was warnyt off Wallace:
Ner Ennerweik chesyt a feild at waill,
90 With nyne hundreth off likly men to waill.
Four hundreth was with Wallace in the rycht,
And sone onon approchit to thair sicht.
Gret fawte thar was of gud trety betweyn,
ol. 58 b To mak concord, and that full sone was seyne.

95 With out raherss off actioun in that tid,
   On athir part to gydder fast thai rid.
   The stour was strang, and wondyr peralous,
   Contenyt làng with dedis chewalrous;
   Mony thar deit off cruell Scottis blud.
100 Off this trety the mater is nocht gud;
   Tharfor I cess to tell the destructioune;
   Peté it was, and all off a natioune.
   Bot erll Patrik the feild left at the last,
   Rycht few with him; to Coburns peth thai past;
105 Agrewit sar that his men thus were tynt.

   Wallace raturnd, and wald no langar stynt,
   Towart Dunbar, quhar suthfast men him tald,
   Na purweance was left in to that hald,
   Nor men off fens; all had beyne with thair lord.
110 Quhen Wallace hard the sekyr trew record,
   Dunbar he tuk all haill at his bandown;
   Gaiff it to kepe to Crystell off Cetoun,
   Quhilk stuffit it weill with men and gud wictall.
   Apon the morn, Wallace that wald nocht faill,
115 With thre hundreth, to Coburns peth he socht:
   Erll Patrik wschyt, for bid him wald he nocht.
   Sone to the park Wallace a range has set;
   Till Bonkill wood Corspatrik fled but let,
   And out off it till Noram passit he.
120 Quhen Wallace saw it mycht na bettir be,
   Till Caudstreym went and lugit him on Tweid.
   Erll Patrik than, in all haist can him speid,
   And passit by, or Wallace power raiss;
   With out restyng, in Atrik forrest gais.
125 Wallace folowed, bot he wald nocht assaill;
   A rang to mak as than it mycht nocht waill:
   Our few he had, the strenth was thik and strang,

Sewyn myill on breid, and tharto twyss so lang.
In till Gorkhelm erll Patrik leiffit at rest.
130 For mar power Wallace past in the west.
Erll Patrik than him graithit hastelye,
In Ingland past to get him thar supplye:
Out throuch the land rycht ernystfully couth pass;
Tald Anton Beik that Wallace cummand was.
135 Wallace him put out off Glaskow befor,
And slew Persye; thair malice was the mor.
The byschope Beik gert sone gret power ryss,
Northummyrland apon ane awfull wyss.
Than ordand Bruce in Scotland for to pass,
140 To wyn his awne; bot ill dissauit he was:
Thai gart him trow that Wallace was rabell,
And thocht to tak the kynryk to hym sel.
Fol. 59 a Full fals thai war, and euir yeit has beyn;
Lawta and trouth was ay in Wallace seyn;
145 To fend the rycht all that he tuk on hand,
And thocht to bryng the Bruce fre till his land.
Off this mater as now I tary nocht.
With strang power Sotheroun to gidder socht;
Fra Owys watter assemblit haill to Tweid.
150 Thar land ost was thretty thousand in deid.
Off Tynnys mouth send schippis be the se,
To kep Dunbar, at nayne suld thaim supplé.
Erll Patrik, with twenty thousand but lett,
Befor Dunbar a stalwart sege he sett.
155 The bischope Beik and Robert Bruce baid still,
With ten thousand, at Noram at thair will.
Wallace be this, that fast was lauborand,
In Lothyane com witht gud men fyve thowsand,
Rycht weill beseyn, all in to armyss brycht;
160 Thocht to reskew the Cetoun bauld and wycht.
Undyr Yhester that fyrst nycht lugit he.

Hay com till him with a gud chewalré;
In Duns forest all that tyme he had beyne;
The cummyng thar off Sotheroun he had seyne.
165 Fyfty he had off besy men in wer;
Thai tald Wallace off Patrikis gret affer.
Hay said; "Forsuth, and ye mycht him our set,
" Power agayne rycht sone he mycht nocht get,
" My consaill is, that we giff him battaill."
170 He thankit him off comfort and consaill,
And said; ' Freynd Hay, in this causs that I wend,
' Sa that we wyn, I rek nocht for till end.
' Rycht suth it is that anys we mon de:
' In to the rycht quha suld in terrour be?'
175 Erll Patrik than a messynger gert pass,
Tald Anton Beik that Wallace cummand was.
Off this tithingis the byschope was full glaid,
Amendis off him full fayne he wald haiff haid.
But mar prolong throuch Lammermur thai raid,
180 Ner the Spot mur in buschement still he baid;
As erll Patrik thaim ordand for to be.
Wallace off Beik wnwarnyt than was he.
Yeit he befor was nocht haisty in deid;
Bot than he put bathe him and his in dreid.
185 Apon swyft hors scurrouris past betweyn.
The cummyng than off erll Patrik was seyn:
The houss he left, and to the mur is gayn,
A playne feild thar with hiss ost he has tayn.
Fol. 59 b Gud Cetoun syne wschet with few menyhe;
190 Part off his men in till Dunbar left he;
To Wallace raid, was on the rychtwyss sid;
In gud aray to the Spot mur thai ryd.
Sum Scottis dred, the erll sa mony wass,
Twenty thousand agayn sa few, to pass.
195 Quhen Jop persauit, he bad Wallace suld bid:

" Tyne nocht thir men, bot to sum strenth ye ryd,
" And I sall pass to get yow power mar;
" Thir ar our gud thus lychtly for to war."
Than Wallace said; ' In trewth I will nocht fle
200 ' For four off his, ay ane quhill I may be.
' We ar our ner, sic purpos for to tak;
' A danger chace thai mycht vpon ws mak.
' Her is twenty, with this power, to day,
' Wald him assay, supposs I war away.
205 ' Mony thai ar, for Goddis luff be we strang;
' Yon Sotheron folk in stour will nocht bid lang.'

The brym battaill, braithly on athir sid,
Gret rerd thar raiss all sammyn quhar thai ryd.
The sayr semblé, quhen thai to gidder met,
210 Feill strakis thar sadly on athir set.
Punyeand speris throuch plattis persit fast;
Mony off hors to the ground doun thai cast;
Saidlys thai teym off horss bot maistris, thar;
Off the soúth sid fyve thousand doun thai bar.
215 Gud Wallace ost the formast kumraid sa,
Quhill the laiff was in will away to ga.
Erll Patrik baid, sa cruell off entent,
At all his ost tuk off him hardiment.
Agayne Wallace in mony stour was he.
220 Wallace knew weill, that his men wald nocht fle
For na power that leiffand was in lyff,
Quhill thai in heill mycht ay be ane for fyfe.
In that gret stryff mony was handlyt hate;
The feill dyntis, the cruell hard debait,
225 The fers steking, maid mony grewous wound,
Apon the erd the blud did till abound.
All Wallace ost in till a cumpaiss baid;
Quhar sa thai turnd full gret slauchtyr thai maid.

M

Wallace and Grayme, and Ramsay full worthi,
230 The bauld Cetoun, and Richard off Lundy,
[And] Adam, als Wallace, off Ricardtoun,
Bathe Hay and Lyll, with gud men off renoun,
Boyde, Bercla, Byrd, and Lauder, that was wycht,
Feill Inglissmen derffly to ded thai dycht.
235 Bot erll Patrik full fersly faucht agayn;
Fol. 60 a Throuch his awin hand he put mony to payn.
Our men on him thrang forthwart in to thra.
Maide throuch his ost feill sloppis to and fra.
The Inglissmen began playnly to fle;
240 Than byschope Beik full sodeynly thai se;
And Robert Bruce, contrar his natiff men:
Wallace was wa, fra tyme he couth him ken.
Off Brucis deid he was agrewit far mar
Than all the laiff that day at semblit thar.
245 The gret buschement at anys brak on breid,
Ten thousand haill that douchty war in deid,
The flearis than with erll Patrik relefd
To fecht agayn, quhar mony war myscheifd.
Quhen Wallace knew the buschement brokyn was,
250 Out off the feild on hors thai thocht to pass.
Bot he saw weill his ost sownd in thair weid;
He thoucht to fray the formast or thai yeid.
The new cummyn ost befor thaim semblit thar,
On athir sid with strakis sad and sar.
255 The worthi Scottis sa fersly faucht agayne,
Off Antonys men rycht mony haiff thai slayne:
Bot that terand so wsit was in wer,
On Wallace ost thai did full mekill der.
And the bauld Bruce sa cruelly wrocht he,
260 Throuch strenth off hand feill Scottis he gert de.
To resist Bruce Wallace him pressit fast,
Bot Inglissmen so thik betuixt thaim past:

And erll Patrik, in all the haist he moucht,
Throuch out the stour to Wallace sone he socht;
265 On the thé pess a felloun strak him gaiff,
Kerwit the plait, with his scharp groundyn glaiff,
Throuch all the stuff, and woundyt him sumdeill.
Bot Wallace thocht he suld be wengit weill,
Folowed on him, and a straik etlyt fast.
270 Than ane Mawthland rakless betwix thaim past:
Apon the heid gud Wallace has him tane,
Throuch hat and brawn in sondyr bryst the bane;
Dede at that straik doun to the ground him drawe.
Thus Wallace was disseuiryt fra the lawe
275 Off hys gud men, amang thaim him allane.
About him socht feill enemyss mony ane,
Stekit his horss; to ground behufid him lycht,
To fend him sclff as wysly as he mycht.
The worthy Scottis, that mycht na langar bid,
280 With sair hartis out off the feild thai ryd.
With thaim in feyr thai wend Wallace had beyne,
On fute he was amang his enemyss keyn.
Fol. 60 b Gud rowme he maid about him in to breid;
With his gud suerd that helpyt him in neid.
285 Was nayne sa strang, that gat off him a strak,
Eftir agayne maid neuir a Scot to waik.
Erll Patrik than, that had gret crafft in wer,
With speris ordand gud Wallace doun to ber.
Anew thai tuk was haill in to the feild;
290 Till him thai yeid, thocht he suld haiff no beild;
On athir sid fast poyntand at his ger.
He hewid off hedys, and wysly coud him wer.
The worthy Scottis off this full litill wyst;
Socht to gud Graym quhen thai thair chyftane myst.
295 Lauder, and Lyle, and Hay, that was full wicht,
And bauld Ramsay, quhilk was a worthy knycht;

Lundy, and Boid, and Crystell off Cetoun,
With fyve hundreth, that war in bargane boun,
Him to reskew full rudly in thai raid,
300 About Wallace a large rowme thai maid.
The byschop Beik was braithly born till erd;
At the reskew thar was a glamrous rerd.
Or he gat wp, feill Sotheroun thai slew.
Out off the press Wallace thai couth raskew;
305 Sone horssit him apon a coursour wicht;
Towart a strenth ridis in all thair mycht,
Rycht wysly fled, reskewand mony man.
The erll Patrik to stuff the chace began.
On the flearis litill harm than he wrocht:
310 Gud Wallace folk away to giddyr socht.
Thir fyve hundreth, the quhilk I spak off ayr,
Sa awfully abawndownd thaim sa sar,
Na folowar durst out fra his falow ga;
The gud flearis sic raturnyng thai ma.
315 Four thousand haill had tane the strenth befor,
Off Wallace ost, his comfort was the mor;
Off Glaskadanc that forrest thocht till hauld.
Erll Patrik twrnd, thocht he was neir sa bauld,
Agayne to Beik, quhen chapyt was Wallace,
320 Curssand fortoun off his myschansit cace.
The feild he wan, and sewyn thowsand thai lost,
Dede on that day, for all the byschoppis bost.
Off Wallace men fyve hundreth war slayne, I gess;
Bot na chyftayne, his murnyng was the less.

325   Ner ewyn it was, bot Beik wald nocht abid;
In Lammermur thai trauuentyt that tid;
Thair lugyng tuk quhar him thocht maist awaill;
For weyll he trowit the Scottis wald assaill.
Apon the feild, quhar thai gaiff battaill last,

330 The contré men to Wallace gaderyt fast.

Fol. 61 a Off Edynburch, with Crawfurd that was wicht,
Thre hundreth come in till thar armour brycht.
Till Wallace raid, be his lugeyng was tayne.
Fra Tawydaill come gud men mony ane,

335 Out off Jedwart, with Ruwane, at that tyd
To giddyr socht fra mony diuerss sid.
Schir Wilyham Lang, that lord was off Douglas,
With him four scor that nycht come to Wallace.
Twenty hundreth off new men met that nycht,

340 Apon thair fais to weng thaim at thair mycht.
At the fyrst feild thir gud men had nocht beyn.
Wallace wachis thair aduersouris had seyn,
In to quhat wiss thai had thair lugeyng maid.
Wallace bownyt eftir soupper, but baid,

345 In Lammermur thai passit hastely;
Sone till aray yheid this gud chewalry.
Wallace thaim maid in twa partis to be.
Schir Jhon the Graym and Cetoun ordand he,
Lawder and Hay, with thre thousand to ryd;

350 Hym selff the layff tuk wysly for to gid;
With him Lundy, bathe Ramsay and Douglace,
Berkla and Boid, and Adam gud Wallace.
Be this the day approchit wondyr neir,
And brycht Titan in presens can apper.

355 The Scottis ostis sone semblit in to sycht
Off thair enemyss, that was nocht redy dycht;
Owt off aray feill off the Sotheroun was.
Rycht awfully Wallace can on thaim pas.
At this entray the Scottis so weill thaim bar,

360 Feill off thair fais to dede was bertnyt thar.
Redles thai raiss, and mony fled away;
Sum on the ground war smoryt quhar thai lay.
Gret noyis and cry was raissit thaim amang.

Gud Grayme come in, that stalwart was and strang:
365 For Wallace men was weill to gyddyr met.
On the south part sa aufully thai set,
In contrar thaim the frayt folk mycht nocht stand;
At anys thar fled off Sotheroun fyve thousand.
The worthi Scottis wrocht apon sic wyss,
370 Jop said hym selff, thai war mekill to pryss.
Yeit byschope Beik, that felloun tyrand strang,
Baid in the stour rycht awfully and lang.
A knycht Skelton, that cruell was and keyn,
Befor him stud in till his armour scheyn,
375 To fend his lord full worthely he wrocht.
Lundy him saw, and sadly on him socht;
With his gud suerd an awkwart straik him gaiff,
Throuch pesan stuff his crag in sondyr draiff;
Quhar off the layff astunyt in that sted,
Fol. 61 b 380 The bauld Skelton off Lundyis hand is dede.
Than fled thai all, and mycht no langar bid;
Patrik and Beik away with Bruce thai ryd.
Fyve thousand held in till a slop away
Till Noram houss, in all the haist thai may.
385 Our men folowed, that worthi war and wicht;
Mony flear derffly to dede thai dycht.
The thre lordis on to the castell socht;
Full feill thai left, that was off Ingland brocht.
At this jornay twenty thousand thai tynt,
390 Drownyt and slayn be sper and suerdis dynt.
The Scottis at Tweid haistyt thaim sa fast,
Feill Sotheroun men in to wrang furdis past.
Wallace raturnd, in Noram quhen thai war;
For worthi Bruce his hart was wondyr sar;
395 He had leuer haiff had him at his large,
Fre till our croun, than off fyne gold to carge,
Mar than in Troy was fund, at Grekis wan.

Wallace than passjt, with mony awfull man,
On Patrikis land, and waistit wondyr fast;
400 Tuk out gudis, and placis doun thai cast.
His stedis sewyn, that mete hamys was cauld,
Wallace gert brek thai burly byggyngis bauld,
Baithe in the Merss, and als in Lothiane;
Except Dunbar, standand he lewit nane.
405 Till Edynburgh apon the auchtand day;
Apon the morn, Wallace with out delay
Till Pert he passit, quhar the consaill was set;
To the barrownis he schawit with outyn let,
How his gret wow rycht weill eschewyt was.
410 Till a maister he gert erll Patrik pass,
Be causs he said off Scotland he held nocht:
Till king Eduuard, to get supplé, he socht.
The lordis was blyth, and welcummyt weill Wallas,
Thankand gret God off this fair happy chass.
415 Wallace tuk state to gowern all Scotland;
The barnage haill maid him ane oppyn band.
Than delt he land till gud men him about,
For Scotlandis rycht had set their lyff in dout.
Stantoun he gaiff to Lauder in his wage;
420 The knycht Wallang aucht it in heretage.
Than Birgeane cruk he gaiff Lyle that was wicht;
Till Scrymgeour als full gud reward he dycht.
Syne Wallace toun, and othir landis thartill,
To worthi men he delt with nobill will.
425 Till hys awne kyn heretage nayne gaiff he,
Bot office haill, at [euer] ilk man mycht se,
For cowatice thar couth na wicht him blayme;
He baid reward quhill the king suld cum hayme.
Fol. 62 a Off all he dyd, he thoucht to bid the law
430 Be for his king, master quhen he him saw.
Scotland was blyth, in dolour had beyne lang:
In ilka part to gud laubour thai gang.

Be this the tyme off October was past;
Ner Nouember approchit wondyr fast.

435 Tithandis than come, king Eduuard grewit was,
With his power in Scotland thocht to pass;
For erll Patrik had gyffyn hym sic consaill.
Wallace gat wit, and semblit power haill,
Fourty thousand on Roslyn mur thar met.

440 "Lordis," he said, "thus is King Eduuard set,
"In contrar rycht to sek ws in our land.
"I hecht to God, and to yow, be my hand,
"I sall him meit, for all his gret barnage,
"With in Ingland, to fend our heretage.

445 "His falss desyr sall on him selff be seyn;
"He sall ws fynd in contrar off his eyn.
"Sen he with wrang has ryddyn this regioun,
"We sall pass now in contrar off his crown.
"I will nocht bid gret lordis with ws fayr;

450 "For myn entent I will playnly declar.
"Our purposs is othir to wyn or de;
"Quha yeildis him, sall neuir ransownd be."
The barrons than him ansuerd worthely,
And said, thai wald pass with thair chewalry.

455 Him selff and Jop prowidyt that menyhé;
Twenty thousand off waillit men tuk he,
Harnes and hors he gert amang thaim waill;
Wappynnys enew, at mycht thaim weill awaill;
Grathyt thar men, that cruell wes and keyn;

460 Bettir in wer in warld coud nocht be seyn.
He bad the laiff on laubour for to bid.
In gud aray fra Roslyn mur thai ryd.
At thair muster gud Wallace couth thaim ass,
Quhat mysteryt ma in a power to pass?

465 "All off a will, as I trow, set ar we,
"In playne battaill can nocht weill scumfit be.

"Our rewme is pur, waistit be Sotheroun blud;
"Go wyn on thaim tresour, and othir gud."
The ost inclynd all in till humyll will,
470 And said, thai suld his commandment fulfill.
The erll Malcome with thir gud men is gayne;
Bot nayme off rewill on him he wald tak nayne.
Wallace him knew a lord and full worthi;
At his consaill he wrocht full stedfastly.
475 Starkar he was, gyff thai had battaill seyn;
For he befor had in gud jornays beyn.
A man off strenth, that has gud wit with all,
Fol. 62 b A haill regioune may comfort at his call:
As manly Ectour wrocht in till his wer;
480 Agayn a hundreth cowntyt was his sper.
Bot that was nocht throuch his strenth anerly;
Sic rewill he led off worthi chewalry.
Thir ensampyllis war noble for to ken.
Ectour I leiff, and spek furth off our men.
485 The knycht Cambell maid hime to that wiage,
Off Louchow cheiff, that was his heretage.
The gud Ramsay furth to that jornay went;
Schir Jhone the Grayme, forthwart in his entent;
Wallace cusyng, Adam, full worthi was,
490 And Robert Boid; full blythly furth thai pass.
Baith Awchynlek, and Richard off Lundy,
Lawder and Hay, and Cetoun full worthy.
This ryall ost, but restyng, furth thai rid,
Till Browis feild, and thar a quhill thai bid.
495 Than Wallace tuk with him fourty, but less,
Till Roxburgh yett raid sone, or he wald cess.
Sotheroun marueld giff it suld be Wallace,
With out souerance come to persew that place.
Off Schyr Rawff Gray sone presence couth he ass;
500 And warnd him thus, forthwart [or] he wald pass.

" Our purposs is in Ingland for to ryd;

" No teyme we haiff off segyng now to bid.

" Tak tent and her off our cummyng agayne;

" Gyff our the houss, send me the keyis in playn.

505 " Thus I commaund befor this witnes large,

" Gyff thow will nocht, ramayne with all the charge.

" Bot this be done, throuch force and I tak the,

" Out our the wall thow sall be hyngit hye."

With that he turnd, and till his ost can wend.

510 This ilk commaund to Berweik sone he send,

With gud Ramsay, that was a worthi knycht.

The ost but mar full awfully he dycht;

Began at Tweid, and spard nocht at thai fand;

Bot brynt befor throuch all Northummyrland.

515 All Duram toun thai brynt wp in a gleid.

Abbays thai spard, and kyrkis quhar thai yeid.

To York thai went but baid, or thai wald blyn;

To byrn and sla off thaim he had na syne.

Na syn thai thocht, the samyn thai leit ws feill;

520 Bot Wilyam Wallace quyt our quarell weill.

Fortrace thai wan, and small castellis kest doun;

With aspre wapynnys payit thair ransoune.

Off presonaris thai likit nocht to kep;

Quhom thai our tuk, thai maid thair freyndis to wepe.

525 Thai sawft na Sotheroun for thair gret riches;

Off sic koffre he callit bot wretchitnes.

Fol. 63 a On to the yettis and faboris off the toun

Braithly thai brynt, and brak thair byggyngis doun;

At the wallys assayed fyfetene dayis;

530 Till king Eduuard send to thaim, in this wayis,

A knycht, a clerk, and a squier of pes;

And prayit him fayr off byrnyng [for] to cess;

And hecht battaill, or fourty dayis war past,

Souerance so lang, gyff him likit, till ass.

535 And als he sperd, quhy Wallace tuk on hand
    The felloun stryff, in defens off Scotland.
    And said, he merweld on his wyt for thy,
    Agayn Inglande was off so gret party;
    " Sen ye haiff maid mekill off Scotland fre.
540 " It war gret tym for to lat malice be."
    Wallace has herd the message say thair will;
    With manly wytt rycht thus he said thaim till:
    ' Yhe may knaw weill that rycht ynewch we haiff;
    ' Off his souerance I kep nocht for to craiff.
545 ' Be causs I am a natyff Scottis man,
    ' It is my dett to do all that I can
    · To fend our kynrik out off dangeryng.
    ' Till his desyr we will grant to sum thing;
    ' Our ost sall cess, for chans that may betid,
550 ' Thir fourty dayis, bargane for till bid.
    ' We sall do nocht, less than it mowe in yow;
    ' In his respyt my selff couth neuir trow.'
    King Eduuardis wrytt wndir his seill thai gaiff,
    Be fourty dayis that thai suld battaill haiff.
555 Wallace thaim gaiff his credence off this thing.
    Thair leyff thai tuk, syne passit to the king,
    And tauld him haill how Wallace leit thaim feill,
    " Off your souerance he rekis nocht adeill;
    " Sic rewllyt men, sa awfull off affer,
560 " Ar nocht crystynyt, than he ledis in wer."
    The king ansuerd, and said; ' It suld be kend,
    ' It cummys off witt enemyss to commend.
    ' Thai ar to dreid rycht gretly in certane;
    · Sadly thai think off harmys thai haiff tane.'
565 Leyff I thaim thus at consell with thair king,
    And off the Scottis agayne to spek sum thing.

    Wallace tranountyt on the secund day;

Fra York thai passyt rycht in a gud aray.
Northwest thai past in battaill buskyt boun,
570 Thar lugcyng tuk besyd Northallyrtoun,
And cryit his pess, thar market for till stand,
Thai fourty dayis, for pepill off Ingland,
Quha that likyt ony wyttaill till sell.
Off all thair fer was mekill for to tell.
Fol. 63 b 575 Schyr Rawff Rymunt, captane off Maltoun was,
With gret power ordand he nycht to pass
On Wallace ost, to mak sum jeperté.
Feyll Scottis men, that duelt in that cuntré,
Wyst off this thing, and gaderyt to Wallace;
580 Thai maid him wyss off all that suttell cace.
Gud Lundy than till hym he callit thar,
And Hew the Hay, off Louchowort was ayr.
With thre thousand that worthely had wrocht,
Syne prewaly out fra the ost he socht.
585 The men he tuk, that come till hym off new,
Gydys to be, for thai the contré knew.
The ost he maid in gud quyet to be;
A space fra thaim he buschyt prewalé.
Schyr Rawff Rymunt with sewyn thousand com in,
590 On Wallace ost a jeperté to begyn.
The buschement brak, or thai the ost come ner;
On Sotheroun men the worthi Scottis thai ster.
Thre thousand haill was braithly brocht to ground;
Jornay thai socht, and sekyrly has found.
595 Schyr Rawff Rymunt was stekit on a sper;
Thre thousand slayn, that worthi war in wer.
The Sotheroun wyst quhen thair chyftayn wes dede;
To Maltoun fast thai fled, and left that sted.
Wallace folowed with his gud chewalry;
600 Amang Sotheroun thai entrit sodeynly,
Ingliss and Scottis in to the toun at anys.

Sotheroun men schot, and braithly kest doun stanys,
Off thar awn rycht feyll thair haiff thai slayn.
The Scottis about, that war off mekill mayn,
605 On grecis ran, and cessyt all the toun.
Derffly to dede the Sotheroun was dongyn doun.
Gud Wallace thair has found full gud ryches,
Jowellis and gold, bathe wapynnys and harnes;
Spoulyeid the toun off wyn, and off wittaill;
610 All off send with caryagis off gret waill.
Thre dayis still with in the toun thai baid;
Syn brak doun werk that worthely was maid.
Wyffis and childre thai put owt off the toun;
Na man he sawft that was off that nacioun.
615 Quhen Scottis had tane to turss at thair desyr,
Wallis thai brak, syn set the layff in fyr,
The temir werk thai brynt wp all in playn,
On the ferd day till his ost raid agayn,
Gert cast a dyk that mycht sum strynthyng be,
620 To kepe the ost fra sodeyn jeperté.
Than Inglissmen was rycht gretly agast,
Fra north and south in to thair king thai past,
Fol. 64 a At Pomfray lay, and held a parlement.
To gyff battaill the lordis couth nocht consent,
625 Less Wallace war off Scotland crownyt king.
Thar consaill fand it war a peralous thing:
For thocht thai wan, thai wan bot as thai war;
And gyff thai tynt, thai lossyt Ingland for euirmar,
A payn war put in to the Scottis hand.
630 And this decret thar wit amang thaim fand;
Gyff Wallace wald apon him tak the croun,
To gyff battaill thai suld be redy boun.
The sammyn message till him thai send agayn;
And thar entent thai tald him in to playn.
635 Wallace thaim chargyt his presens till absent;

His consaill callyt, and schawit thaim his entent.
He and his men desyrit battaill till haiff,
Be ony wayis, off Ingland our the laiff.
He said; " Fyrst, it war a our hie thing,
640 " Agayne the faith to reyff my rychtwis king.
" I am his man, born natiff of Scotland;
" To wer the croun I will nocht tak on hand.
" To fend the rewm it is my dett be skill;
" Lat God abowe reward me as he will."
645 Sum bad Wallace apon him tak the croun.
Wyss men said; ' Nay, it war bot derysioun,
' To croun him king bot woice off the parlyment:'
For thai wyst nocht gyff Scotland wald consent.
Othir sum said, it was the wrangwis place.
650 Thus demyt thai on mony diuerss cace.
This knycht Cambell, off witt a worthi man,
As I said ayr, was present with thaim than,
Herd and ansuerd, quhen mony said thair will;
" This war the best, wald Wallace grant thar till,
655 " To croun him king solemply for a day,
" To get ane end off all our lang delay."
The gud erll Malcome said, that Wallace mycht,
As for a day, in fens off Scotlandis rycht,
Thocht he refusyt it lestandly to ber,
660 Resawe the croun, as in a fer off wer.
The pepill all till him gaiff thar consent:
Malcome off auld was lord off the parlyment.
Yeit Wallace tholyt, and leit thaim say thair will.
Quhen thai had demyt be mony diuerss skill,
665 In his awne mynd he abhorryt with this thing.
The commounis cryit, ' Mak Wallace crownyt king.'
Than smylyt he, and said; " It suld nocht be:
" At termys schort, ye get no mar for me.
" Wndyr colour we mon our ansuer mak:

670 " Bot sic a thing I will nocht on me tak.

Fol. 64 b " I suffer yow to say that it is sa.

" It war a scorn the croun on me to ta."

Thai wald nocht lat the message off Ingland

Cum thaim amang, or thai suld wndirstand.

675 Twa knychtis passit to the message agayn,

Maid thaim to trow Wallace was crownyt in playn;

Gart thaim traist weill that this was suthfast thing.

Delyuyrit thus, thai passit to thair king;

To Pomfrait went, and tald that thai had seyn

680 Wallace crownyt. quharoff the lordis was teyn,

In barrate wox, in parlement quhar thai stud.

Than said thai all; " Thir tithingis ar nocht gud.

" He did so weyll in to thir tymys befor,

" And now thair king, he will do mekill mor.

685 " A fortonyt man, no thing gois him agayn.

" To gyff battaill we sall it rew apayn."

And othir said; ' And battaill will he haiff,

' Or stroy our land; na tresour may ws saiff.

' In his conquest, sen fyrst he coud begyn,

690 ' He sellis nocht, bot takis at he may wyn.

' For Inglissmen he settis no doym bot ded;

' Pryce off pennys may mak ws no ramed.'

And Wodstok said; " Yhe wyrk nocht as the wyss,

" Gyff that ye tak the awnter, off supprice:

695 " For thocht we wyn that ar in till Ingland,

" The laiff ar stark agaynys ws for to stand.

" Be Wallace saiff, othir thai cownt bot small.

" For thi me think this war the best off all,

" To kepe our strynth off castell and off wall toun,

700 " Swa sall we fend the fek off this regioun.

" Thocht north be brynt, bettir off sufferans be,

" Than set all Ingland on a jeperté."

Thai grantyt all, as Wodstok can thaim say;

And thus thai put the battaill on delay;
705 And kest thaim haill for othir gouernance,
Agayn Wallace to wyrk sum ordinance.
Thus Wallace has in playn discumfyt haill,
Agayn king Eduuard, all his strang battaill;
For throucht falsheid, and thar subtilité,
710 Thai thocht he suld, for gret necessité,
And faute off sude, to steyll out off the land.
And this decret thair wytt amang thaim sand;
Thai gert the king cry all thar merket doun,
Fra Trent to Tweid off throchtfayr and fre toun,
715 That in thai boundis na man suld wittaill leid,
Sic stuff, nor wyn, on na less payn bot deid.
This ilk decret thai gaiff in thar parlement.
Off Scottis forsuth to spek is myne entent.
Wallace lay still, quhill fourty dayis was gayn,
Fol. 65 a 720 And fyve atour; bot perance saw he nayn
Battaill till haiff, as thair promyss was maid.
He gert display agayne his baner braid;
Rapreiffyt Eduuard rycht gretlye off this thing;
Bawchillyt his seyll, blew out on that fals king,
725 As a tyrand; turnd bak, and tuk his gait.
Than Wallace maid full mony byggyng hayt.
Thai rassyt fyr, brynt wp Northallyrtoun,
Agayn throucht Yorkschyr bauldly maid thaim boun
Dystroyed the land, als fer as euir thai rid;
730 Sewyn myle about thai brynt on athir sid.
Palyce thai spylt, gret towris can confound;
Wrocht the Sotheroun mony werkand wound.
Wedowis wepyt with sorow in thar sang;
Madennys murnyt with gret menyng amang.
735 Thai sparyt nocht bot wemen and the kyrk.
· Thir worthy Scottis off laubour wald nocht yrk.
Abbayis gaiff thaim rycht largly to thair fud;

Till all kyrk man thai did no thing bot gud.
The temporall land thai spoulyeit at thair will,
740 Gud gardens gay, and orchartis gret thai spill.

To York thai went, thir wermen off renoun;
A sege thai set rycht sadly to the toun.
For gret defens thai garnest thaim within :
A felloun salt with out thai can begyn;
745 Gert woid the ost in four partis about.
With wachys feyll, that no man suld wsche out.
Abowne the toune, apon the southpart sid,
Thar Wallace wald, and gud Lundy, abid.
Erll Malcom syne at the west yett abaid;
750 With him the Boid, that gud jornays had maid.
The knycht Cambell, off Louchow [that] was lord,
At the north yett, and Ramsay, maid thaim ford.
Schyr Jhon the Graym, that worthy was in wer,
Awchinlek, Crawfurd, with full manlik affer,
755 At the est part bauldly thai bowne to bid.
A thousand archaris apon the Scottis sid
Disscueryt thaim amang the four party.
Fyve thousand bowemen in the toun forthi,
With in the wallis, arayit thaim full rycht,
760 Twelf thousand and ma that sembly was to sycht.
Than said Wallace; " Thar yond apon a playn,
" In feild to fecht me think we suld be bayn."
Than sailyeit thai rycht fast on ilka sid.
Fol. 65 b The worthy Scottis that bauldly durst abid,
765 With sper and scheild, for gownnys had thai nayn,
Within the dykys thai gert feill Sotheroun grayn.
Arowys thai schot, als fers as ony fyr,
Atour the wall, that flawmyt in gret ire,
Throuch byrneis brycht, with hedys fyn off steyll.
770 The Sotheroun blud thai leyt no frendschip feyll;

N

Our schefferand harnes schot the blud so scheyn.
The Inglissmen, that cruell was and keyn,
Kepyt thar toun, and fendyt thar full fast.
Fagaldys off fyr amang the ost thai cast;
775 Wp pyk and ter on feyll sowys thai lent;
Mony was hurt or thai fra wallys went.
Stanys and spryngaldis thai cast out so fast,
And gaddys off irne, maid mony goym agast:
Bot neuirtheles, the Scottis that was with out,
780 The toun full oft thai set in to gret dout;
Thar bulwerk brynt rycht brymly off the toun;
Thar barmkyn wan, and gret gerrettis kest doun.
Thus sailyeit thai, on ilk sid, with gret mycht.
The day was gayn, and cummyn was the nycht.
785 The wery ost than drew thaim fra the toun,
Set owt wachis, for restyng maid thaim boun;
Wysche woundis with wyn, off thaim that was w
For nayn wes dede; in gret myrth thai abound.
Feyll men was hurt, bot na murnyng thai maid;
790 Confermyt the sege, and stedfastly abaid.
Quhen that the son on morow raiss wp rycht,
Befor the chyftanys semblyt thai full rycht;
And mendis thocht off the toun thai suld tak,
For all the fens that the Sotheroun mycht mak.
795 Arayit agayn, as thai began afor,
About the toun thai sailye wondyr sor,
With felloun schot atour the wall so scheyn.
Feill Inglissmen, that cruell was and keyn,
With schot was slayn, for all thar targis strang:
800 Byrstyt helmys, mony to erd thai dang.
Brycht byrnand fyr thai kest till cuirilk yet;
The entress thus in perall oft thai set.
The defendouris was off so fell defens,
Kepyt thar toun with strenth and excellens.

805 And thus the day thai dryff on to the nycht:
    To palyounnys bownyt mony wery wycht.
    All yrk off wer; the toun was strang to wyn,
Fol. 66 a Off artailye, and nobill men with gyn.
    Quhen that thai trowyt the Scottis was all at rest,
810 For jeperté the Inglissmen thaim kest.
    Schyr Jhon Nortoun was knawyn worthy and wycht,
    Schyr Wilyham off Leis, graithit thaim that nycht,
    With fyve thowsand welle garnest and sawage;
    Apon the Scottis thai thocht to mak scrymmage;
815 And at [the] yet wschyt owt haistely
    On erll Malcom, and his gud chewalry.
    To chak the wache Wallace and ten had beyn
    Rydand about, and has thair cummyng seyn.
    He gert ane blaw, was in his cumpany;
820 The redy men arayit thaim hastely.
    Feill off the Scottis ilk nycht in harnes baid,
    Be ordinance, for thai sic rewll had maid.
    With schort awyss to gyddyr ar thai went,
    Apon thair fais, quhar feill Sotheroun was schent.
825 Wallace knew weill the erll to haisty was;
    For thi he sped him to the press to pass.
    A suerd off wer in till his hand he bar;
    The fyrst he hyt, the crag in sondyr schar.
    Ane othir awkwart apon the face tuk he;
830 Wysar and frount bathe in the feild gert fle.
    The hardy erll befor his men furth past,
    In to the press, quhar feill war fechtand fast;
    A scherand suerd bar drawyn in his hand;
    The fyrst was fey that he befor him fand.
835 Quhen Wallace and he was to gidder set,
    Thayr lestyt nayn agayn thaim that thai met.
    Bot othir dede, or ellis fled thaim fray.
    Be this the ost. all in [a] gud aray,

With the gret scry assemblit thaim about;
840 Than stud the Sotheroun in a felloun dout.
Wallace knew weill the Inglissmen wald fle;
For thi he preyst in the thikkest to be,
Hewand full fast on quhat sege that he socht;
Agaynys hys dynt fyn steyll awailyeit nocht.
845 Wallace off hand, sen Arthour, had na mak;
Quhom he hyt rycht was ay dede off a strak.
That was weyll knawin in mony place; and thar
Quhom Wallace hyt he deryt the Scottis no mar.
Als all his men did cruelly and weyll,
850 At com to strak; that mycht the Sotheroun feill.
The Inglissmen fled, and left the feild playnly.
The worthy Scottis wroucht so hardely,
Schyr Jhon off Nourtoun in that place was dede,
Fol. 66 b And twelf hundreth, with outyn ony ramede.
855 Thar mony was left in to the feild and slayn:
The layff raturnyt in to the toun agayn,
And rwyt full sar that euyr thai furth coud found;
Amang thaim was full mony werkand wound.
The ost agayn ilkane to thar ward raid,
860 Comaundyt wachis, and no mayr noyis maid,
Bot restyt still quhill that the brycht day dew.
Agayne began the toun to sailye new.
All thus thai wrocht with full gud worthines,
Assailyeit sayr with witt and hardines.
865 The ostis wictaill worth scant, and failyeit fast.
Thus lay thai thair, quhill diuerss dayis war past;
The land waistyt, and meit was fer for to wyn:
Bot that wyst nocht the stuff that was within;
Thai dred full sar for thair awn warysoun.
870 For souerance prayed the power off the toun,
To spek with Wallace thai desyryt fast:
And he aperyt, and speryt quhat thai ast.

The mayr ansuerd, said; "We wald gyff ransoun,
"To pass your way, and der no mayr the toun.
875 " Gret schaym it war that we suld yoldyn be,
" And townys haldyn off less power than we.
" Yhe may nocht wyn ws suthlie, thocht ye bid;
" We sall gyff gold, and yhe will fra ws rid.
" We may gyff battaill. durst we for our king;
880 " Sen he has left, it war ane our hie thing
" Till ws to do, with out his ordinance;
" This toun off him we hald in gouernance."
Wallace ansuerd; 'Off your gold rek we nocht;
'It is for battaill that we hydder socht.
885 ' We had leuir haiff battaill off Ingland,
'Than all the gold that gud king Arthour fand
' On the mont Mychell, quhar he the gyand slew.
' Gold may be gayn, bot worschip is ay new.
' Your king promyst that we suld battaill haiff;
890 ' His wrytt tharto undyr his seyll he gaiff.
' Lettir nor band, ye se, may nocht awaill
' Ws; for this tyme he hecht to gyff battaill.
' Me think we suld on his men wengit be;
' Apon our kyn mony gret wrang wrocht he :
895 ' His dewyllyk deid he did in to Scotland.'
The mayr said; "Schyr, rycht thus we wndyrstand:
" We haiff no charge quhat our king gerris ws do;
" Bot in this kynd we sall be bundyn yow to,
" Sum part off gold to gyff you with gud will,
900 " And nocht efftyr to wait yow with na ill.
Fol. 67 a " Be no kyn meyn, the power off this town ;
" Bot gyff our king mak him to battaill boun."
Into the ost was mony worthi man
With Wallace, ma than I now rekyn can.
905 Bettir it was, for at his will thai wrocht,
Thocht he wes best, no nothir lak we nocht;

All seruit thank to Scotland euirmar,
For manlyk wit, the quhilk thai schawit thar.
The haill consaill thus demyt thaim amang,
910 The toun to sege thaim thocht it was to lang;
And nocht a payn to wyn it be no slycht.
The consaill fand it was the best thai mycht
Sum gold to tak, gyff that thai get no mar;
Syne furth thar way in thar wiage thai far.
915 Than Wallace said; " My selff will nocht consent;
" Bot gyff this toun mak us this playne content;
" Tak our baner, and set it on the wall,
" (For thar power our rewme has ridyn all,)
" Yoldyn to be, quhen we lik thaim to tak,
920 " In till Ingland residence gyff we mak."
This ansuer sone thai send in to the mair.
Than thai consent, the ramayn that was thar,
The baner tuk, and set it in the toun,
To Scotland was hie honour and renoun.
925 That baner thar was fra aucht houris to none;
Thar finance maid, delyuerit gold full sone.
Fyve thousand pund, all gud gold off Ingland,
The ost rasawit, with wictaill haboundland.
Baith breid and wyne rycht gladly furth thai gaiff,
930 And othir stuff at thai likit to haiff.
Twenty dais owt the ost remaynit thar;
Bot want off wictaill gert thaim fra it far.
Yeit still off pees the ost lugyt all nycht,
Quhill on the morn the sone was ryssyn on hycht.

935   In Aperill amang the schawis scheyn,
Quhen the paithment was cled in tendyr greyn,
Plesand war it till ony creatur,
In lusty lyff that tym for till endur.
Thir gud wermen had fredome largly:

940 Bot fude was scant, thai mycht get nayn to by.
Tursyt tentis, and in the contré raid;
On Inglissmen full gret herschipe thai maid;
Brynt and brak doun byggyngis, sparyt thai nocht;
Rycht worthi wallis full law to ground thai brocht.

945 All Mydlame land thai brynt wp in a fyr,
Brak parkis doun, distroyit all the schyr;

Fol. 67 b Wyld der thai slew, for othir bestis was nayn;
Thir wermen tuk off venysoune gud wayn.
Towart the south thai turnyt at the last,

950 Maid byggyngis bar als fer as euir thai past.
The commons all to London ar thai went,
Befor the king, and tald him thar entent;
And said, thai suld, bot he gert Wallace cess,
Forsaik thair faith, and tak thaim till his pess.

955 Na herrald thar durst than to Wallace pass,
Quharoff the king gretly agrewit was.
Thus Eduuard left his pepill in to baill,
Contrar Wallace he wald nocht giff battaill;
Nor byd in feild for nocht that thai mycht say;

960 Gayff our the causs, to London past his way.
At men off wit this questioun her I ass,
Amang noblis gyff euyr ony thar was,
So lang throw force in Ingland lay on cass,
Sen Brudus deit, but battaill, bot Wallace.

965 Gret Julius, the empyr had in hand,
Twyss off force he was put off Ingland.
Wycht Arthour als, off wer quhen that he prewit,
Twyss thai fawcht, supposs thai war myschewit.
Awfull Eduuard durst nocht Wallace abid

970 In playn battaill, for all Ingland so wid.
In London he lay, and tuk him till his rest;
And brak his vow. Quhilk hald ye for the best?
Deyme as ye lest, gud men off discrecioun;

Rycht clayr it is to ransek this questioun:
975 To my sentence breyffly will I pass.
Quhen Wallace thus throw Yorkschyr jowrnat was,
Wictaill as than was nayne left in the land,
Bot in houssis quhar it mycht be warrand.
The ost heroff abaissit was to bid;
980 Fra sude scantyt na plesance was that tid.
Sum bald ryd haym, sum bald ryd forthermar:
Wallace callit Jop, and said till him rycht thar;
" Thow knawis the land, quhar most aboundance is,
" Be thow our gyd, and than we sall nocht myss
985 " Wictaill to fynd, that wait I wondir weill:
" Thow has, I traist, off Ingland mekill feill.
" The kyng and his to stark strenthis ar gayn;
" Bot jeperté, now perell haiff we nayn."
Than Jop said; '[Schir,] be ye gydyt be me,
990 ' The bowndandest part off Ingland ye sall se.
' Off wyn and quhcyt thar is in Rychmwnt schyr,
' And othir stuff off fud that ye desyr;
Fol. 68 a ' Quharoff I trow yhe sall be weyll content.'
The ost was glaid and thiddyrwart thai went.
995 Mony trew Scot was semblyt in that land,
To Wallace com weill ma than nyne thowsand;
Off presone part, sum had in lawbour wrocht,
Fra athir part full fast till him thai socht.
Wallace was blyth off our awn natiff kyn,
1000 That come till him off baill that thai war in:
And all the ost off comforde was the blythar.
Fra thair awn folk was multipliand the mar.

In Richmwnt schyr thai fand a gret boundans,
Breid, ayll and wyn, with othir purweans;
1005 Brak parkis doun, slew bestis mony ane,
Off wild and tayme, forsuth thai sparyt nane.

Throuch owt the land thai past in gud aray;
A sembly place so fand thai in thar way,
Quhilk Ramswaith hecht, as Jop him selff thaim tald;
1010 Fehew was lord and captayne in that hald.
A hundreth men was semblit in that place,
To sawe thaim selff and thar gud fra Wallace;
A ryoll sted, fast by a forest sid,
With turrettis fayr, and garrettis off gret prid,
1015 Beildyt about, rycht lykly to be wicht,
Awfull it was till ony mannis sicht;
Feill men abown on the wallis buskyt beyn,
In gud armour, that burnyst was full scheyn.
The ost past by, and bot wesyt that place;
1020 Yeit thai within on lowd defyit Wallace,
And trumpattis blew with mony werlik soun.
Than Wallace said; " Had we yon gallandis doun,
" On the playn ground, thai wald mor sobyr be."
Than jop said: ' Schyr, ye gart his brodyr de,
1025 ' In harrold weid, ye wait, on Tynto hill.'
Wallace ansuerd; " So wald I with gud will,
" Had I him selff; bot we may nocht thaim der;
" Gud men mon thoill off harlottis scorn in wer."
Schir Jhon the Graym wald at a bykkyr beyn:
1030 Bot Wallace sone, that gret perell has seyn,
Commaundit him to lat his seruice be.
" We haiff no men to waist in sic degré.
" Wald ye thaim harm, I knaw ane othir gait,
" How we throuch fyr within sall mak thaim hait.
1035 " Fyr has beyn ay full felloun in to wer,
Fol. 68 b " On sic a place it ma do mekill der.
" Thar awld bulwerk I se off wydderyt ayk;
" War it in fyr, thai mycht nocht stand a straik.
" Houssis and wod is her enewch plenté;
1040 " Quha hewis best off this forest lat se.

" Pow houssis doun, we sall nocht want adeill;
" The auld temyr will ger the greyn byrn weill."
At his commaund full besyly thai wrocht.
Gret wod in haist about the houss thai brocht.
1045 The bulwerk wan thir men off armys brycht,
To the barmkyn had temyr apon hycht.
Than bowmen schot to kep thaim fra the cast;
The wall about had festnyt firis fast.
Women and barnys on Wallace fast thai cry;
1050 On kneis thai fell, and askit him mercy.
At a quartar, quhar fyr had nocht ourtayn,
Thai tuk thaim out fra that castell off stayn;
Syn bet the fyr with brwndys brym and bauld;
The rude low raiss full heych abown that hauld.
1055 Barrellis off pyk for the defens was hungyn thar;
All strak in fyr, the myscheiff was the mar.
Quhen the brym fayr atour the place was past,
Than thai with in mycht nothir schwt no cast.
Als bestiall, as horss and nowt, within,
1060 Amang the fyr thai maid a hidwyss dyn.
The armyt men in harnes was so hait,
Sum doun to ground duschit but mar debait;
Sum lap, sum fell in to the felloun fyr,
Smoryt to dede, and brynt bathe bayn and lyr.
1065 The fyr brak in at all opynnys about;
Nayn baid on loft, so felloun was the dout.
Fehew him self lap rudly fra the hycht;
Throuch all the fyr can on the barmkyn lycht.
With a gud suerd Wallace strak off his hed,
1070 Jop hynt it wp, and turst [it] fra that sted.
Fyve hundreth men, that war in to that place,
Gat nayne away, bot dede with outyn grace.
Wallace baid still with his power that nycht;
Apon the morn the fyr had failyeit mycht.

1075 Beffor the yett, quhar it was brynt on breid,
A red thai maid, and to the castell yeid,
Strak doun the yett, and tuk that thai mycht wyn,
Jowellys and gold, gret riches was tharin;
Spulyeit the place, and left nocht ellis thar,
1080 Bot bestis, brynt bodyis. and wallis bar.
Than tuk thai hyr, that wyff was to Febew;
Gaiff this commaund. as scho was women trew,
To turss that hed to London to king Eduuard.
Fol. 69 a Scho it rasawyt with gret sorow on hart.
1085 Wallace him selff thir chargis till hyr gaiff;
" Say to your king, bot gyff I battaill haiff,
" At London yettis we sall assailyie sayr;
" In this moneth we think for to be thair.
" Trastis, in treuth, will God, we sall nocht faill;
1090 " Bot I rasyst throw chargis off our consaill.
" The southmaist part off Ingland we sall se;
" Bot he sek pess, or ellis bargan with me.
" Apon a tym he chargyt me on this wyss,
. " Rycht boustously to mak till him seruice:
1095 " Sic sall he haiff, as he ws causs has maid."
Than mowit thai with out langer abaid.
Deliuerit scho was fra this gud chewalry,
Towart London scho socht rycht ernystfully;
On to the tour, but mar process, scho went,
1100 Quhar Eduuard lay sayr murnand in his entent.
His newois hede, quhen he saw it was brocht,
Sa gret sorow sadly apon him socht,
With gret wness apon his feit he stud,
Wepand for wo for his der tendyr blud.
1105 The consaill raiss, and prayit him for to cess;
" We loss Ingland, bot gyff ye purches pess."
Than Wodstok said; ' This is my best consaill:
' Tak pees in tyme as for our awn awaill,

'Or we tyne mar, yeit slaik off our curage;
1110 'Ereſt ye may get help to your barnage.'
The king grantyt, and bad thaim message send;
Na man was thar that durst to Wallace wend.
The queyn apperyt, and saw this gret distance;
Weill born scho was off the rycht blud off France;
1115 Scho trowit weill tharfor to speid the erar,
Hyr selff purpost in that message to far.
Alss scho forthocht that the king tuk on hand,
Agayn the rycht, so oft to reyff Scotland;
And feill said, the wengeance hapnyt thar,
1120 Off gret murthyr his men maid in till Ayr.
Thus demyt thai the consaill thaim amang.
To this effect the queyn bownyt to gang.
Quhen scho has seyn ilk man forsak this thing,
On kneis scho fell, and askyt at the king;
1125 "Souerane," scho said, "gyff it your willis be,
"At I desyr yon chyftayn for to se.
"For he is knawin bath hardy. wyss, and trew;
"Perchance he will erar on wemen rew,
Fol. 69 b "Than on your men; yhe haiff don him sic der,
1130 "Quhen he thaim seis, it mowis him ay to wer.
"To help this land I wald mak my trawaill;
"It ma nocht scaith, supposs it do na waill."
The lordis all off hir desir was fayn;
On to the king thai maid instans in playn.
1135 That scho mycht pass. The king, with aukwart will,
Halff in to yr, has [giffyn] consent thar till.
Sum off thaim said, the queyn luffyt Wallace,
For the gret woice off his hie nobilnes.
A hardy man, that is lykly with all,
1140 Gret fawour will off fortoun till him fall,
Anent wemen is seyne in mony place.
So hapnyt it in his tyme with Wallace.

In his rysyng he was a luffar trew,
And chesyt ane, bot Inglissmen hir slew.
1145 Yeit I say nocht, the queyn wald on hir tak,
All for his luff, sic trawaill for to mak.
Now luff or leiff, or for help off the land,
I mak raherss as I in scriptour fand.
Scho graithit hir apon a gudlye wiss,
1150 With gold, and ger, and folk at hir dewiss;
Ladyis with hir, nane othir wald thai send,
And ald preystis, that weill the cuntré kend.
Lat I the queyn to message redy dycht,
And spek furth mar off Wallace trawaill rycht.
1155 The worthy Scottis amang thar enemyss raid;
Full gret destructioun amang the Sotheron thai maid;
Waistit about the land on athir sid :
Na wer men than durst in thar way abid.
Thai ransoun nane, bot to the dede thaim dycht;
1160 In mony steid maid fyris braid and brycht.
The ost was blith, and in a gud estate,
Na power was at wald mak thaim debate;
Gret ryches wan off gold and gud thaim till,
Leyffyng enewch to tak at thar awn will.
1165 In awfull fer thai trawaill throuch the land,
Maid byggynis bar that thai befor thaim fand;
Gret barmkynnys brak off stedis stark and strang;
Thir wicht wermen off trawaill thocht nocht lang.
South in the land rycht ernystfully thai socht,
1170 To Sanct Awbawnys; bot harm thar did thai nocht.
The pryour send thaim wyn and wenesoun,
Refreschyt the ost with gud in gret fusioun.
The nycht apperyt quhen thai war at the place;
Than herbreyt thaim fra thine a litill space;
1175 Chesyt a sted quhar thai suld bid all nycht,
Tentis on ground, and palyonis proudly pycht;

In till a waill, be a small rywer fayr,
On athir sid quhar wyld der maid repayr;
Set wachis owt, that wysly couth thaim kepe,
Fol. 70 a 1180 To souppar went, and tymysly thai slepe.

Off meit and sleip thai cess with suffisiance.
The nycht was myrk, our drayff the dyrkfull chance.
The mery day sprang fra the oryent,
With bemys brycht enlumynyt the occident.
1185 Eftir Titan, Phebus wp rysyt fayr;
Heich in the sper, the signes maid declayr.
Zepherus began his morow courss,
The swete wapour thus fra the ground resourss;
The humyll breyth doun fra the hewyn awaill,
1190 In euery meide, bathe fyrth, forrest, and daill;
The cler rede amang the rochis rang,
Throuch greyn branchis quhar byrdis blythly sang,
With joyus woice in hewynly armony.
Than Wallace thocht it was no tyme to ly;
1195 He croyssit him, syne sodeynli wp raiss;
To tak the ayr out off his palyon gais.
Maister Jhon Blar was redy to rawess;
In gud entent syne bownyt to the mess.
Quhen it was done, Wallace can him aray,
1200 In his armour, quhilk gudly was and gay.
His schenand schoys, that burnyst was full beyn,
His leg harnes he clappyt on so clene;
Pullane greis he braissit on full fast;
A closs byrny, with mony sekyr clasp;
1205 Breyst plait, brasaris, that worthy was in wer;
Besid him furth Jop couth his basnet ber;
His glytterand glowis grawin on athir sid.
He semyt weill in battaill till abid;
His gud gyrdyll, and syne his burly brand;

1210 A staff off steyll he gryppyt in his hand.
The ost him blyst, and prayit God, off his grace,
Him to conwoy fra all mystymyt cace.
Adam Wallace and Boid furth with him yeid,
By a reuir, throu out a floryst meid.

1215 And as thai walk atour the feyldis greyn,
Out off the south thai saw quhar at the queyn.
Towart the ost, come ridand sobyrly;
And fyfty ladyis was in hyr cumpany.
Wallyt off wit, and demyt off renoun,

1220 Sum wedowis war, and sum off religioun;
And sewyn preistis that entrit war in age.
Wallace to sic did neuir gret owtrage,
Bot gyff till him thai maid a gret offens.
Thus prochyt thai on towart thar presens.

1225 At the palyoun, quhar thai the lyoun saw;
To ground thai lycht, and syne on kneis can faw;
Prayand for pece thai cry with petous cher.
Erll Malcom said; " Our chyftayn is nocht her."

Fol. 70 b He bad hyr ryss, and said it was nocht rycht,

1230 A queyn on kneis till ony lavar wycht.
Wp by the hand the gud erll has hyr tayn;
Atour the bent to Wallace ar thai gayn.
Quhen scho him saw, scho wald haiff knelyt doune;
In armys sone he caucht this queyn with croun,

1235 And kyssyt hyr with outyn wordis mor;
Sa dyd he neuir to na Sotheron befor.
" Madem," he said, " rycht welcum mot ye be;
" How plessis yow our ostyng for to se?"
' Rycht weyll,' scho said, ' off frendschip haiff we neid;

1240 ' God grant ye wald off our nessis to speid.
' Suffyr we mon, supposs it lik ws ill;
' Bot trastis weyll, it is contrar our will.'
" Ye sall remayn, with this lord I mon gang;

" Fra your presens we sall nocht tary lang."

1245 The erll and he on to the palzyon yeid,
With gud awyss to deym mar off this deid.
Till consell son Wallace gart call thaim to:
" Lordys," he said, " ye wait quhat is ado.
" Off thar cummyng my selff has na plesance ;
1250 " Herfor mon we wyrk with ordinance.
" Wemen may be contempnyng in to wer,
" Amang fullis that can thaim nocht forber.
" I say nocht this be thir, nor yeit the queyn ;
" I trow it be bot gud that scho will meyn.
1255 " Bot sampyll tak off lang tym passit by ;
" At Rownsywaill the tresoun was playnly
" Be wemen maid, that Ganyelon with him brocht,
" And Turké wyn ; forber thaim couth thai nocht.
" Lang wss in wer gert thaim desyr thair will,
1260 " Quhilk brocht Charlis to fellon loss and ill.
" The flour off France, withoutyn redempcioun,
" Throuch that foull deid, was brocht to confusioun.
" Commaund your men tharfor in priway wyss,
" Apayn off lyff thai wyrk nocht on sic wyss ;
1265 " Nane spek with thaim, bot wysmen off gret waill,
" At lordis ar, and sworn to this consaill."
Thir chargis thai did als wysly as thai mocht ;
This ordynance throw all the ost was wrocht.

He and the erll bathe to the queyn thai went,
1270 Rasawyt hyr fayr, and brocht hyr till a tent ;
To dyner bownyt als gudly as thai can ;
And serwit was with mony likly man.
Gud purwyance the queyn had with hyr wrocht ;
Fol. 71 a A say scho tuk off all thyng at thai brocht.
1275 Wallace persawyt, and said ; " We haiff no dreid :
" I can nocht trow ladyis wald do sic deid,

" To poysoun men, for all Ingland to wyn."
The queyn ansuerd; 'Gyff poysoun be tharin,
' Off ony thyng quhilk is brocht her with me,
1280 ' Apon my selff fyrst sorow sall ye se.'
Sone aftir meit, a marchell gart [all] absent,
Bot lordis, and thai at suld to consaill went.
Ladyis apperyt in presens with the queyn.
Wallace askyt, quhat hyr cummyng mycht meyn.
1285 ' For pess,' scho said, ' at we haiff to yow socht;
' This byrnand wer in baill has mony brocht.
' Ye grant ws pees, for him that deit on tre.'
Wallace ansuerd; " Madeym, that may nocht be.
" Ingland has doyne sa gret harmys till ws,
1290 " We may nocht pass, and lychtly leiff it thus."
' Yeiss,' said the queyne, ' for crystyn folk we ar.
' For Goddis saik, sen we desyr no mar,
' We awcht pess.' " Madeym, that I deny.
" The perfyt causs I sall yow schaw for quhy;
1295 " Ye seke na pess bot for your awn awaill.
" Quhen your fals king had Scotland grippyt haill,
" For nakyn thing that he befor him fand,
" He wald nocht thoill the rycht blud in our land;
" Bot reft thar rent, syn put thaim selff to ded:
1300 " Ransoun off gold mycht mak [us] na ramed.
" His fell fals wer sall on him selff be seyn."
Than sobyrly till him ansuerd the queyn;
' Off thir wrangis amendis war most fair.'
" Madeym," he said, " off him we ask no mar,
1305 " Bot at he wald byd ws in to battaill;
" And God be juge, he kennys the mater haill."
' Sic mendis,' scho said, ' war nocht rycht gud, think me:
' Pess now war best, and it mycht purchest be.
' Wald yhe grant pess, and trwys with ws tak,
1310 ' Throuch all Ingland we suld gar prayeris mak
O

' For yow, and thaim at in the wer war lost.'
Than Wallace said; "Quhar sic thing cummys throuch bo
" Prayer off fors, quhar so at it be wrocht,
" Till ws helpis [othyr] litill, or ellis nocht."

1315 Warly scho said; ' Thus wyssmen has ws kend,
    ' Ay efftir wer pees is the finall end.
    ' Quharfor ye suld off your gret malice cess;
    ' The end off wer is cheryté and pess.
    ' Pees is in hewyn, with blyss and lestandnas.

1320 ' We sall beseke the Pape, off his hie grace,
Fol. 71 b ' Till commaund pess, sen we may do na mar.'
    " Madeym," he said, "or your purches cum thar.
    " Mendys we think off Ingland for to haiff."
    ' Quhat set yow thus,' scho said, ' so God yow saiff,

1325 ' Fra violent wer at ye lik nocht to duell ?'
    " Madem," he said, "the suth I sall yow tell.
    " Eftir the dayt off Alexandris ryng,
    " Our land stud thre yer desolate but king,
    " Kepyt full weyll at concord in gud stait.

1330 " Throuch twa clemyt, thar hapnyt gret debait.
    " So ernystfully, accord thaim nocht thai can.
    " Your king thai ast for to be thair ourman.
    " Slely he slayd throuch strenthis off Scotland;
    " The kynryk syne he tuk in his awn hand.

1335 " He maid a kyng agayn our rychtwyss law;
    " For he off him suld hald the regioun aw.
    " Contrar this band was all the haill barnage,
    " For Scotland was yeit neuir in to thrillage.
    " Gret Julius, that tribut gat off aw,

1340 " His wynnyng was in Scotland bot full smaw.
    " Than your fals king, wndyr colour but mar,
    " Throuch band he maid till Bruce that is our ayr,
    " Throuch all Scotland with gret power thai raid,
    " Wndyr that king quhilk he befor had maid.

1345 " To Bruce sen syne he kepit na connand:
     " He said, he wald nocht ga and conquess land
     " Till othir men; and thus the cass befell.
     " Than Scotland throuch he demayned him sell;
     " Slew our elderis, gret peté was to se.
1350 " In presoune syne lang tyme thai pynit me,
     " Quhill I fra thaim was castyn out for ded.
     " Thankit be God he send me sum remed!
     " Wengyt to be I prewyt all my mycht;
     " Feyll off thair kyn to dede syn I haiff dycht.
1355 " The rage off youth gert me desyr a wyff;
     " That rewit I sayr, and will do all my liff.
     " A tratour knycht but mercy gert hyr de,
     " Ane Hessilryg bot for dispit off me.
     " Than rang I furth in cruell wer and payn,
1360 " Quhill we redemyt part off our land agayn.
     " Than your curst king desyryt off ws a trew;
     " Quhilk maid Scotland full rathly for to rew.
     " In to that pess thai set a suttell ayr,
     " Than auchtene scor to dede thai hangit thar,
1365 " At noblis war, and worthi off renoun;
     " Off cot armys eldest in that regioun.
     " Thar dede we think to weng in all our mycht.
     " The woman als, that dulfully was dycht,
Fol. 72 a " Out off my mynd that dede will neuir bid,
1370 " Quhill God me tak fra this fals warld so wid.
     " Off Sotheroun syn I can no peté haiff;
     " Your men in wer I think neuir mor to saiff."
     The breith teris, was gret payn to behald,
     Bryst fra his eyn, be he his taill had tald.
1375 The queyn wepyt for peté off Wallace.
     ' Allace,' scho said, ' wa worth the curssyt cace!
     ' In waryit tym that Hesilryg was born!
     ' Mony worthi throuch his deid ar forlorn.

'He suld haiff payn, that saikles sic ane sleuch;
1380 'Ingland sen syn has boucht it der enewch,
      'Thocht scho had beyn a queyn or a prynsace.'
      "Madem," he said, "as God giff me gud grace,
      "Prynsace or queyn, in quhat stait so thai be,
      "In till hir tym scho was als der to me."
1385 'Wallace,' scho said, 'off this talk we will cess;
      'The mendis heroff is gud prayer and pess.'
      "I grant," he said, "off me as now na mayr;
      "This is rycht nocht bot ekyng off our cayr."

      The queyn fand weyll, langage no thing hyr bet;
1390 Scho trowit with gold that he mycht be our set.
      Thre thousand pound, off fynest gold so red,
      Scho gert be brocht to Wallace in that sted.
      "Madeym," he said, "na sic tribut we craiff:
      "A nothir mendis we wald off Ingland haiff,
1395 "Or we raturn fra this regioun agayn,
      "Off your fals blud that has our elderis slayn.
      "For all the gold and ryches ye in ryng,
      "Ye get no pess, but desir off your king."
      Quhen scho saw weill, gold mycht hyr nocht releiff,
1400 Sum part in sport scho thoucht him for to preiff.
      'Wallace,' scho said, 'yhe war clepyt my luff:
      'Mor baundounly I maid me for to pruff;
      'Traistand tharfor your rancour for to slak;
      'Me think ye suld do sum thing for my saik.'
1405 Rycht wysly he maid ansuer to the queyn;
      "Madem," he said, "and verité war seyn,
      "That ye me luffyt, I awcht yow luff agayn.
      "Thir wordis all ar no thing bot in wayn.
      "Sic luff as that is nothing till awance,
1410 "To tak a lak, and syne get no plesance.
      "In spech off luff suttell ye Sothcroun ar;

" Ye can ws mok, supposs ye se no mar."
' In London,' scho said, ' for yow I sufferyt blaym;
' Our consall als will lauch quhen we cum haym;
1415 ' So may thai say, wemen ar ferss off thocht
' To sek frendschip, and syne can get rycht nocht!'
" Madem," he said, " we wait how ye ar send.
" Yhe trow we haiff bot litill for to spend.
" Fyrst with your gold, for ye ar rych and wyss,
72b 1420 " Yhe wald ws blynd, sen Scottis ar so nyss:
" Syn plesand wordis off yow and ladyis fayr,
" As quha suld dryff the byrdis till a swar
" With the small pype, for it most fresche will call.
" Madeym, as yit ye ma nocht tempt ws all.
1425 " Gret part off gud is left amang our kyn;
" In Ingland als we fynd enewch to wyn."
Abayssyt scho was to mak ansuer him till.
' Der schyr,' scho said, ' sen this is at your will;
' Wer or pess, quhat so yow likis best,
1430 ' Lat your hye witt and gud consaill degest.'
" Madem," he said, " now sall ye wndirstand
" The resoune quhy that I will mak na band.
" With yow, ladyis, I can na trewis bynd;
" For your fals king her eftir sone wald fynd,
1435 " Quhen he saw tyme, to brek it at his will;
" And playnly say, he grantyt nocht thartill.
" Than had we nayn bot ladyis to repruff.
" That sall he nocht, be God that is abuff.
" Vpon wemen I will na wer begyn;
1440 " On you in faith no worschip is to wyn.
" All the haill pass apon him selff he sall tak,
" Off pees or wer quhat hapnyt we to mak."
The queyn grantyt his ansuer sufficient;
So dyd the layff in place that was present.
1445 His deliuerance thai held off gret awaill,

And stark enewch to schaw to thair consaill.
Wa was the qweyn hyr trawaill helpyt nocht.
The gold scho tuk, that thai had with hyr brocht;
On to the ost rycht frely scho it gayff.
1450 Till euirylk man that likyt for till haiff.
Till menstraillis, harroldis, scho delt haboundandlé,
Besekand thaim hyr frend at thai wald be.
Quhen Wallace saw the fredom off the queyn,
Sadly he said; "The suth weyll has beyn seyn,
1455 "Wemen may tempt the wysest at is wrocht.
"Your gret gentrice it sall neuir be for nocht.
"We [yow] assure, our ost sall mwff na thing,
"Quhyll tym ye may send message fra your king.
"Gyff it be sa, at he accord and we,
1460 "Than for your saik it sall the bettir be.
"Your harroldys alss sall saiffly cum and ga;
"For your fredom we sall trowbill na ma."
Scho thankit him off his grant mony syss,
And all the ladyis apon a gudly wyss.
1465 Glaidly thai drank, the queyn and gud Wallace;
Thir ladyis als, and lordis in that place.
Fol. 73 a Hyr leyff scho tuk with out langar abaid;
Fyve myile that nycht south till a nonry raid.
Apon the morn till London passit thai,
1470 In Westmenster, quhar at the consaill lay:
Wallace ansuer scho gart schaw to the king.
It nedis nocht her raherss mar off this thing.
The gret commend that scho to Wallace gaiff,
Befor the king, in presens off the laiff,
1475 Till trew Scottis it suld gretly appless,
Thocht Inglissmen tharoff had litill ess;
Off worschip, wyt, manheid, and gouernans,
Off fredom, trewth; key off remembrans
Scho callyt him thar in to thair hye presens;

1480 Thocht contrar thaim he stud at his defens.
"So chyftaynlik," scho said, "as he is seyn,
" In till Inglande, I trow, has neuir beyn.
" Wald ye off gold gyff him this rewmys rent,
" Fra honour he will nocht turn his entent.
1485 "Sufferyt we ar, quhill ye may message mak;
" Off wyss lordis sumpart I reid yow tak,
" To purchess peess, with outyn wordis mar;
" For all Ingland may rew his raid full sayr.
" Your harroldys als to pass to him has leyff,
1490 " In all his ost thar sall no man thaim greiff."
Than thankit thai the queyn for hir trawaill;
The king, and lordis that was off his consaill.
Off hyr ansuer the king applessit was;
Than thre gret lordys thai ordand for to pass.
1495 Thar consaill haill has fownd it was the best
Trewis to tak. or ellis thai get no rest.

A harrold went, in all the haist he may,
Till Tawbane waill, quhar at the Scottis lay,
Condeyt till haiff, quhill thai haiff said thar will.
1500 The consaill sone [ane] condeyt gaiff him till.
Agayn he past with souerance till his king.
Than chesyt thai thre lordis for this thing.
The keyn Clyffurd, was than thar warden haill,
Bewmont, Wodstok, all men off mekill waill;
1505 Quhat thir thre wrocht the layff suld stand thar till;
The kingis seyll was gyffyn thaim at thair will.
Sone thai war brocht to spekyng to Wallace.
Wodstok him schawit mony suttell cace.
Wallace he herd the sophammis euirédeill;
1510 " As yeit," he said, "me think ye meyn bot weill.
" In wrang ye hald, and dois ws gret owtrage,
" Off houssis part that is our heretage.

"Owt off this pees, in playn I mak thaim knawin,

"Thaim for to wyn, sen that thai ar our awin;

1515 "Roxburch, Berweik, at ouris lang tym has beyn

"In to the handis off you fals Sotherone keyn.

"We ask her als, be wertu off this band,

"Our ayris, our king, be wrang led off Scotland.

"We sall thaim haiff, with outyn wordis mar."

1520 Till his desyr the lordis grantis thair;

Rycht at his will thai haiff consentit haill;

For nakyn thing the pees thai wald nocht faill.

The yong Randell, at than in London was,

The lord off Lorn in this band he can ass;

1525 Erll off Bowchane, bot than in tendyr age;

Eftir he grew a man off hycht, wyss and large.

Cummyn and Soullis he gart deliuer alss,

Quhilk eftir was till king Robert full fals.

Wallang fled our, and durst nocht bid that mute,

1530 In Pykardté; till ass him was na bute.

Bot Wallace wald erar haff had that fals knycht,

Than ten thousand off fynest gold so brycht.

The Bruce he askyt, bot he was had away,

Befor that tym, till Calyss, mony day.

1535 King Eduuard prewyt that thai mycht nocht hym get;

Off Glosestir his wncle had him set,

At Calyss than had haly in kepyng.

Wallace that tym gat nocht his rychtwyss king.

The erll Patrik fra London alsua send,

1540 Wyth Wallace to mak, as weill befor was kend,

Off his mater a synaill gouernance;

Till king Eduuard gaiff up his legeance,

And tuk till hald off Scotland euirmar.

With full glaid hart Wallace resauit him thar;

1545 Thai honowryt him rycht reuerendly as lord:

The Scottis was all reiosyt off that conford.

A hundreth horss, with yong lordis off renounc,
Till Wallace com, fred out off that presounc.
Wndyr his scill, king Eduuard thaim gert send
1550 For till gyff our, and mak a fynaill end,
Roxburch, Berweik, quhilk is off mekill waill,
To Scottissmen, and all the boundis haill.
To fyve yer trew thai promyst be thar hand.
Than Wallace said; "We will pass ner Scotland,
1555 "Or ocht be seld; and tharfor mak ws boun
"Agayn we will besid Northallyrtoun,
"Quhar king Eduuard fyrst battaill hecht to me.
"As it began, thar sall it endyt be.
"Gret weyll your queyn," he chargyt the message,
74a 1560 "It is for hyr at we leyff our wiage."
A day he set, quhen he suld meit him thar,
And scill this pees, with outyn wordis mar,
Apon the morn the ost, but mar awyss,
Tranountyt north apon a gudlye wyss,
1565 To the set tryst that Wallace had thaim maid.
The Ingliss message com but mar abaid;
Thai seyllyt the pess with out langar delay.
The message than, apon the secund day,
Till London went in all the haist thai can.
1570 The worthi Scottis, with mony gudly man,
Till Bambwrch com with all the power haill,
Sexté thousand, all Scottis off gret waill.
Ten dayis befor All Halow ewyn thai fur:
On Lammess day thai lycht on Caram mur.
1575 Thar lugyt thai with plesance as thai mocht;
Quhill on the morn at preistis to thaim socht,
In Caram kyrk, and sessyt in his hand
Roxburch keyis, as thai had maid connand;
And Berweik als, quhilk Sothcroun had so lang.
1580 Thai frede the folk, in Ingland for to gang,

For thar lyffis wschet off athir place;
Thai durst nocht weill bid rekynnyng off Wallace.
Capdane he maid, in Berweik, off renoun
That worthy was, gud Crystell off Cetoun.
1585 Kepar he left till Roxburch castell wicht
Schir Jhon Ramsay, a wyss and worthi knycht;
Syne Wallace selff, with erll Patrik in playn,
To Dunbar raid, and restoryt him agayn,
In his castell, and all that heretage,
1590 With the consent off all that haill barnage.
Quhen Wallace was agrëit and this lord,
To rewll the rewm he maid him gudly ford.
Scotlande atour, fra Ross till Soloway sand,
He raid it thryss, and statut all the land.
1595 In the Leynhouss a quhyll he maid repayr;
Schyr Jhon Menteth that tym was captane thar.
Twyss befor he had his gossep beyn;
Bot na frendschip betwix thaim syn was seyn.
Twa monethis still he duelt in Dunbertane;
1600 A houss he foundyt apon the roch off stayne;
Men left he thar till bygg it to the hycht.
Syn to the March agayn he rydis rycht.
In to Roxburch thai chesyt him a place,
A gud tour thar he gert byg in schort space.
Fol. 74 b 1605 The kynrik stud in gud worschip and ess;
Was nayn so gret durst his nychtbour displess.
The abill ground gert laubour thryftely;
Wittaill and froyte thar grew aboundandly.
Was neuir befor, sen this was callyt Scotland,
1610 Sic welth and pess at anyss in the land.
He send Jop twyss to Bruce in Huntyngtoune,
Besekand him to cum and tak his croune.
Conseill he tuk at fals Saxionis, allace!
He had neuir hap in lyff to get Wallace.

1615 Thre yer as thus the rewm stud in gud pess.
Off this sayn, me worthis for to cess:
And forthyr furth off Wallace I will tell,
In till his lyff quhat awentur yeit fell.

A ryoll king than ryngyt in to France,
1620 Gret worschip herd off Wallace gouernance,
Off prowis, pryss, and off his worthi deid,
And forthwart fair, commendede off manheid;
Bathe humyll, leyll, and off his priwyt pryss,
Off honour, trewth, and woid off cowatiss.
1625 The nobill king, ryngand in ryolté,
Had gret delyte this Wallace for to se;
And knew rycht weill schortly to wndyrstand
The gret suppryss and ourset off Ingland.
Als marueld he off Wallace small power,
1630 That but a king tuk sic a rewm to ster,
Agayn Ingland, and gert thair malice cess,
Quhill thai desyryt with gud will to mak pess.
And rycht onon a herrold gert he call,
In schort termys he has rehersit him all
1635 Off his entent completly till ane end;
Syn in Scotland he bad him for to wend.
And thus he wrait than in till gret honour,
To Wilyham Wallace as a conquerour.
" O lowit leid, with worschip wyss and wicht;
1640 " Thow werray help in haldyn off the rycht;
" Thou rycht restorer off thi natyff land;
" With Goddis grace agayn thi fais to stand
" In thi defens, helpar of rychtwyss blud.
" O worthi byrth, and blyssyt be thi fud!
1645 " As it is red in prophecy beforn,
" In happy tym for Scotland thow was born.
" I the besek, with all humylité,

" My closs lettir thow wald consaiff and se,

" As your brodyr, I crystyn king off France,

1650 " To the berer ye her and gyff credance."

The herrold bownd him, and to the schip is gone:

In Scotland sone he cummyn is onon,

Fol. 75 a   Bot harrold lyk he sekis his presens.

On land he went, and maid no residens

1655 In ony steid, quhar he presumyt thar.

So on a day he fand him in to Ayr,

In gud affer, and manlik cumpany.

The harrold than, with honour reuerendly,

Has salust him apon a gudly maner.

1660 And he agayn, with humyll hamly cher,

Rasauit him in to rycht gudly wyss.

The harrold than, with worschip to dewyss,

Be tuk till him the kingis wryt off France.

Wallace on kne, with lawly obeysance,

1665 Rycht reuerendly, for worschip off Scotland.

Quhen he it red, and had it wndirstand,

At this herrold he askyt his credence,

With aspre spech, and manly contenence.

And he him tald, as I haiff said befor,

1670 The kingis desyr; quhat nedis wordis mor?

" The hye honour, and the gret nobilnes

" Off your manheid, weill knawin in mony place,

" Him likis als weill your worschip till awance,

" As yhe war born a liege man off France.

1675 " Sen his regioun is flour off rewmys seyn;

" Als the gret band off kindnes yow betweyn;

" It war worschip his presens for to se,

" Sen at this rewm standis in sic degre."

Wallace consawit, with outyn tarying,

1680 The gret desyr off this gud nobill king;

Syn till him said; ' As God off hewin me sawe,

'Her eftir sone ye sall ane ansuer hawe
'Off your desyr, that ye hawe schawit me till:
'Welcum ye ar with a fre hartly will.'
1685 The harrold baid, on to the twenty day,
With Wallace still, in gud weillfayr and play;
Contende the tyme with worschip and plesance;
Be gud awyss maid his deliuerance.
With his awn hand he wrait on to the king
1690 All his entent, as twyching to this thing.
Rycht rych reward he gaiff the harrold tho,
And him conwoyde, quhen he had leyff to go,
Out off the toun with gudly cumpanye,
His leyff he tuk, syn went on to the se.
1695 Gud Wallace than has maid his prouidance;
His purpos was to se the king off France.
Erest in weyr to Sanct Jhonstoun couth fair;
A consaill than he had gert ordane thar.
In till his sted he chesyt a gouernour
1700 To kep the land, a man off gret walour,
Jamys gud lord, the stewart off Scotland,
Fol. 75 b Quhilk fadyr was, as storys beris on hand,
To gud Waltre that was off hye parage,
[Marjory] the Bruce syne gat in mariage.
1705 Tharoff to spek as now I haiff no space;
It is weill knawin, thankit be Goddis grace:
And to the harrold, with outyn residens,
How he approchyt to the kingis presens.
Fra the Rochell the land sone has he tayn.
1710 Atour the landis he graithit him to gayn,
Sekand the king, als gudly as he may.
So to the court he passit on a day;
To Paryss went, was peirles off renoun.
The king that tym held palace in that toun.
1715 Quhen he hym saw, graithly has wndirstand,

He speryt tithingis, and weyllfayr off Scotland.
The herrold said, in to thir termys schort,
That all was gud; he had the mar comfort.
" Saw thow Wallace, the chyftayn off Scotland?"
1720 And he said; ' Ya; that I dar tak on hand,
' A worthyar this day lyffand is nayn,
' In way off wer, als fer as I haiff gayn.
' The hie worschip, and the gret nobilnes,
' The gud weillfair, plesande and worthines,
1725 ' The rych reward was mychty for to se,
' That for your saik he kythyt apon me;
' And his ansuer in wryt he has yow send.'
The king rasauit it with a lycht attend,
This hie affect and dyt off his writyng.
1730 " O ryoll roy, and rychtwyss crownyt king,
" Yhe knaw this weill, be othir ma than me,
" How that our rewlm standis in perplexité.
" The fals nacioun, that we ar nychtbouris to,
" Quhen plessis thaim, thai mak ws ay ado;
1735 " Thar may na band be maid so sufficians,
" Bot ay in it thai fynd a warians.
" To wait a tym, will God at it may be,
" With in a yer I sall your presens se."
Off this ansuer weill plessyt was the king.
1740 Leyff I him thus in ryolté to ryng,
And glaid comford rycht as I haiff yow tald:
Off Wallace furth I will my process hald.

EXPLICIT LIBER OCTAUUS,
ET INCIPIT NONUS.

In Aperill the one and twenty day,
The hie calend, thus Cancer, as we say,
The lusty tym off Mayus fresche cummyng,
Fol. 76 a Celestiall gret blythnes in to bryng;
5 Pryncypaill moneth forsuth it may be seyn,
The hewynly hewis apon the tendyr greyn,
Quhen old Saturn his cloudy courss had gon,
The quhilk had beyn bath best and byrdis bon:
Zepherus ek, with his suet vapour,
10 He comfort has, be wyrking off natour,
All fructuouss thing in till the erd adoun,
At rewllyt is wndyr the hie regioun:
Sobyr Luna, in flowyng off the se,
Quhen brycht Phebus is in his chemagé,
15 The Bulys courss so takin had his place,
And Jupiter was in the Crabbis face:
Quhen conryet the hot syng coloryk,
In to the Ram, quhilk had his rowmys ryk,
He chosyn had his place and his mansioun,
20 In Capricorn, the sygn off the Lioun:
Gentill [Jupiter,] with his myld ordinance,
Bath erb and tre reuertis in plesance;
And fresch Flora hir floury mantill spreid,
In euery waill, bath hop, hycht, hill, and meide:
25 This sammyn tym, for thus myn auctor sayis,
Wallace to pass off Scotland tuk his wayis.

Be schort awyss he schup him to the se,
And fyfty men tuk in his cumpané.
He leit no word than walk off his passage,
30 Or Inglissmen had stoppit him his wiage:
Nor tuk na leiff at the lordis off the parlement;
He wyst full weill thai wald nocht all consent
To suffyr him out off the land to go.
For thi onon, with outyn wordis mo,
35 He gart forsé, and ordand weill his schip.
And thir war part past in his falowschip;
Twa Wallace, was his kynnys men full ner,
Craufurd, Kneland, was haldyn till him der.
Off Kyrkcubré he purpost his passage;
40 Semen he feyt, and gaiff thaim gudlye wage:
Thai wantyt nocht off wyn, wittaill nor ger;
A fair new barge rycht worthi wrocht for wer.
With that thai war a gudly cumpany
Off waillit men, had wrocht full hardely.
45 Bonalais drank rycht glaidly in a morow,
Syn leiff thai tuk, and with Sanct Jhon to borow.
Bottis was schot, and fra the roch thaim sent;
With glaid hartis, at anys in thai went;
Wpon the schip thai rowit hastely.
50 The seymen than, walkand full besyly,
Fol. 76 b Ankyrs wand in wysly on athir syd;
Thair lynys kest, and waytyt weyll the tyd;
Leyt salys fall, and has thair courss ynom:
A gud gay wynd out off the rycht art com.
55 Frekis in forstame, rewllit weill thar ger,
Ledys on luff burd, with a lordlik fer:
Lansys laid out, to [luik] thar passage sound.
With full sayll thus fra Scotland furth thai found;
Salyt [haill] our the day and als the nycht.
60 Apon the morn, quhen [that] the son raiss brycht,

The ship master on to the top he went;
Sowthest he saw, that trublyt his entent,
Sexten salis arayit all on raw,
In colour reid, and towart him couth draw.
65 The gliterand son apon thaim schawit brycht,
The se about enlumynyt with the lycht.
This mannis spreit was in ane extasy,
Doun went he sone, and said full sorowfully;
"Allace," quoth he, "the day that I was born!
70 "With out rameid our lywys ar forlorn.
"In cursyt tym I tuk this cur on hand;
"The best chyftayn, and reskew off Scotland,
"Our raklesly I haiff tayn vpon me,
"With waik power to bryng him throw the se.
75 "It forsyt nocht, wald God I war torment,
"So Wallace mycht with worschip chaip wnschent."
Quhen Wallace saw, and hard this mannys mon,
To comfort him in gud will is he gon.
'Maister,' he said, 'quhat has amowit the?'
80 "Nocht for my selff, this man said petuislé.
"Bot off a thing I dar weill wndirtane,
"Thocht all war heyr the schippis off braid Bertane,
"Part suld we loss, set fortoun had it suorn.
"The best wer man in se is ws beforn,
85 "Leffand this day, and king is off the se."
Wallace sone sperd, 'Wait yow quhat he may be?'
"The Red Reffayr thai call him in his still.
"That I him saw euyr, waryt worth that quhill!
"For myn awn lyff I wald no murnyng mak;
90 "Is na man born that yon tyran will tak.
"He savis nayn, for gold, nor othir gud,
"Bot slayis and drownys all derffly in the flud;
"He gettis no grace, thocht he war king or knycht.
"This sextene yer he has doyn gret wnrycht.

95 " The power is so strang he has to ster,
" May non eschaip that cummys in his danger.
" Wald we him burd, na but is to begyn;
" The lakest schip, that is his flot within,
Fol. 77 a " May sayll ws doun on to a dulfull ded."
100 Than Wallace said; ' Sen yow can no ramed,
' Tell me his feyr, and how I sall him knaw;
' Quhat is hys oyss; and syn go luge the law.'
The schipman sayis; " Rycht weill ye may him ken,
" Throu graith takynnys, full clerly by his men.
105 " His cot armour is seyn in mony steid,
" Ay battaill boun, and riwell ay off reid.
" This formest schip, that persewis yow so fast,
" Hym selff is in, he will nocht be agast.
" He wyll yow hayll, quhen that he cummys yow ner;
110 " With out tary than mon yhe stryk on ster.
" Hym selff will entir fyrst full hardely.
" Thir ar the syngnys that ye sall knaw him by;
" A bar off blew in till his schenand scheild,
" A bend off greyn desyren ay the feild.
115 " The rede betakynnys blud and hardyment,
" The greyn, curage, encressand his entent;
" The blew he beris, becauss he is a Crystyn man."
Sadly agayn Wallace ansuerd than;
' Thocht he be crystynyt, this war no godlyk deid.
120 ' Go wndyr loft; Sanct Androw mot ws speid!'
Bathe schip maistir, and the ster man also,
In the holl, but baid, he gert thaim go.
His fyfty men with outyn langar rest,
Wallace gart ray in to thar armour prest;
125 Fourty and aucht on luffburd laid thaim law.
Wylyham Crawfurd than till him gert he caw,
And said; " Thow can sumpart off schipman fair;
" Thi oyss has beyn oft in the toun off Ayr.

      " I pray the tak this doctryn [weill] off me;

130 " Luk at thow stand strekly be this tre,

      " Quhen I bid stryk, to seruice be thow bayne;

      " Quhen I the warn, lat draw the saill agayne.

      " Kneland, cusyng, cum tak the ster on hand;

      " Her on the waill ner by the I sall stand.

135 " God gyd our schip! as now I say na mar."

      The barge, be that, with a full werlik far;

      Him selff on loft [was] with a drawyn suord,

      And bad his ster man lay thaim langis the bourd;

      On loude he cryit; ' Stryk, doggis, ye sall de.'

140 Crawfurd leit draw the saill a litill we,

      The capdane sone lap in, and wald nocht stynt.

      Wallace in haist be the gorget him hynt,

      On the our loft kest him quhar he stud,

      Quhill neyss and mowth all ruschit out off blud.

145 A forgyt knyff, but baid, he bradis out.

Fol. 77 b The wer schippis was lappyt thaim about.

      The mekill barge had nocht thaim clyppyt fast;

      Crawfurd drew saill, skewyt by, and off thaim past.

      The Reiffar criyt, with petous woice and cler,

150 Grace off hys lyff, " for him that boucht yow der!

      " Mercy," he said, " for him that deit on rud,

      " Layser to mend! I haiff spilt mekill blud.

      " For my trespas I wald mak sum ramed."

      Wallace wyst weyll, thocht he war brocht to ded;

155 And off his lyff sum reskew mycht he mak.

      A bettir purpos sone he can to tak;

      And als he rewyt him, for his lyff was ill.

      In Latyn tong rycht thus he said him till;

      ' I tuk neuir man, that enemy was to me:

160 ' For Goddis saik thi lyff I grant to the.'

      Bathe knyff and suerd he tuk fra him onon;

      Wp be the hand, and as presoner, has him ton:

And on his suerd scharply he gert him suer,
Fra that day furth he suld him neuir der.

165 'Commaund thi men,' quoth Wallace, 'till our pess;
'Thar schot off gown, that was nocht eith, to cess.'
The cast it was rycht awfull on athir sid.
The Rede Reiffar commaundyt thaim to bid;
Held out a gluff, in takyn off the trew.

170 His men beheld, and weyll that senye knew,
Left off thar schot, that sygn quhen that thai saw,
His grettast barge towart him couth [he] draw.
"Lat be your wer, thir ar our freyndis at ane;
"I traist to God our werst dayis ar gane."

175 He ast Wallace to do quhat was his will.
With schort awyss rycht thus he said him till;
'To the Rochell I wald ye gert thaim saill;
'For Inglissmen I wait nocht quhat may aill.
'For thar, God will, is our purposs to be.

180 'Skour weyll about for scoukaris in the se.'
His commaund thai did in all the haist thai can.
Wallace desyryt to talk mor with this man,
Sadly he sperd; "Off quhat land was thou born?"
'Off France,' quoth he, 'and my eldris beforn;

185 'And thar we had sumpart off heretage:
'Yet fers fortoun thus brocht me in a rage.'
Wallace sperd; "How com thow to this lyff?"
'Forsuth,' he said, 'bot throw a sudan stryff.
'So hapnyt me, in to the kingis presens,

190 'Our raklesly to do our gret offens.
'A nobill man, off gud fame and renoun,
'That throw my deid was put to confusioun,
Fol. 78 a 'Dede off a straik; quhat nedis wordis mor?
'All helpyt nocht, thocht I repentyt full sor.

195 'Throw freyndys off the court I chapyt off that place,
'And neuir sen syn couth get the kingis grace:

'For my saik mony off my kyn gert thai de.
'And quhen I saw it mycht no bettir be,
'Bot leyff the land that me behuffyt o neid,
200 'Apon a day to Burdeous I yeid.
'Ane Ingliss schip so gat I on a nycht,
'For sey lawbour that ernystfully was dycht.
'To me thar semblyt misdoaris, and weill mo;
'And in schort tym we multiplyit so,
205 'That thar wes few our power mycht withstand.
'In tyranry thus haiff we rongyn lang.
'This sexten yer I haiff beyn on the se,
'And doyn gret harm; tharfor full wa is me.
'I savit nayn, for gold nor gret ransoun,
210 'Bot slew and drownyt in to the se adoun.
'Fawour I did till folk off syndry land;
'Bot Franchmen no frendschip with me fand,
'Thai gat no grace als fer as I mycht ryng.
'Als on the se I clypyt was a king.
215 'Now se I weyll that my fortoun is went,
'Vincust with ane; that gerris me sair rapent.
'Quha wald haiff said, this sammyn day at morn,
'I suld with ane thus lychtly doun be born,
'In gret hething my men it wald haiff tayne.
220 'My selff trowit till [haiff] machit mony ane:
'Bot I haiff found the werray playn contrar.
'Her I gyff our roubry for euirmar;
'In sic mysrewll I sall neuir armes ber,
'Bot gyff it be in honest oyss to wer.
225 'Now haiff I told part off my blyss and payn;
'For Goddis saik sum kyndnes kyth agayn.
'My hart will brek, bot I wyt quhat thou be,
'Thus outrageously that has rabutyt me.
'For weill I wend that leyffand had beyn non,
230 'Be fors off strenth mycht me as presoner ton,

' Except Wallace, that has rademyt Scotland,
' The best is callyt this day beltyt with brand.
' In till his wer war worschip for to wak,
' As now in warld I trow he has no mak.'
235 Tharat he smylit, and said; " Frend, weill may be,
" Scotland had mystir off mony sic as he.
" Quhat is thi naym? tell me; so haiff thow seill!"

Fol. 78 b ' Forsuth,' he said, ' Thomas off Longaweill.'
" Weyll bruk thow it! all thus stentis our stryff:
240 " Schaip to pleyss God in mendyng off thi lyff.
" Thi faithfull freynd my selff thinkis to be;
" And als my nayme I sall sone tell to thé.
" For chans off wer thou suld no murnyng mak;
" As werd will wyrk, thi fortoun mon thou tak.
245 " I am that man that you awanss so hie;
" And bot schort tym sen I come to the se:
" Off Scotland born, my rycht name is Wallace."
On kneis he fell, and thankit God of grace;
' I dar awow, that yoldyn is my hand
250 ' To the best man that beltis him with brand.
' Forsuth,' he said, ' this blythis me mekill mor,
' Than off floryng ye gaiff me sexty scor.'
Wallace ansuerd; " Sen thou art her throw chance,
" My purpos is, be this wiage, in France;
255 " And to the king sen I am boun to pass,
" To my reward thi peess I think to ass."
' Pess I wald haiff [fane] of my rychtwiss king;
' And no langar in to that realm to ryng,
' Than to tak leyff, and cum off it agayn.
260 ' In thi seruice I think for to ramayn.'
" Seruice," he said, " Thomas, that may nocht be,
" Bot gud frendschip, as I desir off the:"
Gart draw the wyn, and ilk man mery maid;
Be this the schippis was in the Rochell raid.

265 The rede blasonys thai had born in to wer;
The toun was sone in till a sudane fer.
The Rede Reiffar thai saw was at thair hand,
The quhilk throu strenth mycht nayn agayne him stand.
Sum schippis fled, and sum the land has tayn,
270 Clariownys blew, and trumpattis mony ane.
Quhen Wallace saw the pepill was on ster,
He gaiff commaund na schip suld ner apper;
Bot his awin barge in to the hawyn gart draw.
The folk was fayn quhen thai that senye saw;
275 Rycht weyll thai knew in gold the rede lioun,
Leit wp the port, rasauit him in the toun,
And sufferyt thaim, for all that he had brocht.
The rede nawyn in to the hawyn thai socht;
On land thai went, quhar thai likit to pass.
280 Rycht few thar wyst quhat Scottisman Wallace was;
Bot weyll thai thocht he was a gudly man,
And honouryt him in all the craft thai can.
Bot four dayis still Wallace ramaynyt thar;
Fol. 79 a Thir men he callyt, quhen he was boun to fair.
285 He thaim commaundyt apon that cost to bid,
Quhill he thaim fred for chans at mycht betid.
" Ber yow ewyn; quhat gud that euir yhe spend,
" Leiff on your awin; quhill tithandis I yow send.
" Ger sell thir schippis, and mak yow men off pes;
290 " It war gud tym off wykkitness to cess.
" Your captane sall pass to the king with me,
" Throu help off God I sall his warrand be."
He gert graith him in soit with his awin men;
Was no man thar that mycht weill Thomas ken.
295 Lykly he was, manlik off contenance,
Lik to the Scottis be mekill gouernance,
Saiff off his tong, for Ingliss had he nane;
In Latyn weill he mycht suffice for ane.

Thus past his court in all the haste thai may.
300 To Paris toun thai went apon a day.
Tythingis was brocht off Wallace to the king;
So gret desyr he had off na kyn thing,
As in that tym quhill he had seyn Wallace.
To meyt him selff he waytit apon cace
305 In a gardyng, quhar he gart thaim be brocht.
Till his presence with manly feyr thai socht,
Twa and fyfty at anys kneland doun,
And salust him, as ryoll off most renoun,
With rewllyt spech in so gudly awyss,
310 All France couth nocht [mair] nurtour tham dewyss.
The queyn had leiff, and com in hyr effer;
For mekill scho herd off Wallace deid in wer.
Quhat nedis mor off curtassy to tell?
Thai kepyt weill that to the Scottis befell.
315 Off kingis fer I dar mak no rahers;
My febill mynd, my trublyt spreit rewers.
Off rich scruice quhat nedis wordis mor?
Mycht non be found bot it was present thor.
Sone eftir meit the king to parlour went,
320 With gudly lordis; thar Wallace was present.
Than commound thai off mony syndry thing;
To spek with him gret desyr had the king.
At hym he speryt off wer the gouernance.
He ansuerd him, with manly contenance,
325 Till euery poynt, als fer as he had feill,
In Latyn tong rycht naturaly and weill.
The king consauit, sone throu his hie knawlage,
Quhat wermen oysyt be reyff in thar passage.
In till his mynd the Rede Reiffar than was;
Fol. 79 b 330 Merwell he had how he leit Wallace pass.
Till him he said; " Ye war sum thing to blaym;
" Ye mycht haiff send, be our harrold fra haym,

" Eftir power, to bryng yow throu the se."
' God thank yow, schyr, ynewch tharoff had we.
335 ' Feill men may pass, quhar thai fynd na perell;
' Rycht few may kep, quhar nayn is to assaill.'
" Wallace," he said, " tharoff merwell haiff 1;
" A tyran ryngis, in ire full cruelly,
" Apon the se, that gret sorow has wrocht;
340 " Mycht we him get, it suld not be for nocht.
" Born off this land, a natyff man to me;
" Tharfor on ws the grettar harme dois he."
Than Thomas quok, and changyt contenans;
He hard the king his ewill deidis awans.
345 Wallace beheld, and fenyeit in a part;
' Forsuth,' he said, ' we fand nane in that art,
' That proffryt ws sic wnkyndlynes.
' Bot with your leiff I spek in haymlynes,
' Trow ye be sycht ye couth that squier knaw?'
350 " Full lang it war sen tym that I him saw.
" Bot thir wordis off him ar bot in wayn;
" Or he com her, rycht gud men will be slayn."
Than Wallace said; ' Her I haiff brocht with me,
' Off likly men that was in our countré:
355 ' Quhilk off all thir wald ye call him most lik?'
Amang thaim blent that ryoll roy most ryk,
Wesyit thaim weill, bathe statur and curage,
Maner, makdome, thar fassoun and thar wesage.
Sadly he said, awysit sobyrly;
360 " That largest man, quhilk standis next yow by,
" Wald I call him, be makdome to dewice.
" Thir ar no thing bot wordis off office."
Befor the king on kneis fell gud Wallace:
' O ryoll roy, off hie honour and grace,
365 ' With waist wordis I will nocht yow trawaill;
' Now 1 will spek sum thing for myn awaill.

'Our barnat land has beyn our set with wer,
'With Saxonis blud that dois ws mckill der,
'Slayn our eldris, distroyit our rychtwys blud,
370 'Waistyt our realm off gold and othir gud.
'And ye ar her, in mycht and ryolté,
'Yow suld haiff cy till our aduersité,
'And ws support, throu kyndnes off the band,
'Quhilk is conserwyt betuix yow and Scotland.
375 'As I am her, at your charge, for plesance,
'My lyflat is bot honest chewysance.
'Flour off realmys fersuth is this regioun;
'To my reward I wald haiff gret gardoun.'
Fol. 80 a "Wallace," he said, "now ask quhat ye wald haiff.
380 "Gud gold or land sall nocht be lang to craiff."
Wallace ansuerd; 'So ye it grant to me,
'Quhat I wald haiff it sall sone chosyn be.'
"Quhat euir yhe ask, that is in this regioun,
"Ye sall it haiff, except my wyff and croun."
385 He thankit hym off his gret kyndlynes.
'My reward all sall be askyng off grace,
'Pees to this man I broucht with me throu chans;
'Her I quytcleym all othir gyfftis in Frans;
'This samyn is he, gyff ye knaw him weill,
390 'That we off spak, Thomas off Longaweill;
'Be rygour ye desyryt he suld be slayn;
'I him restor in to your grace agayn.
'Rasaiff him fayr, as liege man off your land.'
The king marweld, and couth in study stand;
395 Perfytly knew that it was Longaweill;
He him forgaiff his trespas euirilkdeill,
Bot for his saik that had him hydder brocht;
For gold or land ellis he gat it nocht.
"Wallace," he said, "I had leuir off gud land,
400 "Thre hundreth pund haiff sesyt in thi hand.

" That I haiff said sall be grantyt in plain;
. " Her I restor Thomas to pes agayn,
" Derer to me than euyr he was befor,
" All for your saik, thocht it war mekill mor.
405 " Bot I wald wyt how that merwell befell."
Wallace answerd; ' The trewth I sall yow tell.'
Than he rahersyt quhat hapnyt on that day,
As ye befor in my autor hard say.
Quhen the gud king had herd this sudan cass
410 Apon the se, be forsicht off Wallace,
The king him held rycht worthi till awans;
He saw in hym manheid and gouernans.
So did the queyn, and all thir othir lordis;
Ilk wicht off hym gret honour than recordis.
415 He purchest pes, for all the power haill,
Fyfteyn hundreth was left in the Rochaill;
Gert cry thaim fre, trew serwandis to the king,
And neuir agayn fautyt in sic thing.
Quhen Thomas was restoryt to his rycht,
420 Off hys awin hand the king has maid him knycht.
Eftir he gaiff stayt to his nerrest ayr;
And maid him selff with Wallace for to fayr.
Thus he was brocht fra naym off reyff, throu cace,
Be sudand chans off him and wicht Wallace.
425 Thus leyff I thaim in worschip and plesance,
At liking still with the gud king off France.
Thai thretty dayis he lugyt in to rest;
Fol. 80 b So to ramayn he thocht it nocht the best.
Still in to pes he couth nocht lang endur;
430 Wncorduall it was till his natur.
Rycht weyll he wyst that Inglissmen occupyit
Gyane that tym; tharfor he has aspyit
Sum jeperté apon thaim for to mak.
A gudly leyff he at the kyng couth tak.

435 Off Franchmen he wald nayne with him call,
At that fyrst tym for auentur mycht fall;
Bot Schyr Thomas that seruice couth persew,
He wyst nocht weyll gyff all the layff was trew.
Off Scottis men thai semblyt hastely

440 Nyne hundyr sum off worthi chewalry;
In Gyan land full haistely couth ryd,
Raissyt feill fyr, and waistyt wonnyngis wid:
Fortrass thai brak, and stalwart byggyngis wan;
Derffly to dede brocht mony Sotheron man.

445 A werlik toun so fand thai in that land,
Quhilk Schenown hecht, that Inglissmen had in hand.
Towart that steid full sadly Wallace wrocht,
Be ony wyss assailye gyff he mocht,
Bargane till haiff and he mycht get thaim out.

450 Gret strenth off wod that tym was thar about;
This toun [stud] als apon a wattir sid.
In till a park, that was bath lang and wyd,
Thai buschit thaim, quhill passit was the nycht.
Quhen the sone raiss, four hundreth men he dycht;

455 The laiff he gert Craufurd in buschement tak,
Gyff thai myster, a reskew for to mak.
Than Longaweill, that ay was full sawage,
With Wallace past, as ane to that scrymmage.
Thir four hundreth rycht wondyr weyll arayit,

460 Befor the toun the playn baner displayit.
This was nocht to thaim weill knawyn in that contré,
The lyoun in gold rycht awfull for to se;
A forray kest, and sessit mekill gud.
Wermen with in, that playnly wndrestud,

465 Sone wschit forth the pray for to reskew.
The worthy Scottis feill Inglissmen thai slew;
The laiff for dreid fled to the toun agayn.
The forray tuk the pray, and past the playn,

Towart the park; bot power off the toun
470 Wschyt agayn in awfull battaill boun,
A thousand hayle wyth men off armys strang;
Few baid tharin that mycht to bargane gang.
Than Wallace gert the forreouris leyff the pray;
Assemblyt sone in till a gud aray.
475 A cruell conterans at that metyng was seyn,
Off wicht wermen in to thair armour cleyn.
Feyll lessyt thar lyff apon the Sotheroun sid,
Bot nocht for thi rycht bauldly thai abyd.
Off the Scottis part worthi men thai slew.
'ol. 81 a 480 Wylyham Craufurd, that weyll the perell knew,
Out off the park he gert the buschement pas,
In to the feild quhar feyll men fechtand was.
At thair entré thai gert full mony de.
The Inglissmen was wondyr laith to fle;
485 Full worthely thai wrocht in to that place.
Baid neuir sa few so lang agayn Wallace,
Wyth sic power as he that day was thar.
On athir syd assailyeit ferly sayr.
In to the stour so fellonly thai wrocht,
490 Rycht worthy men derffly to dede thai brocht;
Wyth poyntis persyt throuch platis burnyst brycht.
Wallace hym selff, and gud Thomas [the] knycht,
Quhom that thai hyt maid neuir mor debait.
The Sotheron part was handlyt thar full hayt.
495 In to that place thai mycht no langar byd;
Out off the feyld with sar hartis thai ryd:
On to the toun thai fled full haistely.
Wallace folowit, and his gud chewalry,
Fechtand so fast in to that thykkest thrang,
500 Quhill in the toun he enterit thaim amang;
With him Crawfurd, and Longaweill off mycht,
And Rychard als, Wallace his cusyng wicht;

Fyfteyn thai war off Scottis cumpany.
Thus hapnyt thai amang the gret party.
505 A cruell portar gat apon the wall,
Powit out a pyn, the portculys leit fall.
Inglissmen saw that entrit was na ma;
Apon the Scottis full hardely thai ga:
Bot tyll a wall thai haiff thar bakkis set,
510 Sad strakys and sayr baulclly about thaim bet.
Rychard Wallace the turngreys weill has seyn;
He folowit fast apon the portar keyn,
A tour the wall dede in the dyk him draiff,
Tuk wp the port, and leit in all the layff.
515 Quhen Wallace men had thus the entré won,
Full gret slauchtir agane thai haff begon;
Thai savit nayn apon the Sotheroun syd,
That wapynnys bar, or harnes in that tid.
Wemen and barnys, the gud thai tuk thaim fra,
520 Syn gaiff thaim leyff in to realm to ga;
And preystis als, that war nocht in the feild.
Off agyt men, quhilk mycht na wapynnis weild,
Thai slew nayn sic, so Wallace chargis was;
Bot maid thaim fre, at thair largis to pass.
525 Ryches off gold thai gat in gret plenté,
Harnes and horss, that mycht thaim weill supplé;
Wyth Franch folk plenyst the toun agayn;
On the tend day the feyld thai tuk in playn;
The riwer doun in to the land thai socht,
530 On Sotheron men full mekill maister thai wrocht.
Quhen to [the] king trew men had tald this taill,
Fol. 81 b Off Franchmen thai semblyt a battaill;
Twenty thousand [off] lele legis off France;
Hys brothir thaim led, was duk of Orlyans.
535 Throu Gyan land in rayid battaill thai raid,
To folow Wallace, and maid but litill baid

For Frans supplé, to help thaim in thair rycht.
Ner Burdeous, or thai our tuk him mycht,
Gud Wallace was, and Thomas had in playn;
540 For sum men tald, that Burdeous, with gret mayn,
With in schort tym thocht battaill for to geyff.
Bot fra thai wyst that Franch folk couth raleiff,
Wyth gret power, with helpyng off Wallace,
Wthyr purpos thai tuk in to schort space.

545   In Pykarté sone message thai couth send;
Off Wallace com thai tald it till ane end.
Off Glosister, captane off Calyss was,
The hardy erll; and maid him for to pass
In Ingland sone; and syne to London went.
550 Off Wallace deid he tald in the parlement.
Sum playnly [said] that Wallace brak the pess.
Wysmen said Nay, and prayit thaim for to cess.
Lord Bowmont said; " He tuk bot for Scotland,
" And nocht for Frans, that sall ye wndyrstand.
555 " Gyff our endentour spekis for ony mair,
" He has doyne wrang, the suth ye may declar."
Wodstok ansuerd; ' Schyr, ye haiff spokyn weill.
' Bot contrar resone that taill is euirilkdeill:
' Gyff yon be he that band for him and his,
560 ' May na man say bot he has wrocht amyss.
' For pryncipaly he band with ws the trew,
' And now agayn begynnys a malice new.
' Schyr king,' he said, ' gyff ye think cuir to mak
' On Scotland wer, on hand now ye sall tak,
565 ' Quhill he is out, or ellis it helpis nocht.'
As Wodstok said, the haill consaill has wrocht;
Power thai raissyt on Scotland for to ryd,
Be land and se; thai wald no langar byd.
Thar land ost thai rayit weyll in deid;

570 Thar wantgard tuk the hardy erll to leid
Off Glosister, that off wer had gret feill;
Off Longcastell the duk demanyt weill
The mydillward; on to the se thai send
Schyr Jhon Sewart, that weyll the northland kend.

575 The knycht Wallang befor the ost in raid;
In sic a way wyth ewyll Scottis men he maid,
Mony castellis he gert sone yoldin be
Till Inglissmen, with outyn mar mellé.
Or the best wyst, that it was wer in playn,

580 Entryt he was in to Bothwell agane.

Fol. 82 a Schyr Jhon Sewart, that com in be the se,
Sanct Jhonstoun sone gat throw a jeperté.
Dundé thai tuk, and putt Scottismen to dede;
In Fyff fra thaim was nocht kepyt a sted;

585 And all the south, fra Cheuyot to the se.
In to the west thar mycht na succour be;
The worthy lord, that suld haiff gouernyt this,
God had hym tayn, we trow, in lestand blyss:
Hys son Walter, that bot a child than was,

590 Trew men him tuk, and couth in Arrane pass.
Adam Wallace than wyst off no supplé,
Till Rawchlé went, and Lindsay off Craggé;
Gud Robert Boid maid no residens;
For haisty desait, thai tuk thaim to defens.

595 Schyr Jhon the Graym in Dundaff mycht nocht bid,
Succour he socht in to the forest off Clid.
The knycht Sewart, a schyrreff maid in Fyff
Schyr Amer Brim; and gaiff, for term off lyff,
The landis haill that Wallang aucht befor.

600 Rychard Lundy had gret dreid off thar schoyr;
He likyt nocht for to cum to thar pess,
For thi in Fyff thai wald nocht lat him cess.
To pass our Tay as than it mycht nocht be,

For Inglissmen so rewllyt that cuntré.
605 Owt off the land he staw away be nycht,
Auchtene with him that worthy war and wycht;
And als his sone, that was off tendyr eild;
Bot eftir sone he couth weill wapynnys weild.
At Sterlyng bryg, quhar at the wach wes set,
610 Thar passyt he away with outyn let.
In Dundaff mur Schyr Jhon the Graym he socht;
A woman tald, as than befor was wrocht;
And till a strenth he drew him on the morn.
Laynrik was tayn with young Thomas off Thorn;
615 So Lundy thair mycht mak no langar remayn:
Besouth Tynto lugis thai maid in playn.
Schyr Jhon the Graym gat wit that he was thair;
Till him he past with outyn wordis mar.
Wallang gart bryng fra Carlele cariage,
620 To stuff Bothwell with wyn and gud warnage.
Lundy and Graym gat wyt off that awaill,
Rycht sudanly thai maid thaim till assaill:
Fyfty thai war off nobill chewalry,
Agayn four scor off Ingliss cumpany.
625 Ane Skelton than kepyt the careage,
All Brankstewat that was his heretage.
Lundy and Graym met with the squier wicht;
Feill Inglissmen to ded derffly thai dycht.
Sexté was slayn apon the tothir sid,
630 And fyve off Scottis, so bauldly thai abid.
Gret gud thai wan, bath gold and othir ger,
Fol. 82 b Wittayll and horss that hapnyt in that wer.
Syn thai haiff seyn weyll lang thai mycht nocht lest
In to that land, tharfor thai thocht it best
635 To seik sum place, in strenth that thai mycht bid,
For Sotheron men had plenyst on ilk sid.
Lundeis luge thai left upon a nycht;

Q

In the Lennox the way thai passyt rycht
Till erll Malcom, that kepyt that cuntré
640 Fra Inglissmen, with help off thar supplé.
Cetoun and Lyll in to the Bass thai baid;
For Sotheroun folk so gret mastryss had maid,
That all the south was tayn in to thar hand.
Gud Hew the Hay was send in to Ingland,
645 And vthir ayris, to presoune at thar will.
The northland lordis, saw na help cum thaim till,
A squier Guthré amang thaim ordand thai,
To warn Wallace in all the haist he may.
Out off Arbroth he passit to the se.
650 And at the Slus, land takyn son had he;
In Flandrys land no residens he maid;
In Frans he past; bot Wallace weill abaid
On his purpos in Gyan at the wer:
On Sotheroun men he had doyn mekill der.
655 Quhill gud Guthré had gottyn his presens,
He haistyt him sone, and maid no residens;
He has him tald, with Scotland how it stud.
Than Wallace said; " Thai tithingis ar nocht gud.
" I had exampill, off tym that is by worn,
660 " Trewys to bynd with thaim that was maynsuorn:
" Bot I as than couth nocht think on sic thing,
" Be causs that we tuk this pess with thar king.
" Be thar chansler the tothir pess was bwn,
" And that full sair our forfadris has fwn;
665 " Wndyr that trew auchtene scor thai gart de,
" At noblis war, the best in our cuntré!
" To the gret God my wow now her I mak,
" Pess with that king I think neuir for to tak.
" He sall repent, that thai this wer began."
670 Thus mowit he, with mony ryoll man,
On to the king, and tauld him his entent.
Till lat him pass the king wald nocht consent,

Quhill [Wallace] thar maid promyss be his hand.
Gyff euir agayn he thocht to leyff Scotland,
675 To cum till him; his gret seyll he him gaiff
Off quhat lordschip that he likit till haiff.
Thus at the king haisty leiff tuk he.
Na ma with him he brocht off that cuntré,
Bot his awn men, and Schyr Thomas the knycht.
680 In Flawndrys land thai past with all thar mycht.

Fol. 83 a Guthreis barg was at the Slus left styll;
To se thai went wyth ane full egyr wyll.
Bath Forth and Tay thai left and passyt by
On the north cost, [gud] Guthré was thar gy.
685 In Munross hawyn thai brocht hym to the land;
Till trew Scottis it was a blyth tithand.
Schyr Jhon Ramsay, that worthi was and wycht,
Fra Ochtyrhouss the way he chesyt rycht,
To meite Wallace with men off armes strang;
690 Off his duellyng thai had thocht wondyr lang.
The trew Ruwan come als with outyn baid;
In Barnart wod he had his lugyng maid.
Barklay be that to Wallace semblyt fast;
With thre hundreth to Ochtyrhouss he past.

695   The later day off August fell this cace;
For the reskew, thus ordanyt wicht Wallace,
Off Sanct Jhonstoun, that Sothroun occupyit.
Fast towart Tay thai passyt and aspyit;
Or it was day wndyr Kynnowll thaim laid.
700 Out off the toun, as Scottis men till hym said,
That serwandys oysyt with cartis hay to leid;
So was it suth, and hapnyt in to deid.
Saxsum thar com, and brocht bot cartis thre.
Quhen thai off hay was ladand most byssé,
705 Guthré with ten in handys has thaim tayn,

Put thaim to dede, off thaim he sawyt nayn.
Wallace gert tak in haist thar humest weid,
And sic lik men thai waillyt, weill gud speid;
Four was rycht rud, Wallace hym selff tuk ane,
710 A rwssyt clok, and with him gud Ruwane.
Guthré with that, and als gud yemen twa,
In that ilk soit thai graithit thaim to ga.
Full sutelly thai coueryt thaim with hay,
Syne to the toun thai went the gaynest way.
715 Fyfteyn thai tuk off men in armes wicht,
In ilk cart fyve thai ordanyt owt off sycht.
Thir cartaris had schort suerdis, off gud steill,
Wndyr thar weidis, callyt furth the cartis weill.
Schyr Jhon Ramsay baid with a buschement still,
720 Quhen mystir war to help thaim with gud will.
Thir trew cartaris past with outyn lett,
A tour the bryg, and entryt throu the yet;
Quhen thai war in, thar clokis kest thaim fra,
Gud Wallace than the mayster portar can ta
725 Wpon the hed, quhill dede he has him left;
Syn othir twa the lyff fra thaim has reft.
Guthré, be that, did rycht weyll in the toun;
Fol. 83 b And Ruwan als dang off thar famen doune.
The armyt men, was in the cartis brocht,
730 Raiss wp, and weill thar dawery has wrocht;
Apon the gait thai gert feill Sothroun de.
The Ramsais spy, has seyn [thaim] get entré,
The buschement brak, bathe bryg and port has won:
Into the toun gret stryff thar was begon.
735 Thai twenty men, or Ramsay come in playn,
Within the toun had saxté Sotheroun slayn.
The Inglissmen on till aray was gayn;
The Scottis as than layser lett them get nayn;
Fra gud Ramsay with his men entryt in,

740 Thai sawit nayn was born off Ingliss kyn.
Als Longaweill, the wycht knycht Schyr Thomas,
Prewyt weill than, and in mony othir place.
Agayn his dynt few Inglissmen mycht stand;
Wallace with him gret faith and kyndnes fand.

745 The Sotheroun part saw weill the toun was tynt,
Fersly thai fled, as fyr dois out off flynt.
Sum fled, some fell in to draw dykis deip,
Sum to the kyrk, thar lywys giff thai mycht keip;
Sum fled to Tay, and in small weschell yeid;

750 Sum derffly deit and drownyt in that steid,
Schir Jhon Sewart at the west port owt past;
Till Meffen wod he sped him wondyr fast.
A hundreth men the kyrk tuk for succour,
Bot Wallace wald no grace grant in that hour.

755 He slay bad all off cruell Sotheroun keyn;
And said thai had to Sanct Jhonstoun enemys beyn.
Four hundreth men in to the toun war ded.
Sewyn scor with lyff chapyt out off that sted.
Wyffis and barnys thai maid thaim fre to ga;

760 With Wallace wyll he wald sla nayn off tha.
Riches thai fand, that Inglissmen had brocht new,
Syn plenyst the toun with worthi Scottis trew.
Schyr Jhon Sewart left Meffen forest strang,
Went to the Gask with feyll Sotheroun amang;

765 And syn in Fyff, quhar Wallang schirreff was;
Send currowris sone out throw the land to pass,
And gaderyt men, a stalwart cumpany.
Till Ardargan he drew him prewaly;
Ordand thaim in bargan reddy boune.

770 Agayn he thocht to sailye Sanct Jhonstoun,
Quhar Wallace lay, and wald no langar rest,
Rewllyt the toun as that him likyt best.
Schyr Jhon Ramsay gret captane ordand he,

Fol. 84 a Ruwan schirreff, at ane accord for to be.

775 This charge he gaiff, gyff men thaim warnyng maid,
    To cum till him with outyn mor abaid:
    And so thai did, quhen tithingis was thaim brocht.
    With a hundreth Wallace furth fra thaim socht.

    To Fyfe he past, to wesy that cuntré,
780 Bot wrangwarnyt off Inglissmen was he.
    Schyr Jhon Sewart, quhen thai were passyt by,
    Fra the Ochell he sped him haistely;
    Vpon Wallace folowit in all his mycht,
    In Abyrnethy tuk lugyng that fyrst nycht.
785 Apon the morn, with fyftene hundreth men,
    Till Black Irnsyde his gydys couth them ken.
    Thar Wallace was, and mycht no message send
    Till Sanct Jhonstoun, to mak this jornay kend;
    For Inglissmen, that full sutell has beyn,
790 Gart wachis walk, that nayn mycht pass betweyn.
    Than Wallace said, " This mater payis nocht me."
    He cald till him the squier gud Guthré,
    And Beset als, that knew full weyll the land;
    And ast at thaim, quhat deid was best on hand,
795 " Message to mak, our pouer for to get;
    " With Sotheroun sone we sall be wndirset.
    " And wykked Scottis, that knawis this forest best,
    " Thai ar the causs that we may haiff no rest.
    " I dred fer mar Wallang, that is thair gyd,
800 " Than all the layff that cummys on that syd."
    Than Guthré said; ' Mycht we get ane or tway
    ' To Saynct Johnstoun, it war the gaynest way;
    ' And warn Ramsay, we wald get succour sone.
    ' Our suth it is, it can nocht now be don.
805 ' Rycht weyll I wait, weschell is lewyt nayn,
    ' Fra the Wood hawyn, to the ferry cald Aran.'

Than Wallace said; " The water cald it is;
" My selff can swym, I trow, and fall na myss.
" But currours oyss, that gaynys nocht for me;
810 " And I leyff yow her, yet had I leuir de.
" Throw Goddis grace we sall bettir eschew;
" The strenth is stark, als we haiff men inew.
" In Elchoch park, bot fourty thar war we,
" For sewyn hundreth, and gert feill Sothron de;
815 " And chapyt weill in mony wnlikly place;
" So sall we her, throw help off Goddis grace.
" Quhill men may fast, thir woddis we may hauld still;
" For thi, ilk man be off trew hardy will;
" And at we do so nobill in to deid,
820 " Off ws be found no lak eftir to reid.
Fol. 84 b " The rycht is ouris, we suld mor ardent be;
" I think to freith this land, or ellis de."
His waillyt spech, with wit and hardyment,
Maid all the layff so cruell off entent;
825 Sum bad tak feild. and giff battaill in playn.
Wallace said; " Nay, thai wordis are in wayn:
" We will nocht leyff that may be our wantage;
" The wod till ws is worth a yeris wage."
Off hewyn temyr in haist he gert thaim tak
830 Syllys off ayk, and a stark barrés mak,
At a foyr frount, fast in the forest syd,
A full gret strenth, quhar thai purpost to bid;
Stellyt thaim fast till treis that growand was,
That thai mycht weyll in fra the barrés pass;
835 And so weill graithit on athir sid about;
Syn com agayn, quhen thai saw thaim in dout.
Be that the strenth arayit was at rycht,
The Inglis ost approchyt to thair sycht.
Than Sewart com, that way for till haiff wend,
840 As thai war wount; so his gydis thaim kend.

At that entré thai thocht till haiff passage;
But sone thai fand that maid thaim gret stoppage.
A thousand he led off men in armes strang,
With fyve hundreth he gert Jhon Wallang gang
845 With out the wod, that nayn suld pass thaim fra.
Wallace with him had fourty archarys thra;
The layff was speris, full nobill in a neid:
On thair enemys thai bykkyr with gud speid.
A cruell cwntyr was at the barrés seyn.
850 The Scottis defens so sykkyr was and keyn,
Sotheroun stud aw to enter thaim amang;
Feill to the ground thai our threw in that thrang.
A rowm was left, quhar part in frount mycht fayr;
Quha entrit in, agayn yeid neuirmar.
855 Fourty thai slew, that formast wald haiff past.
All dysarayit the ost was, and agast;
And part off hors throw schot to dede was brocht,
Brak to a playn, the Sotheroun fra them socht.
The Sewart said; "Allace, how [may] this be;
860 "And do no harm? Our gret rabut haiff we."
He tald Wallang, and askyt his consaill;
"Schyrreff thou art, quhat may be our awaill?
"But few thai ar that makis this gret debait."
John Wallang said; 'This is the best I wait,
865 'To cess her off, and remayn her besyd;
'For thai may nocht lang in this forest byd;
Fol. 85 a 'For fawt off fud, thai mon in the cuntré;
'Than war mar tym on thaim to mak mellé.
'Or thai be won be fors, in to this stryff
870 'Feyll at ye leid sall erar loss the lyff.'
Than Sewart said; "This reid I will nocht tak:
"And Scottis be warnyt, reskew sone will they mak.
"Off this dispyt amendys I think to haiff,
"Or de thar for in nowmyr with the laiff.

875 " In till a rang myselff on fut will fayr."
Aucht hundreth he tuk off liklyest that was thair;
Syn bad the layff bid at the barrés still
With Jhon Wallang, to rewyll thaim at his will.
" Wallang," he said, " be forthwart in this cace;
880 " In sic a swar we couth nocht get Wallace.
" Tak hym or sla; I promess the be my lyff,
" That king Edwart sall mak the erll off Fyff.
" At yon est part we think to enter in;
" I bid no mar, might ye this barress wyn.
885 " Fra thai be closyt graithly amang ws sa,
" Bot merwell be, thai sall na ferrer ga.
" Assailye sayr, quhen ye wit we cum ner;
" On athir sid we sall hald thaim on ster."
Thus semlyt thai apon ane awfull wyss.
890 Wallace has seyn quhat was thair haill dewyss.
" Gud men," he said, " wndirstud ye this deid,
" Forsuth thai ar rycht mekill for to dreid.
" Yon Sewart is a nobill worthy knycht;
" Forthwart in wer, rycht worthy, wyss and wicht.
895 " His assailye he ordannys wondyr sayr
" Ws for to harm, no mannys wyt can do mar.
" Plesand it is to se a chyftane ga
" So chyftanlyk; it suld recomfort ma
" Till his awn men, and thai of worschip be,
900 " Than for to se ten thousand cowartis fle.
" Sen we ar stad with enemyss on ilk syd,
" And her on fors mon in this forest bid,
" Than fray the fyrst, for Goddis saik, cruellye,
" That all the layff off ws abayssyt be."

905 Crawfurd he left, and Longaweill the knycht,
Fourty with thaim, to kepe the barrés wicht:
With him saxté off worthy men in weid,

To meit Sewart with hardy will thai yeid.
A maner dyk in to that wod wes maid,
910 Off thuortour ryss. quhar bauldly thai abaid;
A downwith waill the Sothroun to thaim had.
Son semblyt thai with strakis sar and sad:
Fol. 85 b Scharp sperys, fast duschand on athir sid.
Throw byrnys brycht maid woundis deip and wid.
915 This wantage was, the Scottis thaim dantyt swa,
Nayn Inglissman durst fra his feris ga.
To brek aray, or formast entyr in.
Off crystin blud to se it was gret syn.
For wrangwis causs; and has beyn mony day.
920 Feyll Inglissmen in the dyk deid thai lay.
Speris full sone all in to splendrys sprang;
With scharp suerdys thai hew on in that thrang:
Blud byrstyt out throw fyn harnes off maill.
Jhon Wallang als full scharply can assaill
925 Apon Crawfurd, and the knycht Longaweill,
At thar power kepyt the barrés weill;
Maid gud defens, be wyt, manheid, and mycht;
At the entré feyll men to dede thai dycht.
Thus all at anys assailyeit in that place,
930 Nayn that was thar durst turn fra the barrace
To help Wallace, nor none of his durst pass
To reskew thaim, so feyll the fechtyng was.
At athir ward thai handelyt thaim full hat;
Bot do or de, na succour ellis thai wayt.
935 Wallace wes stad in to that stalwart stour;
Guthré, Besat, with men off gret walour,
Rychard Wallace, that worthi was off hand.
Sewart merweillyt, that contrar thaim mycht stand.
That euyr so few mycht byd in battaill place,
940 Agaynys thaim, metyng face for face.
He thocht him selff to end that mater weill;

Fast pressyt in with a gud suerd off steill;
Into the dyk a Scottis man gert he de.
Wallace tharoff in hart had gret pyté;
945 Amendis till haiff he followit on him fast,
But Ingliss men so thick betwex thaim past,
That apon him a strak get mycht he nocht:
Wthyr worthy derffly to dede he brocht.
Sloppys thai maid throu all that chewalry,
950 The worthy Scottis thai wrocht so worthely.
Than Sothron saw off thar gud men so drest,
Langar to bid thai thocht it nocht the best.
Four scor was slayn, or thai wald leyff that steid,
And fyfty als was at the barrace deid.
955 A trumpet blew, and fra the wod thai draw;
Wallang left off, that sycht fra that he saw.
To sailye mar thaim [thocht] it was no speid,
Withowt the wod to consaill son thai yeid,
The worthy Scottis to rest thaim was full fayn;
Fol.86a 960 Feyll hurtis had, bot few off thaim was slayn.
Wallace thaim bad of all gud comfort be:
" Thankit be God, the fayrer part haiff we!
" Yon knycht Sewart has at gret jornay beyn;
" So fair assay I haiff bot seildyn seyn.
965 " I had leuir off Wallang wrokyn be,
" Than ony man that is off yon menyhe."
The Scottis all on to the barress yeid,
Stanchit woundis that couth full braithly bleid.
Part Scottis men had bled full mekill blud;
970 For faut off drynk, and als wantyng off fud,
Sum feblyt fast, that had feill hurtis thar.
Wallace tharfor sichit with hart full sar.
A hat he hynt, to get water is gayn;
Othir refut as than he wyst off nayn.
975 A litill strand he fand. that ran hym by:

Off cler watter he brocht haboundandly,
And drank him selff, syn said, with sobyr mud;
" The wyn off Frans me thocht nocht halff so gud."
Than off the day thre quartaris was went.

980 Schir Jhon Sewart has castyn in his entent,
To sailye mar as than he couth nocht preiff;
Quhill on the morn that mar men couth raleiff;
And kep thaim in, quhill tha, for hungyr sor,
Cum in his will, or ellis de tharfor.

985 "Wallange," he said, " I charge the for to bid,
" And kep thaim in; I will to Coupar rid.
" Thow sall remayn, with fyve hundreth at thi will,
" And I the morn sall cum with power the till."
Jhon Wallange said; ' This charg I [her] forsaik;

990 ' Eftir this day all nycht I may nocht waik.
' For, trastis weill, thai will ische to the playn,
' Thocht ye bid als, or ellis de in the payn.'
Sewart bad him byd, or wndyrly the blaym;
" I the commaund, on gud king Eduuardis naym.

995 " Or thar to God a wow I mak beforn,
" And thai brek out, to hyng the heych to morn."
Off that commaund Jhon Wallang had gret dreid;
Sewart went fra thaim with nyne scor in to deid
Next hand the wod, and his gud men off Fyff,

1000 That with him baid in all term off thair lyff.
Wallace drew ner, his tym quhen that he saw,
To the wod syd, and couth on Wallang caw;

Fol. 86 b " Yon knycht to morn has becht to hyng the hie.
" Cum in till ws, I sall thi warrand be

1005 " In contrar him, and all king Eduuardis mycht.
" Tak we hym quyk, I sall him hyng on hycht;
" And gud lordschip I sall gyff the hereft
" In this ilk land, that thi brothir has left."
Wallange was wyss, full sone couth wndrestand,

1010 Be lyklynes Wallace suld wyn the land;
And bettir him war in to the rycht to bid,
Than be in wer apon the Sotheroun sid.
With schort wysment to Wallace in thai socht.
Than Sewart cryt, and said; ' That beis for nocht;
1015 ' And fals off kynd thow art in heretage ;
' Eduuard on the has waryt ewill gret wage.
' Her I sall byd, my purpos to fullfill,
' Othir to de, or haiff the at my will."
For all his spech, to pass he wald nocht spar;
1020 Wyth full glaid hart Wallace resawyt thaim thar.

Be that, Ruwan and Ramsay off renown,
Be a trew Scot, that past to Sanct Jhonstoun,
Thaim warnyng maid, that Sewart folowit fast
Apon Wallace; than war thai sayr agast.
1025 Owt off the toun thai wschit with all thair mycht,
With thre hundreth, that worthi war and wicht;
Till Black Irnsid assemblyt in that place,
As Wallang was gayne in to gud Wallace.
The knycht Sewart has weill thair cummyng seyn;
1030 A fayr playn feild he chesyt thaim betweyn.
Elewyn hundreth and four scor than had he;
The Scottismen war fyve hundreth and saxté.
Thai war bot few, a playn feild for to tak.
Out of the wod gud Wallace can thaim mak;
1035 He wyst no thing off thaim that cummyng was;
Mar hardement was fra the strenth to pass.
Bot quhen thai hard Ruwan and Ramsay cry,
Off Ochtyrhous, blyth was that chewalry.
Mycht thai off gold haiff brocht a kingis rent,
1040 To gud Wallace mycht nocht so weyll content.
Than till aray thai yeid on athir sid,
In cruell ire, in battaill bown to byd.

Worthiar men than Sewart semblyt thar,
In all his tym, Eduuard had neuirmar.
1045 Bot Sewart saw his nowmyr was fer ma;
Hys power sone he gart dewyd in twa;
To fecht at anys, rycht knychtlik he thaim kend,
In that jornay othir to wyn or end.
The worthi Scottis ruschyt on thaim, in gret ire.
ol. 87a 1050 With cruell strakis, that flawmyt fers as fyr.
Wallace and his, als Sotheroun that was thar,
Few speris had, for feyll fechtyng and sar
In to the wod at sailye all the day:
Bot new cummyn men weill waillyt speris had thai.
1055 In to the stour thai gart feill Sotheroun de;
Thar cruell deid gret merwell was to se.
Thai worthi Scottis, that fyrst amang thaim baid,
Full gret slauchtir on Inglissmen thai maid;
In to the wod befor had prewyt weill,
1060 Than on the playn thai sonyeit nocht adeill;
In curage grew, as thai war new begon;
Schort rest thai had fra ryssyng off the son.
Be that Ramsay, and with him gud Ruwan,
Throw owt the thykkest off the pres is gan;
1065 Sloppis thai maid throw out the Inglissmen;
Deseueryt thaim be twenty and by ten,
Quhen speris war gayn, with suerdys off metall cler.
Till Inglissmen thar cummyng was sauld full der.
Wallace and his, be worthines off hand,
1070 Feyll Sotheroun blud gart [licht] wpon the land.
The twa feildys togiddyr relyt than
Schyr Jhon Sewart, with mony nobill man,
To help thair lord; thre hundreth in [a] place
About hym stud, and did thair besines;
1075 Defendand him, with mony awfull dynt,
Quhill all the owtwart off the feild was tynt.

Off comowns part into the forest fled
Succour to sek, thair men had thaim so led.
The Scottis, has seyn so mony in a rout
1080 With Sewart stand, na warrand thaim about,
Apon all syd assailyeit wondyr sayr;
Throu polyt platis with poyntis persyt thair.
The Sotheroun made defens full cruelly;
All occupyit was this gud chewalry.
1085 Schyr Jhon Ramsay wald thai had yoldyn beyn.
Wallace said; " Nay, it is all wrang ye meyn.
" Ranson to mak we can nocht now begyn.
" On sic awyss this land we may nocht wyn.
" Yon knycht off auld our enemy has beyn.
1090 " So fell till ws off thaim I haiff nocht seyn.
" Now he sall de, with help off Goddis grace;
" He com to pay his ranson in this place."
The Sotheroun wyst all playnly for to de;
Reskew was nayn, suppos at thai wald fle.
1095 Freschlye thai faucht as thai [had] entryt new;
Apon our sid part worthy men thai slew.
Fol. 87 b Than Sewart said; ' Alace, throw wrangwis thing
' Our lywys we loss, throu desyr off our king.'
The felloun knycht dowtyt his dede rycht nocht;
1100 Amang the Scottis full manfully he wrocht;
Besat he straik to dede with outyn mar.
Wallace prest in, with his suerd burnyst bar,
At Sewart hals he etlyt in gret ire,
Throu pissanis stuff in sondyr strak the swyr;
1105 Dede to the ground he duschit for all his mycht:
Off Wallace hand thus endyt this gud knycht.
The ramaynand with out mercy thai sla;
For gud Besat the Scottis was wondyr wa.
In handis sum thai straik with out remed;
1110 Na Sotheroun past with lyff out off that sted.

Than to the wod, for thaim that left the feild,
A rang [thai] set; thus thai may get na beild.
Yeid nayn away was contrar our punyoun.
Gud Ruwan past agayn to Sanct Jhonstoun.

1115 Schyr Jhon Ramsay to Couper castell raid;
That hous he tuk, for defens nayn was maid.
Wallace, Crawfurd, and with thaim gud Guthré,
Rychard Wallace had lang beyn in mellé,
And Longaweill, in to Lundoris baid still;

1120 Fastyt thai had to lang agayn thar will.
Wallange thai maid thair stwart for to be;
Off meit and drynk thai fand aboundandlé.
The priour fled, and durst na reknyng bid;
He was befor apon the tothir syd.

1125 Apon the morn to Sanct Androwis thai past,
Owt off the toun that byschop turnyt fast.
The king off Ingland had him hydder send;
The rent at will he gaiff hym in commend.
His kingis charge as than he durst nocht hald:

1130 A wrangwys pape that tyrand mycht be cald.
Few fled with him, and gat away be see;
For all Scotland he wald nocht Wallace se.
As than off him he maid bot lycht record.
Gert restor him that thar was rychtwyss lord.

1135 The worthy knycht, that in to Coupar lay,
Gart spulye it apon the secund day,
Syn ordand men, at commaund off Wallace,
But mar process, for to cast doun that place.
Mynouris sone thai gert press throw the wall,

1140 Syn pounciounis fyryt, and to the ground kest all.
Schyr Jhon Ramsay syne to the kyrk can fayr;
Sotheroun was fled, and left bot wallis bayr:
Efter Sewart thai durst nocht tary lang.
Fol. 88 a The Scottis at large [out] throu all Fyff thai rang.

1145 Off Inglissmen nayn left in that cuntré.
Bot in Lochlewyn thair lay a cumpané,
Apon that inch, in a small hous thai dycht;
Castell was nayn, bot wallyt with water wicht.
Besyd Carraill thai semblyt Wallace beforn;
1150 His purposs was for till assay Kyngorn.
A knycht, hecht Gray, than captane in it was;
Be schort awyss purpos he tuk to pas.
Erar he wald bid chalans off his king,
Than with Wallace to rakyn for sic a thing.
1155 That houss thai tuk, and litill tary maid.
Vpon the morn, with outyn mar abaid,
Atour the mur, quhar thai a tryst had set,
Ner Scotlandis Well thair lugyng tuk but let.
Eftir souper Wallace bad thaim ga rest:
1160 " My selff will walk, me think it may be best."
As he commaundyt, but gruching thai haiff don.
In to thar slep Wallace him graithit son,
Past to Lochlewyn as it was ner mydnycht,
Auchtene with him, at he hed warnyt rycht;
1165 Thir men wend weill he come to wesy it.
" Falows," he said, " I do yow weill to wyt;
" Considyr weill this place, and wndirstand,
" That it may do full gret scaith to Scotland.
" Out off the south and power cum thaim till,
1170 " Thai may tak in, and kep it at thair awn will.
" Apon yon inche rycht mony men may be,
" And syn wsche out, thair tym quhen at thai se.
" To bid lang her we may nocht wpon chans,
" Yon folk has fud, trast weill, at sufficians.
1175 " Wattir fra thaim forsuth can nocht be set;
" Sum wthyr wyill ws worthis for to get.
" Yhe sall remayn her at this port all still,
" And I my selff the boit sall bryng yow till."

R

Thair with in haist his weid off castis he:
1180 "Apon yon sid na wachman can I se;"
Held on his sark, and tuk his suerd so gud
Band on his nek, and syn lap in the flud,
And our he swam; for lattyng fand he nocht.
The boit he tuk, and till hys men it brocht;
1185 Arayit him weill, and wald no langar bid,
Bot passyt in, rowit to the tothir sid.
The inch thai tuk with suerdis drawyn in hand,
And sparyt nayn that thai befor thaim fand;
Strak duris wp, stekyt men quhar thai lay;
1190 Apon the Sothroun thus sadly semblyt thai.
Thretty thai slew, that was in that samyn place;
To mak defens the Inglissmen had no space.
Thar women fyve Wallace send off that sted;
Fol. 88 b Woman nor barne he gart neuir put to dede.
1195 The gud thai tuk, as it had beyn thair awyn.
Than Wallace said; "Falowis, I mak yow knawin,
"The purwyance, that is with in this wanys,
"We will nocht tyne; ger sembyll all at anys,
"Gar warn Ramsay, and our gud men ilkane:
1200 "I will remayn quhill this warnstor be gane:"
Send furth a man, thair horsis put to kep,
Drew wp the boit, syne beddys tuk to sleip.
Wallace power, quhilk Scotland Well ner lay,
Befor the son thai myssyt him away.
1205 Sum menyng maid, and merweillyt off that cace.
Ramsay bad, 'Cess, and murn nocht for Wallace.
'It is for gud at he is fra us went;
'It sall ye se, trast weill, in werrament.
'My hed to wed, Lochlewyn he past to se:
1210 'Bot that is thar, no Inglissman knaw we
'In all this land, betwix thir watters left;
'Tithandis off hym ye sall se son hereft.'

As thai about was talkand on this wyss,
A message com, and chargyt thaim to ryss.
1215 " My lord," he said, " to dyner has yow cald
" In till Lochlewyn, quhilk is a ryoll hald.
" Ye sall fair weyll, tharfor put off all sorow."
Thai graithit thaim rycht ayrly on the morow;
And thidder past, off Wallace will to wytt.
1220 Thus semblyt thai in a full blyth falowschip.
Thai lugyt thar till aucht dayis was at end;
Off meit and drynk thai had inewch to spend;
Turssyt furth ger, that Sothroun had brocht thar;
Gert byrn the boit, till Sanct Jhonstoun thai fair.
1225 Byschop Synclar, that worthy was and wyss,
Till Wallace com, and tald him his awyss;
Thus he desyryt Wallace suld with him ryd,
And in Dunkell soiorn that wynter tyd.
Bot he said; " Nay, that hald I nocht the best,
1230 " And Scotland thus; in pess we can nocht rest."
The byschop said, ' Playnly ye may nocht wend;
' In to the north for men I rede yow send.'
" I grant," quoth he, "and cheissit a messynger."
The worthi Jop, was with the byschop ther;
1235 And maister Blair to Wallace cam bot baid,
With that gud lord that nobill cher thaim maid.
Wallace send Blayr, in [to] his priestis weid,
To warn the west, u har freyndys had gret dreid
How they suld pass, or to gud Wallace wyn,
1240 For Inglissmen that held thaim lang in twyn.
Adam Wallace, and Lyndsay that was wycht,
Rawchlé thai left, and went away be nycht.
Fol. 89 a Throu out the land to the Lennox thai cair,
Till erll Malcom, that welcummyt thaim full fair.
1245 Maister Jhon Blair was blith off that semblé;
Gud Graym was thair, and Richard off Lundé;

Als Robert Boid, that out off But thaim socht.
Had thai Wallace, off no thing ellis thai roucht;
Bot Inglissmen betuix thaim was so strang,
1250 That thai in playn mycht nocht weyll to him gang.
Jop passit north, for leiching wald nocht let:
Gret power thar as than he couth nocht get;
The lord Cwmyn, that erll off Bouchane was,
For auld inwy he wald [let] na man pass
1255 That he mycht let, in gud Wallace supplé;
For erll Patrik a playn feild kepyt he.
Yeit pur mén com, and prewyt all thair mycht
To help Wallace, in fens off Scotlandis rycht.
The gud Randell in tendyr age was kend,
1260 Part off men out off Murray he [did] send.
Jop past agayn, and com in presens sone
Befor Wallace, and tauld how he had don.
Bot maister Blayr so gud tithingis him brocht,
That off Cwmyn Wallace full litill roucht.
1265 Als Inglissmen had than full litill dreid;
Fra Fyff was tynt, the war thai trowyt to sped.
The duk and erll, that in Scotland thaim led,
Captanys thai maid, in Ingland syn thaim sped.
Wallace hym bownyt, qwhen he thocht tym suld be,
1270 Off Sanct Jhonstoun, and with him tuk fyfté.
Stewin off Irland, and Kerlé that was wicht,
For Inglissmen thai had haldyn the hycht
In wachman lyff, and fayndyt thaim rycht weill:
Till gud Wallace thai war as trew as steill;
1275 To folow him thai twa thocht neuyr lang.
Throucht the Ochell thai maid thaim for to gang.
Off mar power he taryt nocht that tyd;
To keip the land he gert the laiff abid.
To Styrlyng bryg as than he wald nocht pass,
1280 For strang power of Inglissmen thar was.

Till Erth ferry thai passit prewaly;
And buschit thaim in a dern sted tharby.
A cruell captane intill Erth duelt thar,
In Ingland born, and hecht Thomlyn offįWayr.
1285 A hundreth men was at his ledyng still;
To bruk that land thai did power and will.
A Scottis fyschar, quhilk thai had tayn beforn,
Contrar his will gert him be to thaim suorn.
In thar seruice thai held him day and nycht.
1290 Befor the son Wallace gart Jop him dycht,
And send him furth the passage for to spy.
On that fyschar he hapnyt sodandly,
All him allayn, bot a boy that was thar;
Jop hynt hym son, and for no dreid wald spar,
ol.89 b 1295 Be the collar, and owt a knyff hynt he.
For Goddis saik this man askit mercé.
Jop sperd sone; "Off quhat nacioun art thow?"
'A Scot,' he said, 'bot Sothroun gart me bow.
' In thair seruice, agayn my will full sayr,
1300 ' Bot for my lyff that I remaynit thair.
· To sek fysch I com on this north sid.
' Be ye a Scott, I wald fayn with yow bid.'
Than he him brocht in presens to Wallace.
The Scottis was blyth quhen thai haiff seyn this cace,
1305 For with his bait thai mycht weill passage hawe;
For fery craft na fraucht he thocht to crawe.
Apon that syd langar thai taryed nocht,
Till the south land with glaid hartis thai socht;
Syn brak the bait, quhen thai war landyt thair;
1310 Serwice off it Sotheroun mycht haiff no mayr.
Than throuch the moss thai passit full gud speid
Till the Torwod, this man with thaim thai leid.
The wedow thar brocht tithandis to Wallace,
Off his trew eyme that duelt at Dunypace.

1315 Thomlyn off Wayr in presoun had him set,
    For mar tresour na he befor mycht get.
    Wallace said; " Deym, he sall weill lowsyt be
    " Be none to morn, or ma tharfor sall de."
    Scho gat thaim meit, and in quiet thai baid
1320 Quhill it was nycht, syn redy sone thaim maid;
    Towart Arth hall rycht sodeynly thaim drew.
    A strenth thar was, that weyll the fyschar knew,
    Off draw dykis, and full off watter wan;
    Wysly tharoff has warnyt thaim this man.
1325 On the baksid he led thaim prewalé,
    Fra the watter, as wont to cum was he,
    Our a small bryg.   Gud Wallace entryt in
    In to the hall, hym selff thocht to begyn;
    Fra the sowper as thai war bown to ryss,
1330 He salust thaim apon ane awfull wyss.
    His men hym folowit sodanly at anys,
    Haisty sorow was rassyt in thai wanys;
    With scherand suerdis scharply about thaim dang;
    Feyll on the flur was fellyt thaim amang.
1335 With Thomlyn Wayr Wallace hym selff has met;
    A felloun strak sadly apon him set,
    Throcht hede and swyr all throucht the cost him claiff.
    The worthy Scottis fast stekit off the layff;
    Kepyt duris, and dulfully thaim dycht;
1340 To chaip away the Sotheroun had no mycht.
    Sum wyndowys socht for till haiff brokyn out,
    Bot all for nocht, full fey was maid that rout.
    About the fyr bruschit the blud so red,
Fol. 90 a A hundreth men was slayn in to that sted.
1345 Than Wallace socht quhar his wncle suld be;
    In a dyrk cawe he was set dulfullé,
    Quhar watter stud, and he in yrnyss strang. ·
    Wallace full sone the brassis wp he dang;

Off that myrk holl brocht him with strenth and lyst.
1350 Bot noyis he hard, off no thing ellis he wyst;
So blyth befor in warld he had nocht beyn,
As thair with sycht, quhen he had Wallace seyn.
In dykys owt the dede bodyis thai kest;
Graithyt the place as at thaim likyt best;
1355 Maid still gud cher, and wyss wachis gert set;
Quhill ner the day thai slepe with outyn let;
Quhen thai had lycht, spulycid the place in hy,
Fand gaynand ger, baithe gold and jowelry:
Our all that day in quiet held thaim still.
1360 Quhat Sothroun come, thai rasawyt with gud will;
In that laubour the Scottis was full bayn :
Inglissmen com, bot nayn yeid owt agayn.
Women and barnys put in the presonys cawe;
So thai mycht mak no warnyng to the lawe.
1365 Stewyn off Irland, and Kerlé, that wes wicht,
Kepyt the port apon the secund nycht.
Befor the day the worthy Scottis rayss,
Turssyt gud ger, and to the Torwod gayss;
Remaynyt thar quhill nycht was cummyn on hand,
1370 Syn bownyt thaim in quiet throuch the land.
The wedowis son, fra thai had passit dout,
A serwand send, and leit the women out,
To pass fra Arth quhar at thaim likit best.
Now spek off thaim that went in to the west.

1375   Wallace hym selff was sekyr gyd that nycht;
Till Dunbertane the way he chesyt rycht.
Or it was day, for than the nycht was lang,
On to the toun full prewaly thai gang.
Mekill off it Inglissmen occupyit.
1380 Gud Wallace sone throu a dyrk garth hym hyit,
And till a houss, quhar he was wont to ken,

A wedow duelt was frendfull till our men.
Abone hyr bed, on the baksid, was maid
A dern wyndow, was nothir lang nor braid;
1385 Thar Wallace cauld, and son fra scho him knew,
In haist scho rayss, and prewaly thaim in drew
Till a closs bern, quhar thai mycht kepyt be:
Baith meit and drynk scho brocht in gret plenté.
A gudly gyft to Wallace als scho gaiff,
1390 A hundreth pownd and mar, atour the layff.
Nyne sonnys scho had, was lykly men and wicht;
Ane ayth till him scho gart thaim swer full rycht.
In peess thai duelt, in trubyll that had beyn,
Fol. 90 b And trewbut payit till Ingliss capdanis keyn.
1395 Schir Jhon Menteth the castell had in hand:
Bot sum men said, thar was a prewa band
Till Sotheroun maid, be menys off that knycht,
In thar supplé to be in all his mycht.
Tharoff as now I will no process mak.
1400 Wallace that day a schort purpos can tak;
Quhen it was nycht he bad the wedow pass,
Merk all the duris quhar Sotheroun duelland was.
Syn efftir this, he and his chewalry
Graithyt thaim weill, and wapynnys tuk in hy;
1405 Went on the gayt, quhen Sotheroun was on slep,
A gret oystré our Scottis tuk to kep.
Ane Ingliss captane was sittand wp so lait,
Quhill he and his with drynk was maid full mait.
Nyn men was thar, now set in hye curage;
1410 Sum wald haiff had gud Wallace in that rage;
Sum wald haiff bound Schyr Jhone the Grayme throucht strenth
Sum wald haiff had Boyd at the suerdis lenth;
Sum wyst Lundy, that chapyt was off Fyff;
Sum wychtar was na Cetoun in to stryff.
1415 Quhen Wallace hard the Sotheroun maid sic dyn,

He gart all byd, and hym allayn went in;
The layff remaynyt to her off thar tithans.
He salust thaim with sturdy contenance.
" Falowis," he said, " sen I com last fra haym,
1420 " In trawaill I was our land and wncouth fame.
" Fra south Ireland I com in this cuntré,
" The [new] conquest off Scotland for to se.
" Part off your drynk, or sum gud I wald haiff."
The captane [than] a schrewed ansuer him gaiff;
1425 ' Thow semys a Scot wnlikly, ws to spy;
' Thow may be ane off Wallace cumpany:
' Contrar our king he is ryssyn agane;
' The land off Fyff he has rademyt in plane.
' Thou sall her byd quhill we wyt how it be;
1430 ' Be thow off his, thou sall be hyngyt hye.'
Wallace than thocht it was na tym to stand;
His nobill suerd he gryppyt son in hand;
Aukwart the face drew that captane in teyn,
Straik all away that stud abowne his eyn.
1435 Ane othir braithly in the breyst he bar;
Baith brawn and bayn the burly blaid throcht schar.
The layff ruschyt wp to Wallace in gret ire;
The thryd he feld full fersly in the fyr,
Stewyn off Irland, and Kerlé, in that thrang,
ʋl.91ʌ 1440 Kepyt na charge, bot entryt thaim amang;
And othir ma that to the dur can press;
Quhill thai him saw thar coud no thing thaim cess,
The Sotheroun men full sone was brocht to ded.
The blyth hosteler bad thaim gud ayle and breid.
1445 Wallace said; " Nay, till we haiff laysar mar.
" To be our gyd thow sall befor ws fayr;
" And begyn fyr quhar at the Sotheroun lyis."
The hostellar son, apon a hasty wyss,
Hynt fyr in hand, and till a gret hous yeid,

1450 Quhar Inglissmen was in full mekill dreid.
 For thai wyst nocht quhill that the rud low raiss;
 As wood bestis amang the fyr than gays,
 With paynis fell ruschyt full sorowfully.
 The layff with out, off our gud chewalry,
1455 At ilka houss, quhar the hostillar began,
 Kepyt the duris, fra thaim chapyt na man.
 For all thair mycht, thocht king Eduuard had suorn,
 Gat nayn away that was off Ingland born,
 Bot othir brynt, or but reskew was slayn,
1460 And sum throucht force drywyn in the fyr agayn.
 Part Scottis folk, in seruice thaim amang,
 Fra ony payn frely thai let thaim gang.
 Thre hundreth men was to Dunbertan send,
 To kep the land, as thair lordis thaim kend;
1465 Skaithless off thaim for ay was this regioun.
 Wallace or day maid him out off the toun;
 On to the coyff off Dunbartane thai yeid;
 And all that day [thar] soiornd out off dreid.
 Baith meit and drynk the hostillar gert be brocht.
1470 Quhen nycht was cummyn, in all the haist thai mocht,
 Towart Rossneth full ernystfully thai gang;
 For Inglissmen was in that castell strang.
 On the Garlouch thai purpost thaim to bid,
 Betwix the kyrk, that ner was thar besyd;
1475 And to the castell full prewaly thai draw.
 Wndyr a bray thai buschyt thaim rycht law,
 Lang the wattyr, quhar comoun oyss had thai,
 The castellis stuff, on to the kyrk ilk day.
 A maryage als that day was to begyn.
1480 All wschyt owt, and left na man with in,
 At fens mycht mak, bot serwandis in that place;
 Thus to that tryst thai passyt wpon cace.
 Wallace and his drew thaim full prewaly

Nerhand the place, quhen thai war passyt by,
1485 With in the hauld; and thocht to kep that steid
Fra Sotheroun men, or ellys tharfor be deid.
Fol. 91 b Compleit was maid the mariage in to playn;
On to Rossneth thai raturnyt agayn.
Four scor and ma was in that cumpany,
1490 Bot nocht arayit as was our chewalry;
To the castell thai weynd to pass but let.
The worthy Scottis so hardly on thaim set,
Fourtye at anys derffly to ground thai bar;
The ramaynand affrayit was so sayr,
1495 Langar in feild thai had no mycht to bid,
Bot fersly fled fra thaim on athir sid.
The Scottis thar has weyll the entré woun,
And slew the layff that in that houss was foun;
Syn on the flearis folowid wondyr fast,
1500 Na Inglissman with lyff thar fra thaim past.
The wemen sone thai seysyt in to hand,
Kepyt thaim closs, for warnyng off the land.
The dede bodyes all out off sycht thai kest:
Than at gud ess thai maid thaim for to rest.
1505 Off purwians sewyn dayis thai lugyt thar
At rud costis, to spend thai wald nocht spar.
Quhat Sotheroun come, thai tuk all glaidly in,
Bot owt agayn thai leit nane off that kyn.
Quha tithandis send to the captane off that steid,
1510 Thai seruitouris the Scottis put to ded,
Spulyeid the place, and left na gudis thar,
Brak wallis doun, and maid that byggyng bar.
Quhen thai had spilt off stayne werk at thai mocht,
Syn kendillyt fyr, and fra Rossneth thai socht.
1515 Quhen thai had brynt all tre werk in that place,
Wallace gert freith the wemen, off hys grace;
To do thaim harm neuir his purpos was

Than to Faslan the worthy Scottis can pass,
Quhar erll Malcom was bidand at defence;
1520 Rycht glaid he was off Wallace gud presence.
Than he fand thar a nobill cumpany,
Schir Jhon the Graym, and Richard off Lundy,
Adam Wallace, that worthy was and wyss,
Berklay and Boid, with men mekill to pryss.
1525 At Cristinmess thar Wallace soiornyt still;
Off his modyr tithandis was brocht him till,
That tym befor scho had left Elrislé;
For Inglissmen in it scho durst nocht be.
Fra thine dysgysyt scho past in pilgrame weid,
1530 Sum gyrth to sek to Dunfermlyn scho yeid.
Seknes hyr had so socht in to that sted,
Fol. 92 a Decest scho was, God tuk hir spreit to leid.
Quhen Wallace hard at that tithandis was trew,
How sadness so in ilk sid can persew;
1535 In thank he tuk, be causs it was naturaill,
He lowyt God with sekyr hart and haill.
Bettyr him thocht, that it was hapnyt sa,
Na Sotheroun suld hyr put till othir wa.
He ordand Jop, and als the maister Blayr,
1540 Thiddyr to pass, and for no costis spayr,
Bot honour do the corp till sepultur.
At his commaund thai seruit ilka hour,
Doand thar to as dede askis till haw:
With worschip was the corp graithit in grawe.
1545 Agayn thai turnyt, and schawit him off hir end.
He thankit God quhat grace that euir he send;
He seis the warld sa full off fantasie,
Confort he tuk, and leit all murnyng be;
His most desyr was for to freith Scotland.
1550 Now will I tell quhat new cass com on hand.

Schyr Wilyam lang off Douglace daill was lord;
Off his fyrst wyff, as rycht was to record,
Decest or than out off this warldly cair,
Twa sonnys he had with hyr, that leyffyt thar,
1555 Quhilk likly war, and abill in curage,
To sculle was send in to thair tendre age;
James and Hew, so hecht thir brethyr twa.
And eftir sone thar wncle couth thaim ta,
Gud Robert Keth, had thaim fra Glaskow toun;
1560 Atour the se in Frans he maid thaim boun.
At study syn he left thaim in to Parys,
With a maister that worthy was and wyss.
The king Eduuard tuk thair fadyr that knycht,
And held him thar, thocht he was neuir so wicht,
1565 Till tym he had assentit till his will.
A mariage als thai gert ordane him till,
The lady Ferss, off power and hye blud:
Bot tharoff com till his lyff litill gud.
Twa sonnys he gat on this lady but mar.
1570 With Eduuardis will he tuk his leiff to far;
In Scotland com. and broucht hys wyff on pes,
In Douglass duelt; forsuth this is no les.
Kyng Eduuard trowyt that he had stedfast beyn,
Fast to thair faith; bot the contrar was seyn:
1575 Ay Scottis blud remaynyt in to Douglace,
Agayn Ingland he prewyt in mony place.
Fol. 92 b The Sanchar was a castell fayr and strang;
Ane Ingliss capdane, that dyd feyll Scottis wrang,
In till it duelt, and Bewffurd he was cauld,
1580 That held all waist fra thine to Douglace hauld.
Rycht ner off kyn was Douglace wiff and he;
Tharfor he trowyt in pess off hym to be.
Schyr Wylyham saw at Wallace raiss agayn,
And rycht likly to freyth Scotland off payn.

1585 Till help him part in till hys mynd he kest;
For in that lyff rycht lang he coud nocht lest.
He thoucht na charge to brek apon Ingland;
It was throucht force that euir he maid thaim band.
A young man than, that hardy was and bauld,
1590 Born till him selff, and Thom Dycson was cauld.
" Der freynd," he said, " I wald preyff at my mycht,
" And mak a fray to fals Bewfurd the knycht,
" In Sanchar duellys, and dois full gret owtrage."
Than Dycson said; 'My selff in that wiage
1595 'Sall for yow pass, with Anderson to spek,
' Cusyng to me; frendschip he will nocht brek.
' For that ilk man thar wod ledys thaim till;
' Throucht help off him purpos ye may fullfill.'
Schyr Wilyham than, in all the haist he mycht,
1600 Thretty trew men in this wiage he dycht;
And tauld his wyff till Drumfress he wald fayr,
A tryst, he said, off Ingland he had thair.
Thus passyt he quhar that na Sotheroun wyst,
With thir thretty throw waist land at his lyst.
1605 Quhill nycht was cummyn, he buschit thaim full law
In tyll a clewch ner the wattyr off Craw.
To the Sanchar Dykson allayn he send;
And he son maid with Anderson this end;
Dicson suld tak bathe his hors and his weid,
1610 Be it was day, a drawcht off wod to leid.
Agayn he past, and tauld the gud Dowglace,
Quhilk drew him sone in till a preway place.
Anderson tauld quhat stuff thar was tharin
Till Thom Dicson, that was ner off his kyn :
1615 " Fourty thai ar off men off mekill waill;
" Be thai on fute, thai will yow sayr assayll.
" Gyff thow hapnys the entré for to get,
" On thi rycht hand a stalwart ax is set,

" Thar with thow may defend the in a thrang;
1620 " Be Douglace wyss he bydis nocht fra the lang."
Anderson yeid to the buschement in hy;
Ner the castell he drew thaim prewaly
In till a schaw; Sotheroun mystraystit nocht.

Fol. 93 a To the next wode, wyth Dycson, syn he socht,
1625 Graithyt him a drawcht, on a braid slyp and law,
Chargyt a horss, and to the houss can caw.
Arayit he was in Andersonnis weid,
And bad haiff in. The portar com gud speid;
" This hour," he said, " thow mycht haiff beyn away:
1630 " Wntymys thow art, for it is scantly day."
The yet yeid wp, Dicson gat in but mar;
A thourtour bande, that all the drawcht wpbar.
He cuttyt it; to ground the slyp can ga,
Cumryt the yet, stekyng thai mycht nocht ma.
1635 The portar son he hynt in to that stryff,
Twyss throuch the hede he stekit him with a knyff.
The ax he gat, that Anderson off spak;
A bekyn maid, tharwith the buschement brak.
Douglace him selff was formest in that press,
1640 In our the wod entryt, or thai wald cess.
Thre wachmen sa, off wallis was cummyn new,
With in the closs the Scottis son thaim slew.
Or ony scry was raissyt in that stour,
Douglace had tane the yet off the gret tour;
1645 Rane wp a grece, quhar at the capdane lay.
On fut he gat, and wald haiff beyn away.
Our lait it was; Dowglace strak up the dur,
Bewfurd he fand in to the chawmyr flour;
With a styff suerd to dede he has him dycht.
1650 His men folowit, that worthy was and wycht.
The men thai slew, that was in to thai wanys;
Syn in the closs thai semblit all at anys.

The hous thai tuk, and Sotheroun put to ded;
Gat nane, bot ane, with lyff out off that sted,
1655 For that the yet so lang wnstekit was.
This spy he fled, till Durisder can pass;
Tauld that captane, that thai had hapnyt sa.
Ane other he gert in to the Enoch ga;
And Tybris mur was warnyt off this cass;
1660 And Louchmaban all semblyt to that place.
The cuntré raiss, quhen thai herd off sic thing,
To sege Douglace, and hecht thai suld him hyng.
Quhen Douglace wyst na wayis fra thaim [to] chaip,
To sailye him he trowyt thai wald thaim schaip,
1665 Dicson he send, apon a cursour wycht,
To warn Wallace, in all the haist he mycht.
Off Lewynhouss Wallace had tayn in playn,
Witht thre hundreth gud men off mekill mayn;
Kylsith a castell, he thocht to wesy it,
1670 Ane Rawynsdaill held; bot trew men leit him wyt,
Fol. 93 b That he was out that tym off Cummyrnauld;
Lord Cumyn duelt on tribut in that hauld.
Quhen Wallace wyst, he gert erll Malcom ly
With twa hundreth in a buschement ner by,
1675 To kep the houss, that nayn till it suld fayr;
He tuk the layff, and in the wod ner thar
A scurrour set, to warn quhen he saw ocht.
Son Rawynsdaill com, off thaim he had na thocht.
Quhen he was cummyn the twa buschementis betweyn,
1680 The scurrour warnd the cruell men and keyn;
Than Wallace brak, and folowit on thaim fast.
The Sotheroun fled, for thai war sar agast.
Rawynsdaill had than bot fyftye men;
Amang the Scottis thar deidis was litill to ken.
1685 Quhen erll Malcom had bard thaim fra the place,
Na Sotheroun yeid with lyff that thai did grace.

Part Lennox men thai left the horss to ta;
On spulyeyng than thai wald na tary ma.
To sege the houss than Wallace coud nocht bid;
1690 Throu out the land in awfull feyr thai ryd.
Than Lithquow toun thai brynt in to thair gayt;
Quhar Sotheroun duelt, thai maid thair byggyngis hayt.
The peyll thai tuk, and slew that was tharin;
Off Sotheroun blud the Scottis thocht na syn.
1695 Syn on the morn brynt Dawketh in a gleid;
Than till a strenth in Newbottyll wod thai yeid.
Be that Lawder, and Crystall off Cetoun,
Com fra the Bass, and brynt Northallyrtoun;
For Inglissmen suld thar na succour get:
1700 Quham thai ourtuk, thai slew with outyn let.
To meit Wallace thai past with all thair mycht,
A hundreth with thaim off men in armes brycht.
A blyth metyng that tym was thaim betweyn,
Quhen erll Malcom and Wallace has thaim seyn.
1705 Thom Dycson than was met with gud Wallace,
Quhilk grantyt sone [for] to reskew Douglace,
" Dicson," he said, " wait thow thair multiplé?"
' Thre thousand men thair power mycht nocht be.'
Erll Malcom said; " Thoucht thai war thousandys fyffe,
1710 " For this actioun me think that we suld stryff."
Than Hew the Hay, that duelt wndyr trewage,
Off Inglissmen son he gaiff our the wage;
Mar for to pay as than he likyt nocht.
With fyfté men with Wallace furth he socht;
1715 To Peblis past, bot no Sotheroun thar baid,
Thar at the croice a playn crya thai maid.
Fol. 94 a Wallace commaund, quha wald cum to his pess,
And byd tharat, reward suld haiff but les.
Gud Ruthirfurd, that euir trew has beyn,
1720 In Atryk wode, agayn the Sotheroun keyn,

Bydyn he had, and done thaim mekill der;
Saxté he led off nobill men in wer.
Wallace welcummyt quha com in his supplé
With lordly feyr, and chyftaynlik was he.
1725 Thaim till aray thai yeid with out the toun;
Thar nowmyr was sex hundreth off renoun,
In byrneis brycht, all men off mekill waill;
With glaid hartis thai past in Clyddisdaill.
The sege be than was to the Sanchar set;
1730 Sic tithingis com, quhilk maid tharin a let.
Quhen Sotheroun hard that Wallace was so ner,
Throw haisty fray the ost was all on ster;
Na man was thar wald for ane othir byd,
Purpos thai tuk in Ingland for to ryd.
1735 The chyftane said, sen thair king had befor
Fra Wallace fled, the causis was the mor.
Fast south thai went; to bid it was gret waith.
Douglace as than was quyt [thus] off thair scaith.
In Crawfurd mur be than was gud Wallace,
1740 Quhen men him tauld, that Sotheroun apon cace
Was fled away, and durst nocht him abid.
Thre hundreth than he chessyt with him to rid,
In lycht harnes, and hors at thai wald waill.
The erll Malcom he bad byd with the staill.
1745 To folow thaim, a bakgard for to be,
To stuff a chace in all haist bownyt he.
Throw Durisder he tuk the gaynest gayt;
Rycht sayn he wald with Sotheroun mak debait.
The playnest way abone Mortoun thai hald,
1750 Kepand the hycht, gyff that the Sotheroun wald
Houss to persew, or turn to Lochmaban.
Bot tent thar to the Inglissmen tuk nan;
Doune neth thai held, graith gydys can thaim leyr,
Abon Closburn Wallace approchyt ner.

1755 In ire he grew, quhen thai war in his sycht;
　　　To thaim thai sped with wyll and all thair mycht.
　　　On a out part the Scottis set in that tyd;
　　　Sewyn scor at erd thai had sone at a syd.
　　　The Sotheroun saw that it was hapnyt sa,
1760 Turnyt in agayn [sum] reskew for to ma.
　　　Quhen thai trowyt best agayn Scotland to stand.
　　　Erll Malcom com [than] rycht ner at thair hand.
Fol. 94 b The hayll power tuk playn purpos to fle.
　　　Quha was at erd Wallace gert lat thaim be;
1765 Apon the formest folowit in all his mycht.
　　　The erll and his apon the layff can lycht,
　　　Dyd all to ded wnhorssyt was that tyd.
　　　Feyll men was slayn apon the Sotheroun sid.
　　　Fyve hundreth larg, or thai past Dawswyntoun,
1770 On Sotheroun sid to ded was brocht adoun.
　　　The Scottis horss mony began to tyr,
　　　Supposs thaim selff was cruell fers as fyr.
　　　The flearis left bathe wode and watterys haill;
　　　To tak the playn thai thocht it most awaill.
1775 In gret battaill away full fast thai raid;
　　　In to strenthtis thai thocht to mak na baid.
　　　Ner Louchmaban and Lochyrmos thai went,
　　　Besyd Crouchmaid, quhar feyll Sotheroun was schent.
　　　Rycht mony horss, at ronnyn had so lang,
1780 And trawalyt sayr, thai mycht no forthir gang.
　　　Schyr Jhon the Graym apon his fut was set;
　　　Than Wallace als lychtyt with outyn let.
　　　Thir twa on fute amang the enemyss yeid;
　　　Was nayn, but hors, mycht fra thaim [pas] throw speid.
1785 On Inglissmen so cruelly thai socht,
　　　Quhom thai ourtuk agayn harmyt ws nocht.
　　　To Wallace com a part off power new,
　　　On restyt horss, that partly couth persew;

Adam Corré, with gud men off gret waill,
1790 And Jhonstoun als, that duelt in [to] Housdaill;
And Kyrkpatrik was in that cumpany,
And Halyday, quhilk semblyt sturdely.
Quhar thai entryt, the sailye was so sayr,
Dede to the ground feill frekis doun thai bayr.
1795 Sewyn scor was haill off new cummyn men in deid;
The south party off thaim had mekill dreid.
Wallace was horssyt apon a cursour wicht,
At gud Corré had brocht in to thair sycht,
To stuff the chas with his new chewalry.
1800 He commaundyt Graym, and all his men for thi,
To gydder byd, and folow as thai mycht.
Thre capdanys thar full son to dede he dycht.
That restyt horss so wondyr weill him bayr,
Quhom he our tuk agayn raiss neuir mar.
1805 Raithly he raid, and maid full mony wound,
Thir thre capdanis he stekit in that stound,
Off Durisdeyr, Enoch, and Tybyr mur.
Lord Clyffurdis eym away to Clyffurd fur,
The quhilk befor that kepyt Lowchmaban;
1810 Na landyt man chapyt with him bot ane.
Fol. 95 a For Maxwell als, out off Carlauerok com,
On to the Sotheroun the gaynest wayis nom.
In to the chass so wysly thai rid,
Few gat away that com apon that sid.
1815 Besyd Cokpull full feyll fechtand thai fand;
Sum drownyt was, sum slayn wpon the sand;
Quha chapyt was, in Ingland fled away.
Wallace returnd; na presoner tuk thai.
In Carlauerok restyng that nycht thai maid,
1820 Apon the morn till Drumfres blythly raid.
Thar Wallace cryid, quha wald cum to his pes,
Agayn Sotheroun, thar malice for to cess.

Till trew Scottis he ordand warysoun;
Quha fawtyt had, he grantyt remissioun.
1825 In Drumfress than he wald no langer byd.
The Sotheroun fled off Scotland on ilk sid,
Be sey and land, without langar abaid.
Off castellys, townys, than Wallace chyftanys maid
Rewlyt the land, and put it to the rest,
1830 With trew keparys, the quhilk he traistyt best.
The trew Douglace, that I yow tauld off ayr,
Kepar was maid fra Drumlanryk till Ayr.
Becauss he had on Sotheroun sic thing wrocht,
Hyss wyff was wraith; but it scho schawit nocht,
1835 Wndyr cowart hyr malice hid perfyt,
As a serpent watis hyr tym to byt.
Till Douglace eft scho wrocht full mekill cayr;
Off that as now I leyff quhill forthirmar.

Bot Sotheroun men durst her no castell hald,
1840 Bot left Scotland, befor as I yow tald,
Saiff ane Morton, a capdane fers and fell,
That held Dundé.   Than Wallace wald nocht duell;
Thiddyr he past, and lappyt it about.
Quhen Morton saw, that he was in sic dout,
1845 He askyt leyff with thar lywys to ga.
Wallace denyit, and said; " It beis nocht sa;
" The last capdane off Ingland that her was,
" I gayff him leyff with his men for to pass.
" Thow sall forthink sic maister for to mak;
1850 " All Ingland sall of the exemple tak.
" Sic men [I wend] fra thine now to haiff worn;
" Thow sall be hangyt, supposs thi king had suorn."
He gert commaund na Scottis suld to thaim spek;
" Conferme the sege, and so we sall ws wrek
1855 " On Inglissmen, has sic will off Dundé."

Scrymiour he maid thar constable for to be.
A ballingar off Ingland, that was thar,
Past out off Tay, and com to Whitbé far,
Fol. 95 b Till London send, and tauld off all this cace;
1860 Till hyng Morton wowyt had Wallace.
Befor this tym Eduuard with power yeid
To wer on Frans, for than he had no dreid;
Before he trowyt Scotland suld be his awn.
Quhen thai him warnyt how his men was ourthrawn,
1865 Agayn he turnyt till Ingland haistely,
And left his deid all fykit in to fy.
Gascon he clemyt as in to heretage,
He left it thus, for all his gret barnage;
And Flandris als he thocht till tak on hand;
1870 And thir he left, and come to reyff Scotland.
Quhen that this king in Ingland was cummyn hayme,
Sowmoundis thai maid, and chargyt Bruce be nayme,
And all wthir, that leyffyt wndir his croun,
Byschop, barroun, to cum at thair sowmoun.
1875 Quhen Wallace twyss, throw grace, had fred Scotland,
This tyran king tuk playnly wpon hand,
For sic desyr that he mycht haiff no rest,
He thocht till hym of it to mak conquest.
In cowatice he had rongyn so lang,
1880 Chyftanis he maid; at thai suld nocht pas wrang,
Gydis thai chessyt, fra strenthis thaim to ghy,
Thai thocht no mor to byd at juperty.
In playn battaill, and thai mycht Wallace wyn,
He trowyt off wer thai wald no mor begyn.
1885 Lat I this king makand hys ordinans;
My purpos is to spek sum thing off Frans.
The Inglissmen, that Ghyan held at wer,
Till Franch folk thai did full mekill der.
King and consaill sone in thar wyttis kest,

1890 To get Wallace thai thocht it was the best.
    For Gyan land the Inglissmen had thai;
    Thai schup thaim thus in all the haist thai may:
    For thai traistyt, and Scotland war weill stad,
    Wallace wald cum, as he thaim promyst had.

1895 The sammyn harrald, befor in Scotland was,
    Thai him commaundyt, and ordand he suld pas
    In to Scotland, with out langar delay,
    Out off the Slus, as gudly as he may.
    Redy he was, in schip he went on cace,

1900 In Tayis mowth the hawyn but baid he tais,
    Quhar Wallace was than at the saylye still;
    And he rasawyt the harrold with gud will.
    Thar wryt he raid, and said him on this wyss,
    Ane ansuer sone he couth thaim nocht dewyss.

1905 Till honest in the harrold than he send,
    On Wallace cost rycht boundandly to spend,
Fol. 96 a Quhyll tym he saw how [othir] materis yeid;
    Ane ansuer he suld hawe with outyn dreid;
    The wyt off Frans thocht Wallace to commend;

1910 In to Scotland, with this harrold, thai send
    Part off his deid, and als the discriptioune
    Off him tane thar, be men off discretioun,
    Clerkis, knychtis, and harroldys, that him saw;
    Bot I hereoff can nocht reherss thaim aw.

1915 Wallace statur, off gretnes, and off hycht,
    Was jugyt thus, be discretioun off rycht,
    That saw him bath dissembill and in weid;
    Nyne quartaris large he was in lenth indeid;
    Thryd part lenth in schuldrys braid was he,

1920 Rycht sembly, strang, and lusty for to se;
    Hys lymmys gret, with stalwart paiss and sound,
    Hys browys hard, his armes gret and round;
    His handis maid rycht lik till a pawmer,

Off manlik mak, with naless gret and cler:
1925 Proportionyt lang and fayr was his wesage;
Rycht sad off spech, and abill in curage;
Braid breyst and heych, with sturdy crag and gret;
His lyppys round, his noyss was squar and tret;
Bowand bron haryt, on browis and breis lycht,
1930 Cler aspre eyn, lik dyamondis brycht.
Wndyr the chyn, on the left syd, was seyn.
Be hurt, a wain; his colour was sangweyn.
Woundis he had in mony diuerss place,
Bot fayr and weill kepyt was his face.
1935 Off ryches he kepyt no propyr thing;
Gaiff as he wan, lik Alexander the king.
In tym off pes, mek as a maid was he;
Quhar wer approchyt the rycht Ector was he.
To Scottis men a gret credens he gaiff;
1940 Bot knawin enemyss thai couth him nocht disayff.
Thir properteys was knawin in to Frans,
Off him to be in gud remembrans.
Maistir Jhon Blayr that patron couth rasaiff,
In Wallace buk brewyt it with the layff.
1945 Bot he her off as than tuk litill heid,
His lauborous mynd was all on othir deid.
At Dundé sege thus ernystfully thai lay;
Tithandis to him Jop brocht on a day,
How Eduuard king, with likly men to waill,
1950 A hundyr thousand, com for to assail;
Than Scotland ground thai had [tane] apon cace.
In to sum part it grewyt gud Wallace.
He maid Scrymiour still at the houss to ly,
With twa thousand; and chargyt him forthi,
96 b 1955 That nayn suld chaip with lyff out off that sted,
At Sotheroun war, bot do thaim all to ded.
Scrymgeour grantyt rycht faithfully to bid:

With aucht thousand Wallace couth fra him ryd
To Sanct Jhonstoun; four dayis he graithit him thar;
1960 With sad awyss towart the south can fayr.
For king Eduuard that tym ordanıt had
Ten thousand haill to pass, that was full glad,
With yong Wodstok, a lord off mekill mycht.
At Sterlyng bryg he ordand thaim full rycht,
1965 And thar to byd, the entré for to wer;
Off Wallace than he trowit to haiff no der.
Thar leyff thai laucht, and passit bot delay,
Rycht far alyand, in a gud aray;
To Sterlyng com, and wald nocht thar abyd;
1970 To se the north furth than can he ryd.
Sic new curage so fell in his entent,
Quhilk maid Sotheron full sar to rapent.

BUKE TEND.

This Wodstok raid in to the north gud speid;
Off Scottis as than he had bot litill dreid;
For weyll he trowyt for to reskew Dunde;
Thar schippys com to Tay in be the se.
5 His gydys said, thai suld him gyd in by ·
Saynct Jhonstoun, quhar passage was playnly.
The hycht thai tuk, and lukit thaim about,
So war thai war off Wallace and his rout.
In sum part than he remordyt his thocht,
10 The kingis commaund becauss he kepyt nocht:
Bot quhen he saw thai war fewar than he,
He wald thaim byd, and othir do or de.
Schyr Jhon Ramsay formest his power saw,
He said; "Yon is, that yhe se hydder draw,
15 "Othir Sotheroun, that cummys sa cruellye,
"Or ellis erll Malcom to sek yow for supple."
Than Wallace smyld, and said; 'Ingliss thai ar;
'Ye may thaim ken rycht weyll, quhar euir thai far.'
On Schyrreff mur Wallace the feild has tane,
20 With aucht thousand, that worthy was in wane.
The Sotheroun was rycht douchty in thair deid,
To gydder straik, weyll stuffyt in steyll weid.
Than speris sone all in to splendrys sprent.
The hardy Scottis throw out the Sotheroun went;
25 In reddy battaill sewyn thowsand doun thai bar,
Dede on the bent, that recoueryt neuir mar.

Fol. 97 a With fell fechtyng off wapynnys groundyn keyn,
  Blud fra byrneis was bruschyt on the greyn.
  The felloun stour, that awfull was and strang,
 30 The worthy Scottis so felloun on thaim dang,
  At all was dede within a litill stound;
  Nane off that place had power for to found.
  Yong Wodstok has bathe land and lyff forlorn.
  The Scottis spulyeit off gud ger thaim beforn,
 35 Quhat thaim thocht best, off fyn harnes thai waill,
  Bath gold and gud, and horss that mycht thaim waill.
  To Sterlyng bryg, with out restyng, thai raid,
  Or ma suld com; Wallace this ordinans maid;
  Past our the bryg; Wallace gert wrychtis call,
 40 Hewyt trastis; wndyd the passage all.
  Sa tha sam folk he send to the dep furd,
  Ger set the ground with scharp spykis off burd.
  Bot nyne or ten he kest a gait befor,
  Langis the schauld, maid it bath dep and schor.
 45 Than Wallace said; " On a sid we sall be,
  " Yon king and I, bot gyff he southwart fle."
  He send Lawder, quhilk had in hand the Bass,
  Langis the cost, quhar ony weschell wass,
  And men with him, that bysily couth luk;
 50 Off ilka boyt a burd or twa out tuk.
  Schippys thai brynt off strangearis that was thar,
  Cetoun and he; to Wallace thus thai fayr,
  In Sterlyng lay apon his purpos still,
  For Inglissmen to se quhat way thai will.
 55 The erll Malcom Sterlyng in kepyng had;
  Till him he com with men off armes sad,
  Thre hundreth haill, that sekyr war and trew,
  Off Lennox folk, thair power to renew.
  Schir John the Graym, fra Dundaff prewaly,
 60 Till Wallace com with a gud chewalry;

Tithandis him brocht, the Sotheroun com at hand,
In Torfychan king Eduuard was lugeand;
Stroyand the place off purwiance that was thar;
Sanct Jhonys gud for thaim thai wald nocht spar.
65 The gud Stewart of But com to the land,
With him he ledys weill ma than twelf thowsand;
Till Cumyn past, was than in Cummyrnald.
Apon the morn bownyt the Stewart bald
Sone till aray, with men off armes brycht;
70 Twenty thowsand than semblyt to thair sycht.
The lord Stewart and Cumyn furth thai rid
To the Fawkyrk, and thar hecht to abid.
Fol. 97 b The Scottis chyftane than owt off Sterlyng past;
To the Fawkyrk he sped his ost full fast.
75 Wallace and his than till aray he yeid,
With ten thousand off douchty men in deid.
Quha couth behald thair awfull lordly wult,
So weill beseyn, so forthwart, stern, and stult;
So gud chyftanys, as with sa few thar beyn,
80 With out a king, was neuir in Scotland seyn.
Wallace him selff, and erll Malcom that lord,
Schir Jhon the Graym, and Ramsay at accord,
Cetoun, Lawder, and Lundy that was wicht,
Adam Wallace to that jornay him dycht,
85 And mony gud, quhilk prewyt weill in press;
Thar namys all I may nocht her rehress.
Sotheroun or than off Torfychan fur,
Thar passage maid in to Slamanan mur;
In till a playn set tentis and palyon,
90 South hald Fawkyrk, a litill abon the ton.
And Jop him selff jugit thaim, be his sycht,
In haill nowmyr a hundyr thousand rycht.
Off Wallace com the Scottis sic confort tuk.
Quhen thai him saw, all raddour thai forsuk:

95 For off inwy was few thar at it wyst;
 Tresonable folk thair mater wyrkis throu lyst.
 Poyson sen syn at the Fawkyrk is cald,
 Throu treson and corruption off ald.
 Lord Cumyn had inwy at gud Wallace,
100 Fer erll Patrik that hapnyt vpon cace.
 Cunttas off Merch was Cumyns sister der;
 Wndyr colour he wroucht in this maner,
 In to the ost had ordand Wallace dede,
 And maid Stewart with him to fall in pled;
105 He said that lord, at Wallace had no rycht
 Power to leid, and he present in sycht.
 He bad him tak the wantgard for to gy;
 So wyst he weyll that thai suld stryff forthi.
 Lord Stewart ast at Wallace his consaill,
110 Said; " Schyr. ye knaw quhat may ws maist awaill;
 " Yon felloun king is awfull for to bid."
 Rycht wnabasyt Wallace ansuerd that tyd;
 ' And I haiff seyn may twyss in to Scotland,
 ' With yon ilk king, quhen Scottismen tuk on hand
115 ' With fewar men than now ar hydder socht,
 ' This realm agayn to full gud purpos brocht.
 ' Schyr, we will fecht, for we haiff men inew,
 ' As for a day; sa that we be all trew.'
 The Stewart said, he wald the wantgard haiff.
120 Wallace ansuerd, and said; " Sa God me saiff,
Fol. 98 a " That sall ye nocht, as lang as I may ryng;
 " Nor no man ellis, quhill I se my rycht king.
 " Gyff he will cum, and tak on him the croun,
 " At his commaund I sall be reddy boun.
125 " Throw Goddis grace I reskewed Scotland twyss;
 " I war to mad to leyff [it] on sic wyss,
 " To tyn for bost that I haiff gowernd lang."
 Thus halff in wraith frawart him can he gang.

Stewart tharwith all bolynt in to baill.

130 'Wallace,' he said, 'be the I tell a taill.'
    "Say furth," quoth he, " off the farrest ye can."
    Wnhappyly his taill thus he began.
    'Wallace,' he said, 'thow takis the mekill cur;
    'So feryt it, be wyrkyng off natur,

135 'How a howlat complend off his fethrame,
    'Quhill deym natur tuk off ilk byrd, but blame.
    'A fayr fethyr, and to the howlat gaiff;
    'Than he throuch pryd reboytyt all the laiff.
    'Quhar off suld thow thi senye schaw so he?

140 'Thow thinkis nan her at suld thi falow be.
    'This makis it, thow art cled with our men,
    'Had we our awn, thin war bot few to ken.'
    At thir wordis gud Wallace brynt as fyr;
    Our haistely he ansuerd him in ire:

145 "Thow leid," he said; "the suth full oft has ben,
    "Thar haiff I baid, quhar thow durst nocht be seyn
    "Contrar enemys, na mar, for Scotlandis rycht,
    "Than dar the howlat quhen that the day is brycht.
    "That taill full meit thow has tauld be thi sell;

150 "To thi desyr thow sall me nocht compell.
    "Cwmyn it is has gyffyn this consaill;
    "Will God, ye sall off your fyrst purpos faill.
    "That fals traytour, that I off danger brocht,
    "Is wondyr lyk till bryng this realm till nocht.

155 "For thi ogart othir thow sall de,
    "Or in presoun byd, or cowart lik to fle.
    "Reskew off me thow sall get nane this day."
    Tharwith he turnd, and fra thaim raid his way.
    Ten thousand haill fra thaim with Wallace raid;

160 Nan was bettyr in all this warld so braid,
    As off sic men, at leiffand was in lyff.
    Allace, gret harm fell Scotland throucht that stryff!

Past till a wod fra the Fawkyrk be est,
He wald nocht byd for commaund na request;
165 For charge off nan, bot it had ben his king,
At mycht that tym bryng him fra his etlyng.
The tothir Scottis, that saw this discensioun,

Fol. 98 b For disconford to leiff the feild was boun;
Bot at thai men, was natyff till Stwart,
170 Principaill off But, tuk hardement in hart.
Lord Stewart was at Cumyn grewyt thar,
Hecht, and he leiffd, he suld repent full sar
The gret trespace, that he, throw raklesnace,
Had gert him mak to Wallace in that place.
175 For thair debait it was a gret peté;
For Inglissmen than mycht na treté be,
Haistyt sa fast a bataill to the feild,
Thretty thowsand that weill coud wapynnys weild.
Erll off Harfurd was chosyn thair chyftane.
180 The gud Stewart than till aray is gane;
The feild he tuk, as trew and worthy knycht.
The Inglissmen come on with full gret mycht.
Thar fell metyng was awfull for to se,
At that countour thai gert feill Sotheroun de.
185 Quhen speris was spilt, hynt owt with suerdis son;
On athir sid full douchty deid was don.
Feill on the ground was fellyt in that place:
Stewart and his can on his enemys race;
Blud byrstyt out throuch maill and byrneis brycht.
190 Twenty thowsand, with dredfull wapynnys dycht,
Off Sotheroun men derffly to ded thai dyng;
The remanand agayn fled to thair king.
Ten thousand thar, that fra the ded eschewyt,
With thair chyftane in to the ost relewyt.
195 Agayn to ray the hardy Stwart yeid.
Quhen Wallace saw this nobill worthi deid,

Held wp his handys, with humyll prayer prest,
To God he said; " Gyff yon lord grace to lest,
" And power haiff his worschip till attend,
200 " To wyn thir folk, and tak the haill commend.
" Gret harm it war at he suld be ourset;
" With new power thai will on him rebet."
Be that the Bruce ane awfull battaill baid,
And Byschop Beik, quhilk oft had been assayd,
205 Fourty thowsand, apon the Scottis to fair,
With fell affer; thai raissit wp rycht thair
The Bruce baner, in gold off gowlis cler.
Quhen Wallace saw battallis approchyt ner,
The rycht lyon agayn his awn kynryk,
210 " Allace," he said, " the warld is contrar lik!
" This land suld be yon tyrandis heretage,
" That cummys thus to stroy his awn barnage.
" Sa I war fre off it that I said ayr,
" I wald forswer Scotland for euirmair;
99 a 215 " Contrar the Bruce I suld reskew thaim now,
" Or de tharfor, to God I mak a wow."
The gret debait in Wallace wit can waid,
Betwix kyndnes and wyllfull wow he maid.
Kyndness him bad reskew thaim fra thair fa.
220 Than Wyll said; ' Nay, quhy, fuyll, wald thow do sa?
' Thow has na wyt with rycht thi selff to leid;
' Suld thow help thaim that wald put the to deid?'
Kyndnes said; " Yha, thai ar gud Scottis men."
Than Will said; ' Nay; weryté thow may ken;
225 ' Had thai bene gud, all anys we had ben.
' Be reson heyr the contrar now is seyn;
' For thai me hayt ma na Sotheroun leid.'
Kyndnes said; " Nay, that schaw thai nocht in deid.
" Thocht ane off thaim be fals in till his saw,
230 " For causs off him thow suld nocht loss thaim aw.

" Thai haiff done weill in to yon felloun stour;
" Reskew thaim now, and tak a hye honour."
Wyll said; 'Thai wald haiff reft fra me my lyff;
' I baid for thaim in mony stalwart stryff.'
235 Kyndnes said; " Help, thair power is at nocht;
" Syn wreik on hym that all the malice wrocht."
Wyll said; ' This day thai sall nocht helpyt be;
' That I haiff said, sall ay be said for me
' Thai ar bot dede; God grant thaim off his blys!
240 ' Inwy lang syn has done gret harme but this.'
Wallace tharwith turnyt for ire in teyn,
Braith teris for baill byrst out fra bathe his eyn.
Schyr Jhon the Graym, and mony worthi wicht.
Wepyt in wo for sorow off that sycht.
245 Quhen Bruce his battaill apon the Scottis straik,
Thair cruell com maid cowardis for to quaik;
Lord Cwmyn fled to Cummyrnauld away.
About the Scottis the Sotheroun lappyt thay.
The men off But befor thair lord thai stud,
250 Defendand him, quhen fell stremys off blud
Wer thaim about in flothis quhar thai yeid.
Bathid in blud was Bruce suerd and his weid,
Throw fell slauchtyr off trew men off his awn.
Son to the dede the Scottis was ourthrawn;
255 Syn slew the lord, for he wald nocht be tayn.
Quhen Wallace saw quhen thir gud men was gayn,
" Lordis," he said, " quhat now is your consaill?
" Twa choyss thar is, the best I rede ws waill.
" Yondyr the king this ost abandonand;
260 " Heyr Bruce and Beyk, in yon battaill to stand.
Fol. 99 b " Yon king in wer has wyss and felloun beyn;
" Thar capdans als full cruell ar and keyn;
" Bettyr off hand is nocht leiffand, I wyss,
" In tyrandry; ye trow me weill off this.

T

265 " Than Bruce and Beik to quhat part thai be set,
    " We haiff a choiss, quhilk is full hard but let.
    " And we turn est, for strenth in Lowthiane land,
    " Thai stuff a chass rycht scharp, I dar warrand.
    " Tak we the mur, yon king is ws befor.
270 " Thar is bot this, with outyn wordis mor;
    " To the Torwod; for our succour is thar.
    " Throuch Brucis ost forsuth fyrst mon we far;
    " Amang ws now thar nedis no debayt,
    " Yon men ar dede, we will nocht stryff for stayt."
275 Thai consent haill to wyrk rycht as he will;
    Quhat him thocht best thai grantyt to fullfill.
    Gud Wallace than, that stoutly couth thaim ster,
    Befor thaim raid in till his armour cler,
    Rewellyt speris all in a nowmyr round;
280 " And we hawe grace for to pass throw thaim sound,
    " And few be lost, till our strenth we will ryd.
    " Want we mony, in faith we sall all byd."
    Thai hardnyt horss fast on the gret ost raid;
    The rerd at rayss, quhen sperys in sondyr glaid,
285 Duschyt in gloss, dewyt with speris dynt.
    Fra forgyt steyll the fyr flew out but stynt.
    The felloun thrang, quhen horss and men remowyt,
    Wp drayff the dust quhar thai thair pichtis prowyt.
    The tothir ost mycht nocht no deidis se,
290 For stour at raiss, quhill thai disseuyrit be.
    The worthy Scottis aucht thousand doun thai ber;
    Few war at erd at gud Wallace brocht thar.
    The king cryt horss apon thaim for to ryd;
    Bot this wyss lord gaiff him consaill to bid,
295 The erll off York, said; " Schyr, ye wyrk amyss.
    " To brek aray; yon men quyt throucht thaim is.
    " Thai ken the land, and will to strenthis draw;
    " Tak we the playn, we ar in perell aw."

The king consawyt at his consaill was rycht,
300 Rewllyt his ost. and baid still in thair sycht.
Or Bruce and Beik mycht retorn thair battaill,
The Scottis was throucht, and had a great awaill.

Wallace commaund the ost suld pass thair way
To the Tor wod, in all the haist thai may;
305 Hym selff and Graym, and Lawdir, turnyt in
Betwex battaillys, pryss [and] prowys for to wyn;
And with thaim baid in that place hundrys thre
Off westland men was oysyt in jeperté.
Apon wycht horss that weselé coud ryd.
ol. 100 a 310 A slop thai maid, quhar thai set on a syd;
Na speris thai had, bot suerdys off gud steyll;
Thar with in stour thai leit thair enemyss feill,
How thai full oft had prewyt beyn in press;
Off Inglissmen thai maid feill to decess.
315 Or Bruce tharoff mycht weill persawyng haiff,
Thre hundreth thar was graithit to thair graiff.
The hardy Bruce ane ost abandownyt;
Twenty thowsand he rewllyt be force and wit,
Wpon the Scottis men for to reskew:
320 Serwyt thai war with gud speris enew;
And byschop Beik a stuff till him to be.
Quhen gud Wallace thair ordinans coud se;
" Allace!" he said, " yon man has mekill mycht,
" And our gud will till wndo his awn rycht."
325 He bad his men towart his ost in ryd,
Thaim for to sayff he wald behynd thaim byd.
Mekill he trowys in God, and his awn weid;
Till sayff his men he did full douchty deid.
Wpon him selff mekill trawaill he tais;
330 The gret battaill compleit apon him gais.
In the forbreyst he retornyt full oft:

Quham euir he hyt, thair sawchnyng was wnsoft.
That day in warld knawin was nocht his maik;
A Sotheroun man he slew ay at a straik.

335 Bot his a strenth mycht nocht agayn thaim be:
Towart his ost behwffyd for to fle.
The Bruce him hurt at the returnyng thair,
Wndyr the halss a deip wound and a sayr.
Blude byrstyt owt braithly at speris lenth;

340 Fra the gret ost he fled towart his strenth.
Sic a flear befor was neuir seyn;
Nocht at Gadderis, off Gawdyfer the keyn,
Quhen Alexander reskewed the foryouris,
Mycht till him be comperd in tha houris,

345 The fell turnyng on folowaris that he maid,
How bandounly befor the ost he raid:
Nor how gud Graym wyth cruell hardement,
Na how Lawder, amang thair fayis went:
How thaim allayn in to that stour thai stud,

350 Quhill Wallace was in stanchyng off his blud.
Be than he had stemmyt full weill his wound,
With thre hundreth in to the feild can found,
To reskew Graym and Lawder that was wicht.
Bot byschop Beik com with sic force and slycht,

355 The worthy Scottis weryt fer on bak.
Fol. 100b Sewyn akyrbreid, in turnyng off thair bak.
Yeit Wallace has thir twa delyueryt weill
Be his awn strenth and his gud suerd off steill.
The awfull Bruce amang thaim with gret mayn,

360 At the reskew, thre Scottismen has he slayn:
Quham he hyt rycht, ay at a straik was ded.
Wallace preyst in tharfor to set ramied.
With a gud sper the Bruce was serwyt but baid:
With gret inwy to Wallace fast he raid;

365 And he till him assonyeit nocht for thi.

The Bruce him myssyt as Wallace passyt by,
Awkwart he straik with his scharp groundyn glawe,
Sper and horsscrag in till sondyr he drave;
Bruce was at erd or Wallace turned about.
370 The gret battaill off thousandis stern and stout,
Thai horssyt Bruce with men off gret walour.
Wallace allayn was in that stalwart stour.
Graym pressyt in, and straik ane Ingliss knycht,
Befor the Bruce, apon the basnet brycht.
375 That seruall stuff, and all his othir weid,
Bathe bayn and brayn, the nobill suerd throuch yeid.
The knycht was dede; gud Graym retornet tyte.
A suttell knycht tharat had gret despyt,
Folowyt at wait, and has persawyt weill
380 Gramys byrny was to narow sumdeill,
Be neth the waist, that closs it mycht nocht be.
On the fyllat full sternly straik that sle,
Persyt the bak, in the bowalys him bar,
Wyth a scharp sper, that he mycht leiff no mar.
385 Graym turnd tharwith, and smate that knycht in teyn,
Towart the wesar, a litill be neth the eyn.
Dede off that dynt, to ground he duschyt doun.
Schyr Jhon the Graym swonyt on his arsoun.
Or he our com, till pass till his party,
390 Feill Sotheroun men, that was on fute him by,
Stekit his horss, that he no forthir yeid;
Graym yauld to God his gud speryt, and his deid.
Quhen Wallace saw this knycht to dede was wrocht,
The pytuouss payn so sor thryllyt his thocht,
395 All out off kynd at alteryt his curage;
Hys wyt in wer was than bot a wod rage.
Hys horss him bur in feild quhar so him lyst;
For off him selff as than litill he wyst.
Lik a wyld best that war fra reson rent,

400 As wytlace wy in to the ost he went,
        Dingand on hard; quhat Sotheroun he rycht hyt,
        Straucht apon horss agayn mycht neuir syt.
        In to that rage full feill folk he dang doun;
Fol. 101 a All hym about was reddyt a gret rowm.
405 Quhen Bruce persawyt with Wallace it stud sa,
        He chargyt men lang sperys for to ta,
        And sla hys horss, sa he suld nocht eschaip.
        Feyll Sotheroun than to Wallace fast can schaip,
        Persyt hys hors with sperys on athir syd;
410 Woundys thai maid that was bathe deip and wyd.
        Off schafftis part Wallace in sondyr schayr,
        Bot fell hedys in till his horss left thair.
        Sum wytt agayn to Wallace can radoun,
        In hys awn mynd so rewllyt him resoun;
415 Sa for to de him thocht it no waslage.
        Than for to fle he tuk no taryage;
        Spuryt the horss, quhilk ran in a gud randoun
        Till his awn folk was bydand at Carroun.
        The sey was in, at thai stoppyt and stud;
420 On loud he cryt and bad thaim tak the flud;
        "To gyddyr byd, ye may nocht loss a man."
        At his commaund the watter thai tuk than.
        Hym returned, the entré for to kepe,
        Quhill all his ost was passyt our the depe;
425 Syn passyt our, and dred his horss suld faill,
        Hym selff hewy cled in to plait off maill.
        Set he couth swom, he trowit he mycht nocht weill.
        The cler watter culyt the horss sumdeill;
        Atour the flud he bur him to the land,
430 Syn fell doun dede, and mycht no langar stand.
        Kerlé full son a cursour till him brocht;
        Than wp he lap, amang the ost he socht.
        Graym was away, and fyftene othir wicht;

On Magdaleyn day thir folk to ded was dycht.
435 Thretty thousand off Ingliss men, for trew,
The worthy Scottis vpon that day thai slew.
Quhat be Stwart, and syn be wicht Wallace,
For all his pryss, king Eduuard rewyt that race.

To the Torwod he bad the ost suld ryd;
440 Kerlé and he past wpon Caroun syd,
Behaldand our wpon the south party.
Bruce formast com, and can on Wallace cry.
" Quhat art thow thar?" ' A man,' Wallace can say.
The Bruce ansuerd, " That has thow prewyt to day.
445 " Abyd," he said, " thow nedis nocht now to fle."
Wallace ansuerd; ' I eschew nocht for the.
' Bot that power has thi awn ner fordon;
' Amendis off this, will God, we sall haiff son.'
" Langage off the," the Bruce said, " I desyr."
450 ' Say furth,' quoth he; ' thow may for litill hyr.
Fol. 101 b ' Ryd fra that ost, and gar thaim bid with Beik.
' I wald fayn her quhat thow likis to speik.'
The ost baid styll, the Bruce passyt thaim fra;
He tuk wyth him bot a Scot that hecht Ra.
455 Quhen that the Bruce out off thair heryng wer,
He turned in, and this question can sper:
" Quhy wyrkis thow thus, and mycht in gud pess be?"
Than Wallace said; ' Bot in defawt off the.
' Throuch thi falsheid thin awn wyt has myskend.
460 ' I cleym no rycht, bot wald this land defend,
' At thow wndoys throu thi fals cruell deid.
' Thow has tynt twa had beyn worth fer mair meid,
' On this ilk day, with a gud king to found,
' Na fyve mylyon off fynest gold so round,
465 ' That euir was wrocht in werk or ymage brycht.
' I trow in warld was nocht a bettir knycht,

'Than was the gud Graym off trewth and hardement.'
Teris tharwith fra Wallace eyn doun went.
Bruce said; " Fer ma on this day we haiff losyt."
470 Wallace ansuerd; 'Allace, thai war ewill cosyt,
'Throuch thi tresson, that suld be our rycht king,
'That willfully dystroyis thin awne off spryng.'
The Bruce askyt; " Will thow do my dewyss?"
Wallace said; 'Nay; thow leyffis in sic wyss.
475 'Thow wald me mak at Eduuardis will to be;
'Yeit had I leuir to morn be hyngyt hye.'
" Yeit sall I say, as I wald consaill geyff;
" Than, as a lord, thow mycht at liking leiff,
" At thin awn will in Scotland for to ryng,
480 " To be in pece, and hald off Eduuard king."
'Off that fals king I think neuir wage to tak,
'Bot contrar him with my power to mak.
'I cleym no thing as be titill off rycht;
'Thocht I mycht reiff, sen God has lent me mycht.
485 'Fra the thi crowne off this regioun to wer;
'Bot I will nocht sic a charge on me ber.
'Gret God wait best, quhat wer I tak on hand
'For till kep fre that thow art gaynstandand,
'It mycht beyn said, off lang gone her off forn,
490 'In cursyt tym thow was for Scotland born.
'Schamys thow nocht, that thow neuir yeit did gud,
'Thou renygat deuorar off thi blud?
'I wow to God, ma I thi maistyr be
'In ony feild, thow sall fer werthar de
495 'Than sall a Turk, for thi fals cruell wer.
'Pagans till ws dois nocht so mekill der.'
Than lewch the Bruce at Wallace ernystfulnas,
Fol. 102 a And said; " Thow seis at thus standis the cass.
" This day thow art with our power our set,
500 " Agayn yon king warrand thow may nocht get."

Than Wallace said; ' We ar, be mekill thing,
' Starkar this day in contrar off yon king,
' Than at Beggar, quhar he left mony off his,
' And als the feild; so sall he do with this,
505 ' Or de thar for, for all hys mekill mycht.
' We haiff nocht losyt in this feild bot a knycht:
' And Scotland now in sic perell is stad,
' To leyff it thus my selff mycht be full mad.'
" Wallace," he said, " it prochys ner the nycht,
510 " Wald thow to morn, quhen that the day is lycht,
" Or nyn off bell, meit me at this chapell,
" Be Dunypass, I wald haiff your consell."
Wallace said; ' Nay; or that ilk tyme be went
' War all the men, hyn till [the] orient,
515 ' In till a will with Eduuard, quha had suorn,
' We sall bargane be nyne houris to morn :
' And for hys wrang reyff othir he sall think schaym,
' Or de tharfor, or fle in Ingland haym.
' Bot and thow will, son be the hour off thre,
520 ' At that ilk tryst, will God, thow sall se me.
' Quhill I may lest, this realme sall nocht forfar.'
Bruce promest hym with twelf Scottis to be thar;
And Wallace said; ' Stud thow rychtwyss to me,
' Cownter palyss I suld nocht be to the.
525 ' I sall bryng ten, and, for thi nowmer ma,
' I gyff no force thocht thow be freynd or fa.'
Thus thai depertyt; the Bruce past his way,
Till Lithqwo raid, quhar that king Eduuard lay,
The feild had left, and lugyt a south the toun,
530 To souper set; as Bruce at the palyoun
So entryt in, and saw wacand his seit.
No wattir he tuk, bot maid him to the meit.
Fastand he was, and had beyn in gret dreid;
Bludyt was all his wapynnys and his weid.

535 Sotheroun lordys scornyt him in termys rud,
    And said; Behald, yon Scot ettis his awn blud."
    The king thocht ill thai maid sic derisioun,
    He bad haiff watter to Bruce off Huntyntoun.
    Thai bad him wesche; he said, that wald he nocht:
540 "This blud is myn, that hurtis most my thocht."
    Sadly the Bruce than in his mynd remordyt
    Thai wordis suth that Wallace had him recordyt.
    Than rewyt he sar, fra resoun had him knawin,
Fol. 102 b At blud and land suld all lik beyn his awin.
545 With thaim he was lang or he couth get away;
    Bot contrar Scottis he faucht nocht fra that day.
    Lat I the Bruce sayr mowyt in his entent:
    Gud Wallace sone agane to the ost went,
    In the Torwod quhilk had thair lugyng maid.
550 Fyris thai bett, that was bath brycht and braid;
    Off nolt and scheip thai tuk at sufficiens,
    Tharoff full sone that get thaim sustinens.
    Wallace slepyt bot a schort quhill and raiss;
    To rewll the ost on a gud mak he gais
555 Till erll Malcom, Ramsay, and Lundy wicht;
    With fyve thousand in a battaill thaim dycht.
    Wallace, Lawder, and Crystell off Cetoun,
    Fyve thousand led, and Wallace off Ricardtoun,
    Full weyll arayit in till thair armour clen,
560 Past to the feild quhar that the chass had ben;
    Amang the ded men sekand the worthiast,
    The corss off Graym, for quham he murned mast.
    Quhen thai him fand, and gud Wallace him saw,
    He lychtyt doun, and hynt him fra thaim aw
565 In armyss vp; behaldand his paill face,
    He kyssyt him, and cryt full oft; " Allace!
    " My best brothir in warld that euir I had!
    " My afald freynd quhen I was hardest stad!

"My hop, my heill, thow was in maist honour!
570 "My faith, my help, my strenthiast in stour!
"In the was wyt, fredom, and hardines;
"In the was treuth, manheid, and nobilnes;
"In the was rewll, in the was gouernans;
"In the was wertu with cutyn warians;
575 "In the lawté, in the was gret largnas;
"In the gentrice, in the was stedfastnas.
"Thow was gret causs off wynnyng off Scotland;
"Thocht I began, and tuk the wer on hand.
"I wow to God, that has the warld in wauld,
580 "Thi dede sall be to Sotheroun full der sauld.
"Martyr thow art for Scotlandis rycht and me;
"I sall the wenge, or ellis tharfor de."
Was na man thar fra wepyng mycht hym rafreyn
For loss off him, quhen thai hard Wallace pleyn.
585 Thai caryit him with worschip and dolour;
In the Fawkyrk graithit him in sepultour.

Wallace commaundyt his ost tharfor to byd;
Hys ten he tuk, for to meit Bruce thai ryd.
Sowthwest he past, quhar at the tryst was set;
590 The Bruce full son and gud Wallace is met.
For loss off Graym, and als for propyr teyn,
He grewyt in ire, quhen he the Bruce had seyn.
Thar salusyng was bot boustous and thrawin.
"Rewis thow," he said, "thow art contrar thin awin?"
595 'Wallace,' said Bruce, 'rabut me now no mar;
'Myn awin dedis has bet me wondyr sayr.'
Quhen Wallace hard with Bruce that it stud sua,
On kneis he fell, far contenans can him ma.
In armes son the Bruce has Wallace tane;
600 Out fra thair men in consalle ar thai gane.
I can nocht tell perfytly thair langage;

Bot this was it thair men had off knawlage:
Wallace him prayit; "Cum fra yon Sotheroun king."
The Bruce said; 'Nay, thar lattis me a thing.

605 ' I am so boundyn with wytnes to be leill,
' For all Ingland I wald nocht fals my seill.
' Bot off a thing, I hecht to God and the.
' That contrar Scottis agayn I sall nocht be;
' In till a feild, with wapynnys that I ber,

610 ' In thi purpos I sall the neuir der.
' Gyff God grantis off ws ourhand till haiff,
' I will bot fle myn awin selff for to saiff;
' And Eduuard chaip, I pass with him agayn,
' Bot I throu force be othir tane or slayn.

615 ' Brek he on me; quhen that my terme is out,
' I cum to the, may I chaip fra that dout.'
Off thair consaill I can tell yow no mar.
The Bruce tuk leyff, and can till Eduuard fayr,
Rycht sad in mynd for Scottis men that war lost.

620 Wallace in haist prouidyt son his ost.
He maid Crawfurd the erll Malcom to gid,
The lauch way till Enrawyn thai ryd;
For thar wachis [than] suld thaim nocht aspy.
The tothir ost him selff led haistely

625 Be south Manwell, quhilk that thai war betweyn;
Off the out watch thus chapyt thai wnseyn.
The erll Malcom on Lithquow entris in;
Our haistely a stryff thai can begyn.
Wallace was nocht all to the battaill boun,

630 Quhen that thai hard the scry raiss in the toun.
On Eduuardis ost thai set full sodandly:
Wallace and his maid litill noyis or cry,
Bot occupyd with wapynnys in that stour;
Feill fallen war ded that was with out armour.

.103b 635 All dysarayit the Inglis ost was than;

Amang palyounis the Scottis, quhar mony man
Cuttyt cordys, gart mony tentis fall.
Nayn sonyeid than; at anys fechtand was all,
Bath Wallace ost, and erll Malcom, wyth mycht.
640 King Eduuard than, with awfull fer on hycht,
Cryit till aray, on Bruce. so stern and stout,
Twentye thousand in armys him about,
In to harness had biddyn all that nycht.
Bot frayit folk so dulfully was dycht,
645 On ilk sid thai fled for ferdnes off thar deid;
Wallace and his so rudly throw thaim yeid,
Towart the king, and fellyt feill to grounde:
Quha baid thaim thair, rycht fell fechtyng has found.
That awfull king rycht manfully abaid;
650 Till all his folk [a] gret conford he maid.
The worthy Scottis, agayn him in that stour,
Feill Sotheroun slew in to thair fyn armour;
So forthwartlye thai pressyt in the thrang,
Befor the king maid sloppis thaim amang.
655 Ingliss commounis than fled on athir sid;
Bot noble men nane other durst abid.
The Bruce as than to Scottis did no grewans:
A juge he was with fenyeid contenans:
Sa did he neuir in na battaill ayr,
660 Nothyr yeit eftir, sic deid as he schew thar.
The erll Malcom be than in to the toun,
The erle Herfurd to fle thai had maid boun.
The Lennox men set thar lugyng in fyr;
Then ferdly fled full mony Sotheroun syr.
665 The king Eduuard, that yeit was fechtand still.
Has seyn thaim fle; that likit him full ill.
The worthi Scottis fast towart him thai press:
Hys brydyll ner assayit or thai wald cess.
His banerman Wallace slew in that place:

670 And sone to ground the baner doun he race.
　　The erll off York consaillyt the king to fle;
　　Than he ratornd, sen na succour thai se.
　　The Ingliss men has seyn thair banner fall;
　　Without confort, to fle thai purpost all.
675 Elewyn thousand in toun and feild was ded
　　Off Eduuardis folk, or his selff left the sted.
　　Twentye thousand away to giddyr raid;
　　King and chyftans na langar tary maid.
　　The Scottis in haist than to thair horss thai yeid,
680 To stuff the chass with worthi men in weid.

Fol. 104 a The Lennox folk, that wantyt horss and ger,
　　Tuk thaim at will, to help thaim in that wer;
　　At stragyll raid quhat Scot mycht formest pas,
　　Off Sotheroun men quhar off gret slauchtyr was.
685 Wallace has seyn the Scottis wnordourly
　　Folow the chass, he maid chyftanis in hy
　　Thaim for to rewll, and all to gyddyr ryd;
　　Comaundyt thaim ilk ane suld othir bid.
　　" In to fleyng the Sotheroun suttaill ar,
690 " Se thai the tym thai wyll syt on ws sar;
　　" Feill scalyt folk to thaim will son ranew,
　　" For ye se weyll that thai ar men enew."
　　The folowaris was rewllyt weill with skill;
　　In gud aray thai raid all at his will,
695 And slew doun fast; quhat Sotheroun thai ourtak,
　　Contrar the Scottis com neuir maistrice to mak.
　　In to the chaiss thai haistyt thaim so ner,
　　Na Inglissman out fra the ost durst ster.
　　The frayit folk, at stragill that was fleand,
700 Drew to the king weill ma than ten thousand.
　　Thretty thousand in nowmyr than war thai;
　　In till aray to gyddyr passyt away.
　　Feill Scottis horss was drewyn in to trawaill,

Forrown that day so irkyt can defaill.

705 The Sotheroun was with horss serwyt full weill;
Off Wallace chaiss the lordis had gret feill:
Off horss thai war purwaide in gret wayn;
The king changyt on syndry horss off Spayn.
Than Wallace said; "Lordis, ye may weill se,

710 " Yon folk ar now all that yon king may be.
" For falt off stuff we loiss our mekill thing,
" War we wyth horss to pass befor this king,
" We suld mak end off all this lang debait.
" Yeit sum off thaim sall handelyt be full hayt.

715 " Part off our horss ar haldyn fresche and wicht;
" Set on thaim sar quhill we ar in this mycht."
Tharwith the Scottis so hard amang thaim drew,
Off the outward thre thousand thair thai slew.
In Crawfurd mur mony man was slayn,

720 Eduuard gart call the Bruce mekill off mayn,
Than said he thus; 'Gud erll off Huntyntoun,
' Ye se the Scottis puttis feill to confusioun,
' Wald ye wyth men agayn on thaim raleiff,
' And mer thaim anys, I sall, quhill I may leiff,

Fol. 104 b 725 ' Low yow fer mar than ony othir knycht;
' And for all this sall put yow to your rycht.'
Than said the Bruce; "Schyr, loss me off my band;
" Than I sall turn, I hecht yow be my hand."
The king full son consideryt in his mynd,

730 Quhen he hard Bruce ansuer him in sic kynd,
Fra Inglissmen the Brucis hart set is.
Than kest he thus, how he suld mend that myss;
And so he dyd, in Ingland at his will
Na Scottis man he leit with Bruce bid still;

735 Bot quhar he past held him in subiectioun
Off Inglissmen, held him in gret bandoun.
He turned nocht, na na mar langage maid;

In raid battaill the king to Sulway raid,
With mekill payn, fast vpon Ingland cost,
740 Fyfty thousand in that trawaill he lost.

Quhen Wallace saw he chapyt was away.
Vpon Annand agayn returnyt thai
Till Edynburch, with outyn tary mor;
Put in Crawfurd that captane was befor;
745 Off heretage he had in Mannuell land.
Wallace commaund, ilk man suld hald in hand
Thair awin office, as thai befor had had.
Thus in gud pece Scotland with rycht he stad.
On the tent day to Sanct Jhonstoun he went,
750 Semblyt lordis, syn schawyt thaim his entent.
Scrymgeour com, at than had woun Dundé;
Wallace commaund that tym weill kepyt he.
He sailyeid so, quhill strang hungyr thaim draiff;
Sa feblyst war, the hous till him thai gaiff.
755 The wageourss sone he put to confusioun;
Syn brocht Mortoun, to mak a conclusion,
Befor Wallace; and son fra he him saw,
He gert hyng hym, for all king Eduuardis aw.
Masons, minouris, with Scrymgeour furth he send.
760 Kest down Dundé, and tharoff maid ane end.
Wallace, sadly quhen thir dedis war don,
The lordis he cald, and his will schawit thaim son.
" Gud men," he said, " I was your gouernour;
" My mynd was set to do yow ay honour,
765 " And for to bryng this realme to rychtwysnes;
" For it I passit in mony paynfull place.
" To wyn our awin my selff I neuir spard,
" At the Fawkyrk thai ordand me reward.
Fol. 105 a " Off that reward ye her no mor throu me;
770 " To sic gyftis God will full weill haiff E.

" Now ye ar fre, throu the Makar off mycht;
" He grant yow grace weill to defend your rycht!
" Als I preswme, gyff harm be ordand me,
" Thai ar Scottis men at suld the wyrkaris be.
775 " I haiff enewch off our ald enemys stryff;
" Me think our awin suld nocht inwy my lyff.
" My office our her playnly I resing;
" I think no mar to tak on me sic thing.
" In France I will, to wyn my leffyng thar,
780 " As now awysd, and her to cum no mar."
Lordis gaynstud, bot all that helpyt nocht;
For ony thar he did as him best thocht.
Byschop Synclar was wesyd with seknas
In till Dunkell; and syn throu Goddis grace
785 He recoueryt, quhen Wallace past away;
Eftir the Bruce he lestyt mony day.
Gud Wallace thus tuk leiff in Sanct Jhonstoun.
Auchtene with him, till Dundé maid him boun.
Longaweill past, that douchty was indeid,
790 The barrounyss sone off Breichyn with him yeid.
Twa brethir als with thair wncle thaim dycht,
Symon Wallace, and Richard that was wicht.
Schir Thomas Gray, this preist can wyth thaim fair,
Eduuard Litill, gud Jop, and maister Blayr.
795 Amang merchandis gud Wallace tuk the se;
Pray we to God, that he thair ledar be!

Thai saylyt furth by part off Ingland schor,
Till Hwmbyr mowth quhen at thai com befor,
Out off the south a gret rede saile thai se,
800 Into thar top the leopardis standand hye.
The merchandis than, that senye quhen thai saw
Cummand so neir, thai war discumfyt aw;
For weill thai wyst. that it was Jhon off Lyn,

U

Scottis to slay, he said, it was no syn.
805 Thir frayit folk yeid son to confessioun.
Than Wallace said; "Off sic deuotioun
"Ycit saw I neuir in no place quhar I past.
"For this a schip me think yow all agast,
"Yon wood cattis sall do ws litill der;
810 "We saw thaim faill twyss in a grettar wer,
"On a fair feild; so sall thai on the se:
Fol. 105 b "Dispyt it is to se thaim stand so hye."
The ster man said; 'Schyr, will ye wndirstand,
'He saiffis nane that is born off Scotland.
.815 'We may nocht fle fra yon barge wait I weill,
'Weyll stuft thai ar with gwn ganye off steill.
'Apon the se yon rewar lang has beyn;
'Till rychtwyss men he dois full mekill teyn.
'Mycht we be saiff, it forst nocht off our gud.
820 'This wyss he has, in schort, for to conclud;
'A flud he beris apon his cot armour,
'Ay drownand folk, so payntyt in figour.
'Supposs we murn, ye suld haiff no merwaill.'
Than Wallace said; "Her is men off mar waill
825 "To saill thi schip; tharfor in holl thow ga,
"And thi feris. Na mar cummyr ws ma."
Wallace and his than sone till harnes yeid.
Quhan thai war graithit in to thair worthi weid,
Him selff and Blayr, and the knycht Longaweill,
830 Thir thre has tane to kepe the myd schip weill.
Befor ws sewyn, and sex be eft ws kend;
Syn twa he chesd the top for to defend;
And Gray he maid thair sterman for to be.
The merchandis than saw thaim sa manfullé
835 To fend thaim selff; be causs thai had no weid,
Out off the howll thai tuk skynnys gud speid,
Ay betwix two stufft woll as thai mycht best,

Agayn the straik at thai suld sum part lest.
Than Wallace lewch, and commendyt thaim aw;
840 Off sic harness befor he neuir saw.
Be than the barge com on thaim wondyr fast,
Scwyn scor in hyr, that was no thing agast.
Quhen Jhon off Lyn saw thaim in armour brycht,
He lewch, and said thir haltyn words on hycht;
845 'Yon glakyt Scottis can ws nocht wndyrstand;
'Fulys thai ar, is new cummyn off the land.'
He cryit, 'Stryk;' bot no ansuer thai maid.
Blayr with a bow schot fast with outyn baid;
Or thai clyppyt, he schot bot arowis thre,
850 And at ilk schot he gert a rewar de.
The brygandis than thai bykerit wondyr fast,
Amang the Scottis with schot and gownnys cast;
And thai agayn with speris hedyt weill,
Feill woundis maid throuch plattis off fyne steill.
855 Athir othir festynyt with clippys keyn;
Fol. 106 a A cruell cowntyr thar was on schipburd seyn.
The derff schot, draiff as thik as a haill schour,
Contende tharwith the space ner off ane hour.
Quhen schot was gayn, the Scottis gret confort had;
860 At hand strakys thai war sekyr and sad.
The merchandis als, with sic thing as thai mycht,
Prewyt full weill in defens off thair rycht.
Wallace and his, at ner strakis quhen thai be,
With scharp swerdys thai gert fell brygandis de;
865 Thai in the top so worthi wrocht with hand,
In the south top thar mycht no rewar stand.
All the mydschip off rewers was maid waist,
That to geiff our thai war in poynt almaist.
Than Jhon off Lyn was rycht gretly agast,
870 He saw his folk failyie about him fast:
With egyr will he wald haiff beyn away,

Bad wynd the saill in all the haist thai may;
Bot fra the Scottis thai mycht nocht than off skey
The clyp so sar on athir burd thai wey.

875 Thai saw nothing that mycht be to thaim ess;
Crawfurd on loft thair saill brynt in a bless.
Or Jhon off Lyn schup for to leyff that sted,
Off his best men saxté was brocht to ded.
Thar schip by owris a burd was mar off hycht.

880 Wallace lap in amang thai rewaris wycht;
A man he straik our burd in to the se;
On the our loft he slew son othir thre.
Longaweill entryt, and als the maistir Blair;
Thai gaiff no gyrth to frek at thai fand thar.

885 Wallas him self with Jhon off Lyn was met;
At his coler a felloun straik he set;
Bathe helm and hed fra the schuldris he draiff;
Blayr our burd in the se kest the layff
Off his body; and all the remaynand

890 Entryt, and slew the brygandis at thai fand.
The schip thai tuk, gret gold and othir ger
At thai reiffaris had gaderyt lang in wer;
Bot maister Blayr spak nothing off himsell,
In deid off armes quhat awentur he fell.

895 Schir Thomas Gray, was than preyst to Wallace,
Put in the buk how than hapnyt this cace
At Blayr was in, [and] mony worthi deid,

Fol. 106 b Off quhilk him selff had no plesance to reid.
Wallace rewllyt the schip with his awin men;

900 And saillyt furth the rycht courss for to ken.
In the Sloice hawyn quhill that thai entryt be,
The merchandis weill he kepyt in sawfté;
Off gold and ger he tuk part at thai fand,
Gaiff thaim the schip, syn passyt to the land;

905 Throuch Flandrys raid vpon a gudly wyss,

Entryt in France, and socht vp to Paryss.
The glaid tithing at to the king was brocht
Off Wallace com, it conford all thair thocht.
Thai trowyt be him to get redress off wrang
910 The Sotheroun had in Gyane wrocht so lang.
The peryss off France was still at thair parlement;
The king commaund with trew and haill entent,
Thai suld forsé a lordschip to Wallace.
The lordis all than demyt off this cace;
915 For Gyane was all haill owt off thair hand,
Thai thocht it best for to geyff him that land.
For weill thai trowyt he had so wrocht befor,
He suld it wyn, or ellis de tharfor;
Alsua off it thai mycht no profyt haiff.
920 This was the causs to Wallace thai it gaiff.
This decret son thai schawit to the king:
Displessyd he was thai maid him sic a thing.
Off Gyane, thus, quhen Wallace hard a feill,
" No land," he said, " likit him halff so weill.
925 " My chance is thus for to be ay in wer;
" And Inglissmen has done our realme most der.
" It was weill knawin my defens rychtwyss thar;
" Rycht haiff I her, my confort is the mar.
" I thank your lordis, maid sic reward to me;
930 " Thar purposs is I sall nocht ydill be."
The king bad him be duk off Gyan land:
To that commaund Wallace was gaynstandand,
Becauss that land, was haly [to] conquace,
He thocht to wyn erar throw Goddis grace:
935 Bot neuyrtheless the king had maid him knycht,
And gaiff him gold for to maynteme his mycht:
Syn gaiff playn charge till his wermen off France,
Thai suld be haill at Wallace ordinaunce;
Fol. 107 a And als off him he bad him armes tak.

940 Wallace forsuk sic changyng for to mak:
    "Sen I began, I bar the reid lyoun;
    "And thinkis to be ay trew man to that croun.
    "I thank yow, schyr, off this mychty reward;
    "Your gyft herfor sall nocht rycht lang be spard.
945 "I think to quyt sum part ye kith on me
    "In your seruice, or ellis tharfor to de."
    Gud Wallace thocht, his tym he wald nocht waist;
    On to the wer he graithit him in haist.
    All Scottismen, that was in to that land,
950 Till him thai socht with thair fewté and band.
    Langaweill als a gret power can rass;
    In Wallace help this gud knycht glaidly gais.
    Ten thowsand haill off nobill men thai war,
    The braid baner off Scotland displayed thar.
955 Thir wermen sone apon Gyane thai fwr,
    Brak byggyngs doun quhilk had bene stark and stur.
    Sotheroun thai slew, agayn thaim maid debait;
    Braithly on breid thai rasyt fyris hait.
    Schynnoun thai tuk, at Wallace fyrst had woun,
960 And slew all men off Sotheroun was thar foun.
    In to that toun Wallace his duellyng maid;
    All thar about he wan the contré braid.
    The worthy duk, off Orliance was lord,
    Semblyt his folk in till a gud accord.
965 Twelf thousand than he had in armour brycht,
    And thocht to help gud Wallace in his rycht.
    Leyff I thaim thus, the duk and Wallace baithe,
    And spek sum part how Scotland tuk gret scaithe.

    The fals inwy, the wykkyt fell tresoun
970 Amang thaim selff brocht fcill to confusioun.
    The knycht Wallang in Scotland maid repair;
    The fals Menteth, Schir Jhon, with outyn mair.

Betwix thaim twa was maid a prewa band;
So on a day thai met in till Annand.
975 Off the Leynhouss Schyr Jhon had gret desyr:
Schyr Amer hecht he suld it haiff in hyr
Till hald in fe, and othir landis to,
Off king Eduuard, so he wald pass him to.
Thus cordyt thai, and syn to London went;
980 Eduuard was glaid for to hald that payment.
Fol. 107 b Menteth was thar bound man to that fals king,
Till forthir him till Scotland in all thing;
Syn passyt haym, and Wallang with him fur,
Quhill he was brocht agayn our Carleill mur.
985 King Eduuard than in ire and fers owtrage,
Be thretty dayis raissit his barnage;
In Scotland past, and thar na stoppyng fand,
Na chyftane thar that durst agayn him stand.
For Menteth tald, thai thocht to mak Bruce king;
990 All trew Scottis wald be plessyd off that thing.
Yeit mony fled and durst nocht bid Eduuard,
Sum in to Ross, and in the Ilis past part.
The byschop Synclar agayn fled in to But;
With that fals king he had no will to mut.
995 Thus, wyth out straik, the castellis off Scotland
King Eduuard haill has tane in his awin hand;
Deuidyt syn, to men that he wald lik,
Strenthis and toun to Ross throuch this kynrik.
Baith hycht and waill obeyed all till his will,
1000 As he commaund thai purpos to fullfill.
The byschoprykis inclynyt till his croune,
Bathe temperalité and all the religioune.
The Roman [bukis] that than was in Scotland,
He gart be brocht to scham, quhar thai thaim fand;
1005 And, but radem, thai brynt thaim thar ilkan;
Salysbery oyss our clerkis than has tane.

The lordis he tuk, that wald nocht off him hald,
In Ingland send full nobill blud off ald.
Schyr Wilyam lang Douglace to Londe he send,
1010 In strang presoun quhar throuch he maid his end.
The erll Thomas, that lord was off Murray,
And lord Frysaill fra him he send away;
Als Hew the Hay, and othir ayris ma,
He gert Wallang with thaim in Ingland ga.
1015 Na man was left all this mayn land within;
Fra Eduuardis peess, was knawin off ony kyn.
Cetoun, Lawder, duelt still in to the Bass,
With thaim Lundy, and men that worthi was.
The erll Malcom and Cambell past, but let,
1020 In But, succour with Synclar for to get.
Schir Jhon Ramsay and Rowan than fled north,
To thair cusyng that lord was off Fyllorth.
Quhilk past with thaim throw Murray landis rycht;
Fol. 108 a Sa fand thai thar a gentill worthi knycht
1025 At Climace hecht, full cruell ay had beyn,
And fayndyt weill amang his enemys keyn.
He thocht neuir at Eduuardis faith to be;
In till his tym he gert feill Sotheroun de.
He led thir lordis in Ross with outyn mar;
1030 At the Stokfurd a stark strenth byggit thar;
Kepyt that land rycht worthely be wer:
Till thair enemys thai did full mekill der.
Adam Wallace, and Lyndsay off Craggé,
Away thai fled be nycht apon the se;
1035 And Robert Boid, quhilk was baith wyss and wicht;
Arane thai tuk to fend thaim at thair mycht.
The Corspatrik in to Dunbar baid still;
Fewté full sone he had maid Eduuard till.
Abyrnethé, lord Soullis, and Cummyn als,
1040 And Jhon off Lorn that lang had beyn full fals,

The lord Brechyn, and mony othir, baid
At Eduuardis faith, for gyftis he thaim maid.
Justene off pees for twenty dayis set he
Off Inglissmen in Lorn, at men mycht be
1045 Playn to declayr; bot, for this causs, I wyss,
That all Scotland be conquess than was his.
The lordis than, and byschop gud Synclar.
Sone out off But thai maid a ballingar
To gud Wallace; tald him thair turment haill;
1050 Than wrait thai thus to get bwte off thair baill.
" Our help, our heill, our hop, our gouernour,
" Our gudly gyd, our best chyftane in stour,
" Our lord, our luff, our strenth, our rychtwysnas,
" For Goddis saik radeym anys to grace,
1055 " And tak the croun; till ws it war kyndar,
" To bruk for ay, or fals Eduuard it war."
The wryt he gat; bot yeit suffer he wald,
For gret falsheid that part him did off ald.
Mekill dolour it did him in his mynd,
1060 Off thair mysfayr; for trew he was and kynd.
He thocht to tak amendis off that wrang:
He ansuerd nocht, bot in his wer furth rang.
Off king Eduuard yeit mar furth will I meill,
In to quhat wyss that he couth Scotland deill.
1065 In Sanct Jhonstoun the erll off York he maid
Fol. 108 b Capdane to be off all thai landis braid,
Fra Tay to Dee; and wndyr him Butlar.
His grantschyr had at Kynclewin endit thar,
His fadyr als; Wallace thaim bathe had slayn;
1070 Eduuard tharfor maid him a man off mayn.
The lord Bewmound in to the north he send.
Thai lordschippys all thai gaiff him in commend.
To Sterlyn syn fra Sanct Jhonstoun he went.
Thair for to fulfill the layff off his entent.

1075 The lord Clyffurd he gaiff than Douglace daill,
Rewllar to be off the south marchis haill;
All Galloway than he gaiff Cumyn in hand:
Wyst nayn bot God how lang that stait suld stand.
The gentill lord, gud byschop Lammyrtoun,
1080 Off Sanct Androwss, had Douglace off renoun.
Befor that tyme Jamyss, wicht and wyss,
Till him was cummyn fra scullis off Paryss.
A prewa fauour the bischop till him bar;
Bot Inglissmen was so gret maisteris thar,
1085 He durst nocht weill in playn schaw him kyndnes,
Quhill on a day he tuk sum hardines.
Douglace he cald, and couth to Sterlyng fayr,
Quhar king Eduuard was deland landis thair.
He proferd him in to the kingis seruice
1090 To bruk his awin; fra he wist, in this wyss,
Douglace he was, than he forsuk planlé,
Swor be Sanct George; "He brukis na landis off me.
" His fadyr was in contrar off my crown;
" Tharfor as now he bidis in our presoun."
1095 To the byschop nane othir grant he maid;
Bot as he plesd, delt furth thai landis braid.
To the lord Soullis all haill the Merss gaiff he,
And captane als off Berweik for to be.
Olyfant than, that he in Sterlyng fand,
1100 Quhen he him had, he wald nocht kep his band,
The quhilk he maid or he him Sterlyng gaiff.
Desaitfully thus couth he him dissayff;
In till Ingland send him till presoun strang:
In gret distress he lewyt thar full lang.
1105 Quhen Eduuard king had delt all this regioun,
His leyff he tuk, in Ingland maid him boun.
Out off Sterlyng southward as thai couth ryd,
Cumyn hapnyt ner hand the Bruce to bid.

Thus said he; "Schyr, and yhe couth keip consaill,
1110 "I can schaw her quhilk may be your awaill."
Fol. 109 a The Bruce ansuerd; ' Quhat euir yhe say to me,
' As for my part sall weill conseillyt be.'
Lord Cumyn said; "Schyr, knaw ye nocht this thing,
'. That off this realm ye suld be rychtwyss king?"
1115 Than said the Bruce; 'Supposs I rychtwyss be,
' I se no tym to tak sic thing on me.
' I am haldin in to my enemyss hand,
' Wndyr gret ayth, quhen I com in Scotland,
' Nocht [to] part fra him for profyt nor request,
1120 ' Na for na strenth, bot gyff ded me arest.
' He hecht agayn to gyff this land to me;
' Now fynd I weill it is bot sutleté:
' For thus thow seis he delys myn heretage,
' To Sotheroun part, and sum to traytouris wage.'
1125 Than Cumyn said; " Will ye her to accord?
" Off my landys and ye lik to be lord,
" Ye sall thaim hawe, for your rycht off the croun:
" Or and ye lik, schyr, for my warisoun,
" I sall yow help with power at my mycht."
1130 The Bruce ansuerd; ' I will nocht sell my rycht;
' Bot on this wyss, quhat lordschip thou will craiff
' For thy supplé, I hecht thou sall it haff.'
" Cum fra yon king, schyr, with sum jeperté;
" Now Eduuard has all Galloway geyffyn to me,
1135 " My newo Soullis, that kepis Berweik toun,
" At your commaund his power sall be boun.
". My newo als, a man off mekill mycht,
" The lord off Lorn, has rowme in to the hycht.
" My third newo, a lord off gret renoun,
1140 " Will ryss with ws, off Breichin the barroun."
Than said the Bruce: ' Fayr thar sa far a chance,
[' That we mycht get agayn Wallace fra France,]

'Be witt and force he couth this kynryk wyn.
'Allace, we haiff our lang beyn haldin in twyn!'
1145 To that langage Cumyn maid na record;
Off ald deidis in till his mynd remord.
The Bruce and he completyt furth thar bandis;
Syn that samyn nycht thai sellyt with thar handis.
This ragment left the Bruce with Cumyn thar,
1150 With king Eduuard haym in Ingland can far:
And thar remaynyt quhill this ragment war knawin,
Thre yer and mar, or Bruce persewyt his awin.
Sum men demys that Cwmyn that ragment send;
Sum men tharfor agaynys makis defend.
Fol. 109 b 1155 Nayn may say weill Cumyn was saklasing,
Becauss his wiff was Eduuardis ner cusing.
He serwyt dede be rycht law off his king,
So raklelsy myskepyt sic a thing.
Had Bruce past by but baid to Sanct Jhonstoun,
1160 Be haill assent he had resawyt the croune;
On Cumyn syn he mycht haiff done the law.
He couth nocht thoill, fra tym that he him saw:
Thus Scotland left in hard perplexité.
Off Wallace mar in sum part spek will we.

EXPLICIT DECIMUS PASSUS,
ET INCIPIT VNDECIMUS PASSUS.

BUKE ELEUENTH.

THE sayr trawaill, the ernystfull besynes,
The feill labour had in mony place,
To wyn the land at the gud king him gaiff,
In till his ryng he wald no Sotheroun saiff.
5 In Gyan land Wallace was still at wer;
Off Scotlandis loss it did his hart gret der;
Off trew Scottis in mynd he had peté,
He thocht to help quhen he his tym mycht se.
Off set battaillis fyve he dyscumfyt haill,
10 But jeperté and mony strang assaill.
Syn thai forsuk, and durst him nocht abid;
The Sotheroun fled fra him on athir sid
To Burdeouss, in gret multiplye;
Than com thai stufft with wictaill be the se.
15 All Gyan land Wallace brocht till his peess;
To Burdeouss yit he past or he wald cess.
On out byggyngis full gret maister thai maid;
Still saxté dayis at sar sailyie thai baid.
Fortrace, and werk that was with out the toun,
20 Thai brak, and brynt, and put to confusioun:
Hagis, alais, be laubour that was thar,
Fulyeit and spilt; thai wald no froitis spar.
The Inglissmen maid gret defens agayn
With schot and cast, for thai war mekill off mayn.
25 Off gownnys thai war, and ganyies, stuffyt weill,
All artailye and wapynnys off fyn steill;

With men and meit within war buskit beyn;
Thair gret capdane was wyss, cruell and keyn.
Off Glosyster that huge lord and her,
30 This erll had beyn weill vsyt in to wer,
Kepyt his men be wit and hardement;
Fol. 110 a With out the toun thar durst nane fra him went.
The landis with out wer ner waistyt away,
Wermen so lang in to the contré lay.
35 In Wallace ost so scantyt the wictaill,
Thai mycht nocht bid [na] langar till assaill.
Than this wiss lord, the duk off Orlyance,
To Wallace said; "Schyr, ye suld knaw this chance.
"It standis our weill with this fals Sotheroun blud;
40 "For on no wayis we can nocht stop thair fud.
"The hawin thai haiff and schippis at thair will;
"Off Ingland cummys enewch off wittaill thaim till.
"This land is purd off fud that suld ws beild;
"And ye se weill als thai forsaik the feild.
45 "Thai will nocht fecht, thocht we all yher suld bid;
"Ye may off pess plenyss thir landis wid.
"My consaill is in playn, anent this thing,
"At ye wald pass with worschip to the king.
"Be his assent, ye may at lasar waill
50 "With prouisioun agayn for till assaill."
Wallace inclynd, and thankit this wyss lord.
Than thai tranontyt all in a gud concord;
Past wp in France with honour to the king,
And schawit him haill the verité off this thing;
55 And he tharoff in hart was wondyr glad.
Franch men befor that hundreth yer nocht haid
Off Gyan halff sa mekill in to thair hand.
Wrytting be than was new cumyn off Scotland,
Fra part off lordis and byschop gud Synclar,
60 Besocht the king in [to] thair termys fair,

Off his gentrice, and off his gudlye grace,
For thair supplé, to consaill gude Wallace
To cum agayne, and bring thaim off bandoun,
And tak to wer the croun off that regioun.
65 This wrytt as than he wald nocht till him schaw;
Rycht laith he war for frendschip, feik, or aw,
Wallace suld pass sa son fra his presens:
To duelling place he tuk to residens.
In Schynnown still Wallace his duelling maid,
70 And held about rycht likand landis braid.
A keyn capdane than clemyt in heretage
Office off it, and gret landis in wage;
Tharfor he thocht gud Wallace for to sla.
Wndyr colour sic maistrie for to ma,
75 Lang tym he socht to get a day and place;
Fol. 110 b Said he desyrd in seruice to Wallace.
A tryst thai set with sexteyn on the sid;
Fyfty thar by he gert in buschement byd
Off men in armys. Quhen he with Wallace met,
80 Rycht awfully he bad thaim on him set.
Na armour had Wallace men in to that place,
Bot suerd and knyff thai bur on thaim throw grace.
Parteis beyn met ner a fayr forest sid,
Rycht boustously this capdane said that tyd,
85 At Wallace held off his landis vnrycht.
Rycht sobyrly he said to that Franch knycht;
" I haiff no land bot quhilk the king gaiff me;
" My lyff tharfor has beyne in jeperté."
The knycht ansuerd; ' Thi lyff thow sall forlorn,
90 ' Or ellis that land, the contrar quha had suorn.'
On bak he lap, and owt his suerd he drew;
The buschement brak, quhen he that takyn schew.
Gud Wallace thocht that mater stud nocht weill.
He gryppyt sone a scherand suerd off steill,

95 And at a straik the knycht to ded he draiff;
About sexteyn sone lappyt all the layff.
Wallace and his so worthely thai wrocht,
Full feill thai slew that sarest on them socht.
The knychtis brodyr rycht stalwart was and strang;
100 And thocht he suld be wengyt or thai gang.
Off Wallace men sum part thai woundyt sair.
Mawand thar was in till a medow fair
Nyne stout carllis, all serwandis to that knycht;
Sythis thai hynt, and ran in all thair mycht
105 To the fechtaris. Or thai com ner that place,
Off thaim persawyt rycht weill was gud Wallace.
Sa awfull thing off sic he neuir saw;
Thaim to rasyst him selff can to thaim draw,
In to the stour left his men fechtand still,
110 To meit thai carllis that com with egyr will.
The fyrst leit draw at Wallace with his sith;
Deliuer he was, and heich our lappyt swyth,
And awkwart straik that churl apon the hed;
Derffly on ground he has him left for ded.
115 The tothir he met, our lap his syth so keyn,
On the schuldir als straik him in that teyn;
Throuch all the cost the noble suerd doun schair.
The thrid he met, with a rycht awfull fayr
The groundyn syth at Wallace he leit draw.
120 This gud chyftan cleynly our lap thaim aw.
Fol. 111 a With his gud suerd he maid a hidwyss wound,
Left thaim for ded, syne on the ferd can found:
On the wan bayn with gret ire can him ta.
Cleyffyt the cost rycht cruelly in twa.
125 Thre formast sythis thus gud Wallace our lap,
And four he slew; thai saw sic was his hap;
[For] a man ay he slew at euirilk straik.
The layff fled fast; thus can the power slaik.

Wallace folowed, and sone the fyrst our tais;
130 Straik him to ded, that na forthyr he gais;
Syn sped him fast till his awn men agayn.
Be than thai had the knychtis brothyr slayn.
Sexté and sex sexteyn to ded has dycht,
Bot saiff sewyn men at fled out off thair sycht;
135 Fyve malwaris als, that Wallace selff with met.
To Franch men syn na sic trystis he set,
Be causs that thai him brocht to sic a cace.
The king hard tell weill chapyt was Wallace;
Send for him sone, and prayit him for to be
140 Off his housshald, so leyff in gud saufté.
For weill he saw thai had him at inwye;
Still with him selff he gert him bid forthi.
Twa yeris thus with myrth Wallace abaid
Still in to Frans, and mony gud jornay maid.
145 The king him plessed in all his gudly mane,
Fra him he thocht he suld nocht part agayn.
Lordys and ladiis honoryd him reuerently,
Wrechys and schrewis ay had him at inwy.

Twa campiowns that tyme duelt with the king,
150 Had gret despyt at Wallace in all thing.
To giddyr ay yeid thir twa campiowns,
Off felloun fors and frawart attenciouns.
Rycht gret despyt thai spak oft off Scotland;
Quhill on a day it hapnyt apon hand,
155 Wallace and thai was lewit all thaim allayn,
Be awentur, in till a hous off stayne.
Thai oysyt to ber na wapynnys in that hall,
Thai trowyt thar for a myss thai mycht nocht fall.
Thar commownd thai off Scotland scornfully.
160 Than Wallace said; " Ye wrang ws owtragely,
" Sen we ar bownd in frendschip to your kyng;

X

" And he off ws is plessed in all thing.

" Als Scottis men has helpyt this realme off dreid.

" Me think ye suld gcyff gud word for gud deid.

165 " Quhat may ye spck off your enemys bot ill ?"

In lychtlynes thai maid ansucr him till ;

And him dispysyt in thar langage als;

' Ye Scottis,' thai said, ' has euir yeit beync fals.'

Wallace tuk ane on the face in his teyn

170 With his gud hand, quhill ness, mouth, and eyn.

Throuch the braith blaw, all byrstyt owt off blud;

Butless to ground he smat him quhar he stud.

The tothir hynt to Wallace in that sted;

For weill he wend his falow had beyne ded.

175 And he agayn in greiff him grippyt sayr,

Quhill spretis failyeid ner; he mycht do no mayr.

The fyrst frek raiss, and smat on Wallace fast;

Bathe to the ded he brocht thaim at the last.

Apon a pillar thair harnys owt he dang,

180 Bot with his handis, syn owt at the dur thaim flang;

And said; " Quhat dewyll mowyt yon churllys at me?

" Lang tyme in France I wald haiff lattyn thaim be."

Traistis for trewth, thus war thai ded in deid;

Thocht Franchmen [now] likis it nocht to reid.

185 Als I will cess and put it nocht in rym :

Bettir tharis quha rycht can luk in tym.

Mony gret lord was displessyd in Frans,

Bot the gud king, that knew all haill the chans.

Oft gret dispyt off Scotland spokyn had thai.

190 This passyt our, quhill eftir a nothir day.

Was nayn off thaim that durst it wndirtak

He had done wrang, nor tharfor battaill mak.

This ryoll roy a hie worschip him gaiff;

As conquerour him honowryd our the layff.

195 A fell lyoun the king has gert be brocht

With in a barrace, for gret harm that he wrocht,
Terlyst in yrn, na mar power him gaiff.
Off wodness he excedyt all the layff;
Bot he was fayr, and rycht felloun in deid.

200 In that strang strenth the king gert men him feid;
Kepyt him closs fra folk and bestiall.
In the court duelt twa squieris off gret waill,
At cusyngis war on to thir campiounis twa,
The quhilk befor Wallace hapnyt to sla.

205 A band thai maid in prewa illusioun,
At thair power to wyrk his confusioun,
Be ony meyn, throw frawd or sutelté;
Eftir, tharfor, thai roucht nocht for to de,

Fol. 112a To ded or schaym sa that thai mycht him bryng.
210 Apon a tym thai went on to the king;
" This man," thai said, " at ye sa welthfull mak,
" He seis nocht her bot he wald wndyrtak,
" Be his gret fors, to put to confusioun.
" Now he desyris to fecht on your lyoun;

215 " And bad ws ask at yow this battaill strang,
" Ye grant him leyff in that barrace to gang."
Sadly agayn to thaim ansuerd the king;
' Sayr me forthinkis at he desiris sic thing;
' Bot I will nothir for greyff, nor gret plesance,

220 ' Deny Wallace quhat he desiris off France.'
Than went thai furth, and sone met with Wallace;
A fygourd taill thai tald hym off this cace.
" Wallace," thai said, " the king desiris that ye
" Doren battaill sa cruell be to se,

225 " And chargis you to fecht on this lioun."
Wallace ansuerd in haisty conclusioun,
And said; ' I sall, quhat be the kingis will,
' At my power rycht glaidly to fullfill.'
Than passit he on to the king but mair.

230 A lord off court, quhen he approchyt thar,
  Wnwisytly sperd, with outyn prouisioun;
  "Wallace, dar ye go fecht on our lioun?"
  And he said; 'Ya, so the king suffyr me;
  'Or on your selff, gyff ye ocht bettyr be.'
235 Quhat will ye mar? this thing amittyt was,
  That Wallace suld on to the lyoun pas.
  The king thaim chargyt to bryng him gud harnas:
  And he said; "Nay, God scheild me fra sic cass.
  "I wald tak weid, suld I fecht with a man;
240 "Bot [for] a dog, that nocht off armes can,
  "I will haiff nayn, bot synglar as I ga."
  A gret manteill about his hand can ta,
  And his gud suerd; with him he tuk na mar;
  Abandounly in barrace entryt thar.
245 Gret chenys was wrocht in the yet with a gyn,
  And puld it to quhen Wallace was tharin.
  The wod lyoun, on Wallace quhar he stud,
  Rampand he braid, for he desyryt blud;
  With his rude pollis in the mantill rocht sa.
250 Aukwart the bak than Wallace can him ta,
  With his gud suerd, that was off burnyst steill,
  His body in twa it thruschyt euirilkdeill.
Fol. 112 b Syn to the king he raykyt in gret ire,
  And said on lowd; "Was this all your desyr,
255 "To wayr a Scot thus lychtly in to wayn?
  "Is thar ma doggis at ye wald yeit haiff slayne?
  "Go, bryng thaim furth, sen I mon doggis qwell,
  "To do byddyng, quhill that I with yow duell.
  "It gaynd full weill I graithit me to Scotland;
260 "For grettar deidis thair men has apon hand,
  "Than with a dog in battaill to escheiff.
  "At you in France for cuir I tak my leiff."
  The king persawyt Wallace agrewyt was,

So ernystfully he askyt leiff to pass;
265 Rewid in his mynd at it was hapnyt sa,
Sa lewd a deid to lat him wndyrta.
Knawand the worschip, and the gret nobilnace
Off him, quhilk sprang that tym in mony place,
Hwmblely he said; ' Ye suld displess you nocht;
270 ' This ye desyryt, it mowyt neuir in my thocht.
' And, be the faith I aw the croun off France,
' I thocht neuyr to charge you with sic chance
' Bot men off waill, at askyt it for yow.'
Wallace ansuerd; "To God I mak awow,
275 "I likyt neuir sic battaill to be in;
"Apon a dog na worschip is to wyn."
The king consawyt how this falsheid was wrocht.
The squiers bath, was till his presens brocht,
Coud nocht deny quhen thai com him befor;
280 All thair trespas thai tald with outyn mor.
The king commaundyt thai suld be don to ded;
Smat off thair hedys with out ony rameid.
The campiounis, lo, for inwy causlace,
To sodand dede Wallace brocht thaim throu cace;
285 The squiers als, fra thair falsheid was kend,
Inwy thaim brocht bathe till a sodand end.
Lordis, behald, inwy the wyle dragoun,
In cruell fyr he byrnys this regioun.
For he is nocht, that bonde is in inwy;
290 To sum myscheiff it bryngis hym haistely.
Forsaik inwy, thow sall the bettir speid.
Heroff as now I will no forthir reid;
Bot in my mater, as I off for began,
I sall conteyn als playnly as I can.

295   Quhen Wallace saw thai had him at inwy,
Langar to byd he coud than nocht apply.

Bettir him thocht in Scotland for to be,
And awntur tak othir to leiff or de.

Fol. 113 a Till help his awn he had a mar plesance,

300 Than thar to byd with all the welth off France.
Thus his haill mynd, manheid, and hye curage.
Was playnly set to wyn out off bondage
Scotland agayn fra payn and felloun sor;
He woude he suld, or ellis de tharfor.

305 The king has seyn how gud Wallace was set;
The lettir than him gaiff with outyn let,
The quhilk off lait fra Scotland was him send.
Wallace it saw, and weill thair harmys kend;
Be the fyrst wryt tharto accordiall,

310 Thaim to supplé he thocht he wald nocht faill.
Quhar to suld I her off lang process mak?
Wallace off France a gudly leiff can tak.
The kyng, has seyn it wald nocht ellis be,
To chawmyr went, and mycht nocht on him se:

315 Gret languor tuk quhen Wallace can ramuff:
That king till him kepit kyndnes and luff.
Jowallis and gold, his worschip for to saiff,
He bad thaim geyff, als mekill as he wald haiff.
Lordys and ladyis wepyt wondyr fast,

320 Quhen Wallace thar so tuk his leyff, and past.
Na men he tuk bot quhilk he hydder brocht;
Agayn with him gud Longaweill furth socht:
For payn nor blyss that gud knycht left him neuir.
For cace befell, quhill ded maid thaim deseuyr.

325 Towart the Sluce in gudly fer past he;
A weschell gat, and maid him to the se.
Aucht schipmen feit, and gudly wage thaim gaiff;
To Scotland fur; the Fyrth off Tay thai haiff.
Apon a nycht Wallace the land has tane

330 At Ernyss mouth, and is till Elchok gane.

He gert the schip in cowert saill away;
So out off sycht thai war or it was day.
At Elchok duelt ane, Wallace cusyng der,
At Craufurd hecht; quhen thai the houss com ner,
On the baksyd Wallace a window fand,
And in he cald. Sone Craufurd com at hand,
Fra tym he wyst that it was gud Wallace.
In till his bern he ordand thaim a place:
A mow off corn he bygit thaim about,
And closyt weill, nane mycht persawe without,
Bot at a place, quhar meit he to thaim brocht,
And bedyn to, als gudly as he mocht.
A dern holl furth, on the north syd, thai had
To the watter, quhar off Wallace was glad.
Four dayis or fyve in rest thai soiornd thar,
Quhill meit was gayn; than Craufurd bownd for mar
Till Sanct Jhonstoun, thar purwyance for to by.
Inglissmen thocht he tuk mar boundandly
Than he was wount at ony tym befor;
Thai haiff him tane, put him in presone sor.
Quhat gestis he had, to tell thai mak raquest.
He said, it was bot till a kyrkyn fest.
Yeit thai preiff sone the cumyng off Wallace;
Knawlage to get thai kest a sutell cace.
Thai latt him pass with thing that he had bocht;
Syn eftir sone, in all the haist thai mocht,
To harnes yeid the power off the toun.
Aucht hundreth men with Butler maid thaim boun,
Folowed on dreich, quhill at this man com hame.
Wallace him saw, and said, he serwit blame.
" In my sleping a fell visioun me tauld,
" Till Inglissmen that thow suld me haiff sauld."
Craufurd him said, he had bene turment sair
With Inglissmen, that had him in dispair;

365 ' Tharfor ryss wp, and for sum succour se,
      ' I dreid full sair, thai set wachis on me.'
      The worthi Scottis thai graithit thaim in gud weid;
      Thar wapynnys tuk, syn off that houss furth yeid.
      Thus sodandly the fell Sotheroun thai saw;

370 To few thai war to bid agayn thaim aw,
      At keynly com with yong Butler the knycht.
      Than Wallace said; " A playn feild is nocht rycht;
      " Bot Elchok park is ner hand her besid,
      " The fyrst sailyie we think thar to abid."

375 Nynetene thai war, and Craufurd, with gud will,
      The twentyd man, the nowmer to fullfill.
      The park thai tuk; Wallace a place has seyn
      Off gret holyns, that grew bathe heych and greyn.
      With thuortour treis a maner strenth maid he;

380 Or that war wone, thai trowit to gar feill de.
      The wod was thyk, bot litill off breid or lenth;
      Had thai had meit, thai thocht to hald that strenth.
      The Inglissmen passyt to Craufurdys place,
      Fand in the bern the lugeyng off Wallace;

385 Than Crawfurdis wyff in handys haiff thai tayne,
      And ast at hyr quhat way the Scottis war gayne.
      " Rycht weill thai trowyt at Wallace suld thar be;
      " Off France in Tay he was cumyn be the se."
      Scho wald nocht tell, for bost, nor yeit reward.

390 Than Butler said; ' Our lang thow has beyn spard?'
      Thar with he grew in matelent and ire,
      And gert thaim byg a bailfull braid brym fyr.
      The Sotheroun suor tharin scho suld brynt be.
      Than Wallace said; " Scho sall nocht end for me;

Fol. 114 a 395 " Gret syn it war yon saikless wicht to sla.
      " Or scho suld end, in faith thar sall de ma."
      He left the strenth, and the playn feild can ta;
      On lowd he cryt, and said: " Lo. her I ga.

" Thinkis thow no schaym for to turment a wyff?
400 " Cum fyrst to me, and mak end off our stryff."
Fra Butler had apon gud Wallace seyn,
Throuch auld malice he wox ner wod for teyn;
Apon the Scottis schup thaim all with gret mayn:
Bot Wallace son the strenth he tuk agayn.
405 A fell bykkyr the Inglissmen began,
Assailyeid sayr with mony cruell man:
Bot thai with in, war nobill at defens,
Maid gret debait be force and wiolens.
At the entra fyftenc thai brocht to ded;
410 Than all the lawe, ramowit fra that sted,
Yeid till aray agayn to sailye new.
Wallace beheld, quhilk weill in weir him knew:
" Falowis," he said, " agayn all at this place
" Thai will nocht saill: but thus standis the cace;
415 " Yon knycht thinkis for to dewid his men
" In seir partis, the suth ye sall weill ken,
" Agayn on ws to preiff how it may be.
" Ws worthis now sum wayis for thaim to se,
" Contrar thair mycht a gud defens to mak.
420 " Now, Longaweill, thow sall sex with the tak,
" Wilyam my eym, als mony sall with yow ga,
" And fyve with me; as now we haiff no ma."
Knycht Butler than partyt his men in thre.
Wallace wesyd quhar Butler schup to be;
425 Thidder he past that entré for to wer:
On ilka syd thai sailye with gret fer.
Wallace leit part in the entré begyn;
Bot nane yeid out that on the Scottis com in.
Sewyn formast was, quhilk in the forest yeid,
430 Wallace fyve men, quhilk douchty was in deid,
Ilkane slew ane, and Wallace gert twa de.
Butler was next, and said; ' This will nocht be.'

On bak he drew, and leit his curage slaik:
The worthi Scottis prewyt weill for Scotlandis saik.

435 Gud Longaweill his cowntyr maid sa sar,
And Craufurd als, thai sailyeid than no mar.
Rycht ner be than approchyt to the nycht;
And sternys wp peyr began in to thair sycht.
Sotheroun set wach, and to thair souper went.

440 The Butler was sayr grewyt in his entent;
Yeit fur thai weill off stuff, wyn, aill, and breid.
Wallace and his thai wyst off no rameid
Bot cauld watter, that ran throu owt a strand;
Fol. 114 b In that lugeyng nane othir fud thai fand.

445 Than Wallace said; " Gud falowis, think nocht lang;
" Will God, we sall be sone out off this thrang.
" Supposs we fast a day our, and a nycht,
" Tak all in thank this payn for Scotlandis rycht."
The erll off York, was in Sanct Jhonstoun still,

450 To Butler send, and bad him byd at will;
Till him full sone thar suld cum new power,
And als him selff; thus tald the messynger.
Butler wald fayn Wallace had yoldyn beyn
Or the erll com: for thir causis was seyn;

455 His grant schyr bathe and his fadyr he slew.
This knycht thar with towart the park him drew;
Quhat cher thai maid, apon the Scottis cald;
Than Wallace said; " Fer bettyr than thow wald."
The Butler said; ' I wald fayn spek with the.'

460 Wallace ansuerd; " Thow may for litill fe."
' Wallace,' he said, ' thow has done me gret scaith;
' My rycht fadyr and grant schyr thow slew baith.'
Than Wallace said; " For stait at thow art in,
" It war my det for till wndo thi kyn.

465 " I think als, sa God off hewin me saiff!
" At my twa handis sall graith the to thi graiff."

The Butler said; ' That is nocht likly now:
' In my credence and thow will fermly trow,
' Off this I ask and thow will mak me grant,
470 ' Quhat I the hecht, that thing thow sall nocht want.'
" Sa furth," quoth he, " be thi desyr resonable,
" I sall it grant with outyn ony fable."
The Butler said; ' Wallace thow knawis rycht,
' Thow may nocht chaip for power nor for slycht.
475 ' And sen thou seis it may no bettir be;
' For thi gentrice, thow will yeild the to me.'
Than Wallace said; " Thi will wnskillfull is;
" Thow wald I did quhilk is our hie a myss.
" Yoldin I am to bettir, I can pruff;
480 " To mychty God, that Makar is, abuff.
" For euir ilk day, sen I had wit off man,
" Befor my werk, to yeild me I began;
" And als at ewyn, quhen that I failyeid lycht,
" I me be tuk to the Makar off mycht."
485 The Butler said; ' Me think thow has done weill,
' Yeit off a thing, I pray the, lat me feill.
' For thi manheid this forthwart to me fest
' Quhen that thow seis thow may no langer lest
' On this ilk place, quhilk I haiff tane to wer,
490 ' At thow cum furth, and all othir forber.'
Than Wallace leuch at his cruell desyr;
And said; " I sall, thocht thow war wod as fyr,
" And all Ingland contrar tharoff had suorn.
" I sall cum out at that ilk place to morn,
Fol 115a 495 " Or ellys to nycht; traist weill quhat I the say:
" I byd nocht her quhill nyne houris off the day."
Butler send furth the chak wache on ilka syd;
In that ilk place bauldly he bownyt to bid.
Thus still thai baid quhill day began to peyr;
500 A thyk myst fell, the planet was nocht cleyr.

Wallace assayd at all placis about,
Leit as he wald at ony place brek out;
Quhill Butleris men sum part fra him can ga
To helpe the lawe, quhen thai saw it was sa.

505 Wallace and his fast sped thaim to that sted
Quhar Butler baid; feill men thai draiff to ded.
The worthy Scottis sone past throucht that mellé:
Craufurd, thar oyst, was sayr hurt on the kne,
At erd he was; gud Wallace turnd agayn.

510 And at a straik he has the Butler slayn;
Hynt wp that man wndyr his arm sa strang,
Defendand him out off that felloun thrang,
Gud rowm he maid amang thaim quhar he gais,
With his rycht hand he slew fyve off thair fais;

515 Bur furth Crawfurd, be force off his persoun,
Nyne akyrbreid, or cuir he set him doun.
The Sotheroun fand at thair capdane was ded,
All him about; bot than was no rameid.
Thretty with him off the wychtast thai brocht,

520 Ded at that place quhar at the Scottis furth socht.
Wallace and his be than was off thair sycht;
Sotheroun baid still for sor loss off that knycht.
The myst wes myrk; that Wallace likit weill;
Him selff was gyd, and said to Longaweill;

525 " At Meffan wood is my desyr to be,
" On bestiall thar, for meit, that we may se."
Be than thai war weill cumyn to the hicht,
The myst scalyt, the son schawyt fayr and brycht.
Son war thai war, a litill space thaim by,

530 Four and twenty was in a cumpany.
Than Wallace said; " Be yon men freynd or fa,
" We will to thaim, sen at thai ar na ma."
Quhen thai com ner, a nobill knycht it was,
The quhilk to name hecht Elyss off Dundass;

535 And Schyr Jhon Scot ek, a worthi knycht,
In to Straithern a man off mekill mycht:
For thar he had gret part of heretage;
Dundass syster he had in mariage.
Passand thai war, and mycht no langar lest,
540 Till Inglissmen, thair fewté for to fest.
Lord off Breichyn sic connand had thaim maid.
Off Eduuard thai suld hald thair landys braid;
Fol. 115 b Bot fra thai saw that it was wicht Wallace,
Heyfiyt wp thar handis, and thankit God off grace,
545 Off his gret help quhilk he had sende thaim thair.
To Meffen wod with ane assent thai far,
Sone gat thaim meit off bestiall at thai fand;
Restyt that day; quhen nycht was cumyn on hand,
To Byrnane wode, but restyng, ar thai gayne,
550 Quhar thai found the squier gud Ruwayn.
In vtlaw oyss he had lang lewyt thair
On bestiall, quhill he mycht get no mair.
Thai taryit nocht, bot in till Adell yeid,
Quhar mete was scant; than Wallace had gret dreid,
555 Past in till Lorn, and rycht litill fand thair:
Off wyld and taym that contré was maid bair.
Bot in strenthis, thar fud was lewyt nayn;
The worthi Scottis than maid a petouss mayn.
Schir Jhon Scot said, he had fer leuir de
560 In till gud naym, and leyff his ayris fre,
Than for till byd as bond in subiectioun.
Quhen Wallace saw thir gud men off renoun
With hungyr stad, almast mycht leiff no mar,
Wyt ye, for thaim he sichit wondyr sar.
565 " Gud men," he said, " I am the causs off this;
" At your desyr I sall amend this myss,
" Or leyff you fre sum chewysans for to ma."
All him allayn he bownyt fra thaim to ga:

Prayit thaim to byd quhill he mycht cum agayn.
570 Atour a hill he passit till a playn.

Out off thair sycht, in till a forest syd,
He sat him doun wndyr ane ayk to bid;
His bow and suerd he lenyt till a tre,
In angwyss greiff, on grouff so turned he.
575 His petows mynd was for his men so wrocht,
That off him selff litill as than he roucht.
" O wrech!" he said, "that neuir couth be content
" Off our gret mycht that the gret God the lent;
" Bot thi fers mynd, wylfull and wariable,
580 " With gret lordschip thow coud nocht so byd stable;
" And wyllfull witt, for to mak Scotland fre;
" God likis nocht that I haiff tane on me.
" Fer worthyar off byrth than I was born,
" Throuch my desyr wyth hungyr ar forlorn.
585 " I ask at God thaim to restor agayn;
" I am the causs, I suld haiff all the payn."
Quhill studeand thus, quhill flitand with him sell,
Quhill at the last apon slepyng he fell.
Thre dayis befor thar had him folowed fyve,
ol. 116 a 590 The quhilk was bound, or ellis to loss thair lyff:
The erll off York bad thaim so gret gardoun,
At thai be thyft hecht to put Wallace doun.
Thre off thaim was all born men off Ingland,
And twa was Scottis, that tuk this deid on hand;
595 And sum men said, thar thrid brothir betraissed
Kyldromé eft, quhar gret sorow was raissed.
A child thai had, quhilk helpyt to ber mett
In wildernes amang thai montans grett.
Thai had all seyn disseuyryng off Wallace
600 Fra his gud men, and quhar he baid on cace;
Amang thyk wod in cowert held thaim law,

Quhill thai persawyt he couth on sleping faw.
And than thir fyve approchit Wallace neir;
Quhat best to do, at othir can thai speir.
605 A man said thus; ' It war a hie renoun,
' And we mycht qwyk leid him to Sanct Jhonstoun.
' Lo, how he lyis; we may our grippis waill;
' Off his wapynnys he sall get nane awaill.
' We sall him bynd in contrar off hys will;
610 ' And leid him thus on baksyd off yon hill,
' So that his men sall nothing off him knaw.'
The tothir thre assentyt till his saw;
And than thir fyve thus maid thaim to Wallace,
And thocht throw force to bynd him in that place.
615 Quhat, trowit thir fyve for to hald Wallace doun?
The manlyast man, the starkast off persoun,
Leyffand he was; and als stud in sic rycht,
We traist weill, God his dedis had in sycht.
Thai grippyt him, than out off slepe he braid;
620 " Quhat menys this?" rycht sodandly he said.
About he turnyt, and wp his armys thrang;
On thai traytouris with knychtlik fer he dang.
The starkast man in till his armys hynt he,
And all his harnys he dang out on a tre.
625 A sword he gat son eftyr at he rayss,
Campiounlik amang the four he gais;
Euyr a man he gert de at a dynt.
Quhen twa was ded, the tothir wald nocht stynt,
Maid thaim to fle; bot than it was na but,
630 Was nane leyffand mycht pass fra him on fut.
He folowed fast, and sone to ded thaim brocht;
Than to the chyld sadly agayn he socht.
" Quhat did thow her?" The child, with [ane] paill face,
On kneis he fell, and askyt Wallace grace.
116 b 635 ' With thaim I was, and knew no thing thair thocht;

‘ In to seruice, as thai me bad, I wrocht.’

“ Quhat berys thow her?” ‘ Bot meit, the child can say.’

“ Do, turss it wp, and pass with me away.

“ Meit in this tym is fer bettyr than gold.”

640 Wallace and he furth foundyt our the fold.

Quha brocht Wallace fra his enemyss bauld?

Quha, bot gret God, that has the warld in wauld?

He was his help in mony felloun thrang.

With glaid cheyr thus on till his men can gang.

645 Bathe rostyt flesche thar was, als breid, and cheis,

To succour thaim that was in poynt to leiss.

Than he it delt to four men and fyfté,

Quhilk had befor fastyt our dayis thre;

Syn tuk his part, he had fastyt als lang.

650 Quhar herd ye euir ony in sic a thrang,

In hungyr so slepand, and wapynlass,

So weill recouer as Wallace did this cass;

Playnly befors vencust his enemyss fyve?

Yhe men off wit, this questioun dyscryve :

655 Wythoutyn gloiss I will tell furth my taill.

‘ How com this meit?’ the falowschip askyt haill.

To thar desyr Wallace nane ansuer yald :

Quhar fyve was ded he led thaim furth, syn tauld.

Gretly displessyd was all that chewalry :

660 Till a chyftane, thai held it fantasy

To walk allayn. Wallace, with sobyr mud,

Said ; “ As her off is no thing cummyn bot gud.”

To the law land full fast agayn thai socht ;

Sperd at this child, gyff he couth wyss thaim ocht,

665 Quhar thai mycht best off purviance for to wyn.

Off nane he said was that cuntré within ;

‘ Nor all about, als fer as I can knaw,

‘ Quhill that ye cum down to the Ranoucht hawe.

‘ That lord has stuff, breid, aill, and gud warnage :

670 ' Off king Eduuard he takis full mekill wage.'
Than Wallace said; " My selff sall be your gyd;
" I knaw that sted about on athir syd."
Throuch the wyld land he gydyt thaim full rycht;
To Ranouch hall thai com apon the nycht.

675 A wach was owt, and that full sone thai ta;
For he was Scottis, that man thai wald nocht sla,
Bot gert him tell the maner off that place.
Thus entryt thai with in a litill space.
The yett thai wan, for castell was thar nayn,

680 Bot mudwall werk withoutyn lym or stayn.
Wallace in haist straik wp the chawmir dur
Bot with his fut, that stalwart was and stur.

Fol. 117 a Than thai within sa walknyt sodeynly;
The lord gat wp, and mercy can him cry.

685 Fra tym he wyst that gud Wallace was thar,
He thankyt God, syn said thir wordis mar;
' Trow man I was, and woun agayn my will
' With Inglissmen, supposs I likit ill.
' All Scottis we ar that in this place is now;

690 ' At your commaund all playnly we sall bow.'
Off our natioun gud Wallace had peté;
Tuk aythis off thaim, [and] syne meit askyt he.
Gud cheyr thai maid quhill lycht day on the morne.
This trew man than sone semblit him beforne

695 Thre sonnys he had, that stalwart was and bauld,
And twenty men off his kyn in houshauld.
Wallace was blyth thai maid him sic supplé,
Said; " I thank God, that we thus multiplé."
All that day our in gud liking thai rest;

700 Wachys thai waill to kep thaim, at coud best.
Apon the morn, the lycht day quhen thai saw,
Than Wallace said; " Our power for to knaw,
" We will tak feild, and wp our baner raiss

Y

"Off rycht Scotland, in contrar off our fais.
705 "We will no mar now ws in couert hid;
"Power till ws will sembill on ilk syd."
Horsis thai gat, the best men at was thar;
Towart Dunkell the gaynest way thai far.
The byschope fled, and gat till Sanct Jhonstoun
710 The Scottis slew all was thar off that nacioun,
Baith pur and rych, and serwandis at thai fand;
Left nane on lyff that born was off Ingland.
The place thai tuk, and maid thaim weill to fayr,
Off purwiance that byschop had brocht thair.
715 Jowellis thai gat, bathe gold and syluer brycht;
With gud cheyr thar fyve dayis thai soiornd rycht.
On the sext day Wallace to consaill went,
Gert call the best, and schew thaim his entent:
"Na men we haiff to sailye Sanct Jhonstoun;
720 "In to the north tharfor lat mak ws boun.
"In Ross, ye knaw, gud men a strenth has maid;
"Her thai off ws, thai cum with outyn baid.
"Alss in to But the byschope gud Synclar,
"[Fra he get wit, he cummis with outyn mar.]
725 "Gud westland men off Aran and Rauchlé,
"Fra thai be warnd, thai will all cum to me."
This purpos tuk, and in the north thai rid;
Nan Inglissman durst in thair way abid.
Quham Wallace tuk, thai knew the ald ransoun;
730 Fra he com haym, to fle thai mak thaim boun.
Fol. 117 b And Scottis men semblyt to Wallace fast;
In awfull feyr throuch owt the land thai past;
Strenthis was left, witt ye, all desolate;
Agayn thir folk thai durst mak no debate.
735 In raid battaill thai raid till Abyrdeyn,
The haill nowmyr, sewyn thousand than was seyn.
Bot Inglissmen had left that toun all waist;

On ilka syd away thai can thaim haist;
In all that land left nothir mar nor less.
740 Lord Bewmond tuk the sey at Bowchan ness.
Throu Scotland than was manifest in playn,
The lordis that past in hart was wondyr fayn.
The knycht Climés off Ross com sodeynly
In Murray land with thair gud chewalry.
745 The houss off Narn that gud knycht weill has tayne,
Slew the capdane and strang men mony ane;
Out off Murray in Bowchane land com thai
To sek Bewmound, be he was past away;
Than thir gud men to Wallace passyt rycht.
750 Quhen Wallace saw Schyr Jhon Ramsay the knycht,
And othir gud at had bene fra him lang,
Gret curag than was rasyt thaim amang.
The land he reullyt as at him likit best;
To Sanct Jhonstoun syn raid or thai wald rest.

755   At euirilk part a stalwart wach he maid;
Fermyt a sege, and stedfastly abaid.
Byschop Synclar in till all haist him dycht,
Com out off Bute with symly men to sycht;
Owt off the ilys off Rauchlé and Aran,
760 Lyndsay and Boid, with gud men mony ane.
Adam Wallace, barroun off Ricardtoun,
Full sadly socht till Wallace off renoun,
At Sanct Jhonstoun baid at the sailye still.
For Sotheroun men thai mycht weill pass at will:
765 For in thar way thar durst na enemys be,
Bot fled away be land, and als be se.
About that toun thus semblyt thai but mor;
For thai had beyn with gud Wallace befor.
Cetoun, Lauder, and Richard off Lundé,
770 In a gud barge thai past about be se;

Thair ankyr in Sanct Jhonstoun hawyn set.
Twa Inglyss schippys thai tuk with outyn let;
The tane thai brynt, syn stuffyt the tothir weill
With artailye, and stalwart men in steyll,
775 To kep the port, thar suld com na wictaill
In to that toun, nor men at mycht thaim waill.
Fra south and north mony off Scotland fled,
Left castellys waist, fcill left thar lyff to wed.

Fol. 118 a The South byschop, befor that left Dunkell,
780 Till London past, and tald Eduuard him sell,
In Scotland thar had fallyn a gret myschance.
Than send he son for Amar the Wallance,
And askyt him quhat than war best to do.
He hecht to pass, and tak gret gold tharto,
785 In to Scotland sum menys for to mak
Agane Wallace; on hand this can he tak.
Thai said, he wald wndo king Eduuardis croun,
Bot gyff thai mycht throu tresoun put him doun.
King Eduuard hecht, quhat thing at Wallang band,
790 He suld it kep, war it bathe gold and land.
Wallange tuk leyff, and is in Scotland went;
To Bothwell com; syn kest in his entent,
Quhat man thar was mycht best Wallace begyll:
And sone he fand, with in a litill quhill,
795 Schyr Jhon Menteth Wallace his gossop was.
A messynger Schyr Amar has gert pass
On to Schyr Jhon, and sone a tryst has set;
At Ruglyn kyrk thir twa to gydder met.
Than Wallang said; "Schyr Jhon, thow knawis this thing,
800 "Wallace agayn ryssis contrar the king;
"And thow may haiff quhat lordschip thow will waill,
"And thou wald wyrk as I can gyff consaill.
"Yon tyrand haldys the rewmys at troubill bathe,
"Till thryfty men it dois full mekill scaith.

805 " He traistis the, rycht weyll thow may him tak;
    " Off this mater ane end I think to mak.
    " War he away, we mycht at liking ryng
    " As lordys all, and leiff wndyr a king."
    Than Menteth said; ' He is our gouernour;
810 ' For ws he baid in mony felloun stour,
    ' Nocht for him selff, bot for our heretage:
    ' To sell him thus it war a foull owtrage.'
    Than Wallang said; " And thow weill wndyrstud,
    " Gret neid it war, he spillis so mekill blud
815 " Off Crystin men, puttis saullis in peraill;
    " I bynd me als, he sall be haldyn haill
    " As for his lyff, and kepyt in presoune;
    " King Eduuard wald haiff him in subiectioun."
    Than Menteth thocht, sa [thai] wald kepe connand,
820 He wald full fayn [haiff] had him off Scotland.
    Wallange saw him intill a study be,
    Thre thowsand pundys off fyn gold leit him se;
    And hecht he suld the Lewyn-houss haiff at will.
    Thus tresonably Menteth grantyt thartill;
b825 Obligacioun with his awn hand he maid;
    Syn tuk the gold, and Eduuardis seill so braid,
    And gaiff thaim his, quhen he his tym mycht se
    To tak Wallace our Sulway, giff him fre
    Till Inglissmen; be this tresonabill concord
830 Schyr Jhon suld be off all the Lennox lord.
    Thus Wallace suld in Ingland kepyt be,
    So Eduuard mycht mak Scotland till him fre.
    Thar cowatyss was our gret maystir seyn;
    Nane sampill takis, how ane othir has beyn
835 For cowatice put in gret paynys fell;
    For cowatice, the serpent is off hell.
    Throuch cowatice, gud Ector tuk the ded;
    For cowatice thar can be no ramed.

Throuch cowatice gud Alexander was lost;
840 And Julius als, for all his reiff and bost.
Throuch cowatice deit Arthour off Bretane.
For cowatice thar has deit mony ane.
For cowatyce, the traytour Ganyelon
The flour off France he put till confusion.
845 For cowatice thai poysound gud Godfra
In Antioche, as the autor will sa.
For cowatice, Menteth, apon falss wyss,
Betraysyt Wallace, that was his gossop twyss.

      Wallang in haist, with blyth will and glaid hart,
850 Till London past, and schawit till king Eduuart.
Off this contrak he had a mar plesance,
Than of fyn gold had geyffyn, in ballance,
A grettar wecht na his ransoun mycht be.
Off Wallace furth sum thing spek will we,
855 At Sanct Jhonstoun was at the segeyng still.
In a mornyng Sotheroun, with egyr will,
Fyve hundreth men in harnas rycht juntly,
Thai wschet furth to mak a jeperty;
At the south port, apon Scot and Dundass,
860 Quhilk in that tym rycht wyss and worthy was,
Agayn thair fayis rycht scharply focht and sayr.
In that cowntyr sewyn scor to ded thai bayr.
Yeit Inglissmen, at cruell war and keyn,
Full ferely faucht, quhar douchty deid was seyn.
865 Fra the west yett drew all the Scottis haill
To the fechtaris; quhen Sotheroun saw na waill,
Bot in agayn full fast thai can thaim sped;
The knycht Dundass prewyt so douchty deid.
Our neyr the yett full bandounly he baid,
ol. 119a 870 Wyth a gud suerd full gret maister he maid;
Nocht wittandly his falowis was him fra.

In at the yett the Sotheroun can him ta,
On to the erll thai led him haistelé.
Quhen he him saw, he said he suld nocht de;
875 "To slay this ane it may ws litill rameid."
He send him furth to Wallace in that steid.
On the north syd his bestials had he wrocht;
Quhill he him saw, off this he wyst rycht nocht;
Send to the erll, and thankit him largelé;
880 Hecht for to quyt quhen he sic cace mycht se.
Bot all her for souerance he wald nocht grant,
Thocht thai yoldin wald cum as recreant;
For gold na gud, he wald no trewbut tak.
A full strang salt than he begouth to mak.
885 The erll of Fyf duelt wndyr trewage lang
Off king Eduuard; and than him thocht it wrang,
At Wallace sa was segeand Sanct Jhonstoun,
Bot gyff he com in rycht help off the croun.
Till Inglissmen he wald nocht kep that band,
890 Than he come sone with gud men off the land.
And Jhon Wallang, was than schyreff off Fyff,
Till Wallace past, starkyt him in that stryff.
That erll was cummyn off trew haill nobill blud,
Fra the ald thane, quhilk in his tym was gud.
895 Than all about to Sanct Jhonstoun thai gang,
With felloun salt, was hydwyss scharp and strang.
Full feill fagaldys in to the dyk thai cast,
Hadyr and hay bond apon flakys fast;
Wyth treis and erd a gret passage thai maid;
900 Atour the wallis thai yeid with battaill braid.
The Sotheroun men maid gret defens agayn,
Quhill on the wallys thar was a thousand slayn.
Wallace yeid in, and his rayit battaill rycht;
All Sotheroun men derffly to ded thai dycht.
905 To sayff the erll Wallace the harrald send,

Gud Jop him selff, the quhilk befor him kend.
For Dundass saik thai said he suld nocht de;
Wallace him selff this ordand for to be.
A small haknay he gert till him be tak,
910 Siluer and gold his costis for to mak;
Set on his clok a takyn for to se,
The lyoun in wax that suld his condet be;
Conwoyit him furth, and na man him withall.
Wemen and barnys Wallace gert freith thaim all:
915 And syn gert cry trew Scottis men to thair awn;
Fol. 119 b Plenyst the land quhilk lang had been ourthrawn.
Than Wallace past the southland for to se.
Eduuard the Bruce, in his tym rycht worthé.
That yer befor he had in Irland ben,
920 And purchest thar off cruell men and keyn.
Fyfty in feyr, was off his modrys kyn,
At Kirkwbré on Galloway entryt in.
With thai fyfté he had vencust nyne scor,
And syn he past, withoutyn tary mor,
925 Till Wygtoun sone, and that castell has tayne;
Sotheroun was fled, and left [it] all allayne.
Wallace him met with trew men reuerently;
To Lowmabane went all that chewalry.
Thai maid Eduuard bath lord and ledar thar.
930 This conditioun Wallace him hecht but mar,
Bot a schort tym to bid Robert the king;
Gyff he come nocht in this regioun to ryng,
At Eduuard suld resaiff the croun but faill.
Thus hecht Wallace, and all the barnage haill.
935 In Louchmabane prynce Eduuard lewyt still;
And Wallace past in Cumno with blith will.
At the Blak Rok, quhar he was wont to be,
Apon that sted a ryall hous held he.
Ingliss wardans till London past but mar.

940 And tauld the king off all thair gret mysfar;
    How Wallace coud Scotland fra thaim reduce,
    And how he had resawyt Eduuard the Bruce.
    The commouns suor thai suld cum neuir mar
    Apon Scotland, and Wallace leiffand war.
945 Than Eduuard wrayt till Menteth prewalie,
    Prayit him till haist; the tym was passit by
    Off the promess the quhilk at he was bund.
    Schyr Jhon Menteth in till his wit has fund,
    How he suld best his purpos to fullfill.
950 His syster son in haist he cald him till,
    And ordand him in duellyng with Wallace.
    Ane ayth agayn he gert him mak on cace,
    Quhat tym he wyst Wallace in quiet draw,
    He suld him warne, for awentur mycht befaw.
955 This man grantyt at sic thing suld be done;
    With Wallace thus he was in seruice sone.
    As off tresoun Wallace had litill thocht;
    His laubourous mynd on othir materis wrocht.
    Thus Wallace thryss has maid all Scotland fre;
960 Than he desyryt in lestand peess to be.
    For as off wer he was in sumpart yrk,
    He purpost than to seruc God and the kyrk,
    And for to leyff wndyr hys rychtwyss king;
    That he desyryt atour all erdly thing.

965   The harrold Jop in Ingland sone he send,
Fol. 120 a And wrayt to Bruce rycht hartlie this commend,
    Besekand him to cum and tak his croun;
    Nane suld gaynstand, clerk, burges, na barroun.
    The harrald past; quhen Bruce saw his credans,
970 Tharoff he tuk a perfyt gret plesans;
    With hys awn hand agayn wrayt to Wallace,
    And thankyt him off lauta and kyndnas,

Besekand him this mater to conseill;
For he behuffyd owt off Ingland to steill;
975 For lang befor was kepyt the ragment,
Quhilk Cwmyn had, to byd the gret parlement
In to London; and gyff thai him accuss,
To cum fra thaim he suld mak sum excuss.
He prayit Wallace in Glaskow mur to walk
980 The fyrst nycht off Julii for his salk;
And bad he suld bot in to quiet be,
For he with him mycht bryng few chewalré.
Wallace was blyth quhen he this wrytyng saw;
His houshald sone he gert to Glaskow draw.
985 That moneth thar he ordand thaim to byd;
Kerlé he tuk ilk nycht with him to ryd;
And this youg man that Menteth till him send;
Wyst nane bot thir quhat way at Wallace wend;
The quhilk gart warn his eym the auchtand nycht.
990 Sexté full sone Schyr Jhone [Menteth] gert dycht
Off hys awn kyn, and off alya born;
To this tresoun he gert thaim all be suorn.
Fra Dunbertane he sped thaim haistely,
Ner Glaskow kyrk thai bownyt thaim priwaly.
995 Wallace past furth quhar at the tryst was set,
A spy thai maid, and folowed him but let
Till Robrastoun, was ner be the way syd,
And bot a howss quhar Wallace oysyt to byd.
He wouk on fut quhill passyt was myd nycht;
1000 Kerlé and he than for a sleip thaim dycht.
Thai bad this cuk, that he suld wach hys part,
And walkyn Wallace, com men fra ony art.
Quhen thai slepyt, this traytour tuk graith heid,
He met his eym, and bad him haiff no dreid:
1005 "On sleip he is, and with him bot a man,
"Ye may him haiff, for ony craft he can;

" With owt the houss thair wapynnys laid thaim fra."
For weill thai wyst, gat Wallace one off tha,
And on his feyt, hys ransoun suld be sauld.
1010 Thus semblyt thai about that febill hauld.
This traytour wach fra Wallace than he stall
Bathe knyff and suerd, his bow and arowis all.
Eftyr mydnycht in handis thai haiff him tane,
ol. 120 b Dyschowyll on sleipe, with him na man bot ane.
1015 Kerlé thai tuk, and led him off that place,
Dyd him to ded with outyn langar space.
Thai thocht to bynd Wallace throu strenthis strang;
On fute he gat the feill traytouris amang,
Grippyt about, bot no wapyn he fand.
1020 Apon a syll he saw besyd him stand,
The bak off ane he byrstyt in that thrang;
And off ane othir the harness out he dang.
Than alss mony as handis mycht on him lay,
Beforce hym hynt for till haiff him away.
1025 Bot that power mycht nocht a fute him leid
Owt off that houss, quhill thai or he war deid.
Schir Jhon saw weill beforce it coud nocht be;
Ur he war tayne he thocht erar to de.
Menteth bad cess, and thus spak to Wallace;
1030 Syn schawyt him furth a rycht sutell fals cace.
" Yhe haiff so lang her oysyt yow allane,
" Quhill witt tharoff is in till Ingland gane.
" Tharfor her me, and sobyr your curage.
" The Inglissmen, with a full gret barnage,
1035 " Are semblyt her, and set this hous about,
" That ye, be force, on na wayis may wyn out.
" Supposs ye had the strenth off gud Ectour,
" Amang this ost ye may nocht lang endour.
" And thai you tak, in haist your ded is dycht.
1040 " I haiff spokyn with lord Clyffurd that knycht,

" Wyth thair chyftanys weill menyt for your lyff.

" Thai ask no mar bot be quyt off your stryff.

" To Dunbertane ye sall furth pass with me;

" At your awn houss ye may in saifté be."

1045 Sotheroun sic oyss with Menteth lang had thai,

That Wallace trowyt sum part at he wald say.

Menteth said; " Schyr, lo, wappynnys nane we haiff;

" We com in trayst, your lyff gyff we mycht saiff."

Wallace trowyt weill, and he his gossep twyss,

1050 That he wald nocht, be no maner off wyss,

Him to betrayss for all Scotland so wyd.

Ane ayth off him he askit in that tid.

Thar wantit wit; quhat suld his aythis mor?

Forsuorn till him he was lang tym befor.

1055 The ayth he maid; Wallace com in his will;

Rycht frawdfully all thus schawyt him till.

" Gossep," he said, " as presoner thai mon yow se,

" Or thai throu force wyll ellis tak yow fra me."

A courch with slycht apon his handys thai laid,

1060 And wndyr syn with seuir cordys thai braid,

Bath scharp and tewch, and fast to gyddyr drew.

Allace, the Bruce mycht sayr that byndyng rew,

Quhilk maid Scotland sone brokyn apon cace,

Fol. 121 a For Cumeinis ded, and loss off gud Wallace!

1065 Thai led him furth in feyr amang thaim aw.

Kerlé he myst, off na Sotheroun he saw:

Than wyst he weyll that he betraysyt was,

Towart the south with him quhen thai can pass.

Yeit thai him said, in trewth he suld nocht de;

1070 King Eduuard wald kep him in gud saufté,

For hie honour in wer at he had wrocht.

The sayr bandys so strowblyt all his thocht,

Credence tharto forsuth he coud nocht geyff;

He wyst full weyll thai wald nocht lat him leiff.

1075 A falss foull causs, thai Menteth for, him tauld,
Quhen on this wyss gud Wallace he had sauld.
Sum off thaim said, it was to saiff thair lord;
Thai leid all out that maid that fals racord.
At the Fawkyrk the gud Stewart was slayn,
1080 Our corniclis reherss that in [to] playn,
On Madelan day, that auchtand yer befor;
Comynis ded tharoff it wytness mor.
At Robrastoun Wallas was tresonabilly
Thus falsly stowyn fra his gud chewalry,
1085 In Glaskow lay, and wyst nocht off this thing;
Thus he was lost in byding off his king.
South thai him led, ay haldand the west land,
Delyuerit him in haist our Sullway sand.
The lord Clyffurd and Wallang tuk him thar;
1090 To Carleyll toun full fast with him thai fayr;
In presoun him stad, that was a gret dolour;
That houss efter was callyt " Wallace tour."
Sum men sen syn said, that knew nocht weill the cass,
In Berweik thai to ded put gud Wallace.
1095 Contrar is knawin, fyrst be this opinioun;
For Scottis men than had haly Berweik toun,
And Scotland fre, quhill that Soullis it gaiff
For lord Cumyn till Ingland with the laiff.
Ane othir poynt is, the traytouris durst nocht pass,
1100 At sauld him sa, quhar Scottis men maistris was.
The thrid poynt is, the commouns off Ingland,
Quhat thai desyr, thai will nocht wndirstand
That thing be done, for wytness at may be,
Na credence geyff, forthyr than thai may se.
1105 To se him de Eduuard had mar desyr,
Than to be lord off all the gret empyr.
For thir caussis thai kepyt him sa lang,
Quhill the commouns mycht on to London gang.

Allace, Scotland, to quhom sall thow compleyn!
1110 Allace, fra payn quha sall the now restreyn!
Allace, thi help is fasslie brocht to ground,
Fol. 121 b Thi [best] chyftane in braith bandis is bound!
Allace, thow has now lost thi gyd off lycht!
Allace, quha sall defend the in thi rycht?
1115 Allace, thi payn approchis wondyr ner,
With sorow sone thow mon bene set in feyr!
Thi graciouss gyd, thi grettast gouernour,
Allace, our neir is cumyn his fatell hour!
Allace, quha sall the beit now off thi baill?
1120 Allace, quhen sall off harmys thow be haill?
Quha sall the defend? quha sall the now mak fre?
Allace, in wer quha sall thi helpar be?
Quha sall the help? quha sall the now radem?
Allace, quha sall the Saxons fra the flem?
1125 I can no mar, bot besek God off grace
The to restor in haist to rychtwysnace;
Sen gud Wallace may succour the no mar.
The loss off him encressit mekill cair.
Now off his men in Glaskow still at lay,
1130 Quhat sorow raiss, quhen thai him myst away?
The cruell payn, the wofull complenyng,
Tharoff to tell it war our hewy thing,
I will lat be, and spek off it no mar;
Litill riherss is our mekill off cair:
1135 And principaly quhar redempcioun is nayn,
It helpys nocht to tell thar petous mayn;
The deid tharoff is yeit in remembrance,
I will lat slaik off sorow the ballance.
Bot Longawell to Louchmabane couth pass,
1140 And thar he hecht, quhar gud prince Eduuard was,
Out off Scotland he suld pas neuirmor;
Loss off Wallace socht till his hart so sor.

The rewlm off France he wowit he suld neuir se,
Bot weng Wallace, or ellis tharfor to de.
1145 Thar he remaynd, quhill cummyn off the king;
With Bruce in wer this gud knycht furth can ryng.
Remembrance syn was in the Brucys buk;
Secound he was quhen thai Saynct Jhonstoun tuk :
Folowed the king at wynnyng off the toun;
1150 The Bruce tharfor gaiff him full gret gardoun.
All Charterys land the gud king till him gaiff;
Charterys sen syn off his kyn is the laiff.
Quhar to suld I [fer] in that story wend?
Bot off my buk to mak a fynaill end :
1155 Robert the Bruce com hame on the ferd day
In Scotland, eft Wallace was had away,
Till Louchmabane, quhar that he fand Eduuart,
Quharoff he was gretlie reiossyt in hart :
Bot fra he wyst Wallace away was led,
122a 1160 So mekill baill with in his breyst thar bred,
Ner out off wytt he worthit for to weyd.
Eduuard full sone than till hys brothir yeid.
A sodane chance this was in wo fra weill.
Gud Eduuard said; " This helpys nocht adell :
1165 " Lat murnyng be, it may mak na remeid;
" Ye haiff him tynt, ye suld rawenge his deid.
" Bot for your causs he tuk the wer on hand,
" In your defens; and thryss has fred Scotland,
" The quhilk was tynt fra ws and all our kyn :
1170 " War nocht Wallace, we had neuir entryt in.
" Merour he was off lauta and manheid :
" In wer the best that euir sall power leid.
" Had he likyt for till haiff tane your croun,
" Wald nane him let that was in this regioun.
1175 " Had nocht beyne he, ye suld had na entress
" In to this rewlm, for tresoun and falsnes.

" That sall ye se; the traytour that him sauld,
" Fra yow he thinkys Dunbertane for till hauld;
" Sum confort tak, and lat slaik off this sorou."

1180 The king chargyt Eduuard, apon the morou,
Radress to tak off wrang that wrocht him was.
Till Dallswyntoun he ordand him to pas,
And men off armys; gyff thai fand Cumyn thar,
Put him to ded; for na deid thai suld spar.

1185 Thai fand him nocht.   The king him selff him slew
In till Drumfress, quhar witnes was inew.
That hapnys wrang our gret haist in a king,
Till wyrk by law it may scaith mekill thing.
Me nedis heroff na forthyr for till schaw;

1190 How that was done it was knawin to yow aw.
Bot yong Douglace fyrst to the king can pas,
In all hys wer bath wicht and worthi was.
Nor how the king has tane on him the croun;
Off all that her I mak bot schort mencioun:

1195 Nor how lord Soullis gaiff Berweik toun away;
How eftyr syn sone tynt was Galloway;
How Jhon off Lorn agayn his rycht king raiss;
On athir sid how Bruce had mony fais;
How bauld Breichin contrar his king coud ryd,

1200 Rycht few was than in wer with him to byd:
Nor how the north was gyffyn fra the gud king,
Quhilk maid him lang in paynfull wer to ryng.
Ay trew till him was Jamys the gud Douglace,
For Brucis rycht baid weill in mony place;

1205 Wndyr the king he was the best chyftayn.
Bot Wallace raiss as chyftane him allayn;
Tharfor till him is no comparisoun,
As off a man, sauff reuerence off the croun.
Bot sa mony as off Douglace has beyn

Fol. 122 b 1210 Gud off a kyn, was neuir in Scotland seyn:

Comparisounys that can I nocht weill declar.
Off Brucis buk as now I spek no mar.
Master Barbour, quhilk was a worthi clerk,
He said the Bruce amang his othir werk.

1215 In this mater prolixit I am almaist;
To my purpos breiffly I will me haist,
How gud Wallace was set amang his fayis.
To London with him Clyfford and Wallang gais;
Quhar king Eduuard was rycht fayn off that fang.

1220 Thai [haiff] him stad in till a presone strang.
Off Wallace end my selff wald leiff, for dredis
To say the werst; bot rychtwysnes me ledis.
We fynd his lyff all swa werray trew,
His fatell hour I will nocht fenye new.

1225 Menteth was fals, and that our weill was knawin:
Feill off that kyn, in Scotland than was sawyn,
Chargyt to byd wndyr the gret jugement,
At king Robert ackyt in his parlement.
Tharoff I mak no langar contenuans.

1230 Bot Wallace end in warld was displesans;
Tharfor I cess, and puttis it nocht in rym.
' Scotland may thank the blyssyt happy tym
At he was born, be prynsuall poyntis two.
This is the fyrst, or that we forthyr go;

1235 Scotland he fred, and brocht it off thrillage,
And now in hewin he has his heretage;
As it prewyt be gud experians.
Wyss clerkyss yeit it kepis in remembrans,
How that a monk off Bery abbay than,

1240 In to that tym a rycht religiouss man;
A yong monk als with him in ordour stud,
Quhilk knew his lyff was clene, perfyt, and gud.
This fadyr monk was wesyd with seknace,
Out off the warld as he suld pass on cace.

z

1245 His brothyr saw the spret lykly to pass;
A band off him rycht ernystly he coud ass,
To cum agayn, and schaw him off the meid,
At he suld haiff at God for his gud deid.
He grantyt him, at his prayer to preiff
1250 To cum agayn, gyff God wald geiff him leiff.
The spreyt, changyt out off this warldly payn,
In that sammyn hour cum to the monk agayn.
Sic thing has beyn, and is be woice and sycht.
Quhar he apperyt, thar schawyt sa mekill lycht,
1255 Lyk till lawntryns it illumynyt so cler,
At warldly lycht tharto mycht be no peyr.
A woice said thus; "God has me grantyt grace
Fol. 123 a "That I sall kep my promess in this place."
The monk was blyth off this cler fygur fayr;
1260 Bot a fyr brand in his forheid he bayr,
And than him thocht it myslikyt all the lawe.
'Quhar art thow, spreyt? ansuer, sa God the sawe.'
"In purgatory." 'How lang sall thow be thair?'
"Bot halff ane hour to com, and litill mair.
1265 "Purgatory is, I do the weill to wit,
"In ony place quhar God will it admyt.
"Ane hour of space I was demed thar to be;
"And that passis, supposs I spek with the."
'Quhy has thow that, and all the layff so haill?'
1270 "For off science I thocht me maist awaill.
"Quha pridys tharin, that laubour is in waist,
"For science cummys bot off the haly Gaist."
'Eftir thi hour, quhar is thi passage ewyn?' .
"Quhen tym cummys," he said, "to lestand hewin."
1275 'Quhat tym is that? I pray the now declar.'
"Twa ar on lyff mon be befor me thar."
'Quhilk twa ar thai?' "The verité thow may ken.
"The fyrst has bene a gret slaar off men.

"Now thai him kep to martyr in London toun

1280 "On Wednyssday, befor king and commoun.

"Is nayn on lyff at has sa mony slayn."

'Brodyr,' he said, 'that taill is bot in wayn;

'For slauchtyr is to God abhominabill.'

Than said the spreyt; "Forsuth, this is no fabill.

1285 "He is Wallace, defendour off Scotland,

"For rychtwyss wer that he tuk apon hand.

"Thar rychtwysnes is lowyt our the lawe;

"Tharfor in hewyn he sall that honour hawe.

"Syn, a pure preyst, is mekill to commend;

1290 "He tuk in thank quhat thing that God him send.

"For dayly mess, and heryng off confessioun,

"Hewin he sall haiff to lestand warysoun.

"I am the thrid, grantyt throw Goddis grace."

'Brothir,' he said, 'tell I this in our place,

1295 'Thai wyll bot deym, I othir dreym or rawe.'

Than said the spreyt; "This wytness thow sall hawe.

"Your bellys sall ryng, for ocht at ye do may,

"Quhen thai hym sla, halff an hour off that day."

And so thai did, the monk wyst quhat thaim alyt;

1300 Throuch braid Bretane the woice tharoff was scalyt.

The spreyt tuk leyff at Goddis will to be.

Off Wallace end to her it is peté:

And I wald nocht put men in gret dolour,

Bot lychtly pass atour his fatell hour.

1305   On Wednysday the fals Sotheroun furth brocht,

Till martyr him as thai befor had wrocht.

Fol. 123 b Rycht suth it is, a martyr was Wallace,

Als Osauold, Edmunt, Eduuard, and Thomas.

Off men in armes led him a full gret rout.

1310 With a bauld spreit gud Wallace blent about:

A preyst he askyt, for God at deit on tre.

King Eduuard than cummandyt his clergé,
And said; " I charge, apayn off loss off lywe,
" Nane be sa bauld yon tyrand for to schrywe.
1315 " He has rong lang in contrar my hienace."
A blyst byschop sone, present in that place,
Off Canterbery he than was rychtwyss lord,
Agayn the king he maid this rycht record;
And [said]; ' My selff sall her his confessioun,
1320 ' Gyff I haiff mycht, in contrar off thi croun.
' And thou throu force will stop me off this thing,
• ' I wow to God, quhilk is my rychtwyss king,
' That all Ingland I sall her enterdyt,
' And mak it knawin thou art ane herretyk.
1325 ' The sacrement off kyrk I sall him geiff ;
' Syn tak thi chos, to sterwe or lat him leiff.
' It war mar waill, in worschip off thi croun,
' To kepe sic ane in lyff in thi bandoun,
' Than all the land and gud at thow has refyd.
1330 ' Bot cowatice the ay fra honour drefyd.
' Thow has [thi] lyff rongyn in wrangwis deid;
' That sall be seyn on the, or on thi seid.'
The king gert charge thai suld the byschop ta;
Bot sad lordys consellyt to lat him ga.
1335 All Inglissmen said, at his desyr was rycht;
To Wallace than he rakyt in thar sicht,
And sadly hard his confessioun till ane end.
Hvmbly to God his spreyt he thar comend;
Lawly him serwyt with hartlye deuocioun
1340 Apon his kneis, and said ane orysoun.
His leyff he tuk, and to West monastyr raid.
The lokmen than thai bur Wallace but baid
On till a place, his martyrdom to tak;
For till his ded he wald na forthyr mak.
1345 Fra the fyrst nycht he was tane in Scotland,

Thai kepyt him in to that sammyn band.
Na thing he had at suld haiff doyn him gud;
Bot Inglissmen him seruit off carnaill fud.
Hys warldly lyff desyrd the sustenance,
1350 Thocht he it gat in contrar off plesance.
Thai thretty dayis his band thai durst nocht slaik,
Quhill he was bundyn on a skamyll off ayk,
With irn chenyeis that was bath stark and keyn.
A clerk thai set to her quhat he wald meyn.
1355 "Thow Scot," he said, "that gret wrangis has don,
" 'Thi fatell hour, thow seis, approchis son.
" Thow suld in mynd remembyr thi mysdeid,
" At clerkis may, quhen thai thair psalmis reid
" For Crystyn saullis, that makis thaim to pray,
1360 " In thair nowmyr thow may be ane off thai;
" For now thow seis on fors thou mon decess."
Than Wallace said; ' For all thi roid rahress,
' Thow has na charge, supposs at I did myss;
' Yon blyst byschop has hecht I sall haiff blis;
1365 ' And trew [I] weill, that God sall it admyt:
' Thi febyll wordis sall nocht my conscience smyt.
' Conford I haiff off way that I suld gang,
' Maist payn I feill at I bid her our lang.'
Than said this clerk; " Our king oft send the till;
1370 " Thow mycht haiff had all Scotland at thi will,
" To hald off him, and cessyt off thi stryff;
" So as a lord rongyn furth all thi lyff."
Than Wallace said; ' Thou spekis off mychty thing.
' Had I lestyt, and gottyn my rychtwyss king,
1375 ' Fra worthi Bruce had rasauit his croun,
' I thocht haiff maid Ingland at his bandoun.
' So wttraly it suld beyn at his will,
' Quhat plessyt him, to sauff thi king or spill.'
" Weill," said this clerk, " than thow repentis nocht:

1380 " Off wykkydness thow has a felloun thocht.
　　" Is nayn in warld at has sa mony slane;
　　" Tharfor till ask, me think thow suld be bane,
　　" Grace off our king, and syn at his barnage."
　　Than Wallace smyld [a] litill at his langage.

1385 ' I grant,' he said, ' part Inglissmen I slew
　　' In my quarrel, me thocht nocht halff enew.
　　' I mowyt na wer bot for to win our awin;
　　' To God and man the rycht full weill is knawin.
　　' Thi frustyr wordis dois nocht bot taris me,

1390 ' I the commaund, on Goddis halff, lat me be.'
　　A schyrray gart this clerk sone fra him pass;
　　Rycht as thai durst, thai grant quhat he wald ass.
　　A Psaltyr buk Wallace had on him euir;
　　Fra his childeid fra it wald nocht deseuir.

1395 Bettyr he trowit in wiage for to speid.
　　Bot than he was dispalyeid off his weid.
　　This grace he ast at lord Clyffurd that knycht,
　　To lat him haiff his Psaltyr buk in sycht.
　　He gert a preyst it oppyn befor him hauld,

1400 Quhill thai till him had done all at thai wauld.
　　Stedfast he red, for ocht thai did him thar:
　　Feyll Sotheroun said, at Wallace feld na sayr.
　　Gud deuocioun sa was his begynnyng,
　　Conteynd tharwith, and fair was his endyng;

1405 Quhill spech and spreyt at anys all can fayr
　　To lestand blyss, we trow, for euirmayr.
　　I will nocht tell how he dewydyt was
　　In fyve partis, and ordand for to pass;
　　Bot thus his spreit be liklynes was weill.

1410 Off Wallace lyff quha has a forthar feill,
　　May schaw furth mair with wit and eloquence;
　　For I to this haiff don my diligence,
　　Eftyr the pruff geyffyn fra the Latyn buk,

Quhilk Maister Blayr in his tym wndyrtuk,
1415 In fayr Latyn compild it till ane end;
With thir witnes the mar is to commend.
Byschop Synclar than lord was off Dunkell,
Fol. 124 b He gat this buk, and confermd it him sell
For werray trew; thar off he had no dreid,
1420 Himselff had seyn gret part off Wallace deid.
His purpos was till haue send it to Rom,
Our fadyr off kyrk tharon to gyff his dom.
Bot Maistir Blayr, and als Schir Thomas Gray,
Eftir Wallace thai lestit mony day,
1425 Thir twa knew best off gud Schir Wilyhamys deid,
Fra sexteyn yer quhill nyne and twenty yeid.
Fourty and fyve off age Wallace was cauld,
That tym that he was to [the] Southeroun sauld.
Thocht this mater be nocht till all plesance,
1430 His suthfast deid was worthi till awance.
All worthi men at redys this rurall dyt,
Blaym nocht the buk, set I be wnperfyt.
I suld hawe thank, sen I nocht trawaill spard;
For my laubour na man hecht me reward;
1435 Na charge I had off king nor othir lord;
Gret harm I thocht his gud deid suld be smord.
I haiff said her ner as the process gais;
And fenyeid nocht for frendschip nor for fais.
Costis herfor was no man bond to me;
1440 In this sentence I had na will to be,
Bot in als mekill as I rahersit nocht
Sa worthely as nobill Wallace wrocht.
Bot in a poynt, I grant, I said amyss,
Thir twa knychtis suld blamyt be for this,
1445 The knycht Wallas, off Craggé rychtwyss lord,
And Liddaill als, gert me mak [wrang] record.
On Allyrtoun mur the croun he tuk a day,

To get battaill, as myn autour will say.
Thir twa gert me say that ane othir wyss;
1450 Till Maister Blayr we did sumpart off dispyss.

Go nobill buk, fulfillyt off gud sentens,
Supposs thow be baran off eloquens,
Go worthi buk, fullfillit off suthfast deid;
Bot in langage off help thow has gret neid.
1455 Quhen gud makaris rang weill in to Scotland,
Gret harm was it that nane off thaim ye fand.
Yeit thar is part that can the weill awance;
Now byd thi tym, and be a remembrance.
I yow besek, off your beneuolence,
1460 Quha will nocht low, lak nocht my eloquence;
(It is weill knawin I am a bural man,)
For her is said as gudly as I can: ·
My spreyt felis na termys asperans.
Now besek God, that gyffar is off grace,
1465 Maide hell and erd, and set the hewyn abuff,
That he ws grant off his der lestand luff.

EXPLICIT VITA NOBILISSIMI DEFENSORIS SCOTIE,
VIDELICET WILLIELMI WALLACE MILITIS, PER
ME JHOANNEM RAMSAY, ANNO DOMINI MILLE-
SIMO QUADRINGENTESIMO OCTUAGESIMO OC-
TAVO.*

* Two or three words, apparently eucharistic, which have been added
here, are mutilated in the MS.

NOTES ON WALLACE.

2 A

NOTES ON WALLACE.

NOTES ON THE FIRST BOOK.

His forbearis, quha likis till wndrestand,
Of hale lynage, and trew lyne of Scotland, &c.—V. 21.

Of *auld* linnage, &c. Edit. 1594; *olde*, 1620; *old*, 1648, 1673, and 1714.

Go reid the fyrst *rycht lyne of the fyrst Stewart.* MS.—V. 34.

But both the rhyme and sense point out the word in Roman characters as an error of the copier. It also disagrees with all the copies I have seen, except that of 1714.

Till hald of hym the toun.—V. 64. MS.

This is obviously another error, and opposed to all the copies.

And thar he gat ymage *of Scotland* swne. MS.—V. 116.

It is *homage* in all the copies, except that of Perth.

And Bruce, out of Scotland.—V. 134.

All the copies before that of 1714 connect this with v. 140 ;—

That office than he brukyt bot schort tyme.

The editor of the first edition I have seen might have overlooked the six intervening lines, by fixing his eye on the conclusion of v. 134, which closes with the same words as that of v. 140—*of Scotland*. But the sense requires these lines; as no *office* was given to Bruce, but merely his heritage.

> *Schir Ranald knew weill a mar quiet sted,*
> *Quhar Wilyham mycht be bettir fra thair fede,*
> *With his wncle Wallas of* Ricardtoun,
> *Schir Richard hecht, that gud knycht off renoun.*—V. 353.

" Riccartoun is evidently a corruption of Richardtoun. It is generally supposed to have been so called from a Sir Richard Wallace, who lived in the vicinity of the village, and who is said to have been uncle to the celebrated patriot, Sir William Wallace. Of his house no vestige now remains; the place, however, where it stood is well known. The village of Riccartoun is within one English mile of the market-place of Kilmarnock." V. Riccartoun, Stat. Acc. V. 117.

> *And with the swerd* awkwart *he him gawe.*—V. 407.

In Edit. 1594,—ane *ackwart* straik him gaif.
This is followed by subsequent editions. The line, as it stands in MS. is both clumsy and nonsensical. But perhaps Blind Harry used this for athwart; as it occurs in the same sense, II. 109.

> *Went till his eyme, and tauld him of this* drede. MS.—V. 437.

Of the *deid*, Edit. 1594. Of the *deed*, Edit. 1620.
This is more in character, than to suppose that Wallace, after so chivalrous an achievement, should run to his uncle, and tell him in what terror he was for the vengeance of the English. The term here used, indeed, seems to reduplicate on the phrase which occurs v. 434, "this worthi werk."

NOTES ON THE SECOND BOOK.

> Aboundandely *Wallace amang thaim yeid;*
> *The rage of youth maid him to haf no dreid.*—V. 27.

This is most probably for *abandounly;* signifying, "without regard to danger," as it is indeed explained in the following line. In Edit. 1594, it is rendered,—All but *abaissing;* 1620 and 1648, *abasing.*

> *He bar a* sasteing *in a boustous poille.*—V. 33.

A *sting* signifies a pole; but this *sasteing* must have been something fixed in a larger *poille* or pole. Norw. *sjaastang* is explained, "a pole wherewith skins are taken off or laid on smoky vents." *Sjaa* itself signifies the skin taken from the stomachs of animals, of which parchment is made. V. Hallager Ordsamling. But as Scottish *say* signifies a water bucket, this may refer to the pole used for carrying it. The following definition might seem to throw light on this singular term. "*So* or *soa*, a tub with two ears to carry on a *stang*." Ray's Collection of North Country Words. The term was most probably pronounced *saysting*: as *a*, in our old writers, must often have been sounded *ai*.

The Aperse of Scotland left in cayr.—V. 170.

In MS. it is,—*Prophesye out* Scotland is left, &c. As this has no meaning, I have altered it, according to the reading of Edit. 1594, 1620, and 1648:

The *Apersie* of Scotland is in greit cair.

Celinus was maist his gayder now.—V. 234.

In editions *Cellinus*. In MS. the initial letter is wanting, as is generally the case in MSS. which were afterwards to be illuminated. But from the copies it appears probable that it was C. This name is certainly given figuratively, or in reference to some jailor, celebrated in the romances then in vogue. Or could the Minstrel allude to *Celaeno*, one of the fabled harpies? If so, *Cellinus* would perhaps be the original reading.

> *Thomas Rimour in to the* Faile *was than,*
> *With the mynystir, quhilk was a worthi man:*
> *He wsyt offt to that religiouss place.*—V. 288.

This passage has been strangely misunderstood. So early as 1594 it had been made to bear quite a different meaning:—

Thomas Rymour *withouttin still* was than
With the minister, &c.

This error has been followed in subsequent editions. In Edit. Perth, 1790, it is, *in to the ayle*: although it had been properly given, *in to the Faile*, Edit. 1714.

This was a cell or priory of the Cluniacenses in Kyle, Ayrshire, depending on Paisley. Spottiswoode writes it *Feale*. "Our history," he says, "only remarks, that the prior of this place was one of those who hindred the castle of Dumbarton from being surrendered to the English, anno 1544, in opposition to the Earl of Lenox, then governor of it." But besides this curious passage, which shows that it was an ancient foundation; it may be added, that "the right of the patronage of the kirk of *Fale*, in the county of Ayr," is given to James de Lindsay, apparently the ancestor of the Earls of Crawford, in a charter by Robert II. Registr. Mag. Sigill. p. 172. N. 13. The miln of *Faill*, and the crofthead of *Fail*, in the lordship of *Fail-*furd, are mentioned in a retour regarding William Wallace, heir of William Wallace, minister of Failfurd, A. 1617. Inquis. Retour. Ayr, N. 162.

Thar man that day had in the merket bene.—V. 297.

In Edit. 1594, 1620, 1714, and Perth, it is *that* man; in 1648 and 1673, *this* man; either of which would immediately refer to Thomas of Ercildon. But *thar*, i.e. *their* man, respects the servant of the religious fraternity of Faile, as appears from v. 299, which cannot respect True Thomas;

His mastyr speryt, quhat tithingis at he saw.

NOTES ON THE THIRD BOOK.

And fra the tyme that he of presoune four,
Gude souir *weide dayly on him he wour:*
Gude lycht harness, fra that tyme, wsyt he euir.—V. 83.

Instead of *And* fra the tyme, read, *Ay* fra the tyme, as in MS.

It is remarkable that in all the copies, without exception, as far as I know, it is *somer* or *summer weid*, or *weed*. Of what use could this have been to Wallace, when in "sodeyn stryff?" The term is the same with E. *sure*, i.e. secure armour, although light.

His face he kepit, for it was euir bar,—
In to his weid, and he come in a thrang.—V. 91.

I have pointed this passage according to what seems the sense. Having so many enemies, when he was accidentally "in a crowd, he muffled up his face," that his features might not be recognised. Hamilton of Gilbert-field, although in many instances he has given an air of ridicule to this ancient poem, by the grossness of his phraseology, seems to have hit the true sense here, which is totally lost by the mode of punctuation in most of the editions. He renders it ;—

His face, when he came in among strange folk,
He held it best to hide within his cloak.—P. 42.

Send twa skowrrouris *to wesy weyll the playn.*—V. 103.

Scurriours, Edit. 1620. In that of Perth, *thowrrouris;* but in MS. it may be read *tkowrrouris, t* or *c* being put for *s.* We have *skonriouris,* IV. 431.

> *The knycht* Fenweik *conwoide the caryage.*—V. 117.
> —*The knycht* Fenweik, *that cruell was and keyne;*
> *He had at dede off Wallace fadyr beyne.*—V. 169.

" Among other antiquities there may be mentioned, a place called *Beg,* above Allinton, where the brave Wallace lay in a species of rude fortification with only fifty of his friends, yet obtained a complete victory over an English officer of the name of *Fenwick,* who had two hundred men under his command. This gallant hero, it is well known, had several places of retirement towards the head of this parish and in the neighbourhood, some of which retain his name unto this day; *Wallace-hill* in particular, an eminence near the Galla-law, and a place called *Wallace-Gill,* in the parish of Loudoun, a hollow glen, to which he probably retired for shelter when pursued by his enemies." P. of Galston. Stat. Acc. II. 74.

Schir Amar Wallange, a falss traytour strange, &c.—V. 261.

The Minstrel, it has been said by Lord Hailes, "always speaks of Aymer de Valloins, Earl of Pembroke, as *a false Scottish knight."* Annals, I. 245. But, as Kerr has observed, although he designs him "a false traitor," &c. his country is no where mentioned; unless this should be viewed as implied in what is said, B. VII. 1097, concerning his forsaking *" his awne land* for euirmar." Kerr views this, however, as referable to his quitting Bothwell, the heritage of Moray, which had been given to Valloins. V. Hist. Bruce, I. 115.

NOTES ON THE FOURTH BOOK.

> *So sodcynly at Hesilden he saw*
> *The Perseys sowme, in quhilk gret ryches was.*—V. 26.

In MS. *that* Hesilden; but I have followed the judicious alteration made in Edit. 1714. In that of 1594 it is completely changed:

Sa suddainlie that time himself he saw, &c.

This is adopted by Hart, Edit. 1620.

Hesilden is evidently a local name, and must be the same place that is now called *Hezilton-head*, a farm, situated on high ground, in the parish of Mearns, on the direct road from Ayr to Glasgow, about nine miles to the south-west of the latter. This appears unquestionable, from the necessity under which Sir Ranald Crawfurd was laid, in consequence of his sumpter-horse being carried off by the English, of sleeping that night at Mearns, v. 70.

> Schyr Ranald was wiss, and kest in his entent;
> And said, " I will byde at the *Mernys* all nycht."

Schir Ranald said, ' That is bot litill der.'—V. 60.

In MS. *her*, which is followed by Edit. 1714. But I prefer *der* or *deir*, the reading of 1594, signifying "injury, loss." In Edit. 1620, *deare.*

> *Befor Persye* than seir men *brocht war thai:*
> *Thai* folowit *him of felouny that was wrocht.*—V. 122.

> Befoir the Persie *and his men* brocht were thai.—Edit. 1594.

It is the same as given by Hart.

The phrase "*folowit* him of," signifies, pursued him for. It frequently occurs in this sense in our old statutes.

> *For thai war* strang: *yeitt he couth nocht thaim dreid.*—V. 179.

Strang here signifies, "strange; persons with whom he was not acquainted."

Thocht they were *strangers*, &c. Edit. 1594. *Though* they were *strangers*, 1620.

> *A bown* Lekle, *&c.* MS.—V. 211.

It is *Lekkie* in all the editions; which is still the name of the place, (V. Stat. Acc. XVIII. 98. 116.) and was so in the time of Robert Bruce. Robertson's Ind. 8, 90.

> *On* Gargownno *was byggyt a small* peill, &c.—V. 213.

" A little southward of the village there is a conical height called the Kier-hill, which is evidently artificial, and seems to have been a military work. There are remains of a ditch or rampart of a circular form, which proves that it is not of Roman origin. It is probably of later date, and appears to have been the place from which Sir William Wallace sallied forth on the night when he took by surprise the *Peel* of *Gargunnock*." Stat. Acc. XVIII. 116, 117.

Wallace with hyr in secre *maid him glaid.*—V. 403.

I have retained the word as in MS. although it is *secret* in all the copies. Perhaps it might be from O. Fr. *en secré*.

Wemen and preistis wpon the wall *can wepe.*—V. 480.

In MS. *wpon Wallace.* But the reading of Edit. 1594 is preferable ; especially as they did not then know that their enemy was Wallace. Perhaps it might originally be, " wpon the *wallis*," whence the blunder might easily be made, as the word would be read as two syllables.

No man was thar that Wallace bow mycht draw.—V. 550.

In MS. we find *all* as the last word in the preceding line, and *drall* here. But the error has arisen from the resemblance of *w* to *ll*.

To Cargyll wood thai went that samyn nycht.—V. 677.

In MS. *Gargyll.* But it is *Cargill*, Edit. 1594; and this must be the true reading, Shortwoodshaw being in the parish of Cargill. V. Stat. Acc. XIII. 532. This is evidently spoken of as the same with Cargyll-wood.

NOTES ON THE FIFTH BOOK.

In Gyllisland *thar was that brachell brede.—*
So was scho vsyt on Esk and on Ledaill:
Quhill scho gat blude no fleyng mycht awail.—V. 25.

Gilderland, Edit. 1594; *Gelderland,* 1620, 1648, 1673, &c., also 1714. But this must be *Gillesland* or *Gilsland*, a barony in Cumberland. The Minstrel having said that the hound was *bred* here, immediately speaks of her being used to track in Esk and Liddisdale, in the vicinity of Cumberland. So late as the reign of James I. of England, there is an order dated A. 1616, that no less than nine bloodhounds should be kept on the Border, upon Esk, and other places mentioned. V. Pennant's Tour, 1772 ; I. 77, II. 397.

Bellenden, after Boece, gives a particular description of these blood-hounds, which agrees with the facts mentioned above, and has considerable interest.

"The thrid kynd is mair than ony rache. Red hewit or ellis blak with small spraingis of spottis, and ar callit be the peple sleuthhundis. Thir doggis hes sa meruellous wit, that thai serche theuis, and followis on thaym allanerlie be sent of the guddis that ar tane away. And nocht allanerlie fyndis the theif, bot inuadis hym with gret cruelté. And thocht the theuis oftymes cors the watter, quhair thai pas, to caus the hound to tyne the sent of thaym and the guddis, yit he serchis heir and thair with sic deligence, that be his fut he fyndis baith the trace of the theiff and the guddis. The meruellous nature of thir houndis wil haue na faith with vncouth peple. Howbeit the samyn ar rycht frequent and ryfe on the bordouris of Ingland and Scotland. Attour it is statute be the lawis of the bordouris, he that denyis entres to the sleuthound in tyme of chace and serching of guddis, sal be haldin participant with the cryme and thift com-mittit." Discription of Albion, chap. XI.

This extract throws light on a passage in *The Bruce*, where the king is made to refer to the vulgar idea as to the means necessary for making the blood-hound lose his scent ; although the statement given by Boece opposes the opinion which had been generally received.

> Bot Ik haiff herd oftymys say,
> That quha endland a watter ay
> Wald waid a bowdraucht, he suld ger
> Bathe the slouth hund, and his leder,
> Tyne the sleuth men gert hym ta.
> THE BRUCE, B. v. 317.

John Hardyng has given a curious account of the means used by Edward I. for taking Bruce, similar to that here said to have been employed against Wallace.

> The king Edward with hornes and *houndes* him soght,
> With menne on fote, through marris, mosse, and myre,
> Through wodes also and mountens [wher they fought]
> And euer the kyng Edward hight men greate hyre,
> Hym for to take and by might conquere;
> But thei might hym not gette by force ne by train,
> He satte by the fyre when thei [went] in the rain.

In the stanza immediately following he indeed ascribes the death of Edward to his disappointment, in never being able to get our king into his hands :—

> The kyng Edward *for anger* fell in accesse,
> And homeward came full sycke and sore annoyed.—
> At Burgh vpon the sande he died anone, &c.
> *Chronicle*, p. 303, 304.

Kerly beheld on to the bauld Heroun,
Vpon Fawdoun as he was lukand doune.—V. 145.

This appears to have been the head of the ancient family of Heron, who held Ford Castle in Northumberland. In the reign of Henry III. it was in possession of Sir William Heron, who was governor of the castles of Bamborough, Pickering, and Scarborough, lord warden of the forests north of Trent, and sheriff of Northumberland for eleven successive years. V. Hutchinson's Northumb. II. 19. This castle has attracted much attention, as having been the scene of the enchantments of its fair mistress, by means of which our infatuated James IV. was disarmed before the fatal battle of Flodden ; and it has acquired additional celebrity from the no less bewitching Muse of the author of Marmion.

To Dawryoch *he knew the* forss *full weill.*—V. 265.

This is *Dalreoch*, on the south bank of the Earn, four or five miles west from Forteviot. A bridge across the Earn is called that of Dalreoch. By the *forss* seems to be meant *ford*. V. Etym. Dict. in vo.

Our thwort the Kerss to the Torwode *he yeide.*—
The rone wes thik that Wallace slepyt in.—V. 319—357.

"In Dunipace parish is the famous Torwood, in the middle of which there are the remains of Wallace's Tree, an oak which, according to a measurement, when entire, was said to be about twelve feet diameter. To this wood Wallace is said to have fled, and secreted himself in the body of that tree, then hollow, after his defeat in the north." Stat. Acc. III. 336.

This "is still dignified by the name of *Wallace's Tree*. It stands in the middle of a swampy moss, having a causeway round its ruins ; and its destruction has been much precipitated by the veneration in which the Scottish hero has been long held, numerous pieces having been carried off, to [be] convert[ed] into various memorials of the champion of Scotland." Kerr's Hist. Bruce, I. 127.

Throuch the Oychall thai had gayne all that nycht,
Till Airth *ferry, or that the day was brycht.*—V. 411.

In MS. it is *Qwenys* ferry ; but the word first written has been scraped out, and *Qwenys* substituted on the head margent above it. The term deleted seems to have been *erd ;* most probably written by mistake for *Airth,* in a copy which may have been taken from recitation. The term

Qwenys indeed is apparently in the same hand with the rest of the MS.; but the transcriber, thinking only of *erd* as signifying the earth, had indulged the idea that it must be an error. As the companions of Wallace were on their way to Dunipace in quest of him, to have gone from Gask to Queensferry would have been to take a very circuitous course without any apparent necessity. *Airth* is the reading of editions 1594, 1620, 1648, and 1673. In Edit. 1714 it is *Queens-ferry*, as would seem on the authority of the MS.

> In Dundaff *mur that sammyn nycht he raid.*
> *Schir Jhone the* Grayme, *quhilk lord wes of that land,*
> *Ane agyt knycht had maid nane othir band ;*
> *Bot purchest pess in rest he mycht bide still,* &c.—V. 436.

The castle of *Dundaff*, of which there are still some remains, was situated in Stirlingshire, near the source of Carron. This old knight, by some called David, by others John, was proprietor not only of Dundaff, but of the lands of Strathblane and Strathcarron. V. Nimmo's Stirlingshire, p. 358. A fabulous antiquity has been ascribed to this family; it having been asserted that the wall of Antonine vulgarly received the name of *Graham's Dike*, because in a very early period of our history it was penetrated by a valorous chief, from whom those of this celebrated name had their origin. We have no written evidence of the existence of this family before the reign of David I., when William de Grahame appears as witness to the charter of the foundation of Holyrood-house. Sir J. Dalrymple's Coll. p. 397. From it originated many distinguished families, as that of Montrose, Menteith, Fintry, Balgowan, &c. It was the son of this "agyt knycht" who was the faithful friend of Wallace, and who fell at the battle of Falkirk.

> " *Quhat worth of him? I pray you graithlye tell.*"—V. 498.

By misapprehension, in all the printed copies, *word;* as if the question were, "What intelligence is there concerning him?" But the meaning is, "What *became* of him?"

> *Bot weyle I wait, quhar gret ernyst is in thocht,*
> *It lattis wer in the wysest wys be wrocht.*--V. 642.

i. e. "Where there is great anxiety of mind, it prevents the carrying on of war in the wisest" or "most proper manner."

The meaning is lost in Edit. 1594,—

It lettis weir that in wise men is wrocht.

Edit. 1620.

It letteth war, that in wise men is wrought.

> *The trewth I knaw off this, and hyr lynage;*
> *I knew nocht hyr, tharfor I lost a gage.*—V. 654.

That is, "I know the character and descent of *this* lady; but being a stranger to my *former* sweetheart, at Perth, I lost my stake." *Hyr* in v. 655 is opposed to *this* in the preceding line.

> *To the* Corhed *with out restyng he raid.*—V. 724.
> *At the* Corheid *full fayne thai wald haif beyne.*—V. 816.

I prefer this to *Torhed*, Edit. 1714 and Perth. It agrees equally well with the MS.; and it is that of 1594 and of the other old editions. Besides, I find *Corheid* given as the name of a property in Annandale, belonging to the Johnstouns, Inquis. Retorn. A. 1608, N. 63; but no such place as *Torheid* in Dumfries-shire.

> *In the* Knok *wood he lewyt all bot thre.*—V. 735.

In the parish of Kirkmichael, county of Dumfries, there is "a small fort in the *Knock Wood*, called *Wallace's House*, said to have been thrown up by Sir William Wallace, after he had slain Sir Hugh of Moreland and five of his men, at a place still named, from that event, the *sax corses*, i. e. the six corpses." Stat. Acc. I. 63. It has been ingeniously remarked, that "the *sax corses* more probably signify six crosses, in allusion to some religious monument so decorated." Kerr's Hist. Bruce, I. 125.

> *Ane* Kyrk Patryk, *that cruell was and keyne,*
> *In Esdaill wood that half yer he had beyne.*
> *With Ingliss men he couth nocht weyll accord.*—V. 920.

This, it appears, was the ancestor of the Kirkpatricks of Closeburne, who appear on record so early as the year 1141. Alexander II. grants a confirmation charter of Closeburne to one of this name, A. 1332, which is still in the possession of the family.

Kirkpatrick Sharpe of Hoddam is a descendant of the Closeburne family in the fourth generation; the name of Sharpe having been added, as attached, by the deed of the possessor, to the estate of Hoddam.

> *For* Jhonstoune *send, a man off gud degre:*
> *Secund dochtir forsuth weddyt had he*
> *Off Halidays, nere neuo to Wallace.*—V. 1050.

This was the ancestor of the Marquisses of Annandale.

Thai trew that he has found hys name *agayne.*—MS.   V. 1092.

NOTES ON THE SIXTH BOOK.

Than passit was wtass *off Feuiryher.*—V. 1.

In MS., *wtast;* Edit. 1594, &c. *octaues* of Februar; *octaves,* Edit. 1714.

> *—Nympheus, in beldyn off his bour,*
> *With oyle and balm fullfillit off snet odour,*
> Faunis *materis, as thai war wount to gang,* &c.—V. 12.

In Edit. 1594, l. 14, it is thus given,—

> *Canettis in trace* as they wer wont to gang.

In Edit. 1620,—*Caneittis,* &c.; in that of 1714, *Famous.* In MS. it may
be read either *Famus* or *Faunis.* Although I cannot make sense of the
line, there seems to be an allusion to the *Fawns* of heathen mythology; as
the illiterate Minstrel might allude to the *Nymphs* in the term *Nympheus.*

> *Begynnyng band, with graith witnes besyd,*
> *Myn auctor sais, scho was his* rychtwyss wyff.—V. 47.

After ver. 72, a whole stanza is found in Edit. 1594 and 1620, which
does not appear in MS.

> This vther maid wedded ane Squyar wicht,
> Quhilk was weill knawin cummin of Balliols blude,
> And thair airis be lyne succeeded richt
> To Lammintoun and vther landis gude.
> Of this mater the richt quha vnderstude,
> Heirof as now I will na mair proceid;
> Of my sentence schortlie to conclude,
> Of vther thing my purpois is to reid.

I hesitate very much as to the authenticity of this stanza. It would not
of itself be a sufficient proof that it is wanting in MS., because we meet

with similar deficiences; but it does not tally well with the stanza preceding, which speaks only of *a child*, that is, most probably, one to the exclusion of others. As little does it agree with the stanza immediately following in the copies which have adopted it; for it begins with these words ;—

Rycht gudly men come of this lady ying, &c.

For this supposes either that there was but one young lady referred to, or that she, who is previously mentioned as having been married to Squire Shaw, had no family.

It has been said, that Wallace "left no legitimate issue; but had a *natural* daughter, who married Sir William Baillie of Hoprig, the progenitor of the Baillies of Lammington." Caledonia, I. 579. From the reference here made in a foot-note to Crawfurd's Hist. Renfrew, 61, and Ruddiman's Index Dipl. Scotiæ, 121, one might have supposed that these writers had brought some proof of the illegitimacy of this daughter. But it does not appear that the idea of illegitimacy had once entered into the mind of Crawfurd. He merely says of Wallace : " He left issue only one daughter, who was married to Sir William Baillie of Hoprig," &c.; adding, "the lands of Elderslee returned to the family of Craigie." Ruddiman merely says; "Reliquisse unam filiam Willelmus dicitur, quam uxorem duxit D. Willelmus Baillie de Hoprig," &c.

The only thing that has the semblance of a proof that Wallace was not married, is what follows in the same note. "The estate of Ellerslie went to the Wallaces of Ricardton, as his nearest male heirs." But their being *male* heirs might be the reason of their inheriting this property. Besides, it does not seem fully ascertained, whether our illustrious champion was ever personally vested in these lands. It is admitted by the author of Caledonia, in a preceding note, p. 578, that "both Wyntoun and Harry concur in speaking of the great Wallace as the *second* son of Sir Malcolm." Lord Hailes says : " He was the younger son of a gentleman in the neighbourhood of Paisley. Such is the opinion generally received." Annals, I. 245. It must be admitted, however, that Bower, in his continuation of Fordun, says that " Andrew, the elder brother of William, and honoured with the order of knighthood, being guilefully slain by the English, William succeeded to a sufficient patrimony in lands for his state, which he left to be held by his posterity." Scotichron. II. Lib. xi. c. 28.

Unless we should suppose the Minstrel determined to lie in the face of evidence, his appeal, in the passage quoted, to his *auctor,* shews the general belief of the country at the time of his writing, and even during the life of Mr. John Blair, to whom he seems to appeal, that Wallace was married. Now, it is well known that Blair was the bosom friend and the faithful associate of Wallace; and, being a priest, it may reasonably be conjectured that he was the person who celebrated the marriage.

Pinkerton remarks, "that the murder of Wallace's wife, which seems the first cause which excited him to arms," (he means, most probably, after remaining for several months in peace,) "was committed at Lanark by Heselrig or Hislop, governor of the castle" of Lanark, "whom Wallace after slew. See Fordun, XI. 28. Henry the Minstrel in this instance accords with history, and with tradition; a large cave in Cartland Craigs near Lanark, where Henry says that Wallace lurked, being called *Wallace's Cave* to this day. It is remarkable that Sir D. Dalrymple should have omitted this important circumstance, for which Fordun [Bower, his continuator,] was surely good authority." The Bruce, II. 20, N.

The "important circumstance" referred to must be that of Wallace having slain the governor of the castle of Lanark; for Bower does not say that the reason of this was the murder of the wife of Wallace. But undoubtedly this was a remarkable omission on the part of our learned and accurate annalist.

I do not say, that the account given by Bower of the slaughter of Hesilgir, or, as he calls him, *Hesliope*, amounts to a proof of the marriage of Wallace, or even certainly intimates the reason of the deed; but it authenticates the fact of Wallace having been at Lanark at this time, and renders it highly probable that he had met with some special excitement. According to the testimony of Bower, it was from this time forward that he openly appeared as the avenger of the wrongs of his country.

The memory of Wallace is still so fresh in the town of Lanark, that the inhabitants point out the place where he was wont to lodge.

"Tradition tells that the house where Wallace resided was at the head of the Castlegate, opposite the church, where a new house has lately been erected. It also acquaints us, that a private vaulted archway led from this house to Cartlane Craigs, but seemingly without the smallest probability." P. Lanark, Stat. Acc. XV. 33.

> *And thai oft syss feill causis till him wrocht,*
> *Fra that tyme furth, quhilk mowit* [hym sa sar,
> That neuir in warld out of his mind was brocht.]—V. 78.

In MS. ver. 79 is;

> *Fra that tyme furth, quhilk mouit* hyr fer mar.

The following line, as printed in the text, which is the concluding one of the stanza, is totally omitted. Most probably it had been wanting in the

MS. from which Ramsay copied ; as he seems to have altered the three last words of ver. 79, so as apparently to complete the sense, by transferring the language, which obviously regards Wallace, to his wife. I have given the reading of Edit. 1594. It is the same in Hart's, with a slight change of the orthography.

> *He salust thaim, as it war bot in scorn;*
> " Dewgar, *gud day, bone Senyhour, and gud morn* !"—V. 131.

It is thus given in Edit. 1594 and 1620;

> Dew gaird, gude day bon Senyour, and gude morne.

Fr. *Dieu garde*, a salutation, God save you.

> *Gud deyn, dawch Lard, bach lowch banyoch a de.*—V. 140.

> Gud euin daucht Lord, Ballanch, Banyenochade.—Edit. 1594.
> Good euin daucht Lord, Ballanch, Banyenochadie.—Edit. 1620.

As the former salutation consists of a ridiculous mixture of French and Scottish, this seems to be composed of Scottish and Gaelic. *Gud deyn* is evidently for " Good evening." *Dawch Lard* may signify lazy laird. The latter words have been viewed as Gaelic, *l'ail, luibh, beannach a De*, "if you please, God bless you !" V. Etym. Dict. vo. DAWCH.

> *Off gret statur, and sum part gray wes he;*
> *The Inglissmen cald him bot* Grymmysbé.—V. 311.

Bot Grymmysbé, i.e. by no other name ; and this, it appears, was a nickname, from his gray or grim complexion.

> *The awfull ost, with Eduuard off Ingland,*
> *To* Beggar *come, with sexté thousand men.*—V. 342.

This is the mode in which Ramsay gives the name of *Biggar*, a village in Lanarkshire. " There is a tradition of a battle having been fought at the east end of the town, between the Scots, under the command of Sir William Wallace, and the English army, who were said to be 60,000 strong, wherein a great slaughter was made on both sides, especially among the latter." Stat. Acc. P. Biggar, I. 336.

> *A yong squier was brothir to Fehew.*—V. 363.

It is *Schir Hew*, Edit. 1594 and 1620; the same in that of 1714. But in Edit. 1648, it is, as here, *Fehew*. In MS. *Schyr hew* seems to have been first written, and afterwards deleted, the letter *s* or *f* being left singly, with a blank before *hew*. But in ver. 397, it is clearly *Fehew;* as also in B. VIII. 1010, 1067, 1081, where the fate of this squire is referred to. Whether such a person ever existed, I can find no trace in the Fœdera, or in any history of that period. For the honour of Wallace, it may well be supposed that the whole story is fabulous.

> *Off* Anadderdaill *he had thaim led that nycht.*—V. 536.

This denotes Annandale. But it seems to be an error of the copier, for Ananderdaill, the more ancient designation of this district, watered by the river Annan.

> —*Haistit thaim nocht, bot sobyrly couth fair*
> *Till Townbery; thar captane was at Ayr*
> *With lord Persie, to tak his consaill haill.*—V. 835.

In Edit. 1594, 1620, 1714, and Perth 1790;

To Turneburie *that* captaine was *of* Air.

This passage does not seem to have been hitherto given intelligibly, in any one edition. *Townbery* has still been viewed as the name of the person who was "captain of Ayr." But this deprives the passage of any reasonable meaning. How could this supposed person be "captain of Ayr" *with* Lord Percy, who had the charge of the whole district? Thus, also, these words, "to tak his consaill haill," according to the construction, apply equally well to Wallace and his troops, as to the supposed "captain of Ayr." But Turnbery is the name of a place, particularly mentioned in The Bruce, V. Note, III. 829. The line must have been written as given in this edition. *At Aire* is the reading, Edit. 1648 and 1673; and what has been rendered *that*, in MS. may be read *thar*, i.e., their. This shews the reason why the Scots did not hurry on, but went *sobyrly* to Turnbery. They had learned that *their* captain, the captain of those who had the defence of "Turnbery castle," as it is denominated by Barbour, was *at* Ayr with Lord Percy, to take his advice about the state of public matters.

> *Apon the morn in* Cumno *sone thai socht.*—V. 846.

This is Cumnock, in Ayrshire, whence two parishes now take their name.

> *He will nocht bow to na* part *off your kyn.*
> Sufferyt *ye ar, I trow yhe may spek weill.*—V. 884.

In Edit. 1594 and 1648 ;—to na *prince* of your kin.

Instead of *Sufferyt*, it is *Assouerit*, i.e. assured, having security, Edit. 1594 and 1620; and ridiculously, *All ordered*, Edit. 1648 and 1673. *Soueryt* is adopted, Edit. 1714. This term is more adapted to the sense than that of MS., as illustrated by the words that follow, expressive of Wallace's strict adherence to any safe conduct given by him.

> *Wallace said; " Schyr, we jangill* bot *in wayne."*—V. 920.

In MS. it is *" nocht* in wayne;" which contradicts the obvious design of the language of Wallace. In Edit. 1594 and 1620;

> —— we jangill *all* in vaine.

It seems most probable, that in the more ancient MS. whence Ramsay took his copy, *bot* had been written indistinctly, and read by Ramsay as *not*, the contraction for *nocht*.

NOTES TO THE SEVENTH BOOK.

> *Than demyt he, the fals Sotheroun amang,*
> *How thai best mycht the Scottis barownis hang.*
> *For gret* bernys *that tyme stud in till Ayr,*
> *Wrocht for the king, quhen his lugyng wes thar;*
> *Byggyt about, that no man entir mycht,*
> *Bot ane at anys, nor haiff off othir sicht.*
> *Thar ordand thai thir lordis suld be slayne.*—V. 23.

Here the Minstrel introduces his account of the savage transaction ascribed to Edward I., in causing the greatest part of the barons of the west of Scotland to be hanged, without trial, under the semblance of peace; and of the vengeance taken by Wallace, in what has been usually called "the burning of the BARNS OF AYR."

Before examining this account, I may observe, that instead of *For gret bernys*, as in MS., Edit. 1594 reads, *Four* greit barnis; and that of 1620, to the same purpose, *Foure greit barnes*. Perhaps I ought to have adopted this reading, especially as the conjunction *for*, with which ver. 25 commences, does not seem necessary as marking the connection with the words preceding.

The story of the destruction of these buildings, and of the immediate reason of it, is supported by the universal tradition of the country to this day; and local tradition is often entitled to more regard than is given to it by the fastidiousness of the learned. Whatever allowances it may be necessary to make for subsequent exaggeration, it is not easily conceivable that an event should be connected with a particular spot, during a succession of ages, without some foundation.

Sir D. Dalrymple deems this story "inconsistent with probability." He objects to it, because it is said "that Wallace, accompanied by Sir John Graham, Sir John Menteth, and Alexander Scrymgeour, constable of Dundee, went into the west of Scotland to chastise the men of Galloway, who had espoused the part of the Comyns and of the English;" and that, "*on the* 28*th August* 1298, they set fire to some granaries in the neighbour-hood of Ayr, and burned the English cantoned in them." Annals, I. 255, N. Here he refers to the relations of Arnold Blair, and to Major, and produces three objections to the narrative. One of these is, that " Comyn, the younger of Badenoch was the only man of the name of Comyn who had any interest in Galloway, and he was at that time of Wallace's party." The other two are ; that " Sir John Graham could have no share in the enterprize, for he was killed at Falkirk, 22d July, 1298;" and that " it is not probable that Wallace would have undertaken such an enterprize im-mediately after the discomfiture at Falkirk." Although it had been said by mistake that Graham and Comyn were present, this could not invalidate the whole relation ; for we often find that leading facts are faithfully narrated in a history, when there are considerable mistakes as to the persons said to have been engaged.

But although our annalist refers both to Major and Blair, it is the latter only who mentions either the design of the visit paid to the west of Scotland, or the persons who are said to have been associates in it.   The whole of Sir David's reasoning rests on the correctness of a date, and of one given *only* in the meagre remains ascribed to Arnold Blair.   If his date be accurate, the transaction at Ayr, whatever it was, must have taken place thirty-seven days afterwards.   Had the learned writer exercised his usual acumen here, had he not been resolved to throw discredit on this part of the history of Wallace; it would have been most natural for him to have supposed that this event was post-dated by Blair.   It seems, indeed, to have been long before the battle of Falkirk.   Blind Harry narrates the former in his Seventh, the latter in his Eleventh Book.   Sir David himself, after pushing the argument from the date given by Blair as far as possible, virtually gives it up, and makes the acknowledgment which he ought to have made before.   "I believe," he says, "that this story *took its rise* from the pillaging of the English quarters, about the time of the treaty of Irvine, in 1297, which, as being an incident of little consequence, I omitted in the course of this history." Here he refers to Hemingford, T. I. p. 123.

Hemingford says, that "many of the Scots and men of Galloway had in a hostile manner made prey of their stores, having slain more than five hundred men, with women and children." Whether he means to say that this took place at Ayr, or at Irvine, seems doubtful. But here, I think, we have the nucleus of the story. The *barns*, according to the diction of Blind Harry, seem to have been merely "the English quarters," erected by order of Edward for the accommodation of his troops. Although denominated *barns* by the Minstrel, and *horreas* by Arnold Blair, both writers seem to have used these terms with great latitude, as equivalent to what are now called *barracks*. It is rather surprising, that our learned annalist should view the loss of upwards of five hundred men, besides women and children, with that of their property, "as an incident of little consequence," in a great national struggle.

Major gives nearly the same account with that of Blair. Speaking of Wallace, he says: "Anglorum insignes viros apud *horrea* Aerie residentes de nocte incendit, et qui a voraci, flamma euaserunt ejus mucrone occubuerunt." Fol. LXX.

There is also far more unquestionable evidence as to the cause of this severe retaliation than is generally supposed. Lord Hailes has still quoted Barbour as an historian of undoubted veracity. Speaking of Crystal of Seton, he says :—

> It wes gret sorow sekyrly,
> That so worthy persoune as he
> Suld on sic maner hangyt be.
> Thusgate endyt his worthynes.
> And off Crauford als Schyr Ranald wes,
> And Schyr Bryce als the Blar,
> *Hangyt in till a berne in Ar.*
> *The Bruce*, III. 260. V. Note.

This tallies very well with the account given by the Minstrel.

> *Four thousand haill that nycht was in till Ayr.*
> *In gret* bernyss, *biggyt with out the toun,*
> *The justice lay, with mony bald barroun.*
> *Wallace*, VII. 334.

The testimony of the *Complaynt of Scotland*, a well known national work, written A. 1548, concurs. Speaking of the king of England, the writer says:

Ony of you that consentis til his fals conques of your cuntre, ye sal be recompenssit as your forbears var at the blac perliament at *the bernis of Ayre*, quhen kyng Eduard maid ane conuocatione of al the nobillis of

Scotland at the toune of Ayre, vndir culour of faitht and concord, quha comperit at his instance, nocht heffand suspitione of his tresonabil consait. Than thai beand in his subiectione vndir culour of familiarite, he gart hang, cruelly and dishonestly, to the nummer of sexten scoir of the maist nobillis of the cuntre, tua and tua ouer ane balk, the quhilk sextene scoir var cause that the Inglismen conquest sa far vithtin your cuntre." Compl. Scotl. p. 144.

The author refers to this as a fact universally acknowledged among his countrymen, although, it must be recollected, no edition of the Life of Wallace was printed for more than twenty years after this work was written. He introduces it again, as a proof of treachery and cruelty, which still continued to excite national feeling.

"Doubtles thai that ar participant of the cruel inuasione of Inglis men contrar thar natyue cuntreye, ther craggis sal be put in ane mair strait yoik nor the Samnetes did to the Romans, as kyng Eduard did til Scottis men at the blac parlament at *the bernis of Ayr*, quhen he gart put the craggis of sexten scoir in faldomis of cordis, tua and tua, ouer ane balk, of the maist principal of them," &c. Ibid. p. 159, 160.

> Schir Ranald *fyrst, to mak fewté for his land,*
> *The knycht, went in, and wald na langar stand.—*
> Schyr Bryss *the* Blayr *next with his eyme in past:*
> *On to the ded thai haistyt him full fast.*—V. 205.

Schir Ranald is Sir Reginald Craufurd of Loudoun, maternal uncle to Wallace. He was heritable sheriff of the county of Ayr. The grand-daughter, the heiress of the property, was married to Sir Duncan Campbell, the son of Sir Donald of Redcastle, from whom the noble family of Loudoun is descended. Reginaldus de Craveford is one of the persons chosen on the part of Robert Bruce to judge between him and John Baliol, as to their respective claims, A. 1292. V. Fœdera, II. 555. But whether this was the *Ranald* here mentioned, or his father, who was then alive, is doubtful; because our author gives the name of *Ranald* to his father, while others call him *Hugh. John* and *Hugh* de Craufurd are mentioned in two rescripts of Edward I., as barons received under his protection, A. 1255. Ibid. I. 559. 567.

Schyr Bryss the Blayr was the ancestor of the Blairs of that ilk in Ayrshire. There was a *Bryce* Blair of Blair in the seventeenth century; whence it appears that this ancient christian name was retained in the family. V. Crawfurd's Renfrew, p. 203. Nisbet, I. 211.

It deserves observation, that these are the two persons particularly named by Barbour, among those who suffered that cruel martyrdom for liberty which was inflicted by the English tyrant. *Syr Brice* is the reading of Edit. 1594 and 1620: and I am now convinced that the name ought to have stood *Bryce* in the Bruce, B. III. ver. 265; as it is corrected in the extract made in the preceding Note. But I was misled by the appearance of the letter *y* in the MS., which differs so much from its usual form, as at first view to resemble *u*.

Sir D. Dalrymple remarks; "Barbour says that Sir Brice Blair was executed in company with Sir Reginald Crawfurd; but he erroneously supposes this to have happened in Scotland." Ann. II. 19, N. Kerr follows him in this assertion. Hist. Bruce, I. 284.

But our worthy senator is so averse to give credit to anything that tends to confirm what he calls "the famous story of *the Barns of Air*," that he prefers the single testimony of Matthew of Westminster to that of Barbour; not to mention the later but concurrent one of the Minstrel. The English historian says that Reginald de Crawfurd, with Thomas and Alexander *de Brus*, "brothers of the pseudo-king," having been defeated and taken prisoners, were presented to Edward at Carlisle, "wounded and half-dead, and that he immediately ordered their execution;" and that "to this their heads bare witness, being placed on the castle and gates" of that city. Hist. p. 458.

It is surprising, however, that the difference of the dates did not make Sir David hesitate to oppose the united testimony of our oldest Scottish writers on this point: especially as the account given by Matthew of Westminster is, by his own confession, at variance with that of Robert of Langtoft. The butchery at Ayr is said to have taken place, A. 1298; this at Carlisle in the year 1306-7, about nine years after. The fact seems to be, that the Reginald he refers to was the son of the other Reginald who had suffered in "the blac parlament" at Ayr. It was he who left a daughter, his only child and heir, who, as is mentioned above, was married to Sir Duncan Campbell. V. Nisbet's Ragm. Roll. p. 18.

The third entrit, that peté was for thy,
A gentill knycht, Schyr Neill *off* Mungumry.—V. 213.

Worthi occurs in the line; but this word being under-doted, *gentill* appears on the margent. The latter is the reading of Edit. 1594, and of 1620. This person seems to have been one of the family now represented by the Earl of Eglinton. One of this family had the same christian name in the reign of James IV. V. Nisbet, I. 375.

> *Kerlé turnyt with his mastir agayne,*
> *Kneland and* Byrd, *that mekill war off mayne.*—V. 249.

All the editions have *Boyd*. It appears, however, from ver. 287, that Boyd was left in the town:

> '*Der wicht*,' he said, '*der God, sen at thou knew*
> '*Gud Robert* Boid, *quhar at thou can him se.*'

Besides, the name *Byrd* occurs B. VIII. 233, where the person thus denominated is conjoined with Boyde:

> Boyde, *Bercla*, Byrd, *and Lauder, that was wycht.*

In Edit. 1594, 1620, and 1648, this is *Baird*, apparently the ancestor of the Bairds of Newbyth, descended from Baird of Auchmedden, a very ancient family. To this family, as proprietors in Lanarkshire, Fergus, John, and Robert *Bard*, mentioned in Ragman Roll, are supposed to have belonged. V. Nisbet's Rem. p. 42. 46. Robert de *Boyd* was ancestor of the family of Kilmarnock.

> *At the* Roddis *thai mak full mony ane,*
> *Quhilk worthy ar, thocht landis haiff thai nane.*—V. 403.

This refers to the knights of St. John then made at Rhodes.

> *In all the warld na grettar payne mycht be,*
> *Than thai with in,* insufferit *sor to duell,* &c.—V. 442.

This, if not from O. Fr. *ensuairé*, wound up, lapt in, may be equivalent to *ensured ;* as the Minstrel uses *sufferance* for *souerance* or *assurance.*

> *Till* Crage Vuyn *with thre hundir he yeid.*—V. 649.

To *Craghumyre*, Edit. 1594, 1620, 1648, and 1673. *Cragunyn*, 1714 ; *Crage Vyum*, Edit. Perth. As this is connected with Lochow, it may be *Crage Ewan* in Lochdochart, as laid down in Bleau's Atlas.

> *Fast vpon* Aviss *that was bathe depe and braid.*—V. 654.

This is obviously the word in MS. But I suspect that it is an error for *Awfe*, which occurs in Edit. 1594, 1620, 1648, and 1673. It is undoubtedly the river *Awe* that is meant, whence the name of *Lochawe* or Lochow.

> *Dunkan off Lorn his* leyff *at Wallace ast;*
> *On Makfadyane with worthi men he past.*—V. 861.

In MS. it is *lyff*, apparently denoting *life*, which would render the passage self-contradictory. In Edit. 1594 and 1620, *leine;* 1648, *leave.* The meaning is ; " Duncan asked permission of Wallace to pursue Macfadyane."

Of nobill blud, and alss haill ancestré.—V. 893.

The term is not *ancestré* in MS. but may be read *imcrasé, imtrasé, uncrasé,* or *untrasé.* But as neither of these give any known sense, I have retained the word which occurs in all the editions. The only word that seems to have any resemblance is O. Fr. *entraisser* (*s',*) s'animer, s'exciter ; Gl. Roquefort.

Tharfor I will bot lychtly ryn that cace.—V. 918.

Edit. 1594, *rais;* i. e. as in Edit. 1648, *race;* which is a more natural mode of expression.

A trew squier, quhilk Rwan *hecht be nayme.*—V. 1009.

Ruthuen, Edit. 1594, i. e. Ruthven, the ancestor of the unfortunate family of Gowrie. As it is said that Wallace made him captain and hereditary sheriff of Perth, it deserves observation that his descendants for several generations seem almost exclusively to have possessed authority in that town. V. Cant's Hist. Perth, vol. II.

At Crummadé *feill Inglissmen thai slew.*—V. 1085.

This is *Cromartie,* Edit. 1594, &c.

Hew Kertyngayme *the wantgard ledis he,*
With twenty thousand off likly men to se.—V. 1171.

This refers to the battle of Stirling-bridge. He is called *Kirkinghame* in editions. But the person meant was *Cressingham,* an ecclesiastic, who was the king's treasurer, "a pompous and haughty man," says Hemingford, who hurried on the battle in opposition to the counsel of Lundie and others. Hist. p. 118. 127. 129.

In Jedwort *wod for saiffgard he had beyne.*—
Jedwort *thai tuk; and Rwan lewit he,*
At Wallace will captane off it to be.—V. 1277. 1289.

It is *Iedbrugh* in Edit. 1594 and 1620. The name of this place assumes a great variety of forms ; Gedword, Geddeworde, Gedewrde, Geddewerde, Gedworth, Gedeworth, Gedewurth, Gedewrze ; Jedworth, Jedwurth, Jed-word, Jedwort, Jedewrth, Jedwod, Jeddeburch. V. Macpherson's Geogr. Illustr. The latter is merely the modern name. The vulgar, and indeed almost universal, pronunciation, q. *Jethart*, points out what was the original designation. Here were two monasteries, one of them founded so late as A. 1513; the other was established in the year 1147. Another place, not far distant, retains the name of *Auld Jedworth*. According to Simeon of Durham, these two Jedworths were built by Ecgred, bishop of Lindis-farn, about the year 840. Dec. Script. 13. 28. 119. 121. Simeon writes it *Geddeword*.

The name, it has been conjectured, might be traced to the *Gadeni*, a tribe who anciently inhabited the whole tract of country that lies between Northumberland and the river Tiviot. Stat. Acc. I. 1. But the Gadeni have been placed, with far more probability, in Dunbartonshire. V. Pin-kerton's Enquiry, I. p. 35. 224. 320. It is obvious, that the name of the place is formed from that of the stream, which probably claims a British origin. *Gwyth* signifies a channel or drain. But whatever might be the origin of *Ged*, or *Jed*, Ecgred having chosen this river as the seat of his mansion, had given it a name by adding the Saxon term *weorth*, or *worth*, denoting a possession, or hamlet; Fundus, praedium; vicus; Lye. In the same manner the names of many places in England have been formed; as *Worth*am, *Worth*ington, Wands*worth*, Kenel*worth*, &c. Old German *wart*, and Alemannic *werts*, signify locus.

NOTES ON THE EIGHTH BOOK.

—" *He had sic message seyldyn seyne,*
" *That Wallace now as gouernowr sall ryng:*
" *Her is gret faute off a gud prince or kyng.*
" *That* kyng *off* Kyll *I can nocht wndirstand;*
" *Off him I held neuir a fur off land."*—V. 18.

That Corspatrick, Earl of Dunbar, used this provoking language, appears highly probable; as it is certain from other documents that, "when sum-moned by the guardian of Scotland, to attend a convention at Perth," he "contemptuously refused. Blind Harrie is supported by the Tower Records." Caledonia, II. 246.

I need scarcely say, that the earl had given Wallace this contemptuous designation, as being a native of the district of Kyle in Ayrshire.

" *In lyff or dede, in faith, him sall we haiff,*
" *Or ger him grant quhom he haldis for his lord :*
" *Or ellis war* schaym *in story to racord.*"—V. 44.

In MS. *schapin ;* but undoubtedly from inadvertency. It had perhaps been written *schaym.*

In till Gorkhelm *erll Patrik leiffit at rest.*
For mar power Wallace past in the west. V. 129.

Edit. 1594,—*Cokholme:* followed by 1620, and other editions. But Macpherson says that Gorkhelm, here mentioned, is "in Etrik forest." Geogr. Illustr.

Was nayne sa strang, that gat off him a strak,
Eftir agayne maid neuir a Scot to waik.—V. 285.

In Edit. 1594, *wraik,* i. e. wreck. Perhaps this is the true reading. As in MS., it may signify, "to be deficient," or "wanting," as used for *vaik.* Here we have the double negative, common in Scottish.

This ryall ost, but restyng, furth thai rid,
Till Browis feild, *&c.*—V. 493.

In Edit. 1594, *Brokis feild :* Edit. 1648, *Browes.* D. Macpherson refers to *Browis-feld* as in Teviotdale. Geogr. Illustr.

Gud Lundy *than till hym he callit thar,*
And Hew *the* Hay, *off Louchowort was ayr.*—V. 581.

"Richard de *Lundie, Lundin,* or *London,* was a powerful baron in the shire of Fife. He brought five hundred men to Wallace's aid in the encounter with Macfadyan near Craigmore, in Perthshire.—Lundie, having become dissatisfied with some of the Scottish leaders, was on the side of the English in the battle of Stirling Bridge, September 11, 1297.

"In a charter by King William the Lion to the town of Perth, 1210, one of the witnesses is Robert de *London,* the king's son. This natural son of the king had married the heiress of Lundin in Fife, and from her lands took his surname. Richard was their lineal descendant.

"In 1679, the family of Lundie, because of their descent, obtained liberty to bear the royal arms of Scotland. Afterwards the heiress married John Drummond, Earl of Melfort," second son of James, Earl of Perth. This family is now represented by the Hon. R. P. Burrel Drummond of Perth.

I have extracted the greatest part of this note from those added to the Perth Edit. of Wallace, by my worthy friend the late Reverend James Scott of Perth, well known as an accurate and indefatigable antiquary. V. also Nisbet, I. p. 64. 107.

Hew the Hay seems to be the same person who afterwards married a sister of King Robert the Bruce, the widow of Laurence Lord Abernethy. He was descended from William Hay of Errol, and was ancestor to the family of Tweeddale. V. Nisbet, I. 182. He is designed Hay of Locharret, or Lochquharret, county of Edinburgh. The ancient orthography was *Lochuswerword, Locherworn.* Sir James Dalrymple's Coll. Pref. 76 ; also *Locherward,* Ind. Chart. I. 26,—16. 9. 13.

> *All* Mydlame *land thai brynt wp in a fyr,*
> *Brak parkis doun, distroyit all the schyr.* —V. 945.

In MS. *mydlen.* This I have explained as signifying middle, or denoting lands lying in the interior of a county or district. V. Etym. Dict. But I have here adopted the reading of Edit. 1594. Wallace being represented as at this time in Yorkshire, this is probably the honour or town of Middleham in the northern part of this county. In Blean's Atlas, it is written *Midlam.* It afterwards belonged to the Nevilles, who were Earls of Richmond.

> *Amang noblis gyff cuyr ony thar was,*
> *So lang throw force in Ingland lay on cass,*
> *Sen* Brudus *deit, but battaill, bot Wallace.*—V. 962.

In editions *Brutus:* i. e. he who is called *the Brute.*

> *Than had we nayn bot ladyis to repruff.*
> *That sall* he nocht, *be God that is abuff.*
> *Vpon wemen I will na wer begyn.*—V. 1437.

In Edit. 1594, ver. 1438 is thus given ;

> That sall *not be,* be God that sitis abufe.

This might at first view seem to correspond better with the preceding line, as signifying the determination of Wallace to make no retaliation on the female sex for the treachery of men ; but as the author perhaps refers back to what is said in v. 1435, as to the king breaking any truce, made by women, as soon as he found it convenient, and then proceeds to declare that he would make no war on them, I have retained the verse as it is in MS. Thus, it expresses a determination that Edward should have no opportunity of acting so treacherous a part.

> *A harrold went, in all the haist he may,*
> *Till* Tawbane *waill, quhar at the Scottis lay.*—V. 1497.

In Edit. 1594, *Auane.* The place is the same mentioned before, v. 1170, Sanct *Awbawnys,* i. e. St Albans. If we might suppose the *Tautonie bell* to be a corruption of "St Antony's bell," we could easily account for the introduction of the letter *T* here, as an abbreviation for *Sauct.*

> *We ask her als, be wertu off this band,*
> *Our* ayris, *our king, be wrang led off Scotland.*—V. 1517.

In Edit. 1594;—

> Our *awin young* king, be wrang led fra Scotland.

Ayris is the word in MS. This may be an *erratum* for *ayr,* in singular, as Bruce is thus designed, v. 1342—*our ayr,* i.e. "heir of our kingdom." But I have retained it in plural, as by *ayris* the Minstrel might not only mean the king, but the heirs of noble families, then kept prisoners in England; as Randell, Lorn, Bowehane, &c. mentioned in connexion.

> *In the* Leynhouss *a quhyll he maid repayr—*
> *Twa monethis still he duelt in Dunbertane.*—V. 1595. 1599.

In Edit. 1594,—*Lenox,* vulgarly pronounced *Lennoss.* The mention of *Dunbertane* immediately after shows that this district is meant. V. Note on the Bruce, B. II. 40.

> *His purpos was to se the king off* France.—V. 1696.

It is undoubtedly a problematical question, whether Wallace ever was in FRANCE. Some, among whom we must reckon our historian Major, think that this is improbable. The Minstrel, it must be acknowledged, has interspersed so much fable in his narrative, as to bring discredit even on what might otherwise have been readily admitted as fact. It seems unlikely that Wallace should have left his native country twice; and the exploits ascribed to him while in France must generally be rejected, especially those said to have been performed by him in Guienne; because it is incredible that, if he had done so much injury to the English in their recent conquests there, not the slightest notice should have been taken of this by any of their historians.

But I do not see the same reason for deeming it improbable that he should ever have been in France.

1. From the great intercourse between Scotland and France, as well as from the great celebrity of the achievements of our hero, it seems very natural to suppose that Philip King of France should express an earnest desire to see him, and even send him an invitation to this purpose; and not less so, that while his hands were tied up, during a truce or peace with Edward, he should take the opportunity of gratifying his curiosity, in visiting that kingdom to which so many of his countrymen had been accustomed to resort, as one that had been long in a state of amity and alliance with their own. He might be the more disposed to a temporary change of place, from the envy which his valorous deeds had excited among the nobles of Scotland.

2. The story concerning the capture of Sir Thomas Charteris of Longueville is in so far supported by the known fact that there was a race of this name at Kinfauns; and that a two-handed sword is still shown in the castle of Kinfauns, which tradition has uniformly ascribed to this Longueville. Henry Adamson, in his Muse's Threnodie, speaking of this castle, describes it as the place,—

> - - ——which famous Longoveil
> Sometime did hold; whose ancient sword of steele
> Remaines unto this day, and of that land
> Is chiefest evident.—— *Book* VI. p. 156.

3. In the Scotichronicon it is said, that "after the battle of Roslin, Wallace, having gone on board a ship, sought to France;" that "he acquired great fame there from the dangers to which he had been exposed, not only from pirates while at sea, but afterwards from the English in France; and that this is attested by certain songs in France as well as in Scotland." The author goes so far as to assert, that Philip had applied to Edward for a truce between him and the Scots, that Philip might have a pretence for retaining Wallace for some time longer in France. Lib. XI. c. 34. MSS. Cupr. et Perth.

4. It is worthy of remark, that Major, after having mustered up several arguments against the probability of Wallace having ever been in France, at once seems to throw them all aside as of little weight, and in conclusion speaks like a man who had hitherto reasoned against his own secret convictions, acknowledging that he is unwilling expressly to deny that Wallace had been there. He closes the account with these remarkable words: Nolo tamen ob has *ratiunculas* constanter *inficias ire* ipsum oras Galliæ visitasse. Hist. Fol. LXXIV, a.

It would appear most probable, that the Charterises of Amisfield, now represented by the Earl of Wemyss and March, were connected with those of Kinfauns; from the similarity of their armorial bearings, if not also from their possession of Elcho, in the immediate vicinity of the latter. There was, however, one family of rank of this name settled in Scotland before the time assigned for the arrival of Longueville. Andrew de Charteris, who is said to have been the ancestor of the Amisfield family, swore fealty to Edward, A. 1296, and William de Charteris in 1306. V. Nisbet, Rem. Ragm. Roll, II. 23. Fœdera, II. 1015.

—Erest in weyr to Sanct Jhonstoun couth fair.—V. 1697.

Neirest but weir, &c. Edit. 1594. This makes nonsense of the passage, and has been an early alteration. Wallace did not go *nearest* to Perth, but went to the town itself. The meaning must be, "In the earliest part of spring." V. VEIR, Etym. Dict.

NOTES ON THE NINTH BOOK.

The barge, be that, *with a full werlik far,* &c.—V. 136.
In Edit. 1594, it is;

> The barge *began* with ane full weirlyke fair.

The language is defective as in MS. But *began* is scarcely the term that we could suppose the Minstrel to use. He would more probably have said;

> The barge, be that, *com* with full werlik far.

I have therefore adhered to the reading of MS. borrowing the word in brackets in the next verse, from the edition quoted above.

> " *For my trespas I wald mak sum ramed.*"
> *Wallace wyst weyll, thocht he war brocht to ded;*
> *And off his lyff sum reskew mycht he mak.*—V. 153.

The passage, as here given from the MS., is evidently deficient in sense. It is given more intelligibly in Edit. 1594.

> For my trespas I wald mak sum remeid,
> Monie saikles I haue gart put to deide.
> Wallace wist weill, thocht he to deith was brocht,
> Fra thame to chaip on na wyse micht he nocht.
> And of his lyfe sum reskew micht he mak,
> Ane better purpois syne sone than can he tak.

Ane Skelton than kepyt the careage,
A Brankstewat *that was his heretage.*—V. 625.   MS.

In Edit. 1594, and 1648;

All Brankistnahait haill, that was his heritage.

A Brankstewat seems an error for *All Brankstewat.*   Both in MS. and in
editions, the name has been evidently corrupted.   I suspect that it ought to
be *Branthwaite.*   For the Skeltons were a family of considerable antiquity
in Cumberland.   John de Skelton was knight of the shire in the reign of
Edward II.   *Armathwaite* was the designation of their property.   But
Richard Skelton, sheriff of Cumberland, in the reign of Henry VI., lived
at *Branthwaite. Brankistnahait,* and *Brankistewat,* have been originally
Brankisthwaite. Thwaite forms the termination of many local names in the
north of England.   Grose explains it; "The shelving part of the side of a
mountain."   Hutchinson's account corresponds: "Down the river of Dudden
stands the manor of *Thwaites,* between the river and the mountains, and the
ancient seat of Joseph Thwaites of Ulnerigg, Esq., and the place being a
stony mountainous country, is not everywhere altogether fit for tillage,
meadow, and pasture.   But in several parts and pieces, as they are marked
by nature, differing in form and quality of soil, or otherwise, by the inhabitants inclosed from the barren wastes of the fells; such pieces of land are
now, and were of old, called *Thwaites* in most places of the shire, sometimes with addition of their quality, as Brackenthwaite, of ferns; Swith-
waite, of rushes; Stonythwaite, of stones; *Brenthwaite,* of its steepness;
Brunthwaite, of burnt with the sun, &c."   Hist. of Cumberland, I. 531,
532. 494.
    I do not find any similar term in AS. conveying the idea of a stony place.
The signification has perhaps been originally more general, as denoting any
place separated from another, as are those "inclosed from wastes;" from
thweot-an, exscindere, q. "a place cut off" from another.

A squier Guthré *amang thaim ordand thai,*
To warn Wallace in all the haist he may.
Out off Arbroth he passit to the se.—V. 647.

    This is understood as referring to the ancestor of the Guthries of Guthrie;
and it is a strong presumption of the justness of the idea, that Arbroath is
the harbour most contiguous to the seat of this ancient family.   He is afterwards in different passages designed "the *gud* Guthré," a character which,
from all that I have seen, appears to have descended to his posterity.

In Barnan *wod he had his lugyng maid.*—V. 692.

Birnanc, Edit. 1594. This is evidently Birname wood, that has derived such celebrity from its connection with the history of Macbeth.

"The hill of Birnam, rendered classic ground by the magic pen of Shakespeare, rises with a rude and striking magnificence to an elevation higher than that of the Sidla hills in Forfarshire, opposite to it. A round mount at the bottom of Birnam hill in the south-east, is worthy of remark. It is faced with steep oaks [q. rocks?] except for a few yards where it was fortified by art. This eminence has been known for time immemorial, by the names of Court-hill, and *Duncan's-hill,* and is believed to have been on some occasions occupied by the unfortunate Scottish king of that name. It looks full in the face, at the distance of about twelve miles, the celebrated Dunsinan-hill, the seat and fortress of Macbeth." Stat. Acc. VII. 355. 374.

Fersly *thai* fled, *as fyr dois out off flynt.*—V. 746.

The reading in MS. is, *Freschly* thai *ferd.* But to this no meaning can be attached. I have therefore given it as in the editions. But I suspect that there has been some corruption of the original here, as *fled* is introduced in the next line.

Till Ardargan *he drew him prewaly.*—V. 768.

This, I suppose, must be the place now called *Ardargie,* in the Ochil Hills, parish of Forgandenny, Perthshire.

Apon the morn, with fyftene hundreth men,
Till Black Irnsyde *his gydys couth them ken.*—V. 785.

"All round this monastery [Lindores, Fife,] was *Earn-side*-wood, where Wallace defeated the English. It was anciently four miles in length, and three in breadth; now there is nothing but some few shrubs to the east of the abbey." Sibbald's Hist. Fife, P. iv. sect. 9. p. 406.

It is added in a note: "Of this wood no vestige remains. The place where it is said to have grown lies along the shore of the Frith, a considerable way below the junction of the Tay and the Earn. The name seems to countenance the tradition, that the Earn alone once flowed by the bottom of the hills of Fife, and did not unite for several miles below this with the Tay, whose course was then along the foot of the hills, forming the northern boundary of the Carse of Gowrie, which lying thus betwixt two rivers, was

frequently overflowed, and only became habitable, when, in a great inunda-
tion, the Tay burst into the Earn, where they now join."

In A. Blair's *Relationes*, this battle is said to have been fought on the
12th of June 1298.

> *Rycht weyll I wait, weschell is lewyt nayn,*
> *Fra the* Wood hawyn, *to the ferry cald* Aran.—V. 805.

Macpherson thinks that this is perhaps the same with *Portnebaryan*,
mentioned by Wyntoun, q. "the haven of bread;" *arran* signifying bread
in Gaelic, and *barra* in Welsh, Cornish, and Armoric. V. Geogr. Illustrations. Shall we add another supposition, —that *Portnebaryan* had been the
ancient name of *Port-on-craigs*, a ferry to the eastward of *Woodhaven*. The
latter still retains its ancient name. It lies opposite to Dundee.

> *—In that jornay othir to wyn or end.*—V. 1048.

The whole passage to ver. 1057, *Thai worthi Scottis*, &c. is wanting in
Edit. 1594, and subsequent editions. Both verses, 1049 and 1057, beginning in a similar manner, the intermediate ones must have been overlooked
by some transcriber for the press. In MS. ver. 1050 is; *The* cruell strakis,
&c. But as the sense requires it, I have substituted *with*, as in Edit. 1714,
followed by that of Perth, 1790.

> *The lord* Cwmyn, *that erll off Bouchane was,*
> *For auld inwy he wald* [let] *na man pass*
> *That he mycht let, in gud Wallace supplé.*—V. 1253.

According to Henry, his son John Comyn, younger of Badenoch, served
himself heir to this envy; as he attributes to him, in a special manner, the
loss of the battle of Falkirk. But the account which he gives of this battle
disagrees with that of the English writers, who give not the slightest hint of
such variance among the chieftains, as, had it really taken place, could
not have been totally unknown to their opponents.

William, one of this family, was Chancellor to King David I., and in the
year 1140, by the grant of the Empress Maud, was made Bishop of Durham.
Crawfurd's Officers, p. 7. So powerful did it become, that in the reign of
Alexander III. there were three earls and one lord of this name, besides
thirty knights of landed property. Nisbet, I. 367.

I need scarcely say that Comyn was competitor with the elder Bruce for
the crown, as boasting the same blood. This ancient and honourable family
is now represented by Sir William Cumyn Gordon, of Altyre and Gordons-
town, Baronet.

A cruell captane intill Erth *duelt thar,*
In Ingland born, and hecht Thomlyn off Wayr.—V. 1283.

It is *Erth* also in Edit. 1594; *Airth* in that of 1620, and those of a later age.

" The tower at Airth was built before Sir William Wallace's time. This tower is in good repair; it makes part of the house of Airth, and bears the name of *Wallace's Tower*." Stat. Acc. III. 493, 494.

Alexander de Airth, or Erth, is one of those whose names are recorded in the Ragman Roll. V. Nisbet, Rem. p. 23.

" The Erths of that ilk were once a very considerable family in this shire, being proprietors of Airth, Elphingstone, Carnock, and Plean. We find Adam de Erth mentioned among the commissioners who were appointed, in 1248, to ratify an agreement with England, concerning the regulations called the *Border-laws*. Bernard de Erth, who was probably a son of this Adam, married before 1271, one of the three daughters and co-heiresses of Finlaus de Campsie, a cadet of the family of Lennox." Nimmo's Stirling-shire, p. 516, 517. In the reign of James I. the eldest daughter of William Airth married " a son of the ancient family of Clackmannan, who thereupon came into possession of the lands of Airth. The family of Erth, like others, took their sirname from their lands; but it is now quite extinct in this country." Ibid.

Than to Faslan *the worthy Scottis can pass,*
Quhar erll Malcom was bidand at defence.—V. 1518.

In editions it is *Falkland*. But this being so distant from the earl's dis-trict, and from Dunbarton, where Wallace was immediately before, it must be an error. Macpherson places Faslan near the head of the Gairloch, above Roseneath, Dunbartonshire. V. Hist. Map of Scotl. In the passage, ver. 1514, Wallace and his party are said indeed to take their course thither from *Roseneath*, now a well known seat of the noble family of Argyle.

And eftir sone thar uncle couth thaim ta,
Gud Robert Keth, *had thaim fra Glaskow toun;*
Atour the se in Frans he maid thaim boun.—V. 1558.

This exactly tallies with the account given by Godscroft. V. p. 20.

A mariage als thai gert ordane him till,
The lady Ferss.—V. 1566.

In editions *Ferres*. On this head Godscroft says; " His next wife was an English lady called *Ferrar*, or *Ferrais*, of which name we find the Earls of Darbie to have beene in the dayes of King Henry the Third." Hist. Dougl. p. 16. In the Fœdera they are designed *De Ferrariis*.

The Sanchar *was a castell fayr and strang.*—V. 1577.

Sanquhair, Edit. 1594. But here, and in the rest of the narrative, I have replaced what must have been the original term, as in Edit. 1620 and 1648, *Sanquhair*. "The wattyr of Craw," ver. 1606, must be the rivulet now called Crawick, which falls into the Nith. V. Stat. Acc. VI. 451. There we are informed, that "the old castle of Sanquhair had been a building of considerable magnitude and extent;" and that "it is said to have been for some time in the possession of the English in the reign of Edward I., and to have been recaptured by Sir William Douglas," as is here related. Ibid. p. 460, N.

And Jhonstoun als, that duelt in [to] Housdaill.—V. 1790.

This, in editions, is rendered *Eskdaill*. But this is undoubtedly a mistake. *Housdaill* is evidently the asperated pronunciation of the name of that district called *Eusdaill*, as being watered by the river *Ewes*, which joins the Esk at Langholm. V. Bleau's Atlas, p. 47. This seems to have been the ancestor of the Marquisses of Annandale.

Thir thre capdanis he stekit in that stound,
Off Durisdeyr, Enoch, and Tybur mur.—V. 1806.

"The vestiges of *Tiber's* castle, which has been a large building, are to be seen on the banks of the Nith. A small part of the wall next the river remains. Fosses are visible, and some entrenchments where it was most accessible. It is supposed that the barony of *Tiber* is named from Tiber, or Tiberius. There is a Roman encampment too. The English had a garrison in this castle in the time of Sir William Wallace, who took it by surprise." Stat. Acc. P. of Penpont, I. 209.

NOTES ON THE TENTH BOOK.

In till a playn set tentis and palyon,
South hald *Fawkyrk.*—V. 89.

I have hesitated whether this be not an erratum for *half* or *halff*, fre-

quently used by our old writers in the sense of quarter; but have retained
the term as in MS. Edit. 1594 has,—

South the Faukirk, &c.

If *hald* be the original term, it may lead us to the sense of the common
termination in vulgar language, as in *Southilt, Wessilt.* V. EΛSSILT, Etym.
Dict. Thus it might be resolved, "*Hald,*" or hold, "to the south of
Falkirk." Isl. *halld-a* signifies, viam dirigere; Haldorsoni Lex.

The lauch way till Enrawyn thai ryd.—V. 622.

Innerauyn, Edit. 1594; *Inneravin,* Edit. 1648. More properly *Inver-
avon,* a village near the mouth of the river Avon in Stirlingshire, a little
to the south of Kinneil. V. Nimmo's Map of Stirlingshire. The rhyme
requires that this should be pronounced as a word of four syllables.

For weill thai wyst, that it was Jhon off Lyn,
Scottis to slay, he said, it was no syn.—V. 803.

It is not improbable that there might be, in that age, some dreaded English pirate, denominated perhaps from *Lynne* in Norfolk, especially as it
is said that his ship was not seen by Wallace and his companions till they
were opposite to the mouth of the Humber. But I have not met with any
historical traces of him.

The Roman [bukis] that than was in Scotland,
He gart be brocht to scham, quhar thai thaim fand;
And, but radem, thai brynt thaim thar ilkan;
Salysbery oyss our clerkis than has tane.—V. 1003.

The Roman *buikes* that then war in Scotland,
He gart thame beir to *cume* quhar thai thaim fand, &c.—Edit. 1594.

The Roman *bookes,* &c.
Hee gart them beare to *Scone* where they them fand.—Edit. 1620.

Although the essential term, *bukis,* has been omitted by Ramsay, the
MS. alone makes sense of the passage. Hart's emendation is equal in
absurdity with the reading of Edit. 1594. By the *Salysbery oyss,* I need
scarcely say, those missals are meant which were formed *secundum usum
Sarisburiensem.* This agrees with the account given by Bellenden.
"He brint all the Cronikles of Scotland, with all maner of bukis als
weill of deuyne seruyce as of othir materis; to that fyne that the memorye
of Scottis suld peris. He gart the Scottis wryte bukis efter *the vse of Sarum,*

and constranit thaym to say efter that *vse*." Cronikle, Fol. CCIX, a. Libros sacros *Anglico ritu* conscribi jussit. Boeth.

> *Schir Jhon Ramsay and Rowan than fled north,*
> *To thair cusyng that lord was off Fyllorth.*
> *Quhilk past with thaim throw Murray landis rycht;*
> *So fand thai thar a gentill worthi knycht*
> *At* Climace *hecht, full cruell ay had beyn,*
> *And fayndyt weill amang his enemys keyn.*—V. 1021.
> *The knycht* Climés *off Ross com sodeynly*
> *In Murray land with thair gud chewalry.*—B. XI. v. 743.

It appears that this knight belonged to the county of Ross; and it has been conjectured that he was a son or brother of the Earl of Ross, who was at this time a prisoner in England. V. Notes to Perth Edit. p. 25, 26. In Edit. 1594 and 1620, it is in both places *Clement*.

NOTES ON THE ELEVENTH BOOK.

> *A mow off corn he* bygit *thaim about.*—V. 339.

This is given according to Edit. 1594, &c. In MS. it is *gyhyt*. But this must certainly be an error; unless we should suppose it to be from AS. *gehyd*, "tectus, abditus, absconditus, hid, hidden, covered." Somner.

> *Fra Butler had* apon *gud Wallace* seyn,
> *Throuch auld malice he wox ner wod for teyn.*—V. 401.

We have here one proof, among many in our old national works, of the danger of editors rashly venturing to change the language. In Edit. 1594, it is ;—

Fra Butteller had *on feild* gude Wallace seyne, &c.

The editor had supposed that *seyn apon*, being an obsolete phrase in his time, must of necessity be improper. He had not known that it is very ancient, being pure Anglo-Saxon. The verb is used in a neuter sense; and *seyn apon* signifies beheld, looked upon. Thus *on se-on* is, intueri, aspicere in. *On* that wundor *seon ;* Istud miraculum intueri.

Quhen thai com ner, a nobill knycht it was,
The quhilk to name hecht Elyss *off* Dundass.—V. 533.

This is the ancestor of the ancient house of Dundas of that ilk. Helias, or as here written *Elyss*, seems to have been a common name in this family. The first on record is Helias, son of Uchtred, who got the lands of Dundas, A. 1124, in the reign of Alexander I. One of the same christian name appears as witness to a charter in the reign of Alexander II. *Serle* de Dundas, probably the father of our Elyss, is mentioned in Ragman Roll. V. Nisbet's Remarks, p. 34, 35, and Heraldry, I. 275.

And Schyr Jhon Scot *ck, a worthi knycht,*
In to Straithern a man off mekill mycht.—V. 535.

"He was probably a descendant of the family of Scott of Balweary in Fife." This "family continued till the reign of Charles I.," and "is now represented by the Scotts of Ancrum, in Roxburghshire." Notes to Edit. Perth, p. 49.

Schyr Jhon Menteth *in till his wit has fund,*
How he suld best his purpos to fullfill, &c.—V. 948.

The account given of the treachery of MENTETH is one of these points on which Sir D. Dalrymple shews his historical scepticism. He introduces it in language calculated to inspire doubt into the mind of the reader; observing that "the popular tradition is, that his *friend* Sir John Menteth betrayed him to the English." Annals, I. 281. It is rather strange that he should express himself in this manner, at the very moment that he quotes the Scotichronicon on the margent; as if this venerable record, when a modern should be disposed to adopt a theory irreconcileable with its testimony, were entitled to no higher regard than is due to "popular tradition."

He adds; "Sir John Menteth was of high birth, a son of Walter Stewart Earl of Menteth." I can perceive no force in this remark, unless it be meant to imply that there never has been an instance of a man of noble blood acting the part of a traitor. On the same ground we might quarrel with all the evidence given of the conspiracies formed against Robert Bruce; and even call in question the murder of that amiable and accomplished prince James I.

But "at this time," we are told, "the important fortress of Dumbarton was committed to his [Menteth's] charge by Edward." Here, it would seem, the learned writer fights the poor Minstrel with his own weapons. For I find no evidence of this fact in the Fœdera, Hemingford, or the

Decem Scriptores; and Lord Hailes has referred to no authority; so that there is reason to suspect, to use his own language, that he here "copies" what "is said by *Blind Harry*, whom no historian but Sir Robert Sibbald will venture to *quote*." If Harry's narrative be received as authority, it is but justice to receive his testimony as he gives it. Now, in the preceding part of his work, he represents Menteth as holding the castle of Dunbarton at least with the consent of Wallace, while acknowledged as governor of Scotland. It would appear, indeed, that the whole district of the Lennox had been entrusted to him.

> In the Leynhouss a quhill he maid repayr ;
> Schyr Jhon Menteth that tym was captane thar.—B. VIII. 1595.

But even at this time there was something dubious in the conduct of Menteth. While he retained the castle, the English held the town under Edward.

> In peess thai duelt, in trubyll that had beyn,
> And trewbut payit till Ingliss capdanis keyn.
> Schir Jhon Menteth the castell had in hand :
> Bot sum men said, thar was a prewa band
> Till Sotheroun maid, be menys off that knycht,
> In thar supple to be in all his mycht.—B. IX. 1393.

It is perfectly conceivable, that, although it was known to Wallace that Menteth had some secret understanding with the English, this artful man might persuade him that he only wished an opportunity of wreaking the national vengeance on them, or at least of more effectively serving the interest of Wallace when he saw the proper time. Although Wallace had been assured that Menteth had taken an oath of fealty to Edward, he would have had no more reason for distrusting him than for distrusting by far the greatest part of the nobility and landholders of Scotland, who, as they believed, from the necessity of despair had submitted to the usurper.

John de Menteth is designed by Arnold Blair *immanis proditor ;* and the writer proceeds to curse him as if with bell, book, and candle. Relationes, p. 8.

Sir David aims another blow at this account in the following words: "That he had ever any intercourse of friendship or familiarity with Wallace, I have yet to learn." But the truth is, the worthy judge does not seem disposed to *learn* this. It is difficult to say what evidence will satisfy him. The incidental hints, in the preceding part of the poem, in regard to Wallace's connection with Menteth, all perfectly agree with the mournful termination. Such confidence had he in him, according to the Minstrel, that he not only resided in Dunbarton castle for two months, while Menteth had the charge of it, but gave orders for building "a house of stone" there, apparently that he might enjoy his society.

Twa monethis still he duelt in Dunbertane ;
A houss he foundyt apon the roch off stayne ;
Men left he thar till bygg it to the hycht.—B. VIII. 1599.

But independently of the testimony of Blind Harry, Bower expressly
asserts the co-operation of Menteth with Wallace, Graham, and Scrymgeour, in the suppression of the rebellious men of Galloway. In hoc ipso
anno [1298], viz., xxviii die mensis Augusti, dominus Wallas Scotiæ custos,
cum Johanne Grhame, et *Johanne de Menteith*, militibus, necnon Alexandro
Scrimzeour constabulario villæ de Dundee, et vexillario Scotiæ, cum quin-
quagentis militibus armatis, rebelles Gallovidiensis punierunt, qui regis
Angliæ et Cuminorum partibus sine aliquo jure steterunt. These words,
which seem to be a quotation in the Relationes of Blair from the Scotichronicon, are not found in the MSS. from which Goodall gave his edition.
They appear to have formed the commencement of the xxxii. chapter of the
eleventh book, one of the two chapters here said to be wanting. Now this,
whether it be the language of Bower, or of Blair, could not have been
borrowed from the Minstrel, for the circumstance is overlooked by him.
It seems to refer to that period of the history of Wallace, in which he is
said to have made a circuit through Galloway and Carrick.

Fra Gamlis peth the land obeyt him haill
Till Ur wattir, bath strenth, forest, and daill.
Agaynis him in *Galloway* hous was nayne, &c.—B. VI. 793.

It is to be observed, that John Major expressly affirms the treachery of
Menteth, as acting in concert with Aymer de Valloins, Earl of Pembroke.
He says that Menteth was considered as his most intimate friend ;—ipsi
Vallaceo putatus amicissimus. Hist. Fol. LXXIII. Now, although he
rejects many of the transactions recited by Blind Harry "as false," so
far is he from insinuating the slightest hesitation as to this business, that
he formally starts an objection as to the imprudence of Wallace in not being
more careful of his person, and answers it by remarking, that "no enemy
is more dangerous than a domestic one." He differs from the Minstrel,
in saying that Wallace was "captured *in* the city of Glasgow."

It may be added, that Bower expressly asserts that Wallace, "suspecting
no evil, was fraudulently and treacherously seized *at* Glasgow by Lord John
de Menteth." Scotichron. XII. 8. Bower again refers to the treacherous
conduct of Menteth towards Wallace when afterwards relating a similar
plan which he had laid for taking King Robert Bruce prisoner, under pretence of delivering up to him the castle of Dunbarton, on condition of his
receiving a hereditary right to the lieutenancy of the Lennox. V. Lib. xii.
c. 16. 17. Vol. II. 243. These two chapters are not in all the MSS., but
are found in those of Cupar, Perth, and Dunblane. Now, Bower was born

A. 1385. Ibid. II. 401. The date assigned to the Scotichronicon, as published with his continuation, is 1447, and that to the Minstrel's poem 1470. V. Pinkerton's Maitland Poems, Intr. LXXXVI. LXXXIX. It is therefore impossible that Bower could have borrowed the account given of Menteth from Blind Harry. Bower was born, indeed, only eighty or eighty-one years after the fact referred to; and, considering the elevation of the character of Wallace, and the great attachment of his countrymen even to this day, as well as the multitude of his enemies, it is totally inconceivable that a whole nation, learned and unlearned, should concur in imputing this crime to one man *without* the most valid reasons.

Wyntown finished his *Cronykil* A. 1418. He, it is generally believed, was born little more than fifty years after the butchery of our magnanimous patriot. Sir D. Dalrymple could not, one would suppose, reasonably object to his testimony. Let us hear it.

> A thousand thre hundyr and the fyft yhere
> Eftyr the byrth of oure Lord dere,
> Schyre Jhon of Menteth in tha days
> Tuk in Glasgw Willame Walays,
> And send hym in-til Ingland swne,
> Thare wes he quartaryd and wndwne
> Be dyspyte and hat inwy:
> Thare he tholyd this martyry.
>
> CRON. VIII. c. 20.

I shall only add an important proof from the Lanercost MS., referred to in the *Preliminary Remarks.* "*Captus* fuit Willelmus Waleis per unum Scottum, scilicet per dominum Johannem de Mentiphe, et usque London ad Regem adductus, et adjudicatum fuit quod traheretur, et suspenderetur, et decollaretur, et membratim divideretur, et quod viscera ejus comburentur, quod factum est; et suspensum est caput ejus super pontem London, armus autem dexter super pontem Novi Castri super Tynam, et armus sinister apud Berwicum, pes autem dexter apud Villam Sanctis Johannis, et pes sinister apud Aberden." Fol. 211. *Mentiphe* is obviously an *erratum* for *Mentithe*.

> *A spy thai maid, and folowed him but let*
> *Till Robrastoun, was ner be the way syd,*
> *And bot a howss quhar Wallace oysyt to byd.* —V. 996.

i. e. Only *one* house, where he was wont to conceal himself, while waiting for Bruce.

"At Robroystone, in this parish, [Cadder, Lanarkshire] on the 11th September 1305, Sir William Wallace was betrayed and apprehended by Sir John Monteath, a favourite of King Edward I. of England. After he was overpowered, and before his hands were bound, it is said he threw his sword into Robroystone Loch. An oaken *couple* or joist, which made part of the barn in which the Scottish hero was taken, is still to be seen in this neighbourhood, and may yet last for ages." Stat. Acc. VIII. 481, 482.

> *Rycht suth it is, a martyr was Wallace,*
> *Als* Osauold, Edmunt, Eduuard, *and* Thomas.—V. 1307.

In Edit. 1620, these lines are thus varied :—

> Wallace was martyred, the trueth to you to tell,
> As were *Osweld, Edmond, Edward* with paine fell.

Osauold must be Osuald, the King of Northumbria, who, having embraced Christianity, was slain by Penda the pagan king of Mercia. Bed. Hist. Eccl. III. 9. Eng. Martyrol. p. 213, 214. *Edmunt* is St Edmund, King of the East Angles, barbarously slain by the Danes of Northumbria for confessing Christ. Martyrol. p. 319. *Eduuard* seems to be St Edward, King of the West Saxons, slain at the instigation of his step-mother. Ibid. p. 72. *Thomas* is most probably the well-known Thomas a Becket.

Wyntown informs us that even in his day, long before that of the Minstrel, various works were written recording the deeds of Wallace; but he concludes that these fell short of the truth, as to their extent at least.

> Of his gud dedis and manhad
> Gret gestis, I hard say, ar made :
> Bot sa mony, I trow, noucht
> As he in-til hys dayis wroucht,
> Quha all hys dedis of prys wald dyte,
> Hym worthyd a gret buk to wryte:
> And all thai to wryte in here
> I want bathe wyt and gud laysere.
> CRON. VIII. c. 15. ver. 79.

The character given to Wallace, by Andro Hart, is worthy of being preserved:

"This was the end of this worthy man's life, who, for high spirit in enterprising dangers, for fortitude in execution, comparable in deed to the most famous chiftains amongst the ancients, for loue to his natiue countrey second to none, he onely free, the rest slaues,—could neither bee bought with benefites, nor compelled by force to leaue the publike cause which he had once profest; whose death appeared more to be lamented, that being inuincible, to his enemy he was betrayed by his familiar, that in no case should have done so." Pref. to Life of Wallace, p. 14.

Such is the affectionate remembrance of this illustrious defender of the liberties of Scotland, that his name is retained in many other places besides those mentioned in the preceding Notes.

On the hill of " Couthboanlaw, now by corruption called Quothquanlaw, —the common people, to this day, point out with much fond admiration, *Wallace's Chair*, where he had his abode, and held conferences with his followers, before the battle of Biggar. The chair is a large rough stone, scooped in the middle." P. Libberton, Lanarkshire, Stat. Acc. II. 235. This is called *Quodquen* in a charter of the Duke of Albany. Robertson's Ind. 167, 21.

In the town of Ayr they still point out the ancient tower* in which Wallace was imprisoned, and so cruelly treated, that he was at length thrown down from the battlements as dead. Common tradition gives the same account of this barbarous conduct as the Minstrel has done:

> Quhen thai presumyt he suld be werray ded,
> Thai gart scrwandys, with outyn langer pleid,
> With schort awiss on to the wall him bar ;
> Thai kest him our out of that bailfull steid,
> Off him thai trowit suld be no mor ramede,
> In a draff myddyn, quhar he remannyt thar.—B. 11. 252.

The building still bears his name, and appears to be the very same as it was in his time. It has been more fully brought into notice by the allusion of a poet, who, whatever were his defects, had power to stamp a deathless name on the subject of his muse, although it had not been otherwise entitled to this distinction.

> The drowsy Dungeon-clock had number'd two,
> And *Wallace-Tower* had sworn the fact was true.
> BURNS'S *Brigs of Ayr.*

" In one of the hills above Wandel mill there is *Wallace's Camp*, so called from that great Scotch warrior, who encamped here." The walls of the castle of Lamington " still remain some stories high, very thick and strong. It was built by a laird of Lamington, of the ancient and honourable name of Baillie, *with* whom the aforesaid Sir William Wallace was *allied by marriage;* in proof of which, and as a piece of curiosity, Wallace's chair is now in Bonnington, in the possession of Lady Ross Baillie, the representative of the family of Lamington, being removed from the tower of that place. The chair is remarkably broad and stout." P. of Lamington, Stat. Acc. VI. 557, 558. V. Note on B. VI. 47, above, p. 374, &c.

I have seen this chair at Bonnington, which is of oak, the posts of it at least, and otherwise corresponding with the description given in the Statistical Account. I am informed that there is a rock in the Pap Craig, a part of Tinto, which is still called *Wallace's Chair;* and that another in

---

* This building was taken down in 1835 and rebuilt.

the parish of Symington bears the same name, in a place called the Castlehill.

On the estate of Gladswood, parish of Mertoun, Berwickshire, are still pointed out what are called the *Camp-braes*, where, according to the harmonious voice of popular tradition, Wallace had his camp before one of his battles. It has had two ditches with ramparts; and being situate on the neck of land at the confluence of Leader with the Tweed, might have been rendered almost unassailable, in that age, by a line of communication between the two rivers.

" On the west side of Clatto-moor, are the traces of a camp. It is generally believed to have been occupied by a part of Agricola's army, and afterwards by Alpin, Wallace, and Monk. Tradition reports that 'Wallace pitched his camp on Clatto-hill, and ground his corn at Philaw's mill,' which is about half a mile from the place where the traces of the camp are seen." P. Strathmartin, Forfarshire, Stat. Acc. XIII. 99.

"Tradition says, that the Figget Whins, formerly a forest, afforded shelter and a place of rendezvous to Sir William Wallace and his myrmidons, when they were preparing to attack Berwick." P. Duddingstone, county of Edinburgh, Stat. Acc. XVIII. 877.

" On the face of the hill " of Kinnoul, " there is a cave in a steep part of the rock, which, it is said, will contain about a dozen of men. It is called the *Dragon-hole*. There is a tradition among the common people, that Sir William Wallace hid himself in this hole of the rock, when he absconded for some time." P. Kinnoul, Perthshire, Stat. Acc. XVIII. 560.

The same useful work contains an anecdote, which, at least from the circumstances, is worthy of insertion here. The article was written A. 1795 or 1796.

"There is a very respectable man in Longforgan, [Perthshire,] of the name of Smith, a weaver, and the farmer of a few acres of land, who has in his possession a stone, which is called *Wallace's Stone*. It is what was formerly called in this country a *bear stone*, hollow like a large mortar, and was made use of to unhusk the bear or barley, as a preparation for the pot, with a large wooden mell, long before barley-mills were known. Its station was on one side of the door, and covered with a flat stone for a seat, when not otherwise employed. Upon this stone Wallace sat on his way from Dundee, when he fled, after killing the governor's son, and was fed with bread and milk by the goodwife of the house, from whom the man, who now lives there, and is proprietor of the stone, is lineally descended, and here his forbeers (ancestors) have lived ever since, in nearly the same station and circumstances, for about 500 years." Stat. Acc. XIX. 561, 562. This refers to what is related in Book I. 257, &c.

In the castle of Dunbarton they pretend to shew the mail, and, if I mistake not, also the sword of Wallace. If he was confined in that fortress by Menteith, before being sent into England, as some have supposed, it is not improbable that his armour might be left there. The popular belief on this head, however, is very strong; of which I recollect a singular proof, which took place many years ago, and of which I was an eye-witness. In the procession of King Crispin, at Glasgow, his majesty was always preceded by one on horseback, appearing in armour, as his *champion.* In former times, this champion of the awl thought it enough to wear a leathern jerkin, formed like one of mail. One fellow, however, was appointed, of a more aspiring genius than his predecessors, who was determined to appear in real mail; and who, having sent to Dunbarton castle, and hired the use of Wallace's armour for a day, made his perambulations with it through the streets of Glasgow. I can never forget the ghastly appearance of this poor man, who was so chilled and overburdened by the armour, that, as the procession went on, he was under the necessity of frequently supporting himself with a cordial. It was said that he took to bed immediately after the termination of this procession, and never rose from it. From that time forward, his successors in office were content to wear the proper badge of their profession.

It is generally admitted that our hero was the son of Sir Malcolm Wallace of Ellerslie in Renfrewshire, by the daughter of Sir Ranald Crawfurd, High Sheriff of Ayr, of whom the Minstrel says;

> Malcolm Wallas hir gat in mariage,
> That *Elrisle* than had in heretage,
> *Auchinbothe*, and other syndry place.—Book I. ver. 27.

It appears that the metre, corresponding with the modern pronunciation, requires that this word should have been accented as above.

Ellerslie, also written *Elderslee*, is about three miles to the south-west of Paisley, Renfrewshire. The old house, called by Crawfurd, "the castle," is still habitable. Near it is a tree, which, according to the account I received on the spot, was planted by Wallace himself: but this, like most other traditions, assumes a very different aspect, according to Semple's narration. "The large oak-tree," he says, "called *Wallace's Tree*, is still growing, standing alone in a little enclosure, a few yards south from the great road between Paisley and Kilbarchan, being on the east side of Elderslee rivulet, the manour of Elderslee being a few yards distant from the rivulet. They say that Sir William Wallace and 300 of his men hid themselves upon that tree among the branches (the tree being then in full blossom) from the English. The tree, indeed, is very large, and well spread in the branches, the trunk being about twelve feet in circumference." Crawfurd's Renfrewshire, p. 260.

About the year 1769, Ellerslie was sold to Alexander Speirs, Esq., who took his designation from it, by Archibald Campbell, Esq., W.S., who had married Helen Wallace, a lady lineally descended from a collateral branch of the family of Wallace.

Auchinbothé is in some old writings called *Auchinbothie-Wallace*, as distinguished from the lands of *Auchinbothie-Blair*. Thus, in an old Valuation Book, made A. 1654, in the time of Cromwell, we have the following account:—" The 5 mark (land) of Auchinbothie-Wallace subdivydit as s^d is, Mastar [the proprietor]

33 lib. 6sh. 8d. Feuars 366 lib. 13sh. 4d.	400	0	0
The 5 m^k land of Auchinbothie-Blair	383	6	8"

It is supposed that Auchinbothie-Blair belonged to Blair, the companion of Wallace, who was of the Blairs of that ilk in Renfrewshire. The lands of Thornley, in the same county, are said to be designed, in some old writs, the lands of *Thornley-Blair*, alias Thornley-Wallace; and it has been also supposed that these lands had been given by Wallace to his companion of this name. But the latter is undoubtedly a mistake; for in our records *Thornylé* or *Thornley*, as it is also written, appears as the property of the Wallaces till the time of Robert III., when it was given, by John Wallace of Craigie, to the Abbey of Paisley. Ind. Chart. 142, 80. V. also 97, 324. —131, 25.

The Valuation Book above quoted also mentions Wallace of Neilstonside, Wallace of Dungraine, Wallace of Bardraine, &c. I am informed that there is now no proprietor of this name in the county of Renfrew, excepting Wallace of Kelly, in the parish of Innerkip, whose ancestors resided in that of Neilston.

In the Edinburgh Evening Courant of May 19, 1817, it is said that "the statue of Sir William Wallace, erected by the Earl of Buchan at Dryburgh, was designed exactly from the authentic portrait of him, painted in watercolours during his residence in France, which was purchased by the father of the late Sir Philip Ainslie of Pilton, knight. The hero is represented in the ancient Scottish dress and armour, with a shield hanging from his left hand, and leaning lightly on his spear with his right."

I shall conclude these miscellaneous notices with the just and beautiful reflection made by a statistical writer. After remarking that the principle cascade, in one of the rivulets in the parish of Greenock, "bears the name of Wallace, our brave and disinterested patriot," he subjoins: " How many monuments, far more durable than statues or columns, has grateful posterity bestowed throughout Scotland on this distinguished friend of liberty ! In this part of the country, steep precipices, high falls of water, huge rocks, and Roman stations and encampments, not unfrequently bear his name." Stat. Acc. V. 566.

The editor takes the liberty of subjoining, as a slender tribute to the memory of one to whom our country owes so much, a few verses written a considerable number of years ago, in consequence of a visit to a place in the vicinity of Lanark, which has acquired celebrity from having afforded Wallace a temporary shelter from the fury of his enemies.

ADDRESS TO CARTLANE CRAIGS.

Ye Cartlane Craigs, your steepy sides
    Let Nature's votaries explore,
To learn what fossils here she hides,
    Or find some plant unknown before.

A far more precious vein I seek;
    And here, I know, 'twas once conceal'd;
A simple—that can nerve the weak,
    And prowess to the fearful yield.

Blest Freedom flourish'd in this wild,
    When banish'd from each cultur'd spot:
Expiring Albin saw, and smil'd,
    And all her wounds and woes forgot.

And still the rugged rock, fair plant,
    Hath been thy lov'd, thy native soil;
Remote from Luxury's deadly haunt,
    Thy dwelling 'mongst the sons of toil.

Thy arms entwin'd around the rock,
    And shrouded by a fleece of snow,
The tyrant-tempest thou canst mock,
    That rudely strives to lay thee low.

Ye towering cliffs, your form upright,
    The awful frown ye downward send,
Seem to portray that faithful knight,
    Who to his foes would never bend.

I love thy gloom, thou cavern drear;
  Such magic influence quite unfelt,
Where lordly domes their turrets rear;
  —Here Freedom and her First-born dwelt.

Hence bursting, like the wrathful blast,
  That issues from thy hollow glade,
To hostile Lanark Wallace pass'd,
  And low the haughty *Southeron* laid.

But why a pledge so precious left?
  Thou, Chieftain, might'st thy foes have known
—Of life thy lovely partner's reft,
  Of life—far dearer than thy own.

Base *Hesilrig*, I hate thy name!
  Thy crime a Pompey's praise would mar:
A woman slay!—thou soldier's shame!
  With women only could'st thou war.

Yet worthy thou of such a lord;
  And school'd his purpose to fulfil,
No right who knowledg'd, but the sword,
  No reason, save his sovereign will:

The forms of justice, if employ'd,
  Who still her sacred essence scorn'd;
Each faithful witness first destroy'd,
  Then Falsehood's base-born brood suborn'd.

An ancient kingdom, could he think,
  The scourge of his,—might thus be won?
Thy name, crown'd traitor, still shall stink,
  While Albin boasts one freeborn son!

Thou, Edward, many a traitor vile,
  —Thy kindred true—didst aggrandize:
Nor force, nor flattery,—dastard guile
  Alone, could Wallace make thy prize.

Him—who could not be taught to crouch,
  Nor grace, nor justice, thine to save:

2 D

Thou knew'st our Lion ne'er would couch,
While Wallace liv'd his keeper brave.

His name, who Scotia's fetters broke,
Shall never lose its power to charm,
Who liv'd to shield her,—dying spoke
The weakness of her spoiler's arm.

ADDITIONAL NOTE TO BOOK FIFTH.

Vpon the morn to the Gilbank *he went;—*
For his deyr eyme, yong Auchinlek, *duelt thar,*
Brothyr he was to the schirreff off Ayr.—V. 467.

It bears the name of *Gilbanke* in Edit. 1594 and 1648. In the Sixth
Book, v. 226, the same person is designed *Awchinlek off Gilbank*.

Macpherson mentions Gilbank, in his Geographical Illustrations, referring
to Blind Harry; but he marks it as a place "the exact position" of which
"is not known."

But there is a property, distant only about half a mile from the Fall of
Stonebyres, below Lanark, which still bears the name of *Gillbank*, as it
is designed in Forrest's Map of Lanarkshire. There is another place called
Gill, belonging to Lockhart of Lee, on the north side of the Mouse, opposite to Jerviswood, about half a mile above Cartlane Craigs. Here are the
remains of a very old castle, the walls of which are very thick. It is seated
on a promontory betwixt two gullies. It has been suggested, that this
might be the place referred to, as there are no vestiges of ancient building
at Gillbank. But the claim undoubtedly belongs to the latter; as it not
only retains the name, but in our old deeds, although with a change of
orthography, is conjoined with a place called Auchinleck.—Terrae de Stane-
byres, *Auchinlek*, Greinrig, Teathes, et *Kilbank*. Inquis. Retornat. Com.
Lanark, (149,) A. 1625. It is given as the property of the Marquis of
Hamilton. The same places are mentioned, with the addition of *Over
Auchinlek*, ibid. (239.)

This place had been honoured to be the head-quarters of our hero, while
he resided in this part of the country, at least before his open attacks on the
English. For it is said ;

In Laynrik oft till sport he maid repair.
Quhan that he went fra Gilbank to the toune,
And he fand men that was off that falss nacioune,
To Scotland thai dyde neuir grewance mar.—B. V. v. 567.

" Yong Auchinlek" could be *eyme* or uncle to Wallace, only on the sup-position that his father had married Wallace's maternal grandmother, the widow of Sir Reginald (or Hugh) Crauford. His chief property was in Ayrshire. The heirs male failing, James IV. gave the lands of Auchinleck to a younger son of Boswell of Balmuto. Thus the family of Boswell of Auchinleck is lineally descended from Auchinleck of that ilk. V. Nisbet, I. 60.

So late as the year 1617, there was a gentleman of this name who held half of the property of Tweedie, in the barony of Stonehouse, distant only a few miles from Gillbank.—Jacobus Auchinleck, haeres Jacobi Auchinleck de Twedie, avi,—in baronia de Stanchous. Inquis. *ut sup.* (117.) It is probable, from the vicinity, Stonehouse being only about six miles from Gillbank, that he might be a descendant from that Auchinleck who is cele-brated by the Minstrel. Gillbank is now the property of a gentleman of the name of Thomson.

ADDITIONAL NOTE TO BOOK SIXTH.

—— *- Syne couth to Braid wood fayr,*
At a consaill thre dayis soiornyt thai.
At Forest kyrk a metyng ordand he;
Thai chesd Wallace Scottis wardand to be.—V. 765.

The tradition at Biggar is, that it was in the old church there that Wal-lace was chosen Guardian of Scotland. But this seems to be a mistake. For we have no proof of the erection of a church there till the year 1545, when the college of this place was founded by Malcolm Lord Fleming. Spottiswood's Relig. Houses, c. 19.

The opinion that by the *Forest kyrk* we are to understand Selkirk, has far greater probability. Thomas Crawford, in his MS. History of the House of Douglas, says that this meeting was held "at the Forest Kirk in the sheriffdom of Selkirk." Comment. in Relat. A. Blair, p. 22. Keith, in his List of Parishes, thus mentions Selkirk : " *Vulg.* Selkrig, *alias* the Forrest." Catalogue of Bishops, p. 223.

In a deed of David, the son of Malcolm, (while he was yet Earl of Hun-tington) founding an abbey here, which was afterwards translated to Kelso, it is called *Scelechyrca* and *Selechyrche.* Sir J. Dalrymple's Collect. p. 403. The name, it is said, in Celtic, "signifies the kirk in the wood or forest; expressing thus, in one word, the situation of the place itself, and the state of the surrounding country." Statist. Acc. II. 434. But there seems to be no authority for this etymon. The last part of the word is undoubtedly from Anglo-Saxon *circ, circe, cyre, cyric*, church. Mr Chalmers's derivation is highly probable. "As the occasion of the church in the forest," he observes, "arose from the circumstance of the king's having a hunting-seat here, the place of his worship may have been called *Sele*-chyrc, from the Saxon *Sele*, a hall, a prince's court." This idea receives a considerable degree of confirmation from what follows: "When a second church was built, nearly on the same site, after the establishment of the monastery at this hunting-seat, the prior place was distinguished by the name of Selkirk-*Regis*, while the village of the monks was called Selkirk-*Abbatis*." Caledonia, II, 963.

ADDITIONAL NOTE TO BOOK NINTH.

—In Gyan land full haistely couth ryd.—
A werlik toun so fand thai in that land,
Quhilk Schenown *hecht, that Inglissmen had in hand.*—V. 441.
—In Schynnown *still Wallace his duelling maid.*—B. XI. 69.

I can find no place in Guienne, bearing any nominal resemblance. Henry's geography, of France especially, could not be expected to be very accurate. He had most probably heard of *Chinon*, a village in Touraine, near Saumur, which was indeed held by the English, and which might be viewed as on the way from Paris to Guienne. Here Henry II. of England died; and here, also, that singular writer Rabelais was born.

EXPLANATION OF THE VIGNETTE IN THE TITLE-PAGE OF THIS VOLUME.

As the cruel and unmerited fate, which terminated the bright career of Wallace, appeared to that ingenious gentleman who furnished me with this design, to be the object on which the mind especially rests in contemplating the history of his life, he has given to the block the principal place here. To this melancholy symbol, the crown of laurel, which, as we learn from the English chroniclers, was contemptuously put on the head of the hero during his trial at Westminster, is with great propriety transferred. Before it appears the fatal axe; also, the target of Wallace, together with the sword of his faithful friend Longueville, exactly copied from that preserved under this name in the house of Kinfauns. The headless body appears from behind. In the back-ground, rays of light are seen to dart forth, giving ground of hope that the dark clouds, which envelope this dismal scene, should be dispelled ; and intimating, according to the sense of the inscription, that this cruel act of the tyrannical Edward, by which he hoped to extinguish the spirit of liberty in our native land, should only excite it anew, —the fall of Wallace being immediately succeeded by the intrepid appearance of Bruce, as asserting his claim to independent royalty.

———

By some of my learned friends, who are acquainted with the manuscripts of the preceding poems, I may be censured, perhaps, because I have rendered the contraction ſ by *ss*, instead of making it to denote *is*. I have not done so unadvisedly; and I could not have acted otherwise without sacrificing my own conviction. I preferred this mode for several reasons.

Another well known contraction, totally different in form, is used throughout these manuscripts, where there can be no doubt that *is* is meant. Had I adopted a different plan, I would have been laid under the necessity of rendering the contraction in a variety of modes. I must frequently have viewed it as signifying *se*. But here, in many places, I met with an obstacle that seemed insurmountable;—a different contraction being employed for denoting a word of this form, sometimes in the same verse, as in *The Bruce*, B. VIII. 353.

> The king thus, that wes wycht and wys,
> And rycht *awise* at *diuiss*, &c.

Here both contractions occur. If I did not give to the sign so ambulatory and indefinite a character, I must often have used a double *i*, where it could not be supposed that the writer meant to introduce it. Thus I must have given *maiss*, makes, in the form of *maiis; raiss*, arose, as *raiis; cheiss*, choose, as *cheiis; pass*, a strait and steep passage, as *pais;* and *leiss*, loss, as *leiis*, &c. &c.

The rhythm, as well as the sense, would also, in different instances, have materially suffered. Thus, in B. IX. 259, where we read;

> And with all thair mycht schot egrely
> Amang the *horss men*, that thar raid;

It would have been,

> Amang the *horsis men* that thar raid.

In reading these poems, it must be observed, that, although *is*, the mark of the plural, is more generally to be viewed as a distinct syllable, this rule does not apply universally. *Scottis*, for example, is sometimes to be read *Scott-is;* at other times, when the rhythm requires an abbreviation, as if *Scots*. Even monosyllables are occasionally to be lengthened; as *armes*, denoting armour, must at times be pronounced *armés*. The same liberty seems to have been taken by Chaucer and other old English poets.

In the following Glossary, I do not pretend to explain all the words that may stumble a reader who is not well acquainted with our ancient language; for this would have almost required a volume. But I have not overlooked a single term that seemed to demand attention. For further elucidation, and for the explanation of some words that may have been overlooked here, I beg leave to refer to my *Dictionary of the Scottish Language*. It will greatly aid the reader of these works, if he recollect that many common words appear here under a disguised orthography, especially by the frequent use of *w* for *v*.

A

GLOSSARY

TO

THE BRUCE AND *WALLACE.*

A

A, *one.*
A, *ah.*
Abad, *abode, delay.*
Abandon, *to subject; to let loose: to destroy.*
Abandonly, *also* at abandoun, *at random.*
Abowyne, *above.*
Ae, *but; and.*
Acquart, *athwart.*
Adew, *done.*
Adheill, *Athol.*
Afaynd, *attempt.*
Afauld, *upright; one.*
Affer, *belong.*
Affer, *condition; warlike preparation; shew.*
Affray, *fear; terror.*
Aforgayn, *opposite to.*
Agait, *on the way.*
Agatis, *uniformly.*
Agyt, *aged.*
Air, ayr, *before; early.*
Air, ayr, *oar.*
Air, ayr, *heir.*

Air, ayre, *itinerant court of justice.*
Airt, *quarter.*
Alais, *alleys.*
All anys, *together.*
Allayne, *alone.*
Allenarly, *only.*
Aller, *entirely: altogether.*
Allgate, *in all ways.*
All out, *beyond comparison.*
Allryn, *constantly progressive.*
All-weildland, *all-governing.*
Als, *as: also.*
Alsone, *as soon.*
Alsua, *also.*
Alswyth, *forthwith.*
Alya, *alliance.*
Alyand, *keeping close together.*
Amang, *among; at intervals.*
Ameysyt, *mitigated; appeased.*
Amittyt, *admitted.*
Ammonyss, *admonish.*
Amowyt, *moved with anger; excited.*
An, and, *if.*
Ane, *one; a, used as the article.*
Aneding, *breathing.*
Anens, *over-against.*
Anerly, *only: alone.*

Angell-hede, *the hooked or barbed head of an arrow.*

Ankyrs, *anchors.*

Antecessour, *ancestor, predecessor.*

Anys, *once.*

Apayn, *reluctantly; scarcely; in case; under pain.*

Apersé, *an incomparable person.*

Apert, *brisk; bold.* In apert, *evidently; openly.*

Apertly, *briskly; boldly.*

Apon, apoun, *upon.*

Apparaill, *furniture for warfare.*

Apperand, *apparent, appearing.*

Appleis, apples, *satisfy, please.*

Ar, *ere; before.*

Ar, are, *formerly; early.*

Ar, *oar.*

Arest, *stop.*

Arettyt, *accused.*

Argoune, *censure; chide with.*

Arly, *early.*

Armyne, *armour.*

Arsoun, *buttocks.*

Artailye, *offensive weapons of any kind.*

Asperans, *lofty; pompous.*

Aspre, *sharp;* aspresper, q. *sharp spear.*

Aspyne, *a boat.*

Ass, *ask.*

Assailyie, *attack; assail.*

Assembill, *engage.*

Assenyhé, *word of war.*

Assoilyeit, *absolved.*

Assonycit, *acquitted.*

At, *that.*

Athys, *oaths.*

Atour, *over; across; above.*

Atour, *warlike preparation.*

Aucht, *owned.*

Aukwart, *athwart.*

Aunter, awntyr, *hazard; adventure.*

Auter, awter, *altar.*

Aw, awe, *owe.*

Awail, awal, *let fall; descend.*

Awail, awailye, *avail; advantage; superiority.*

Awance, *advance.*

Awaward, *vanguard.*

Awblaster, *cross-bow; cross-bow-man.*

Awenand, *convenient.*

Awent, *cool; ventilate.*

Awerty, *cautious; experienced.*

Awin, awyne, *own; proper.*

Awisé, *prudent; considerate.*

Awisely, *prudently.*

Ayk, *oak.*

Aynd, *breath.*

Ayndlesse, *breathless.*

Ayr. *V.* Air.

B

Bade, baid, *delay.*

Bail, bayle, *flame; blaze.*

Baille, *sweetheart.*

Bair, bar, *boar.*

Bakgard, *rearguard.*

Bald, *bold.*

Ball, *blaze. V.* Bail.

Ballingar, *a kind of ship.*

Ballyoune, *Baliol.*

Band, *bond; obligation.*

Bandoune, bandown, *command; orders.*

Bandounly, *courageously.*

Baneour, *standard-bearer.*

Baner-man, *standard-bearer.*

Banyst, *banished.*

Bar, *boar.*

Bar, *naked; bare.*

Barblyt, *barbed.*

Bargane, *fight; contend; battle; skirmish.*

Barmkyn, *rampart of a castle.*

Barnage, *barons.*

Barnat, *native.*

Barne, *same with* Barnage.

Barne, *child.*

Barres, barrais, *barrier; inclosure.*

Barrat, *hostile intercourse.*

Bassynit, *helmet.*

Bataill, battaill, *battle array; battalion.*

Bate, *boat.*
Bath, bathe, *both.*
Battalit, *embattled.*
Bauk, *beam.*
Bauld, *bold.*
Bawchillyt, *treated contemptuously.*
Bawmyt, *embalmed.*
Bayle, *fire; bonefire.*
Bayne, *ready; active.*
Baynly, *readily; cheerfully.*
Bayt, *give food to.*
Be, *by; concerning.* Be than, *by that time.*
Bear on hand, *relate; inform.*
Bearis befor, *ancestors.*
Bedene, *forthwith.*
Beforn, *before.*
Beforouth, *before; formerly.*
Begouth, *began.*
Beild, *supply; place of shelter.*
Beit, *make better.*
Bekand, *basking.*
Belewyt, *delivered up.*
Beliff, *by and by.*
Bellamy, *friend; intimate.*
Bellis. Blyth as bellis?
Benk, *a bench.*
Bern, *barn.*
Bern, *baron.*
Bertane, *Britain.*
Bertynit, bertnyt, *struck; battered.*
Berys, *bury.*
Berynes, *interment.*
Beryt, *roared.*
Best, *beast.*
Best, *struck; beaten.*
Best, *shaken.*
Bestiall off tre, *engine for besieging.*
Bet, bett, *supplied.*
Betane, *inclosed.*
Betech, *commit; consign; pr.* betaucht.
Betrayss, betreyss, *betray.*
Beyn, *splendid; showy.*
Bid, *wait;* bidand, *abiding.*
Big, byg, *build.*
Blaw, *blow; stroke.*
Blaw, *brag; boast.*
Blawand, *blowing.*

Blenkit, *glanced; blinked.*
Blent, *glanced; turned the eye quickly.*
Bless, *blaze.*
Blyne, *cease; desist.*
Blythis, *gladdens.*
Bodward, *message.*
Body, *strength; bodily ability.*
Bodyn, *prepared; matched.*
Boist, *threatening.*
Bon, *bane; injury.*
Bonalais, *parting drink taken with a friend.*
Borch, *surety; become surety for.*
Bot, *but.*
Botand, *but if; except.*
Boun, boune, bown, *ready.*
Bounté, *worth; goodness.*
Bourdand, *jesting.*
Bourn, *rivulet.*
Bow-draught, *bow-shot.*
Bownyt, *made ready.*
Bowrugie, *burgesses.*
Boyis, *fetters.*
Bra, *side of a hill; acclivity.*
Brache, brachell, *dog used for tracking.*
Bradit, *drew out quickly.*
Braid, *brayed.*
Braith, *violent; severe;* braithly, *violently.*
Bran, *brain.*
Brasaris, *vambraces.*
Brassit, *bound; tied.*
Brast, *burst.*
Brawland, *running into confusion.*
Breg, brig, bryg, *bridge.*
Brewyt, *put in writing.*
Brodyr, *brother.*
Brokyll, *fickle; inconstant.*
Browdyn, *displayed; unfurled.*
Brukyt, *enjoyed.*
Brundis, brwndys, *sparks.*
Brusch, *burst forth.*
Brycht, *fair lady.*
Bryg, *bridge.*
Brymly, *fiercely; keenly.*
Brynt, *burned.*
Bundyn, *bound.*
Burd, *board; table.*

2 E

Burdeous, *Bourdeaux.*
Burdowys, *those who fought with batons.*
Burdyn, *of boards.*
Burdys, *boards.*
Burgeans, *buds.*
Burly, *stately; strong.*
Busch, *lay in ambush.*
Buschement, *ambush.*
Busk, *prepare; move rapidly.*
Bustnous, *huge; powerful.*
But, *without; besides.*
But, *isle of Bute.*
Bute, *advantage; boot.*
By, *away from; against.*
Byggynge, *building.*
Bykkyr, *fight with rapid succession of strokes.*
Byrd, *it behoved.*
Burdyngis, *burdens.*
Byrk, *birch-tree.*
Byrn, *burn.*
Byrnys, *corslets.*

C

Caar, *sledge; hurdle.*
Caflis, *lots.*
Caiff, *cave.*
Cair, *return to a place; go.*
Call, *drive; Scot.* caw.
Can, *for* gan, *began.*
Cannell bayne, *collar-bone.*
Cant, *lively; merry.*
Capleyne, *small helmet.*
Carge. To carge, *in charge.*
Carll, *strong man.*
Carnaill, *putrid.*
Carping, *talking; relation.*
Cass, *chance.*
Catour, *caterer; provider.*
Cauld, *cold.*
Cawk, *chalk.*
Cayme, *comb.*
Ceis, *cease;* cest, *ceased.*
Certes, *certainly.*
Chaipe, *escape.*

Chak, *check.*
Chamyr, *chalmer.*
Chapyt, *escaped.*
Char, *carriages.*
Char dout, *murmur distrust.*
Charnaill bandis, *rivetted hinges.*
Chass, *case; condition.*
Chasty, *chastise.*
Chemagé, *chief mansion.*
Chemer, *loose upper garment.*
Chesd, *chose.*
Chewalry, *men in arms; prowess.*
Chewalrous, *brave; gallant.*
Chewyss, *achieve; accomplish.*
Chewysans, *provision; acquirement.*
Child, chyld, *servant; page.*
Childer, *children.*
Child-ill, *pains of child-bearing.*
Chokkeis, *jaws.*
Choss, *choice.*
Chrystismes, *Christmas.*
Clag, *clog by adhesion.*
Clam, *climbed.*
Cleket, *tricker of an engine.*
Clemys, *claims.*
Clemyt, *emptied.*
Clep, clepe, *call; name.*
Cleuch, *precipice; rugged ascent.*
Cleue and law, *higher and lower part.*
Clippys, *grappling irons.*
Clyppyt, *grappled.*
Come, *arrival; advent.*
Conabill, *attainable.*
Conand, connand, *covenant; proffers.*
Conandly, *skilfully.*
Condet, *safe conduct.*
Conn, *know.*
Conquace, *conquest.*
Conquess, *acquire by conquest.*
Conryet, *disposed.*
Conscil, *conceal.*
Contene, *demean;* contenyng, *deportment.*
Contermyt, *firmly set against.*
Conteyne, *continue.*
Contré, *country.*
Contrer, *opposition; mischief.*
Conwoid, *conveyed.*

Conwyne, cowyne, covyne, *paction; condition*.

Cordyt, *agreed; accorded*.

Cornykle, *chronicle*.

Cost, *side of the body*.

Cosyt, *exchanged*.

Courche, *covering for a woman's head*.

Couth, *could*.

Covyne, *same with* Conwyne.

Cowardy, *cowardice*.

Cowart, *covert*.

Cowatyss, *covetousness; ambition*.

Cower, *recover;* coweryng, *recovery*.

Cowntir, *encounter; division of an army engaged in battle*.

Cowntyr palyss, *contrary to*.

Cowyne, *covenant*.

Coynyc, *corner*.

Crakys, *ordnance*.

Crykes, *angles*.

Cruell, *keen in battle; undaunted: terrible*.

Crukis, *windings of a river*.

Cuk, *cook*.

Culter, *coulter of a plough*.

Cummerit, *encumbered*.

Cunsail, *council*.

Cursour, *stallion: charger*.

Cusyng, *accusation*.

Cuwys, *caves*.

D

Dainté, *regard; kindness*.

Dait, *destiny*.

Dang, *struck;* dang to dede, *killed with repeated blows*.

Danger, daunger, *great exertion made by a pursuer*. But daunger, *without apprehension*.

Danger, *perilous*.

Darn, *secret*.

Daw, *dawn*. Doune of daw, *dead*.

Dawch, daw, *lazy*.

Dawing, dawyn, *dawning*.

Debaid, *delay*.

Dede, deid, *death: dead*.

Dedeynyeit, *disdained*.

Defaill, *wax feeble*.

Defawtyt, *forfeited*.

Degesteable, *concocted*.

Deid. *V.* Dede.

Deille, *part, quantity*.

Deit, *deid*.

Deliuer, *light; agile*. Deliuerly, *nimbly*.

Demanyt, *demeaned*.

Dempt, demyt, *judged; doomed*.

Demyng, *judging*.

Den, *dam*.

Depertyt, *divided*.

Der, dere, deir, *hazard; adventure; injury*.

Deray, *disorder; disturbance*.

Derenye, *contest*.

Derf, derff, *active; severe; cruel*.

Derfily, *vigorously*.

Dess, *long seat erected against a wall*.

Dew, *dawned*.

Dewgar, *a salutation*.

Dewilry, *devilry; magic*.

Dewoydede, *divided*.

Dewour, dewory, *duty*.

Ding, *drive; beat*.

Discourrour, *scout*.

Disherys, *disinherit*.

Dispend, *expend: dispending, expenses*.

Dissaiff, *insecurity*.

Dissembill, *unclothed*.

Dissese, *want of ease*.

Distrowblyne, *disturbance*.

Diuiss, *devise*.

Diwysit, *divided*.

Do, *avail*.

Dongyn, *driven*.

Doren, *dare*.

Dosnyt, *stupified by a stroke*.

Douchty, *mighty; powerful*.

Doungeoun, *keep of a castle*.

Dounwith, *downwards*.

Dour, *stern*.

Doute, *fear; apprehension*.

Dowtyt, *feared*.

Draff, *grains.*

Dragoun. Raiss dragoun, *give up to military execution.*

Dre, drey, *suffer; undergo.*

Drefyd, *drove.*

Dreich, *slow.*

Dreiching, drychyn, *tarrying: delay.*

Dressyt, *prepared.*

Drouery, *illicit love.*

Dryw, *drive.*

Duell, *cease; rest; tarry.*

Duelt, *left.*

Duelling, *delay.*

Durwarth, durward, *doorkeeper.*

Dusche, *hard blow.*

Dycht, *prepared; dressed in armour.*

Dyk, *trench.*

Dykit, *fenced with ditches or ramparts.*

Dyner, *dinner.*

Dyng, *honourable; worthy.*

Dynnit, *resounded.*

Dynt, *blow.*

Dyrk, *dark.*

Dyschowyll, *undressed.*

Dyt, *endite.*

Dyttay, *indictment.*

Dytytt, *stopped; blocked up.*

E

Effer, *appearance.*

Effray, effraying, *terror.*

Effrayitly, *under affright.*

Eft, efter, eftir, *after.*

Eftremess, *a dessert.*

Eftsonys, *in a short time.*

Eld, *age.*

Eldaris, *ancestors.*

Eldfader, *grandfather.*

Elys, *eels.*

Ellis, *already; otherwise; else.*

Empriss, *enterprise.*

Emys, *uncles.*

Enbuschment, *ambush.*

Enbuschyt, *placed in ambush; also, ambuscade.*

Enchausyt, *pursued.*

Enchesoun, *reason; cause.*

Endenturis, *instruments; deeds.*

Endfundeyng, *perhaps asthma.*

Endlang, *along.*

Enforcely, *forcibly.*

Engaigne, *indignation.*

Engrewand, *vexing; annoying.*

Enkerly, enerely, *inwardly.*

Enpress, *enterprize.*

Enselyt, *sealed.*

Ensenye, *word of war.*

Ententely, *attentively.*

Ententyve, *earnest; intent.*

Entremellys, *skirmishes.*

Er, *before.*

Erd, *earth.*

Erdyt, *interred.*

Erewyn, *Irvine.*

Erlys, *earls.*

Ersche, *Irish.*

Eschel, *division of an army.*

Escheve, *achieve.*

Eschew, *achievement.*

Esful, *producing ease.*

Etling, *aim: design.*

Etlyt, *aimed.*

Euirilkane, *every one.*

Euirmar, *evermore.*

Ewynly, *equally.*

Eyme, *uncle.*

Eyn, *eyes.*

Eyth, *easy.*

F

Faboris, *suburbs.*

Fader, fadyr, *father.*

Fagaldis, *faggots.*

Faillyt, *wanted.*

Failyhé, *fail.*

Fais, *foes.*

Fallbrig, *bridge used in a siege.*

Falset, *falsehood.*

Falt, faut, faute, *want.*

Famen, *foes.*

Fand, *found.*

Fang, *capture.*

Fantiss, *fancy.*
Far, *expedition.*
Far, *solemn preparation.*
Far, *fair.*
Farand, *appearing;* weill farand, *handsome.*
Faring, *leading of an army.*
Farne, *fared.*
Fassoun, *fashion.*
Fastryngis-ewyn, *Shrove-tide.*
Faw, *fall.*
Fawely, *few in number.*
Fay, *faith: fidelity.*
Faynd, *endeavour; make shift.*
Faynding, *perhaps guile.*
Fayntice, *dissembling.*
Fayr, *solemn preparation.*
Fayr, *proper, expedient.*
Fe, *cattle; possessions in general; hereditary succession.*
Feble, *become weak.*
Feblis, *enfeeble, make weak.*
Fechtar, *warrior.*
Fede, *enmity.*
Feil, feill, fele, *many.*
Feil, *understand.*
Feit, *hired.*
Felcouth, *strange.*
Fell, *cruell: fierce.*
Fell syis, *often, many times.*
Felony, *cruelty.*
Felloun, *fierce; cruell: denoting excess.*
Fend, *tempt.*
Fende, *defend.*
Fenyeyng, *feigning.*
Fer, *preparation.*
Ferd, *fourth: waxed, became.*
Ferdly, ferdely, *fearfully.*
Fer, *far.*
Fer, *entire: sound.*
Fere, *companion: pl.* feris.
Ferly, *wonder.* Ferlyfull, *wonderful.*
Ferrar, *farther.*
Ferraris. Barell ferraris, *casks for carrying liquor.*
Feryt, *became: waxed.*
Feryt, *farrowed.*

Fest, *confirm by promise or oath.*
Feuiryher, *February.*
Fewte, *fealty.*
Fewtir, *rage, violent passion.*
Fey, *on the verge of death.*
Fey, *fief held of a superior.*
Feyrd, *fourth.*
Fichyt, *fixed.*
Flaikis, *hurdles.*
Flatlynys, *flat.*
Flaumyt, *flamed.*
Flawmand, *displaying.*
Flayt, *remonstrated.*
Flearis, *those who flee.*
Flechand, *flattering.*
Flem, *banish.*
Fleting, *sailing.*
Flett, *floated.*
Floryng, *florins.*
Flote, *fleet.*
Flothis, *floods.*
Flouss, *flood.*
Flyt, *transport by water.*
Foison, *abundance.*
Fold, *ground.*
Fond, found, *go.*
Forbeft, *in great perturbation.*
Forby, *past; beyond.*
Forbreist, *van of an army.*
Ford, *way.*
Fordyd, *destroyed.*
Forfar, *perish; forfayr, lost.*
Forfouchtyn, *exhausted with fighting.*
Forly, *ly with carnally.*
Forouch, forouth, *before.*
Forowsein, *foreseen.*
Forowt, foroutyn, *without.*
Forray, *ravage, pillage; ravaging, predatory excursion.*
Forreouris, *foraging party.*
Forrydar, *one who rides before.*
Forrown, *exhausted with running.*
Fors. Off fors, *of necessity.*
Forss, *a current.*
Forst noct, *gave no concern.*
Forsye, *powerful; superl.* forseast.
For thi, *therefore.* Nocht for thi, *nevertheless.*

Forthocht, *repented of.*
Forthwart, *precaution.*
Forthyr, *furtherance.*
Fortrawaillyt, *greatly fatigued.*
Forwondryt, *greatly surprised.*
Fothyr, *load.*
Fra, *from; from the time that; seeing.*
Frawart, *from: froward.*
Fraying, *friction.*
Frayit, *afraid.*
Fre, *noble.*
Freit, *strong man;* frekys, *pl.*
Freith, *liberate.*
Frely, *noble; beautiful woman.*
Frest, *delay.*
Frewall, *fickle.*
Frog, *upper garment, frock.*
Frusch, *break in pieces.*
Frustir, *frustrated.*
Fud, *matrix.*
Fullely, *fully.*
Fulyt, *played the fool.*
Fundyn, *supplied.*
Fur, *furrow.*
Fur, *went; fared.*
Fute hate, *straightway.*
Fwyngyt, *foined; pushed.*
Fygowrd, *figured.*
Fyffe, *five.*

G

Ga, *go.*
Gabyt, *mocked:* gabbing, *mockery.*
Gadryng, *gathering; assembly.*
Gaf, gaff, *gave.*
Gait, *way.* A gait, *a little way.*
Galay, *reel, stagger.*
Galay, *ship, galley.*
Gamyn, *game, mirth.*
Gan, *began.*
Ganand, *becoming.*
Gang, *walk; proceed in discourse.*
Ganging, *going.*
Ganye, *arrow; iron gun.*
Gart, *caused.*
Garth, *inclosure.*

Gayne, *again.*
Gaynest, *nearest.*
Geddis, *pikes, jacks.*
Gentilly, *neatly, completely.*
Gentrice, *genteel manners.*
Ger, *warlike accoutrements.*
Ger, *cause, make.*
Gerettis, *watch towers.*
Gerit, *provided with armour.*
Gestis, *joists.*
Geyeler, *jaylor.*
Giff, *give; if.*
Glaidschip, *gladness.*
Glakyt, *foolish, rash.*
Glamrous, *noisy.*
Gle, glew, *game; fate of battle.*
Gleid, *squint eyed.*
Gleid, *strong or bright fire.*
Glisnyt, *blinked.*
Gloss, *dross; atoms.*
Gome, goym, *a man.*
Gossop, *gossip, sponsor.*
Gouernaill, *government.*
Gowlis, *gules in heraldry.*
Graith, *prompt: not embarrassed; straight, direct: earnest.*
Graithly, *readily.*
Granys, *groans.*
Grathit, *dressed in accoutrements.*
Graunt, *great, grand.*
Grawyn, *interred.*
Gre, *degree.*
Grece, *stair:* grecis, *steps.*
Greis, *greaves.*
Greis, *gray.*
Greit, *great.*
Gret, *cried, wept.*
Greting, gretyng, *act of weeping.*
Gretumly, *greatly.*
Grewing, *grievance.*
Growyt, *shuddered with terror.*
Gruchys, *grudges;* gruching, *repining.*
Grypyt, *griped.*
Gryth, *quarter in battle.*
Grunye, *promontory.*
Gud, *substance: provisions.*
Gud, *good; well-born.*

Guschet, *armour for defending the arm-pit.*
Gy, *guide:* gyit, *guided.*
Gyf, *if.*
Gyde, *attire, weeds.*
Gyn, *engine for war.*
Gynour, *engineer.*
Gyrd, *stroke, blow.*
Gyrdand, *moving expeditiously.*
Gyrning, *grinning.*
Gyrth, *protection: sanctuary.*

H

Haboundanlé, *abundantly.*
Haboundlyt, *abounded.*
Haddyr, *heath.*
Hagis, *hedges.*
Haid, *had.*
Haif, haiff, *have.*
Halche, *low-lying ground.*
Haill, *whole.*
Haldyn, *held.*
Half, *side: quarter.*
Halfindall, *the half.*
Hals, *throat, neck.*
Haltyn, *contemptuous.*
Haly, *wholly.*
Halyst, *saluted.*
Halyt, *haled: drew up.*
Hamely, *familiar; condescending.*
Hamillet, *hamlet.*
Hand. Weill at hand, *in good keeping.*
Hansel, *earnest.*
Hamewarts, *homeward.*
Hard, *heard.*
Harlottis, *scoundrels.*
Harnys, *armour: brains.*
Harn-pan, *the scull.*
Hartlye, *cordial.*
Hartyt, *encouraged.*
Hat, *was called.*
Hat, *keen.*
Hate, *hot.*
Having, *carriage, behaviour.*
Hauld, *stronghold.*

Haylyst, *embraced, saluted.*
He, *high:* heast, *highest.*
He, *dignify, exalt.*
Hecht, *promise.*
Heithing, *scorn: derision.*
Heildyne, *covering.*
Heyld, *give the preference.*
Heklyt, *fastened with a hook.*
Hely, *proud: proudly.*
Hely, *loudly.*
Helyng, *covering.*
Hendre, *past.*
Hendermar, *hindermost.*
Her, *master: magistrate.*
Her, *here: hear.*
Her, *loss; injury.*
Herbery, *military station.*
Herberyt, *stationed.*
Herbriouris, *a piquet.*
Herbryage, *an inn.*
Herdis, *refuse of flax.*
Herdoun, *here below.*
Herd tell, *learned by report.*
Hereft, *hereafter.*
Herschip, *act of plundering.*
Heryit, *plundered, pillaged.*
Hetful, *hot, fiery.*
Hewid, *head.*
Hewit, *hewed to pieces.*
Hewy, *heavy.*
Hewyn, *heaven.*
Hewyt, *tinged.*
Hey, *high.*
Hey-gate, *highway.*
Heyle, *health.*
Heylyt, *covered.*
Hiddillis, *hiding-places.*
Hidwyss, *hideous.*
Hobeleris, *light cavalry.*
Hobland, *wavering.*
Hobynys, *light horses.*
Holyns, *holly trees.*
Hone, *delay.*
Hoo, *delay.*
Hop, *sloping hollow between hills.*
Hostellar, *innkeeper.*
Houss, *a castle.*
How, *hollow.*

How, *a hoe.*
Howe, *lodge, remain.*
How sa, *although.*
Humely, *humbly.*
Humest, *uppermost.*
Hund, *hound.*
Husband, *farmer.*
Hy, *haste.*
Hycht, *trust; expect, promise.*
Hycht, *engagement.*
Hyne, *young man.*
Hynt, hyntyt, *laid hold on.*
Hyrchoune, *hedge-hog.*

I

Ic, Ik, *I.*
Ik, *also.*
Ilka, ilk, *each; every.*
Ilkan, *every one.*
Ill, *disease, malady.*
In, *into.*
In, *the tents of an army.*
Inbasset, *embassy.*
Ineuch, *enough.*
Infar, *entertainment given on newly entering a house.*
Inlumyt, *illuminate.*
Innouth, *within.*
Innys, *lodgings, house.*
Intill, *into.*
Inwey, *envy.*
Jorne, *warlike expedition.*
Irk, *tire, become weary.*
Irusly, *angrily.*
Isch, *issue, go forth.*
Jugisment, *judgment.*
Junctly, juntly, *compactly.*
Juperty, jeperty, *warlike enterprise, implying danger.*
Justry, *justice.*

K

Ken, *instruct; to be acquainted.*
Kepe, *care, heed.*
Kepyt, *met in a hostile way.*

Kers, kerss, *flat ground on the bank of a river.*
Kerwyt, *carved.*
Kest, *cast; contrived.*
Knaw, *know.*
Knave, *a male; a male under age.*
Knyff, *hanger or dagger.*
Kow-yet, *cow-gate.*
Ky, *cows.*
Kyn, *kind.*
Kynrent, *kindred.*
Kynrik, *kingdom.*
Kyrk, *church.*
Kyrkynfest, *feast given when a woman first goes to church after childbirth.*
Kyrneill, *interstice in a battlement.*
Kyth, *shewed; appeared.*

L

Ladys, *loads.*
Laidmen, *men bearing loads.*
Lak, *taunt, scoff.*
Landbryst, *breakers.*
Lansys, *throws out;* lansit, *darted.*
Lap, *leaped.*
Lappyt, *environed in a hostile way.*
Lardner, *larder.*
Larg, *liberal;* largly, *liberally.*
Larges, *liberty, free scope.*
Lat, *suffer, permit; leave.*
Lat off, *esteem, reckon.*
Late, *mein, expression of the countenance.*
Lattyn, *impediment.*
Laucht, *took.*
Laucht, *clothed.*
Lauchtane, *of or belonging to cloth.*
Lave, law, layff, *remainder.*
Law, *low; low ground.*
Lawch, *low.*
Lawit, *brought down, humbled.*
Lawta, lawté, *loyalty.*
Layndar, *laundress.*
Lechis, *physicians.*
Ledaill, *Liddisdale.*
Lege-pousté, *sovereign power.*

Leiching, *recovery, cure.*
Leid, *man, person; people.*
Leid, *safe-conduct.*
Leiff, *leave, permission.*
Leiff, *live.*
Leit, *pretended, made a shew as if.*
Lele, *true.* Lelyly, *faithfully.*
Leman, *mistress.*
Leme, *splendour, brightness.*
Lentryne, *the season of Lent; spring.*
Lenye, *lean, lank.*
Lep, *go rapidly.*
Leryt, *learned.*
Less, *lies.* But less, *in truth.*
Lest, *tarried.*
Lesyng, *lying.*
Lesyt, *lost.*
Let, *hinder; leave.*
Lete, *pretended.*
Letles, *without hindrance.*
Leveré, *delivery; distribution.*
Leuir, *rather.*
Levyt, *left.*
Lewer, *rather.*
Lewyng, *sustenance.*
Lewyss, *leaves of trees.*
Lewyt, *allowed: left.*
Leyff, *live; leave.*
Leynd, *dwell:* leyndyt, *abode.*
Leysche, *leash.*
Leyte, *let, permitted.*
Libart, *leopard.*
Licaym, *dead body, corpse.*
Lik, *the same with* Licaym.
Likand, *pleasing, agreeable.*
Liking, *pleasure, delight.*
Liklines, *appearance.*
Lingand, *going at a long pace.*
Loge, *lodge, booth.*
Loklate, *securing a lock.*
Lokmen, *executioners.*
Lompnyt, *laid with trees.*
Lorn, lorne, *lost.*
Losyngeour, *deceiver.*
Louch, *cavity; lake.*
Louchsid, *side of a lake.*
Loup, *leap, spring.*
Lourdane, *lazy scoundrel.*

Lovyt, *praised.*
Low, *flame.*
Lowe, *love.*
Lowing, *praising.*
Lowsyt, *loosed.*
Lowtyt, *made obeisance.*
Luff, *praise, extol.*
Luffand, *loving.*
Luff-burd, *loof-board.*
Luflely, *lovingly.*
Lugit, *lodged.*
Luk, *look.*
Lwnd, *London.*
Lychtly, *contemptuously.*
Lychtlyness, *contempt.*
Lyflat, *deceased; course of life.*
Lyft, *firmament.*
Lykly, *having a good appearance.*
Lymys, *limbs.*
Lynt, *flax.*
Lyppynyt, *put confidence in.*
Lyr, *flesh, as distinguished from the bones.*
Lysnyt, *listened.*
Lywyt, *lived.*

M

Ma, *more in number.*
Ma, *may; make.*
Macht, *matched.*
Magre, *ill-will; in spite of.*
Mailyeis, *coats of mail.*
Maist, *most.*
Maister, maistry, *dominion; service; resistance.*
Maistryss, *appearance of dominion; service; art; ability.*
Maisterfull, *arduous.*
Maistress, *mistress.*
Mait, *overpowered with drink.*
Mak mayne, *make exertion.*
Makaris, *poets.*
Malice, *bodily disease.*
Malvyté, *vice, wickedness.*
Malwaris, *mowers.*
Man, *vassal.*

Maner, *kind, sort.*
Maner, *manor house.*
Manerlik, *discreetly.*
Mangery, *feast.*
Mank, *maim, mutilate.*
Manland, *mainland.*
Maurent, manredyn, *homage.*
Mar, *more.*
Mar, *hinderance.*
Mar, *mayor, or chief magistrate.*
Marcheand, *bordering on.*
Mare, *longer.*
Mar furth, *furthermore.*
Marrais, *marsh, morass.*
Marschal, *steward.*
Martyr, *hew down.*
Martyrdom, *slaughter.*
Matelent, *rage, fury.*
Maucht, *might, strength.*
Maundment, *order, mandate.*
May, *more.*
Mayne, *might, power.*
Mayne, *moan.*
Mayr, *mayor.*
Mayss, *makes.*
Meill off, *treat of.*
Mekil, *much.*
Mellé, *contest; battle.*
Mellyne, *mixture.*
Mellyt, *mixed, blended.*
Menand, *lamenting;* menys, *moans.*
Menausyt, *menaced.*
Mene of, *or on, reflect.*
Mengye, mengné, *followers of a chieftain; troops in general.*
Menovnys, *minnows.*
Mensk, *manliness; honour.*
Menskly, *decently; respectfully.*
Menyng, *pity, compassion.*
Mer, *put into confusion.*
Merrys, *mars.*
Mess, *mass.*
Message, *ambassadors.*
Mete, *meet.*
Mete hamys, *manors, messuages.*
Mikill, *much.*
Mistry, *strait.*
Mobles, *moveables; goods.*

Mocht, *might.*
Mody, *bold; spirited.*
Modyr, *mother.*
Mole, *promontory.*
Mone, *moon.*
Mone, *take notice of.*
Monestingis, *admonitions.*
Mon, *must.*
Mony, *many.*
Monteyle, *mount.*
Monyss, *admonish.*
More, *a heath.*
Mortfundyit, *cold as death.*
Moss, *marshy place.*
Mounth, *the Grampian ridge.*
Mow, *heap.*
Mowence, *motion, or dependence.*
Multiplé, *number: quantity.*
Mur, *gentle; mild.*
Muryt, *walled.*
Mut, *meet; mute, meeting.*
Mute, *treat of; complain.*
Myddyn, *dunghill.*
Mydlike, *moderate, ordinary.*
Mydwart, *middle ward of an army.*
Myrk, *dark;* myrkness, *darkness.*
Mysel, myselwyn, *myself.*
Mysfall, *miscarry.*
Mysfar, *mischance.*
Myss, *fault, error.*
Myster, *craft, art.*
Myster, *want, necessity; necessary.*
Mysterit, *had need of.*
Mystraistit, *mistrusted.*
Mistrowing, *suspecting; distrust.*

N

Na, *no, not; neither; nor; none; than.*
Nakyn, *no kind of.*
Nanys, *purpose.*
Nathing, *nothing.*
Nawyn, *shipping, navy.*
Ne, *not.*
Nedwayis, *of necessity.*
Neide, o neide, *of necessity.*

Neist, *next.*
Nerhand, *near.*
Neth, *below.*
Nethring, *depression.*
Neuo, nevo, *nephew.*
Newlingis, *newly, recently.*
Newth, *beneath.*
Newys, newffys, *fists.*
Neych, *approach.*
Noblay, *nobility; intrepidity.*
Nocht, *not; nothing.* Nocht for thi, *nevertheless.*
Nome, *taken.*
None, *noon.*
Noryss, *nurse.*
Noryst, *nourished.*
Nothir, *neither.*
Nounys, *nuns.*
Noy, *annoyance.*
Nycete, *folly; simplicity.*
Nygramansour, *necromancer.*
Nyt, *denied.*

O

O, *grandson.*
Obeysant, *obedient.*
Odyr, *other.*
Oftsyss, *often.*
Ogart, *pride; arrogance.*
Omast, *uppermost.*
Onane, *forthwith, anon.*
Or, *ere, before; rather than; lest.*
Ost, *host.*
Ostyng, *encampment.*
Ostrye, *an inn.*
Otherane, *either.*
Our, *over; above.*
Ourhand, *upper hand.*
Ourhyede, *overtook.*
Ourlord, *superior.*
Ourman, *arbiter.*
Ournowne, *afternoon.*
Our rad, *too hasty.*
Ourtane, *overtaken.*
Ourthourth, *athwart.*
Out, *issue; go forth.*

Outcome, *egress.*
Out our, *over: across.*
Outreyng, *extremity.*
Owe, *above.*
Owtakyn, owtane, *except.*
Owting, *expedition.*
Owtouth, *outwith; outwards: out from.*
Owyr mar, *more upperward.*
Oyss, *use; manner of life.*

P

Page, *boy.*
Pailyownys, *pavilions.*
Pantener, *rascally.*
Pape, *Pope.*
Par, *impair: decrease; fail.*
Party, *part; degree.*
Pasch-ewyn, *evening before Christmas.*
Patron, *pattern.*
Pawmer, *palm-tree.*
Pay, *satisfy.*
Pay, *payment; drubbing.*
Pele, *fort, place of strength.*
Pennon, *a small banner.*
Pennystane cast, *distance to which a stone quoit may be thrown.*
Penselys, *small streamers borne in battle.*
Per, *appear.*
Peral, *peril.*
Peralous, *perilous.*
Perfay, *indeed, verily.*
Perquer, *exactly, accurately.*
Perys, *peers.*
Pesabylly, *peaceably.*
Pess. The pess, *covering for the thigh.*
Peth, *steep and narrow way.*
Pettail, pittall, *rabble attending an army.*
Pichtis, *force, strength.*
Pissand, *powerful.*
Pithones, *witch.*
Playne. In playne, *clearly.*

Plenyeit, *complained.*
Plenyss, *supply, furnish.*
Poille, *pole.*
Pollis, *paws.*
Ponyeand, *piercing, pungent.*
Porturat, *portrayed.*
Pottis, *small holes.*
Pouerall, poweraill, *rabble.*
Poutstaff, *pole used in fishing with a small net.*
Powed, *pulled.*
Powsté, *power.*
Poynye, *skirmish.*
Prayit, *made a prey of.*
Preiff, *find by examination.*
Prent, *deep impression.*
Preyne, *pin; thing of no value.*
Prese, *press.*
Prewé, *privy.*
Prikyt, *spurred, rode quickly.*
Prissyt, *praised.*
Prochand, *approaching.*
Pryse, *value.*
Pulaile, *poultry.*
Pullaine greis, *greaves worn in war.*
Pundelayn?
Punye, *small body of men.*
Punyeid, punyeit, *pierced; pricked.*
Punyoun, *side, party.*
Pur, *poor.*
Purches, *procure.*
Purd, *impoverished.*
Pyk, *pitch.*
Pykkis, *picks.*

Q

Quentiss, *elegant device.*
Quer, *choir.*
Quharthrouch, *through which.*
Quhat kyn, *what kind of.*
Quhen, quheyne, quhayne, *few.*
Quhethirand, *whizzing.*
Quhethyr. The quhethyr, *however.*
Quhile, *some time, formerly.*
Quhill, *untill.*
Quhilum, *at times.*

Quhonnar, *fewer.*
Quhytyss, *fine woollen coats.*
Quouk, *quaked.*
Quyt, *requite.*
Quytcleme, *renounce all claim to.*

R

Rabutyt, *repulsed.*
Race, *dashed.*
Racunnyss, *recognize.*
Rad, *afraid.* Raddour, radness, *fear.*
Radoun, *return.*
Ragment, *deed, convention.*
Raid, *rode.*
Raiss, rase, *strong current in the sea.*
Raith, *early.*
Rakyt, *went swiftly.*
Raleiff, *rally.*
Ramayn, *the rest.*
Ramede, *remedy.*
Rampand, *raging.*
Ramuff, *remove.*
Randoun, *swift motion.*
Rang, *rank.*
Range, *van of an army.*
Rangale, *rabble.*
Ransoune, *ransom.*
Rapys, *ropes.*
Rar, *roar.*
Rass, *dashed, threw down violently.*
Raung, *range.*
Raw, *row, rank.*
Rawess, rewess, *to put on the sacerdotal dress.*
Ray, *array; military arrangement.*
Real, *royal.*
Rebaldaill, *mob, rabble.*
Rebaldie, *gross conversation.*
Rebet, *made a renewed attack.*
Rebouris. At rebouris, *contrary to the right way.*
Reboytyt, *rebuked; taunted.*
Red, *separate; rescue; overpower.*
Red, *clearance.*
Rede, *fierce, furious.*

Rede, *voice.*
Rede, *speak at large.*
Redles, *in a confused state.*
Redy, *make ready.*
Refeckit, *repaired, renovated.*
Reff, *spoil, plunder.*
Reid, *red.*
Reide, *counsel.*
Reiffar, reffayr, reyffar, *robber.*
Reist, *support of a warlike instrument.*
Rek, reik, *smoke.*
Releifit, relewid, *re-assembled.*
Relyit, *rallied.*
Remord, *have remorse for; disburden the conscience.*
Rengye, *reins.*
Renkis, *ranges, roams.*
Renommé, renowmé, *renown.*
Renyit, *forsworn.*
Repende, *dispersed.*
Rerd, *noise, clamour.*
Rerit, *fell back.*
Rerward, *rear.*
Resavit, *received.*
Resett, *act of harbouring; he who gives harbour.*
Rescours, *rescue.*
Resourss, *rose again.*
Reth, *fierce, unruly.*
Reueré, *robbery.*
Reuersyt, *struck from behind.*
Reuk, *atmosphere.*
Rew, *repent; have compassion for.*
Rewar, *robber.*
Rewell, *haughty.*
Rewellyt, *revealed.*
Rewess. *V.* Rawess.
Rewid, rewyd, *reaved, bereaved.*
Rewmour, *tumult, clamour.*
Rewmyd, *roared, bellowed.*
Rewth, *pity.*
Rewyn, *torn, riven.*
Rewyss, *streets.*
Reyff, *rob.*
Reyss, *coarse grass in marshes, or on the sea-shore.*
Richt now, *just now.*
Richtwys, *righteous; legitimate.*

Rid, *severe, sharp.*
Rod, *road.*
Roid, *rude, severe; large.*
Romanys, *a genuine history.*
Rumble, *blow, stroke.*
Rone, *a bush; brushwood.*
Rok, *distaff.*
Rouch, *rough.*
Roucht, *reached; cared.*
Rouschede, *rushed.*
Routand, *assembling.*
Rout, *severe blow.*
Rowaris, *moveable wooden bolts, rollers.*
Rowaté, *royalty.*
Rowlyngis, *shoes of untanned leather.*
Rowme, *large, spacious.*
Rowtyt, *snored.*
Roy, *king.*
Rud, *red.*
Ruff, *roof.*
Ruflyt, *annoyed.*
Ruryk, *rural, rustic.*
Ruschyt, *drove, driven back.*
Ruthyr, *rudder.*
Ruys, *streets.*
Rybaldaill, *low dissipation.*
Ryg-bayne, *back-bone.*
Ryk, ryke, *rich; kingly.*
Ryk, *kingdom.*
Ryotyt, *ravaged.*
Ryve, *rob.*

S

Sa, *so.*
Sad, *grave; wise; firm, steady.*
Sadly, *steadily, compactly.*
Saffer, *sapphire.*
Sailye, *assault.*
Sakles, *guiltless.*
Salss, *sauce.*
Salt, *assault.*
Salust, *saluted.*
Samyn, sammyn, *the same; together.*
Sane, sayn, *bless, save.*
Sanyt, *made the sign of the cross.*

Sarde, *vexed, galled.*
Sariely, sarraly, *artfully.*
Sark, *shirt.*
Sary, *sorry.*
Sat, *became, was beseeming.*
Saucht, *reconciled.*
Saw, *discourse, address.*
Sawchnyng, *state of quietness.*
Sawerand, *savouring.*
Sawffly, *safely.*
Sawt, *assault.*
Sawth, *saveth.*
Sawyn, *sown.*
Sawyt, *saved.*
Sax, *six;* saxté, *sixty.*
Say yow, *tell you.*
Sayn, *saying.*
Sayn, *save.*
Saynd, *message; messenger.*
Sayr, *sore; violent; oppressive.*
Sayr, *sorely, as causing pain.*
Scail. *V.* Skail.
Scansyte, *seeming, characterized.*
Schald, *shallow.*
Schapis, *endeavours.*
Schapyn, *qualified.*
Schar, *cut, carved.*
Schaw, *small wood, grove.*
Schawyt, *shewed.*
Sched, *broke; parted.*
Schent, *put to shame.*
Scher, *cut, did shear.*
Scheyff, *escape.*
Scheyne, *beautiful.*
Schiltrum, *host ranged in a round form.*
Schipfair, *navigation.*
Schir, *sir.*
Scho, *she.*
Schonkand, *gushing.*
Schonkit, *shaken.*
Schor, *steep, abrupt; rugged.*
Schor, *threatening.*
Schot, *launched forth.*
Schoyne, *shoes.*
Schraiff, *made confession to a priest.*
Schuip, *attempted.*
Schuldrys, *shoulders.*

Schyr, *clear.*
Schyreffys, *sheriffs.*
Scottis se, *Frith of Forth.*
Scounryt, *shrunk back from fear.*
Scowmar, *pirate.*
Scrip, *a mock.*
Scroggy, *bushy, thorny.*
Scry, *cry.*
Scrymyn, *skirmishing.*
Scrymmage, *a skirmish.*
Scudleris, *scullions.*
Scumfit, *discomfited.*
Scurrour, skurriour, *a scout.*
Se, *see; sea.*
Sedeyn, *sudden.*
Sedull, *schedule.*
Sege, *seat; rank; soldier.*
Seildyn, *seldom.*
Seir, *several.*
Seker, *certain as to effect.*
Sekkis, *sacks.*
Self, selff, *same.*
Sellis, *cells.*
Selwyn, *same.*
Sely, *poor, wretched.*
Semblay, semlay, semle, *meeting; act of assembling; hostile rencontre.*
Sembled, *assembled.*
Semly, *handsome.*
Sen, *since.* Sen syne, *since that time.*
Senon, *sinew.*
Sent, *scent.*
Senyhé, senye, *badge worn in battle.*
Senyhory, *lordship.*
Ser, *several.*
Serd, *served.*
Serwis, *deservest.*
Sessoun, *season.*
Sesyt, *ceased.*
Set, *although.*
Setis, *gins, snares.*
Sey, *trial, attempt.*
Sey, *sea.*
Seyle, *happiness.*
Seyne, *see; also, sinew.*
Sib, *related by blood.*
Sibman, *kinsman.*
Sic, *such.*

Sikerly, *surely*.
Sitfully, *sorrowfully*.
Sittis, *grieves*.
Siyss, *assize*.
Skail, scail, *scattered party*.
Skalyt, *parted from each other; was diffused*.
Skamyll, *bench, form*.
Skath, *harm*.
Skew and reskew, *take and retake*.
Skey off, *fly, remove quickly*.
Sklandyr, *slander*.
Skowurand, *shuddering*.
Skyll, *cause, reason*.
Slaid, *valley*.
Slak, *opening in the higher part of a hill, a sort of pass*.
Slalk, *slake, quench*.
Sle, sley, *skilful; ingenious; an artful person*.
Slely, *in an artful manner*.
Sleuch, *slow*.
Slew fyre, *struck fire*.
Sleuth, *track*. Sleuth hund, *dog that follows the track*.
Slewyt, *slipped*.
Slik, *slime*.
Slink, *mire, ditch, slough*.
Slop, *compact body*.
Sloppys, *gaps, breaches*.
Snell, *keen, severe*.
Snuk, *small promontory, cape*.
Soberyt, *composed, kept under*.
Sodanly, *suddenly*.
Sodiourys, *soldiers*.
Soiournyng, *delaying*.
Solacious, *cheerful*.
Sold, *money in general*.
Somer, *summer*.
Somoun, *summon*.
Sone, *soon; sun*.
Sonkyn, *sunk*.
Sonounday, *Sunday*.
Sonyeit, *was anxious*.
Sonyhe, *care, concern*.
Sop, *a slight meal; a crowd*.
Sophammis, *sophisms*.
Sordid, *defiled*.

Sothly, *truly*.
Sotheroun, *English*.
Souch, *deserted*.
Soucht, *assailed with arms*.
Soudly, *soiled, dirty*.
Souerance, *assurance; safe conduct*.
Souerty, *surety*.
Soupe, *sup*.
Sournome, *surname*.
Sow, *a military engine*.
Sow, *pierce, gall*.
Sowing, *effect of piercing*.
Sowerit, *assured*.
Sowme, *load carried by a horse*.
Sowmir, *sumpter-horse*.
Soyme, *rope which fastens hay on a wain*.
Sparit, *fastened up*.
Spayn, *grasp*. Spaynyt, *grasped*.
Specialté, *peculiar regard*.
Speidfull, *expedient*.
Spek, *speech, discourse*.
Sper, *spear*.
Sperit, spyryt, *searched out*.
Speryng, *information in consequence of inquiry*.
Spill, *defile, deflower*.
Splendris, *splinters*.
Spoyn, *spoon*.
Sprent, *darted forward*.
Spryngald, *ancient warlike engine; the materials thrown from it*.
Spurgyt, *spread itself*.
Spyryt. *V.* Sperit.
Stad, *situated*.
Staff suerd, *sword for thrusting*.
Staill, stale, *body of armed men stationed in a particular place, especially as lying in ambush; any division of an army; compact body of armed men*.
Stalle, *stole*.
Stalwart, *strong*.
Stalwartly, *bravely*.
Stanssour, *iron bar for a window*.
Stapell, *stable, firm*.
Stark, sterk, *strong; strengthen*.
Staw, *stole*.

Stay, *steep.*

Sted, *station.*

Stedys, *horses, steeds.*

Steild, *placed.*

Steing, *a pole.*

Stekyt, *stabbed, stopped.*

Stellyt, *placed, set.*

Stent, *aperture for a bar.*

Stentit, *stretched.*

Ster, *steer; helm; government.*

Stern, *star.*

Stert, *sprung.*

Sterue, *die, perish.*

Stew, *vapour.*

Stewyn, *judgment, doom.*

Stewyn, *voice, sound.*

Stole, *stool, seat.*

Stoney, *astonish.*

Stot, *stop.*

Stound, *blow.*

Stour, *battle; perilous situation.*

Stoutlynys, *stoutly.*

Straik, *engagement in battle.*

Strak, *straight.*

Strakys, *strokes.*

Strand, *gutter.*

Straucht, *straight; stretched.*

Strenthis, *places of strength.*

Strenthly, *by main strength.*

Strenyeit, *constrained.*

Strestely, *perhaps for* trestely, *faith-fully.*

Stuff, *supply with men, in warfare; men placed in a garrison for its defence.*

Stuart, *steward.*

Stuffyt, *lost wind, became stifled.*

Stunay, *astonish.*

Sture, *hardy, robust.*

Sturting, *trouble, vexation.*

Stynt, *delay.*

Styth, *steady; strong.*

Sua, swa, sway, *so.*

Suerd, *sword.*

Suet, *life.* Tynt the suet, *lost the life.*

Suffer, *delay, put off; patient in bearing injurious treatment.*

Sukudry, *presumption.*

Suld, *should.*

Sumdell, *in some degree; respecting quantity or number.*

Sumer, *sumpter-horse.*

Suppowall, *support.*

Suppriss, *oppression.*

Suthfast, *true.*

Suthfastness, *truth.*

Swa. *V.* Sua.

Swagat, *so, in such way.*

Swak, *hard blow; throw.*

Swakit, *cast forcibly.*

Swanys, *swains.*

Swappyt, *drew; threw with violence; struck; rolled or huddled together.*

Swar, *a snare.*

Swarff, *stupor, insensibility.*

Swate, *sweat.*

Swelt, *died.*

Swilk, *such.*

Swing, *stroke.*

Swome, *swim.*

Swycht, *perhaps for* wycht, *powerful.*

Swyth, *quickly.*

Sympill, symple, *low-born; not possessing strength.*

Sympylly, *poorly, meanly.*

Syne, *afterwards; next in order.*

Syng, *sign.*

Synglar, *unarmed.*

Syr, *sir.*

Syss, *assize.*

Syth, *times.* Fele syth, *often.*

Sythyn, *afterwards.*

Syvewarin, *first magistrate of a town.*

T

Ta, *take.*

Ta, *one, after* the.

Ta and fra, *to and fro.*

Tach, *arrest.*

Taile, *flatter one's self.*

Taile, *tax; covenant; entail.*

Tais, *takes.*

Taist, *grope.*

Tak in hand, *make prisoner.*

Tak on hand, *affect state; undertake.*
Takynnyng, *intimation by sign.*
Talent, *desire, purpose.*
Tane, *taken.*
Taucht, *gave, committed.*
Taysyt, *poised, adjusted.*
Tene, teyne, *anger; sorrow.*
Tent, *care, attention.*
Ter, *tar.*
Terand, *tyrant.*
Terlyst, *grated.*
Teyne, *mad with rage.* V. Tene.
Tha, *these.*
Thak-burd, *thatch-board, roof.*
Than, *then, at that time.*
Thar, *there.*
Thar befor, *before that time.*
Tharby, *there about.*
Thar our, *on the other side.*
Tharout, *without.*
Thay, *these.*
The, *thigh.*
Thewtill, *large knife.*
Thing, *affairs of state; meeting.*
Thir, *these.*
Thirldome, *thraldom.*
Thocht, thoucht, *although.*
Thoill, *suffer:* tholyt, *suffered.*
Thortour, thuortour, *cross.*
Thowis, *dost address in the singular number.*
Thowlesnes, *inactivity, torpor.*
Thra, *brave: obstinate: eagerness.*
Thrang, *straits.*
Thraw, *short space of time.*
Thre, *three.*
Threll, *slave.*
Thresum, *three together.*
Thret, *threatened.*
Thretty, *thirty.*
Threw, *struck.*
Thrid, *third.*
Thrillage, *bondage.*
Thring, *press on, or forward.*
Thropell, *windpipe.*
Throuch, *faith, credit.*
Throuch, *thoroughly, entirely.*
Thrusande, *falling with a crash.*

Thruschyt, *did cleave with a crashing noise.*
Thryll, *slave.*
Thurch, *perhaps, force.*
Thurst, *could.*
Thyggyt, *begged.*
Thyne, *thence.*
Tid, *proper time, season.*
Til, till, *to.*
Till, *while, during the time that.*
Tillgyddre, *together.*
Tillit, *allured, enticed.*
To, *too, also.*
Ton, *town.* Of ton, *out of town.*
Torn but, *retaliation.*
Tothir, tothyr, *other: another.*
Towboth, *prison.*
Townnys, *large casks, tuns.*
Traist, *trusty; confident; safe.*
Traist, *appointed meeting.*
Traistly, *securely.*
Traistyt, *trusted.*
Tranont, tranoynt, tranownt, tranent, trawent, *march suddenly in a clandestine manner; march quickly, in general.*
Tranowintyn, *stratagem of war.*
Trast, trest, *a beam.*
Trawaill, *labour.*
Tray, *trouble, vexation.*
Trayn, *draw: entice.*
Tre, *tree, wood.*
Trew, trewis, *truce.*
Trewage, *tribute.*
Trewaill, *labour.*
Trewbut, *tribute.*
Tronsoun, *truncheon.*
Troplys, *troops.*
Trow, *believe; curse.*
Trowentyn. V. Tranont.
Trump, *march, trudge.*
Tryst, *appointed place of meeting.*
Turngreys, *winding stair.*
Turss, *carry off hastily.* Turss furth, *bring out what has been kept in store.*
Tutilling, *blowing of a horn.*
Twa, *two.*
Twal, *twelve.*

Twyn. In twyn, *asunder*.
Twyne, *separate*.
Twyst, *twig, small branch*.
Tymmeris, *crests for helmets*.
Tyne, *lose*. Tynt, *lost*. Tynsaill, *loss*.
Tyrandry, *tyranny*.
Tyre, hat of, *tiara*.
Tyt, *soon, quickly*.
Tyt, *snatch*. Tytt, *snatched*.
Tyttar, *sooner, rather*.

V

Ver, *spring*.
Ulispit, wlispit, *lisped*.
Veyle, *well*.
Umbeset, *beset on all sides*.
Umbethoucht, *considered attentively*.
Umbeweround, *environed*.
Umquhile, *at times;* now, *as contrasted
     with* then; *formerly*.
Uncorduall, *incongruous*.
Undercast, *revolve*.
Unlaw, *a fine*.
Unraboytyt, *not repulsed*.
Unrest, *trouble*.
Unsele, *mischance*.
Unsowerable, *unsufferable*.
Up blinkit, *glanced up*.
Upgang, *ascent, acclivity*.
Upwith, *uphill*.
Ure, *chance*.
Urned, *pained, tortured*.
Utouth, *outwards*.
Unwemmyt, *not scarred*.

W, as a vowel.

Wness, *with difficulty, hardly*.
Wrandly, *without intermission; cr,
     with much contention*.
Wtast, *octaves*.
Wtelawys, *outlaws*.

W, consonant.

Wa, way, *wo; sorrowful.* Comp.
     wäer; *superl.* wayest. Waworth,
     wo befal.
Wageouris, *mercenary soldiers*.
Waik, *watch*.
Waile, waill, *avail; advantage*.
Waill, waille, *valley*.
Wailland, *choosing*.
Wailye, *avail*.
Waine, *vain*.
Wait, waite, *wot*.
Waith, *danger*.
Waith, *the spoil taken in hunting or
     fishing.* Waithyng, *the act of thus
     taking*.
Wala, walé, waley, *valley*.
Walageouss, walegeous, *lecherous*.
Wald, *would; government*.
Wale, *choice, best part*.
Walk, *watch*.
Walopyt, *gallopped*.
Wan, *dark-coloured, gloomy*.
Wan away, *escaped*.
Wan our, *got over, crossed*.
Wan up, *was able to ascend*.
Wanbayn, *cheek-bone*.
Wandyst, *recoiled from fear*.
Wane, *manner, fashion*.
Wane, *opinion, estimation*.
Wane, *habitation; pl.* wanys.
Wanys, *jaws*.
Wapynnys, *weapons*.
War, *were; aware; worse*.
War, *waste, squander*.
War, *wore, did wear*.
War him, *befal him*.
Warand, *place of shelter*.
Ward, *guard*.
Wardan, *guardian, governor*.
Warne, *refuse:* warnyt, *refused*.
Warnstor, *store for a garrison*.
Warnyst, *supplied with provision*.
Warpyt, *threw*.
Warrayand, *warring*.
Warrer, *more aware*.
Waryit, *cursed*.

Warysoun, *reward.*
Wassalage, wasselage, *great achievement; valour.*
Wat, *know.*
Wated, *waited.*
Wauld, *government.* In wauld, *under sway.*
Wawand, *waving.*
Waward, *vanguard.*
Wawys, *waves.*
Way, *sorry.*
Wayn, *plenty, abundance.*
Waywart, a waywart, *in a direction from.*
Wayndit, *cared.*
Wayne. In wayne, *in vain.*
Wayne, *plenty, abundance.*
Wed, *pledge.*
Weddyr, wedder, *weather.*
Wedeis, *withes, twigs.*
Wei, wey, *little.*
Weid, *waxed furious.*
Weild, weld, *manage; enter on possession of an estate.*
Weill, *many.*
Welany, *damage, disgrace.*
Weltre, *roll.*
Wem, *stain.*
Wemmyt, *scarred, disfigured.*
Wencusyt, *vanquished.*
Wend, *imagined, weened.*
Weng, *avenge.*
Went, *to go.*
Wenys, *thinkest.*
Wepit, *wiped.*
Wer, *war; worse; defend.*
Wer, *spring.*
Wer, *doubt.* But wer, *undoubtedly.*
Werdis, *fates.*
Werk, *work.*
Wernage, *provision laid up in a garrison.*
Werray, *make war upon.*
Werray, *very;* werray ded, *truly dead.*
Werrament, *truth.*
Werthar, *more worthy.*
Weryté, *verity.*
Wesand, *windpipe.*

Wesar, wyser, *visor.*
Wesche, *wash.*
Weschel, *vessels.*
Wesely, *cautiously.*
Westland, *western.*
Wesie, *examine narrowly.*
Weyne, *doubt.*
Weyt, *wet.*
Wiage, wyage, *military expedition.*
Wicht, wycht, *strong; valiant.*
Wictailyt, *victualled.*
Will, willis, *use, custom.*
Will, *bewildered.* Will of reide, *destitute of counsel.* Will off wane, *at a loss for a habitation.*
Willfully, *willingly.*
Wincust, *vanquished.*
Withletting, *obstruction.*
Withsay, *gainsay.*
Withset, *beset.*
With that, *thereupon.*
Withthi, *wherefore; provided.*
Wittaill, *grain; provisions.*
Wittand, *knowing.*
Wittryng, wyttring, *information.*
Wocc, *voice.*
Wod, wood, *furious, mad; wild, not domesticated.*
Woid, *divide.*
Wok, *walked.*
Wonnyn, *dried by exposure to the air.*
Wonnyng, *habitation.*
Wonnyt, *dwelt.*
Wor, *guarded, defended.*
Wordis, *behoves, becomes.*
Worschippis, *valorous deeds.*
Worth, *wax, become;* worthit, *became.* Worthit to weide, *became furious.* It worthit, *it was necessary.*
Worthyhed, *valorous conduct.*
Woud, *wood; mad.*
Wouk, *week; watched.*
Woun away, *got off, escaped.*
Wowyn, *woven.*
Woyd, *void.* Woydyt, *emptied.*
Wraithly, *furiously.*
Wrang, *wrong.*
Wrangwis, *not proper; unjust.*

Wrethyt, *was filled with indignation:* or, *writhed.*

Wrokyn, *avenged.*

Wrychtis, *carpenters.*

Wycht. *V.* Wicht.

Wyn, *dry by exposure to the air.*

Wyn to, *reach.* Wyn to gidder, *effect a conjunction.*

Wynland, *whirling.*

Wys, wyss, *wise, prudent.*

Wysk, *quick motion.*

Wyt, *shun, evite.*

Wyttrely, *according to good information.*

Wytt, *blamed.*

Y

Ya, *yea, yes.*

Yarne, *eagerly, diligently.*

Yauld, *yielded.*

Ydill, *idle.*

Yeit, *yet.*

Yede, *went.*

Yemsell, *keeping; guardianship.*

Yemyt, *kept, took care of.*

Yerdit, *interred.*

Yett, *gate, door.*

Yharn, *eagerly to desire.*

Yhemar, *keeper.* *V.* Yemyt.

Yhis, *yes.*

Yhude, *went.*

Yhule-ewyn, *Christmas-eve.*

Yit, *yet.*

Yiwyn, *even.*

Ymage, *homage.*

Yneuch, *enough.*

Ynom, *took.*

Yoldyn, *yielded, surrendered.*

Youde, *went.*

Yowtheid, *stage of youth.*

Yrage, *Irish.*

Ythanly, *without interruption.*

Ythen, *busy; steady, uniform.*

Yuman, *farmer's servant.*

Yumenry, *armed peasantry.*

Printed by Robert Anderson, 22 Ann Street, Glasgow.

WORKS PUBLISHED

BY

MAURICE OGLE & COY.,

GLASGOW.

Now ready, Crown 8vo, 532 pp., Cloth, Price 6s.,

BARBOUR'S BRUCE, Edited from the MS., with Introduction and Notes, by JOHN JAMIESON, D.D. A Reprint of the Celebrated Edition of 1820.

"The Reprint is as good as the original, and therefore worth purchasing at once."—*Athenæum.*

"Messrs. OGLE & Co. have done good service to Scottish Literature by their Reprint of 'The Bruce.'"—*London Scotsman.*

"The present Publishers have just reproduced, in a neat and portable form, 'The Bruce,' a work which has justly been regarded as the Æneid of Scotland. It is the earliest heroic poem produced in any dialect of the Anglo-Saxon tongue, and may be characterised as 'the well of Scottish undefiled.'"—*North British Daily Mail.*

"The Volume is admirably printed, and the taste displayed in its production reflects much credit upon the Publishers."—*Ayrshire Express.*

"We gladly welcome the appearance of the First Volume of a New Edition, in convenient form, of the fine old Poems of 'The Bruce' and 'Wallace.'"—*Scotsman.*

Now ready, Crown 8vo, uniform with Barbour's Bruce, Price 6s.,

BLIND HARRY'S WALLACE, Edited from the MS., with Introduction, Notes, and Glossary, by JOHN JAMIESON, D.D. Reprinted from the Celebrated Edition of 1820.

Now ready, printed for Private Circulation, 1 Vol., Post 8vo,

WATSON'S COLLECTION OF SCOTS POEMS. The three parts, 1706, 1709, 1711, in One Volume. A Reprint in *facsimile* of the scarce Original Editions.

Impression—154 Copies Small Paper, Price 30s.
10 Copies Large Paper (all Sold).
1 Copy Vellum.

www.ingramcontent.com/pod-product-compliance
Lightning Source LLC
Chambersburg PA
CBHW022014110726
47901CB00006B/1521